THE
HEM

THE
HEM

BOOK ONE

DENNIS HAROLD MCKASKEY

LENTEN ROSE PUBLISHING

THE HEM - BOOK ONE
Copyright © 2024 by Dennis Harold McKaskey

This is a work of historical fiction. Although it is based on the story recounted in Mark, chapter 5, all the people and events portrayed in this book are fictitious and any resemblance to real people or events is purely coincidental. The scenes which make up the book were received as most writers become acquainted with the stories pressed upon them and are transcribed as such.

Paperback Edition ISBN: 979-8-9887330-0-3
Hardback Edition ISBN: 979-8-9887330-1-0
Collector's Edition ISBN: 979-8-9887330-3-4

Book design and layout by Julie Hodgins

To my wife and best friend,
Catherine Marie-Therese Girard McKaskey

TABLE OF CONTENTS

Trade Routes of the
ROMAN EMPIRE

OCEANUS ATLANTICUS
NORTH SEA
JUTLAND
BALTIC SEA
MARE CASPIUM
CAUCASUS MTS.
EUXEINOS PONTOS
MARE LIGUSTICUM
RED SEA
ARABIAN DESERT
SAHARA
NORTH AFRICA
LIBYA

BRITANNIA
GAUL
BELGICA
MAGNA GERMANIA
ALPS
HISPANIA
ITALIA
DALMATIA
ILLYRIUM
DACIA
MOESIA
THRACE
MACEDONIA
ACHAEA
CRETE
SICILY
SARDINIA
CORSICA
MAURETANIA
NUMIDIA
ASIA
CAPPADOCIA
ARMENIA
CRIMEA
SYRIA
JUDAEA
CYPRUS
EGYPT

Deva
London
Cologne
Lyons
Narbo
Massilia
Brigantium
Tarraco
New Carthage
Gades
Caesarea
Carthage
Aquileia
Luna
Ancona
Salonae
Rome
Ostia
Puteoli
Dyrrhachium
Thessalonica
Corinth
Byzantium
Ephesus
Tarsus
Myra
Antioch
Damascus
Caesarea
Aelana
Melitene
Alexandria
Memphis
Leptis
Cyrene
Olbia
Panticapeum
Sinope
Amisus
Trapezus
Dioscurias
Potaissa
Ctesiphon
Seleucia

Tin
Lead
Gold
Silver
Grain
Cloth
Pottery
Wine
Glass
Olives
Fish
Horses
Iron
Copper
Metals
Wool
Slaves
Hides
Amber
Salt
Marble
Timber
Carpets
Papyrus
Silphium
Ivory and Incense from Africa
Gold and Ivory from Africa
Routes to China and India

Elbe
Vistula
Rhine
Rhône
Po
Ebro
Danube
Dnieper
Don
Volga
Tigris
Euphrates
Nile

0 200 400 Km.
0 200 400 Mi.

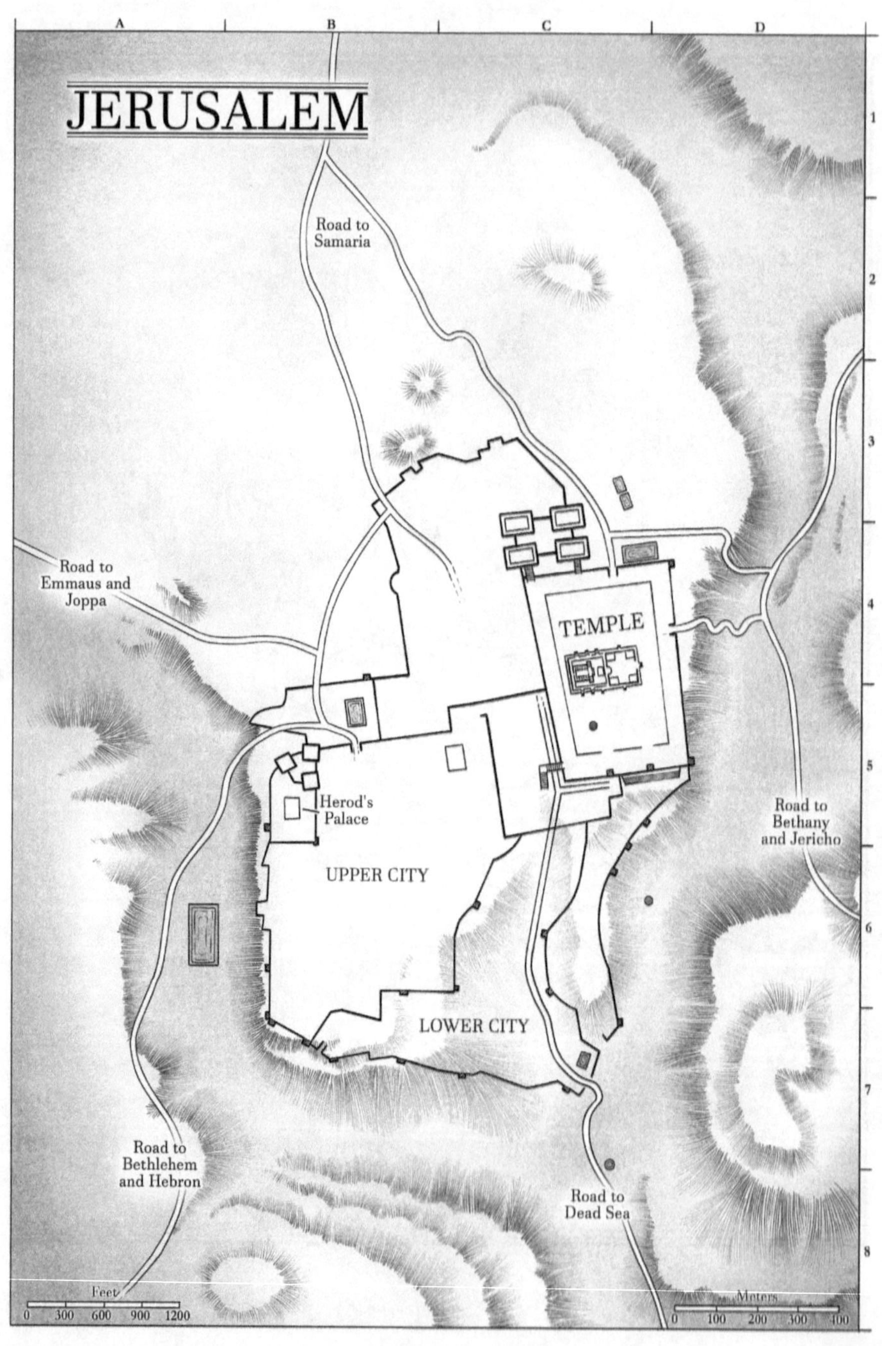

JERUSALEM
A
B
C
D
1
2
3
4
5
6
7
8
Road to Samaria
Road to Emmaus and Joppa
TEMPLE
Herod's Palace
UPPER CITY
Road to Bethany and Jericho
LOWER CITY
Road to Bethlehem and Hebron
Road to Dead Sea
Feet
0   300   600   900   1200
Meters
0   100   200   300   400

INTRODUCTION

THE CAST

I T IS ALWAYS COMFORTING TO be introduced to the characters in any stage or film production ... or book. Some authors are exceptional in their ability to spring characters on the audience when least expected. In this book, we deal with a deep and cohesive history of a covenant people with a common narrative which extends back to the beginning. Having the primary characters known and available for thought allows the story to be more familiar, as if you are standing there watching, smelling, hearing, touching, and feeling the entire production on a personal level.

Here are the three primary characters who each have their own narrative stream:

- **Veronica:** The anonymous New Testament woman with the 12-year issue of blood overcomes tremendous obstacles, decides to act, pushes through the crowd, desperately reaches out in faith, and touches the hem. In this simple act of faith, she is instantly healed by Jesus, is discovered, and then receives the declaration "My daughter, thy faith hath made thee whole."

- **The Young Merchant:** The youngest grandson of a powerful family with international trade holdings and operations across the Mediterranean basin. He is attempting his first long-haul business venture along the trade route previously managed by his grandfather, who taught him how to become respected as an honest and valuable business associate and owner.

- **Dinah:** The senior textile designer for the Jerusalem Temple and primary source for civic textile adornments in public and private spaces. She commands respect and is extremely talented in professional projects as well as in the private development of personal relationships.

There are eight supporting characters who have their own pursuits as they also interact with the primary characters:

- **Sophie:** Dinah's high-energy daughter who is taught sewing and textile design by Veronica. She, like her mother, has a good head on her shoulders and is exceptionally talented.

- **The Camel Herder:** The Young Merchant's long-time friend is also on his first business venture as a transportation specialist with his two personal camels and, on this trip, ten leased cargo camels.

- **Lidia:** Dinah's mother and senior matriarch of the family. She worked for decades at the Temple as it was being reconstructed by King Herod the Great. She sometimes shares memories of familiar and not-so-familiar events that are awe-inspiring. She never gossips but knows what is going on.

- **The Jewish Leader's Senior Assistant:** Operations Manager for building projects including the Temple and the King's Palace, along with the Treasury and other Herod-sponsored temples honoring foreign deities. He works closely with Dinah and the Young Merchant.

- **The Roman Armorer:** The diligent, obedient, and pragmatic Roman Military Officer has been trained in the art of body armor, shields, and weaponry for almost two decades. Working in the background, he keeps the troops' equipment in perfect working order and on occasion, creates special-use instruments of death for clandestine operations large and small.

- **Peter's apprentice:** The heavy fishing business responsibilities thrust upon him without notice compelled him to gain knowledge, experience and strength while facing the challenges caused by Peter's sudden departure.

- **Peter's mother-in-law:** Becomes the watchful eyes of Peter's international fishing business as she confirms the rights and strength of the family business when it is confronted by a self-appointed license regulations committee who wish to erase its legal standing.

- **Various merchants:** Are ever-pesky and always in-the-know as they try to swindle each other and make a dime off what they hope is the Young Merchant's naivete. They bring old legends to the forefront and attempt to invent new ones to keep their minds occupied while growing old.

There are background characters who mostly cause trouble as they influence the main characters:

- **The Jewish Spy**: is ever-present in the background until the Young Merchant catches his eye; he is then intent on destroying the Young Merchant and all he associates with, except the Romans.

- **The Roman Spy**: A perfect specimen of a Roman Military Officer, who keeps watch on the citizenry, the visitors and all young men who can excel in the Roman Army and available to do so ... soon; like the Young Merchant who he stalks to recruit.

- **The Jewish Leader**: Always engaged in important deeds and programs, he has a mysterious background that is not easily discovered, and his current private works are sometimes invisible.

- **The Committee**: Its members are always on the lookout for money-making opportunities whether charging large sums for indispensable services or illegally stealing fishing business licenses of traditional families of the Galilee ... until a powerful matriarch confronts them.

There are several animal characters who provide essential services, entertainment, warning, and rescue:

- **Ognir**: The guard dog is Roman-trained and very good at what he does.

- **Bindi**: The female camel of the Young Merchant, who "turns on him" when Veronica arrives.

- **Revolk**: The old male camel of The Camel Herder, who keeps an eye on his surroundings.

- **Miskah**: The young male camel of The Camel Herder: needed for his future wife if/when she is found.

- **Squishy Lips**: The seasoned Roman-trained war-camel that has been Veronica's companion for over fifteen years.

The Hem is set in the forefront of a powerful New Testament background narrative that is known at its fundamental level by most members of the audience. Whether the scene is on the dusty road to Jerusalem or arriving in Cairo on a camel, readers carry with them their personal experiences, and will warmly relate to Veronica, who makes a life-changing decision and courageously presses through the crowd, reaching in faith and desperation to touch *The Hem*.

As quickly as the Man who heals Veronica arrives, He must walk on to His painful and glorious destiny. This moment changes Veronica's life. She and the multitudes who have read her story will never forget.

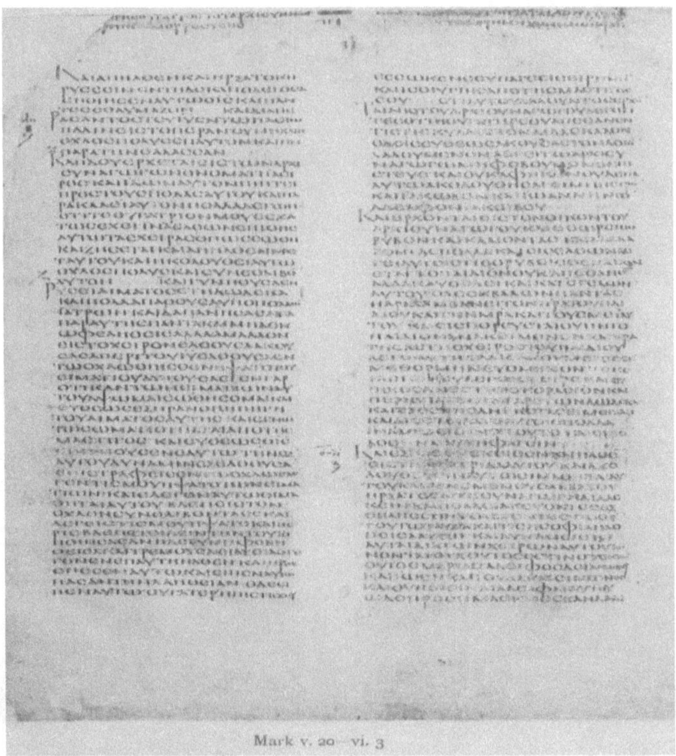

Mark v. 20   vi. 3

Credit: Facsimile of the Codex Alexandrinus (London: British Museum, 1881), pp. 1321–1322.

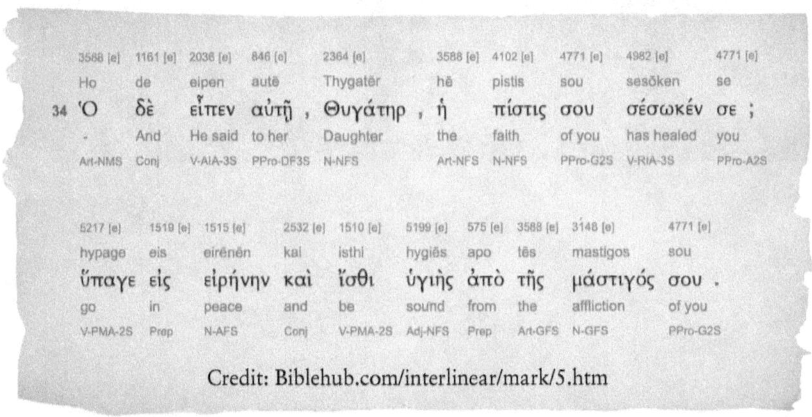

Credit: Biblehub.com/interlinear/mark/5.htm

And he said unto her, Daughter, thy faith hath made thee whole; go in peace, and be whole of thy plague.

Mark 5:34 (King James Version)

THE YOUNG MERCHANT

S TANDING IN THE DOORWAY CRYING, his mother Mariah's long black hair is pulled back and wrapped in a bun, the morning light sparkling in her timeless, green eyes which have watched protectively over her son since she escaped Bethlehem more than ten years ago. The decision was made several weeks ago. The twelve-year-old boy knew there would be tears when his grandfather Nehemiah took him on his first cargo-camel caravan. It is time. He needs to take his place in the family.

Nehemiah strides past the ten camels. They snort with steam coming out of their nostrils, as if to recognize his senior place in the family and in their lives. The camels are calmly lying in the shade, chewing as usual while the morning light reflecting off the sand makes their eyes larger than life, with long eyelashes looking like shade canopies.

The young boy makes sure he is standing straight as his grandfather stops, kicking up dust. With kindness in his eyes, Nehemiah slowly takes a breath, carefully reaches out both arms, and straps a new, full water bladder over the boy's slender left shoulder. It is heavier than the boy expects and reminds him of the new responsibilities he is now carrying. Nehemiah, whose aged face looks like time itself, kneels down and smiles at his grandson who is grinning ear to ear, freckles, and all.

Placing his hand on the boy's shoulder, Nehemiah's face becomes serious again as he counsels, "Life … Truth … Strength. Always keep them with you and always know their source." The excited boy with freckles looks up and shakes his head yes. He then finds himself being hugged and lifted off the ground. Grandmother Ruth joins with her own embrace and offers her enthusiastic well-wishes.

Finding himself back on the sandy ground, the new adventurer walks quickly across the courtyard of the desert homestead in Northern Judea, looks up at his mother, and says, "Thank you for helping me get ready. Please do not worry; grandpa and I are good partners. We will be OK." He is trying to be brave but feels the warmth of his own tear move slowly down his right cheek.

"I know you will be well, Joshua. I love you."

Standing next to Joshua's camel, his grandmother Ruth smiles and suggests, "You'd better climb on, or they will leave without you!"

THAT FIRST CARAVAN TRIP WAS twenty years ago. There were many lessons that followed: predicting weather, learning the trade routes, knowing who to trust, who to avoid, and keeping track of orders with delivery schedules are only a few. Record keeping is an essential, bedrock skill, which had been developed by Nehemiah's family for hundreds of years.

After years of being taught how to read and write the sales record's modified Egyptian/Hebrew text, Joshua received an additional bag from his aging grandfather prior to this trip: several collections of merchant sales records which had been passed down for generations.

The special text ensures that the detailed transaction lines cannot be stolen and used by competitors. The family legend is that they had been used for almost seven hundred years on the great trade routes traveled by their ancestors.

All things prepared. Joshua ponders, *Getting ready for a cargo voyage was, and still is, an amazing combination of planning, skill, tenacity, bravery, and luck. At least my camel provides some amount of consistency.* Bindi snorts as Joshua climbs on, raises her up, and looks around to ensure there is not a mishap while she establishes a sure foothold while standing under weight.

A camel never stands up and goes straight; you need to gently guide them a few steps to the right or left before they agree to move forward.

Bindi prefers going to the right if there is enough room. From up on a camel, the ground looks very far away.

Although Joshua had been standing in the shade, his head is now at least eight or nine feet up, and the full morning sun launching over the rocky horizon makes him feel the heat already.

Joshua thinks to himself, *At least the sand will be cool traveling this direction for another couple of hours. That is a favorable way to begin my very first solo cargo voyage. We will get to Byzantium, meet my longtime Egyptian friend I jokingly call 'the Camel Herder,' lease enough cargo camels to carry a total of about three hundred kilograms, and pack them up for the trip to Jerusalem.*

We need to arrive and fulfill our sales agreements four months prior to Passover. Think of it as a kind of a supply shipment for preparation. The Jews are big on readiness, especially for Passover, when Jerusalem triples its population for several weeks surrounding celebrations, culminating with a sacred holy day.

This trip should account for at least one third of my annual sales to merchants along the two-thousand-mile trade route. Camels are astute navigators based on their experience doing the exact same route on multitudes of occasions. They know what they are carrying and what it is by smell and by weight. With that information, they know the direction, where the water is found, and how long it will take to get there. Bindi has found her stride; she relaxes and carries me with care. I try to not to fall asleep.

BINDI KNOWS THE WAY THROUGH the well-worn road east, then south along the canyon edge over to the foothills. There are hills everywhere in this part of the trip. Locals even call some of them mountains. They have never seen real mountains; however, they feel like mountains because the ancient trails which they built to ascend them are carved straight up and they descend straight down. The reason for that trail-building approach is lost to history, and no one seems interested in correcting the problem any time soon.

The real mountains are north of Italy and east through the Caucus Mountain range. The trail switchbacks go back and forth as they rise above the clouds. Snow can be seen year-round. During portions of the year, the snow descends to well below the trail, making it difficult to navigate, unless you are a camel.

As Bindi continues her slow, steady walk, Joshua's mind wanders through the past, thinking of all that is good about the life of a merchant, *There are certainly challenging times, and even frightening times, but dwelling on those makes me sad and sometimes feel worthless, so I choose to wander in the good times and remember real friends with true hearts.*

When I was a boy traveling with my grandfather, he taught me a way to know that I was being watched over. He said, "You know God is watching over you when you see one of his creatures cross your path. When that happens, you will know that God loves you." I have seen my share of snakes, beetles, and foxes. I have even seen a tortoise, but what reminds me most of what he said are birds. It is marvelous to see them fly.

My friend the Camel Herder has been traveling as long as I have, and he is my age. He is thin but strong and has a natural sense of humor. He has a good relationship with almost everyone and is a natural storyteller and entertainer. His father and my grandfather are friends and have shared many trips together. This is the Camel Herder's first solo trip as well, and I cannot wait to join up with him and get going.

In Byzantium, the Camel Herder is negotiating with the stout and black-bearded Onur, the active camel stock-yard superintendent. They have known each other for many years, and they know the process. The end price to lease ten camels always ends up about the same, but the starting price is always higher. Although they both know where the sometimes loud and boisterous negotiation session will end, the process is followed ... always adhered to.

Such camel negotiations have been done for the last several thousand years; it works, and there seems no reason to change it. Joshua approaches as things are getting tense. The Camel Herder is casting dispersions on the camels he will soon be leasing.

"You know these camels are ugly and they are as temperamental as your almost-dead grandmother," The Camel Herder taunts with arms close to his body, communicating with his fingers and hand gestures, showing he is in control of his emotions while stating the facts of his case. His eyes move from the camels to Onur.

Raising his arms with grand expression, Onur retorts, "The camels trained and leased by this family have been providing excellent services for over one hundred years. They are fit and able ... as long as they are treated with respect." He places his hands on his ample waist and stares back, eyebrows pulled down over his dark eyes.

"Yes, I do not disagree with what you say, and yes, they do look over one hundred years old. Look at their lips; they sag! Inspect their eyes; they are as droopy as an old goat's udders! How do they even see where they are going, my friend?" The Camel Herder asks with enthusiasm, placing his left arm across his chest, holding his right elbow while his right hand touches his well-trimmed goatee. He raises his eyebrows.

This is the most fun part, and Joshua is glad his arrival is timed so he can watch as the supervisor takes an authoritative stance with his sandaled feet apart and comes back with a new and hilarious response....

"They see well, and it is a good thing they do—if they did not, you would get lost before you even left the stockyard because your gallant father is not here to guide you like he has done for the last twenty years! I will give you a deal! You lease these ten camels today, and I will, with no extra charge, blindfold your eyes and strap you on top of one of my excellent camels, and he will take you to Jerusalem without you needing to say a single solitary word!" He remains motionless in anticipation of the next round.

The Camel Herder thinks with amazement, *Yes, maybe he has a point there. Maybe I should take him up on this offer.* He looks the Supervisor in the eye and concludes the deal with a soft conciliatory voice, "So, I will lease your ugly camels even if they are dim-witted and dim-eyed so I can get going and don't have to put up with your slander any longer."

"I will take your money if you promise to respect my camels and treat them well, and remember, you do not have permission to eat any of them, even if you are starving to death ... do you understand this contract?" Onur asks, standing straight up, eyebrows raised and extending his hand to seal the deal.

"Yes, I will bring these useless flea-bitten animals back to you, and they will be so magnificently improved, you will not even recognize them," the Camel Herder says with a huge grin and sparkle in his eyes as he reaches out his hand in agreement.

They shake hands, and with the negotiations completed, embrace each other as Onur counsels, "Take care my young friend. Be safe, and most of all, watch out for Mr. Moneybags here; he is a lonely salesperson, and he looks desperate," as he points to Joshua and takes a few steps in his direction.

The Camel Herder turns toward Joshua, slowly shakes his head up and down, saying, "Ah! Well, there you are! What has been keeping you? All the good camels are taken at the reputable shops, so I was forced to scrape the bottom of the barrel and do business with this scoundrel," pointing to the supervisor.

Joshua shows a wide, approving grin exclaiming, "Good to see you both again! I am thrilled to hear you have come to a business decision in such a short amount of time. I was about to rent a room before I fell asleep listening to the haggle session."

Looking at the supervisor Joshua asks, "How is your family Onur? Your kind wife, Ece, is doing well I hope?" He looks at the supervisor as a long-time friend and feels as if they are family.

Onur looks pleased and replies, "Thank you kindly for asking. All is well with my wife and the children, who are getting older far too quickly for my taste. Speaking of taste, she has prepared a dinner for you both and urges you to come home with me, or she will send evil spirits to haunt you. I told her of the exciting solo trip you have planned, and she wishes to send you off fat and happy." His welcoming grin shows off his marvelously white teeth and bright, kind eyes.

"Come!" is his last offer as he turns and practically runs toward the gate and down the way to his home.

IN BYZANTIUM AT THIS TIME of day, there is always focused activity with people moving in every direction down cobblestone streets and long, straight avenues. Moving toward the residential area the threesome passes ornate buildings with mosaic designs and spectacularly carved and painted entryway doors.

The many sounds include wheeled carts, donkeys, camels, and shopkeepers crying out their sales pitches to passers-by. The smells of spicy cooking fill the air which provides ample reason to hurry in any direction if it leads to a place with great food. Such is the case as they arrive and are warmly greeted and seated on large cushions in the corner of Onur's family-gathering room.

Even though it is still chilly outside, the cooking fires on the low furnace have heated not only the food, but the stone walls as well, which are warm as Joshua leans up against one to position himself comfortably. Onur's three sons and daughter are already in place, sitting respectfully silent as the guests are reintroduced to them. They were younger last time Joshua met them, but their easy engagement in discussion is the same ... like their father's.

"So," the thirteen-year-old boy Altan says in a matter-of-fact way, "You are looking many years older now, and you are getting gray hairs in your beard." He is looking down as he picks up some food, so Joshua assumes, *His comment must have been made to the Camel Herder because I only have a few white hairs in my beard.*

Altan looks up expecting a reaction, and he is looking straight at Joshua ... directly into his eyes with a straight face. Their eyes meet, and Joshua has no clue what to say. Everyone else is instantly quiet as if a deadly standoff is taking place.

"Yes! You are very observant," Joshua says with a grin, "and do you know why I have gained these white hairs and have lost more hair than I should have by this age?"

Altan has a surprised look, caught off guard and searching for a quick response. He had probably been involved in training with his father's business for at least a year since he turned twelve, so Joshua lets him know man-to-man, "I lost some of my hair and gained gray hair because I have had to deal with the stubborn and disobedient camels you have tended without regard to your important customer's well-being. When are you going to change that bad habit you have developed?"

Altan swallows, stares back in disbelief, and cannot find the words to respond. His father lets the man-to-man question hang in the air for a moment and then says, "So son," Altan looks expectantly at his father as Onur continues, "tell your customer you will mend your ways."

The young boy gulps again, looking back at Joshua, and responds in a squeaky thirteen-year-old's voice, "Yes sir. I will do better, and I apologize."

Altan's older brother, Duman, and older sister, Aylin, hold in their laughter. Onur starts laughing, which breaks the spell and causes an explosion of giggling.

Onur catches his breath and says to his youngest, "So, you started something you could not finish?"

The supervisor nods his head in approval, smiles a great big smile, and offers, "Well, at least you are trying." He takes a bite of food and continues in a calm, reassuring voice, "That was very good." He then begins a soft chuckle while still nodding his head as he places a piece of cooked lamb in his mouth.

Onur's wife, Ece, offers Altan a smile, saying, "You can start eating again. I am sure your little joke will not make him hate you the rest of his life." She glances at Joshua with a smile. Joshua reaches over to Altan, puts his arm across his shoulders, and offers a smile of his own.

Within a few minutes, the Camel Herder is having an animated discussion with the children, who seem to enjoy his visit. Seventeen-year-old Duman asks, "I see you brought your own riding camel. I remember you calling him Revolk. Why did you bring a second personal camel? You certainly could have easily leased eleven camels from us instead of only ten. Do you think Revolk will die on the trip?"

The Camel Herder turns to Duman and responds with delight, speaking slowly to enhance the import of what he is going to say to the young man, "I brought the extra camel to be prepared for an adventure every man seeks for."

Duman replies quickly, "What adventure is that? Are you going to enter a race? Is it a champion and you are going to sell him?"

The Camel Herder sits up straight to emphasize the importance of his answer. "I have this fine camel at my side to be prepared when I find my future wife, take her into my arms, and get lost in her wondrous eyes," he says with a self-contented grin.

The seventeen-year-old considers this plan and nods his head like his father does, looks down as he is chewing, and while still nodding, seems to think it is a clever idea. He reaches for some more food as if he has adopted the plan for a future time in his own life.

Simultaneously, the two younger children burst out laughing, almost spitting their food across the platters set in the middle of the gathering. They are still giggling and mimicking finding a spouse when their mother Ece gives them "the look."

Although they stop using their fingers to portray camels and wives, Joshua can tell they have not forgotten how funny the Camel Herder's plan seemed to them. It is a new idea and seems rather comical to Joshua as well, but he says nothing, thinking, *Maybe it will happen, maybe not. I did not bring an extra tent in case it does; I will have to keep an eye out.*

They are fed more than they deserve and eat more than is healthy. On their departure they are blessed with health and success and most of all, with the watchful eye of God to prepare the way before them and protect their rearward.

Back at the inn, as they settle for the night, Joshua thinks again, *Why would a guy ever want a wife? There are so many more important things to do. The Camel Herder finding a wife would be a pain, no matter how "wondrous" her eyes were.* He falls asleep thinking of remarkable success as a lone merchant, traveling the world with ease.

And so, the next day is busy but uneventful. They gather the last of the merchandise and take sales orders from local merchants needing items from Jerusalem and Cairo where they will be traveling. Joshua muses to himself, *I hope that when we come back, we will not need the extra "camel-of-the-bride" as I will now jokingly call the young male camel, whose name is Miskah.*

VERONICA

AT ABOUT THE SAME TIME Joshua was completing his first merchant journey with his grandfather Nehemiah, another bright-eyed twelve-year-old was learning important things.

"Yes, I can do that with pleasure. I will be right back for more," Veronica says as she lifts the crisp linen she has folded with care. She turns her head in the direction she needs to go within the Jerusalem Temple and begins walking quickly. Her quiet smile is contagious, and she walks with perfect posture as if she is floating on the air.

She quietly counts twenty paces, makes a right-hand turn, walks across the end of the outer courtyard of the temple, makes a left-hand turn with precision, walks ten paces, and turns right into the linen pantry, placing her bundle on the table where it is retrieved by an older girl who places the linen on the correct shelf behind her to the right.

From low in the east, the early morning sunlight is about to reach the highest point of the temple's pristine structure, causing it to glow brilliantly. Veronica focuses on her sacred, personal mission; looks straight ahead; and never slows down to chat with or even look at the friends she may pass along the way. This does not bother them. She is always smiling, and they understand that this is how Veronica does her chores. Veronica calls them sacred tasks.

At the appointed time, the sound of the shofar blares and she stops, looks up at the architecture of the temple and waits quietly as the three distinct tones are carried into Jerusalem in one sustained blast. In a moment or two, her face is warmed by the light reflecting off the top of the temple, rays of sun which quickly cascade down to lighten her white temple dress then to her feet. As she looks down, Veronica recites, "The call to Service, Sacrifice and Worship," takes a deep breath, tries to absorb what is happening, lets her breath out slowly, turns her head, and continues on.

Veronica knows every required fold for this pattern of linen and exactly how to stack it, carry it, and place it. She knows it is 144 paces each direction for a total of 288 paces, not including the five steps needed to reach the seat where she waits on the next laundry bundle to fold.

The older workers who associate with her feel she has achieved perfection while the younger workers have mixed feelings, except those she plays with while they are not at their assigned stations.

Veronica spends her time working in the temple as a young assistant to Dinah. Dinah has responsibilities involving the High Priests' activities, their ceremonial robes, and the fabric used in all parts of the temple, including the veil of the Holy of Holies, one of the most sacred items in the temple.

Girls living in Jerusalem and some who are related to dedicated, regularly scheduled adult temple workers can place themselves as willing and able to begin temple service. Young girls begin their service around twelve years of age. A sizable number of those continue serving throughout their lives.

The temple activities include more than is visible to those who visit on pilgrimage, who present offerings throughout the year or during specific celebrations. Nearly seven thousand adults and three thousand youths take turns in officiating, administering, and supporting temple ordinances throughout the year.

VERONICA IS A VERY QUICK study and takes immense joy in learning and mastering each new task. She is not afraid to ask questions and listens intently to the answers. In her first two years, Veronica progresses from linen-washing intern to the linen-folding team to curtain-washing team to curtain-folding team to curtain-hanging team. She is agreeable to even the most mundane tasks and is present and on time for each of her shifts, a rare accomplishment for a young girl.

"So, I see you received a new assignment, Veronica. How do you like it? I would never want to work with the animals. They all are killed, and that would be horrible to see," her close friend Adina says with an exaggerated grimace.

"You already know Adina, I like everything when I am here, even the animals. Besides, I get to see Kaleb occasionally, and you know, he has been working with the animals for almost a year. First the birds, now the lambs," Veronica responds with an upbeat tone.

"Yes, I talked to him the other day. He was extremely interested in what he was doing," Adina pauses then adds, "and he was also extremely interested in you!" Adina pushes Veronica, giggles, and runs away laughing. They are fourteen at the time.

Strict rules govern each responsibility in the temple. The rules come from canonized sacred scrolls handed down from generation to generation. Each act and each prayer's formal process is followed precisely.

Each person who works in the temple has specific duties and is rigorously trained, evaluated, and certified to perform those duties unsupervised. After another year, Veronica is certified to work with each type of animal independently. She offers to do extra work. From time to time, she even does tasks normally left to the boys when her supervisor preapproves her request.

When Adina is asked about her close friend Veronica, she explains in her adult tone, "The interesting thing one can observe if you are familiar with animals is how docile and submissive the animals are when Veronica is around. They do not cower; they always seem at peace. Keep in mind that these animals are sacrificial animals; the firstborn males, unblemished, whole, and pure.

"Veronica speaks to them as she tends to their needs and grooms and prepares them. To witness her kind and loving temperament is a calming and uplifting experience for the animals as well as for the adults who pause to carefully observe, taking the time to experience something unusual, something wondrous. I always learn something when I serve with her." Adina looks up in search of more, then says in a matter-of-fact way, "Yes, that is how I see things at this time in my life." She tries to stay mature, but then grins and smiles as brightly as ever.

"Veronica, hold still so I can fit this apron," Dinah says in a patient voice. "You have grown quite a bit in the last six months. I am surprised no one has remarked that your shift has let your ankles show," Dinah continues as she places hem pins in to ensure the apron falls straight.

"My ankles certainly do not show," Veronica replies with confidence.

"And exactly how could that be?" Dinah asks without losing her spot in the apron hem.

"I added to the hem of course. It is remarkably simple, and the trick you showed me to keep a second hem flat worked perfectly!" Veronica explains what she had done without anyone even noticing, "It was easy to find the fabric, simple to locate the extra thread, and absolutely fascinating to match the patterns. It only took me half the night."

Dinah stops and looks up to see Veronica's endearing smile looking down, encapsulating the pride of a craftswoman mingled with childish innocence.

Veronica is sixteen and so is once again changing responsibilities, joining Dinah fulltime during each of her three-weeks-a-month temple assignments. The apron is a sign that she has reached a new level of service. It is from this time forward that Veronica's talents blossom.

Dinah completes the pins and takes the apron off of Veronica carefully. While folding the apron and placing it on the worktable she announces, looking directly at Veronica, "You are going to learn to ride a camel today. They are mischievous, bad tempered, and sometimes angry, and these are their better temperaments. I will not tell you what they are like when they are in a bad mood, but here is a scar that betrays the results." Dinah extends and raises her left arm, palm down.

Veronica looks and does not see anything, until Dinah turns her hand and shows her forearm, revealing a two-inch scar.

"It must have been very bad!" Veronica exclaims.

"Yes, it was a very bad camel that day," Dinah responds with quiet resilience.

"No, I mean the wound. It must have hurt badly. I feel so sorry that this happened to you," Veronica returns looking up at Dinah.

As she often does, Dinah avoids sharing her feelings. Instead, she responds, "It was a long time ago, and that is why I have arranged for you to have a riding lesson, so when you are my age, you can show the men exactly how it is done, with style and grace."

Veronica smiles knowingly, showing a maturity of understanding not common in a sixteen-year-old. She thinks, *I would replace "style and grace" with "precision and speed." Camels run as fast as racing horses and are able to very easily beat them in sand dunes.... Camels, I cannot wait!*

THE ROMAN TRAINING GROUNDS NORTH of Jerusalem are available for nonmilitary activities if the training is for the affluent or otherwise influential Jews. The training area is wide and long, flat, and mostly grassy. It has watering stations on both sides and can provide enough water for dozens of camels at the same time. It is a display of order and a demonstration of purposeful structure.

Three Roman soldiers meet Dinah and Veronica, one with a camel ready at the end of the reins and the other two soldiers each holding the reins of a fine Roman cavalry horse. "Hello Dinah, we are ready to introduce your young assistant to the fine art of camel dressage," the oldest soldier announces.

Looking at this marvelous scene, Veronica's mind instantly reacts, *I am an assistant to Dinah? Is that how she introduced me? An assistant? Oh my, I never dreamed I was an assistant. Assistants are older people with serious responsibilities. Oh wow!*

"Sir, I introduce Veronica, my primary assistant. I expect you to train her well and to make … absolutely … sure … she is not harmed by one of your camels," Dinah replies, making it clear who is paying handsomely for this training session and who is in charge.

Even the Roman soldiers stand straighter when Dinah is on the training field. "Yes, we will set forward the preliminary training course for advanced students. Please Miss, let me introduce your camel … five-year-old male, has packed cargo for two years, follows well, and has received no disciplinary demerits. His records are available for your inspection," the senior trainer says in a customarily formal manner. He pulls a sheet of paper out of his satchel and holds it up with both hands so Veronica can see it.

She has no clue what she is looking at and thinks, *These people are very, very regimented. I wonder if my camel can read and sing a military tune!* She smiles and says, "Thank you kindly, I am ready to learn what you have to teach. Let us begin."

Veronica then reflects, *I wonder if that sounded like an "advanced student" to them.*

Taking advantage of the moment of silence, Veronica announces with authority, "I will introduce myself to this camel before we start the training." She steps up to the camel.

"It is fair that he should get to know who he will be carrying around, is that not so?" she asks the soldier as she cocks her head to the right, looking him in the eye.

The senior trainer stumbles with an answer, as it is the first time he has ever been presented with such a question. Veronica turns her head, looks the camel in the eyes, places her left hand under his droopy chin and softly says, "I am Veronica, and I want you to know how I appreciate your willingness to teach me what you can do with someone who knows your true worth." The training camel does not respond but continues chewing in a disinterested camel way.

Veronica scratches behind his right ear with her right hand, then scratches behind the left ear. She straightens up and says with commanding enthusiasm, "So, Mister Camel, let us learn from each other and do well together!" Stepping to the mounting side for her first camel dressage lesson, Veronica stops, turns, and looks expectantly at the trainer, "Yes?"

The trainer is somewhat stunned by his new student but immediately engages with his precise instructions from step one through step fifty. Veronica is soon up on her camel. The senior trainer mounts his camel and begins riding next to Veronica. The two camels venture slowly out to the training grounds.

Dinah mounts her horse, and the senior Roman soldier walks over to the side to take his horse so he can provide proper escort. They casually circle the training field, keeping an eye on the "advanced student" collaborating with her senior trainer.

The escort officer looks to Dinah and says, "She certainly is a strong young lady. Most of our young students are in great fear when they are first introduced to a camel. It has only been ten minutes, and it seems as though she has been camel riding for a long time."

Dinah nods her head in agreement, "Yes, she did not even jump up and down when I told her this morning, for fear or delight. Veronica is very pragmatic, yet she takes joy in her every task and is thrilled when given the opportunity to learn something new."

"Yes, she will be a very quick learner," he says with approval.

"I agree, but do not skip anything, including the practice steps. She needs to have a complete and genuine experience and not become too confident. I know what can take place when that happens," Dinah warns.

He responds, "I know what you say. She must have enchanted the camel. Look how he is walking; he is submissive and expert at the same time."

The escort was seeing something he rarely sees as he reflects, *Hmmm, camel and rider becoming one in purpose, seemingly sharing the same mind. Beautiful to watch on the training field ... fearful and horribly effective to face in battle. This student has some amazing gifts, and it is an honor to teach her.* He nudges his horse into a gentle trot as a signal to the trainer to advance to the next stage. Dinah follows along, expertly keeping up with the senior Roman soldier.

This training session ends nicely with both "advanced student" and camel getting along well enough. "Cush, Cush," Veronica says quietly, looking at the back of her camel's head. Her camel stops and lies down upright so Veronica can climb off, an unusually awkward move for most people, especially for new camel riders.

The senior trainer is surprised she knows the command and further astounded when Veronica lights off the camel as if she is a sparrow and pats the camel on the head. She then steps in front of the camel, scratches the animal behind the ears, looks him in the eyes, and says in a formal tone, "Well, I believe we started off on good terms. I thank you, kind camel." Veronica then ends with jiggling the camel's upper lips while adding, in a joking, familiar tone, "Mr. Squishy Lips!" The camel seems pleased, as much as camels can display finer points of emotion.

Veronica is presented with fresh water and a linen towel. After using it, she folds the linen back into the exact pattern it had been presented, places it in the servant's hand, turns once again to the senior trainer, and begins asking him questions about camels.

"How fast can camels run?"

"Sixty kilometers an hour."

"What do you feed camels?"

"Forage, oats, and lettuce, when it is available."

"How much water can a camel drink at one time after a long trip?"

"One hundred liters in ten minutes or one hundred and fifty liters in fifteen minutes."

"Do camels really smell water from far away?"

"Camels familiar with their journey know where the water will be but can smell open water up to five kilometers away."

As the trainer is getting into the cadence of answering easy questions, Veronica changes the beat.

"So, what is the most demanding thing to manage with camels?"

He looks Veronica straight in the eye with the response, "Do ... not ... surprise them, ever."

"How often do they get sick and how can you tell?"

"Not often at all. You need to watch for cuts and missing hair. Their eyes will tell you if they are stressed."

She continues further into unknown territory, "If you were a camel, what is the best thing someone could do for you?"

"They like to be busy. They enjoy having a purpose and accomplishing useful tasks."

Veronica responds, "Thank you sir, that is very good to know." She is touched by that response coming from a Roman soldier and thinks, *So, perhaps these guys actually have hearts. Soul no, but hearts yes.*

Her last question is perfect.

"Thank you once again…. So … one last question for today if you will permit me." He nods yes.

"Do you know any good camel jokes?" She grins ear to ear, and the question, after a stunned silence, makes everyone laugh hysterically.

The senior trainer steps forward with a huge grin. He must answer her question. He looks down at the ground, looks up at Veronica, and says, "So, two camels are on holiday at the beach of the Dead Sea. The bull looks at the cow and asks, 'Do you think I look good in my new swimming trunks?' She does not look at him, brings her drink up, takes a sip, and responds, 'No, I have told you a thousand times. You do not need to cover up. Everyone here has a hairy rear end. All you did was make yourself look like a walking advertisement. Go back to sleep.'"

The senior soldier shakes his head. Dinah smiles and says, "Thank you for not repeating any soldier jokes. I appreciate your time gentlemen. We will see you again soon." She looks at Veronica, who still has a radiating grin, and says, "Let us be on our way. We have business to attend to." So off they go.

At the top of the training grounds steps, Veronica turns to look back and sees the soldiers stowing the gear and taking out brushes for both the horses and camels. She remarks, "I would like to learn to do what they are now doing when we come back … if that is possible."

"Yes," Dinah replies, "You will learn that and much more in your future lessons." She pauses and then adds, "So, exactly how did you know the command to have the camel get down so you could dismount?"

Veronica responds in a matter-of-fact way, "Well, every time I walk across Jerusalem, I try to see and learn something new. On several occasions I have witnessed camel riders stop and dismount. They all say the same thing, so I repeated what they tell their camels … it is quite easy. They all seem to know the same language because 'Cush' is used with camels from the north country as well as from the south countries."

Dinah nods her head with, "Hmph, very observant. We will visit the Project Office on the way and see what they have in mind for the palace draperies."

NOTHING IN JERUSALEM IS FLAT. Yes, the buildings have flat floors thanks to the advanced engineering being used these days, especially when the Roman engineers take on a project. The roads and pathways, though, are always up or down and sometimes both at the same time.

Dinah and Veronica come to the entrance of the Project Office, a multi-story building on the east side of the temple wall, adjacent to the huge Roman military housing building. The Jewish project leader's office is on the top level, from where you can look down at the temple; an impressive view, regardless of what time of day you have a moment to look and pay attention.

As Dinah and Veronica walk along the open passageway on the temple-side of the building, Veronica begins to speak as if she is guiding guests through the temple. Her words are enchanting, allowing you to both hear and imagine.

"In the early morning, before light, there are a few temple workers preparing for morning prayer; placing rugs for dignitaries, lighting incense, shuttling linens and robes and table ornaments to their proper places so everything is in order. I used to carry linen. It was an honor." She continues, "At the same time, the sounds of livestock waking and birds chirping come alive, and prior to the sun rising, they all reach a crescendo of song which no musical celebration can duplicate. It is beautiful and enchanting to be inside the temple walls when this happens. I remember stopping and looking at the highest point of the temple as the sun would reach it, lighting up for the world to see its splendor, God's magnificence."

It is already early evening. As they continue walking, Veronica is still looking down at the temple. Participants for the evening prayer have been gathering, and there is the steady noise of greetings rising into the air. At this time of year, the sun sets early, so the perimeter torches on the temple walls are already lit. Veronica says to Dinah while not losing the pace, "Which time to visit do you like the most, the early morning or the evening?"

Dinah stops, turns toward the temple, and gathers her thoughts, *This is a moment I should not miss. I owe it to her to stop being so busy I bypass what is actually the most important.*

"Thank you for asking that question, Veronica," Dinah says, looking out over the temple grounds as the sun is lowering but still sending its rays over the walls, casting long shadows.

Dinah pauses, then continues thoughtfully, "I love it most when the sun rises to greet the temple each day, illuminating the brightly colored textiles hanging as joyful ornaments to God and His work."

Dinah takes a breath and adds, "It is a strengthening thing to know that out of darkness, we can be warmed by God's love and His kind attention." She lingers a moment still looking out over the temple, "We need to be reminded from time to time to stop, look, and listen to what is beautiful and fulfilling."

Dinah turns to look at Veronica and offers, "Thank you for asking such a profound question," while giving an unusually warm and kind smile.

Veronica feels the truth of what Dinah said. Her heart responds quietly, *Wow, I love that. All I was expecting was a "morning" or "evening" response. I am so glad Dinah thought about the question in a way that was deeper and that she took the time to share that with me. She does not know how important that is to me. I am also thankful for our afternoon adventure. I love to go camel riding. I cannot wait until we do it again!*

They quickly arrive at the senior project manager's office, stop, and knock on the new, ornately carved door. The sound of someone speaking with authority comes before the large door is fully open.

"The king's wife wants something new for her guests to be impressed by when they visit for Passover. She has some very specific designs in mind and has asked, ehm, directed that we move quickly to not miss the installation deadline," the senior project manager says in an almost monotone voice. He sounds perturbed but also as if he has been dealing with similar client conflicts for years and years.

A moment later, as Dinah and Veronica enter, he is already back leaning over a design table, looking up at Dinah with a smile of resignation. He has been through these types of situations with this specific client several times since the death of Herod the Great.

Dinah steps closer, looks at the fabric samples lying on the table. She picks up the dark blue piece, and as she looks at it, says, "Yes Daniel. Having repeat business is always a curse you think? Having multiple projects happening simultaneously is bothering you again?" She emphasizes the word "bothering" and looks up at him for an answer.

"No! I get this way when 'She' summons me, cannot make up her mind, and then when she does, and I repeat it back to her, word for word, she says, 'No, that's not what I said.'" He looks at Dinah in exasperation, "It goes in circles that never end, and wastes so much time!"

Dinah is not impressed and with a straight face, tilts her head and emphasizes her one-word response: "So?" She waits.

As this familiar conversation continues, Veronica is enthralled by all the fabrics on the design table. She walks slowly around the table and notices design drawings of bridges, cornices, stairways, and other projects.

On a smaller table sitting at the end of the design table sits a pile of drawings that look to be an extensive wall project. The senior project manager and Dinah are still in "waiting-for-his-response mode," so Veronica looks up and breaks the silence with, "May I ask a question please?"

The senior project manager turns to look at her. The tension leaves his persona as soon as he focuses on Veronica and replies, "Why yes, of course. What is your question, Veronica?"

Veronica looks from him to the pile of drawings and asks, "Are these drawings for the north wall of the city? The wall that will make Jerusalem really big?"

He walks over to Veronica as his demeanor changes even more. He is pleased someone is interested in his personal project, a serious project that does not need the King's wife's involvement ... ever.

Dinah begins looking through the deep blue fabric while Daniel and Veronica engage in a detailed discussion of all things engineering for walls. They look at drawings for the clearing, underlayment, base, and wall structures as well as the capstone plans. It is a massive project, which is under constant observation and negotiation by and with the Romans. Daniel is thrilled beyond measure to have an intelligent, inquisitive, and energetic audience.

Dinah completes her review of the textiles and design notes for the palace draperies, makes notes of her own, and is almost ready to leave when she overhears Veronica ask, "So, when can we come up to the construction site and look at how your plans are being implemented?"

Dinah thinks, *This young woman is interested in way too many things. She is like a sponge soaking up knowledge every minute. I do not have time to go on tours of every project dealing with plain and dirty rock.* She walks over to the "engineering team," stops, and asks, "Shall I request that the servant bring up dinner?"

Veronica looks up and exclaims as her attention turns toward the source of the voice, "That would be absolutely wonderful, thank ..." In the middle of the last word, her brain adjusts to who had asked the question, realizes they had better get going, and says in submission, "Uh, no. I am very sorry."

She turns to look up at Daniel, who also has a look of submission on his face when he says, looking again at Veronica, "Yes, it is getting late. I have kept you too long, but I enjoyed reviewing this project with you, Veronica. Thank you for your advice and suggestions. I will share them with the committee when they meet next week." He smiles broadly and quickly turns his attention to Dinah, keeping his smile bright.

Dinah keeps her ever-present, regal-looking smile and offers, "Thank you, Daniel," with a glance at Veronica. "We will pay attention to the palace draperies, so have no fear. The wife of the king will get what she has requested." Dinah is thinking, *The wife of the king will (eventually) get what she deserves.* They turn and leave, thanking Daniel for his time and business.

WALKING BACK TO THE STAIRWAY that leads to street level, Dinah and Veronica pass again through the temple-view passageway. Everything has quieted down with most all of those participating in evening prayer having passed back out of the entrance gates. The gate guards continue to stand at their posts while the temple functionaries walk quietly and peacefully from place to place, gathering anything dropped on the temple assembly area floor.

This passageway has a quieting effect on both women, who are intent on returning home after a long day. Veronica is not particularly calmed. Her mind is racing, *We will pay attention to the palace draperies? Did she say that? What did she mean when she said the word "we"? I cannot wait to sort out how to get up to the north wall construction site. Who could take me there?*

I adore riding my Mr. Squishy-Lips camel! I need to make sure we schedule the next lesson as soon as possible. I will need to bring something to feed him and must research what he would like best. Is it turnips? Perhaps bread ... probably not ... OK, lettuce like he said. Who can donate some lettuce to a poor working camel who needs love and attention?... So many items to keep track of.

I hope I wake up on time to get to my station at the temple by five o'clock. I do not want to be late. I need to get my shift ready, and the beautiful apron Dinah sewed for me. She is amazing and does so many thoughtful things for me. I will bring her a grass arrangement when I visit her after my temple shift is done.

So, how will I do my hair? It cannot fly around. Hannah pulled hers up in an adorable bun last week. Do I have enough pins? Should I roll it to the left or the right? How did Hannah do it? Yes, I have a plan and it will look exactly right.... I may see Kaleb. I wonder how he is and what his assignments at the temple are now. Will he become a priest? His father is a priest, so he can if he wants to. Will he have gray in his beard when he gets old? Jacob has already started losing his hair....

I need to show the dress design I made and the sleeves, how they flow down with simplicity. I hope Hannah will be there tomorrow, but maybe it is her week off. I hate weeks off; sometimes it is painful, but the women in the temple tell me once my body gets used to the cycle, it should only have some cramping for a short while. It does not seem fair, but they also said that this process is designed to "create women who can bring forth life." I suppose this is all according to plan. Veronica looks up and asks aloud, "Hmmm, where are we?"

In final preparation for the now weekly camel lesson, Veronica places a bundle of colorful purple beads around her camel's neck. Of course, she introduces herself once again, thanks the camel, and tells him they are still doing well together. Yes, she also scrunches in his two upper lips and affectionately calls him, "Mr. Squishy-Lips."

"Huph Huph," Veronica says. Sitting very straight, she rises as the camel stands erect, holds the reins in one hand, and moves them lightly to the right. The camel responds instantly and looks to be glad that all the brushing and blanketing are completed, with the saddle strapped and cinched, feeling good to do something useful.

A Splendid Life of Service

V ERONICA IS NOW ALMOST TWENTY, has been engaged in temple service since she was twelve, and is now filled with joy while instructing young girls who have lots of energy. Each afternoon they display a vivid curiosity similar to hers at the same age. She is the leader of six young twelve-year-olds who think she is a bit mean from time to time. They do, however, think Veronica is the best big sister they could imagine and love it when she sneaks them into areas they were not assigned to, particularly the area where lambs are kept.

With the young girls sitting around her, Veronica slowly explains, "You each have been prepared for a very long time to serve here in God's temple. You were taught before time began how to be reverent and peaceful and how to learn your tasks," she pauses, "again."

"Again?" the girls ask.

"Yes, again. Neither you nor I remember, but we were spirits before we came down to earth to gain a body, and we learned all about the good things we could choose to do when we arrived. Is that not wonderful?" The girls all shake their heads yes.

Veronica stands and begins walking, "Come, follow me. I want to show you something amazing. Did you know that there is an exact way God wishes temple linens to be folded?" They all walk lightly behind her, trying to mimic Veronica's ballerina-like movement.

Veronica's work as Dinah's assistant is also very fulfilling. Although she gets in trouble for asking so many questions when visiting clients, the clients love her and look forward to her visits. They do, in fact, place orders to create a reason for Veronica to "bless them with her presence," as they say.

The camel riding is an entirely separate subject altogether Veronica is quite a different person when on the camel. After three-and-a-half years of consistent training, she is as good, if not better, than many of the Roman troops she now rides with and sports against. She communicates with her camel in a way that shows sensitivity, but she is clearly in charge.

When Veronica is working with Dinah and visiting many different clients, whose vocations vary widely, Veronica is becoming a studied professional. Her camel life, however, is a true adventure, and her interest is always being fed by enthusiastic and detailed answers by her senior trainer. When on her camel, she is, and has to be, one hundred percent focused. She is in a different world where, for the most part, she is in control of most everything, with, of course, her camel's permission. So different than the rest of her life.

For her safety and the safety of others, Veronica has learned not to entertain any non-camel-related idea or thought that even tries to enter her mind when on the Roman Training Grounds. She knows and practices a no-distractions-allowed frame of mind. From the moment she arrives until the moment she departs, Veronica is all camel master. She has become a master in every aspect of her life: her temple service, her work with textiles, and her camel riding. Life could not be better.

Although the world was as good as it could possibly be for Veronica when her twentieth birthday arrives, it is about to change in a dramatic way.

VERONICA ASKS DINAH IN HER customary way, "Is there anything I can do for you while I am excused this week from temple service?"

Dinah looks up from the red fabric she is measuring for an upcoming project and asks, "You know?" forgetting that Veronica is still young, and her cycles are regular.

"Why yes of course I know. It is always the same. I will certainly have some time. How can I help?"

Dinah is not surprised that Veronica would be asking this question, she has asked it every month since she became a woman; she is touched at Veronica's sincerity and her consistent service of everyone around her. Dinah thinks, *This wonderful young woman is such a joy to have around. I wish she could live here, but that would be selfish.*

Dinah raises her eyes to the ceiling, then looks at Veronica again and says, "Veronica, you are too kind. I do not deserve you in my life, but yes, I have a couple of tunics which you can work on in your spare time."

She gives Veronica a great, big smile to which Veronica says, "I'd love to work on some tunics for you!"

"They are only common tunics for common people, not special at all, and should not be too difficult."

"Yes, that will be fine. I love taking care of 'common people,'" Veronica says and then looks into the air and adds in a wishful tone, "I'd love to work on a special tunic for a very important person." Her finger goes to her chin as she imagines, "If you ever speak to the rich son of the king of Greece, tell him I will make his tunic!"

"Yes, of course. Next time I see him at the Training Grounds or at the palace, I will certainly bring your offer up. Will you require a down payment?" They both giggle and begin their business for the day.

VERONICA'S NEXT SCHEDULED VISIT TO the Roman Training Grounds is different. "So, today is another 'Training Demonstration' day where you will exhibit to our new troops how a camel master is able to do amazing maneuvers on a well-trained camel. As you know, this is a formal presentation, so remember to leave the beads off this time. Confirmed?" the senior trainer instructs.

"Yes, my trainer. Do I repeat what we practiced last week?" Veronica asks.

"Yes, but do not do the last part, which only officers are allowed to perform. It is a battlefield maneuver which is not yet appropriate for the new troops. Cover yourself so they cannot see you are a girl."

Veronica looks straight at him and declares, "I am a woman."

"Yes, a woman," the senior trainer agrees, then turns and walks away without further comment.

Veronica looks at her senior trainer as he departs and surmises, *He must have a lot on his mind to be so abrupt and formal. I hope everything is OK. New recruits are sometimes stressful.*

Veronica completes her and the camel's preparations. She says kind words, then scratches behind his ears. This time, however, as she is jiggling his lips, she advises her camel, "Let us do well, Mister Squishy Lips … Sir." She climbs on without any effort, then commands, "Huph Huph." Her camel stands and begins his assigned movements as she is thinking.

She does not need to move her reins; she communicates with her legs and body position in the saddle. Camels can be very sensitive if given the chance. She pulls her riding hood up and over her head and confidently rides to the north end of the Training Grounds with her well-trained and loyal camel. They wait patiently.

Veronica holds very still and watches as the new Roman soldiers who will be trained are marched in. Veronica considers what she has learned about new recruits; *Thinking about Roman soldiers marching anywhere gives a mind's-eye view that they are 1) all in the exact same uniform, 2) all the same height, and 3) from a well-controlled Italian soldier-breeding program and are delivered in ships to the various Roman outposts across the Mediterranean world.*

As the troops arrive and take their places on the rise next to the eastern side of the Training Grounds, Veronica observes. *It is easy to see none of these expectations are even close to being correct. Number one is all right, but numbers two and three are so far off that they make number one look wrong as well. Romans recruit their troops from everywhere and anywhere they can find them. Not only are many nations represented, their heights, shapes, and hair colors are of every sort.* They are in place and settled to watch the demonstration. What happens next is unusual and surprising. Veronica focuses so she will not be distracted.

Seven mounted cavalry troops in full regalia slowly appear on the south side of where the troops are situated on the east side. They raise their battlefield horns, and the sound is thrilling: "Tah dah dit dit dit dah!"

As Veronica was not informed this was going to happen, she thinks, *I will need to request to be appraised of this type of thing in the future. Ha-ha … that is a joke!*

What also amazes her is that the horns have a magnificent effect on her camel. Master Squishy-Lips instantly stands at attention, and it feels to Veronica as if he gained fifteen centimeters in height and is now poised to be expert at what he and Veronica have refined together. Veronica is transformed with the camel and is poised to teach with authority.

The horns sound again, which signals for a larger cavalcade of mounted troops to enter from the south side. There are four rows of eight horses walking onto the Training Grounds in a very formal manner. At the center, they pivot to the right, continue straight, and then, once at the end near Veronica and her camel steed, turn around, stop for only two seconds, then abruptly explode into a full gallop, all still in perfect rows.

It is a remarkable sight. They slow down and split at the end, forming two single-file rows which turn to the right and to the left, ending with sixteen horses on each side of the Training Ground, each about six feet apart, facing the center. It is Veronica's time. Both she and the camel are ready; they are focused as one.

THE HORNS BLARE AGAIN. VERONICA'S hands are already on her hips. The reins are loosely hanging in a hook to keep them from sliding to either side as she takes her mind through the maneuvers: *Sit straight with open leg space. Walk slowly, straight ahead for seventeen, eighteen, nineteen, twenty paces.*

Press right knee against Master Squishy-Lips to begin a large circle. Lean slightly forward to begin trotting. Keep hands on hips. Complete a full circle. Squeeze your right knee more and lean more forward. Canter to complete another smaller circle.

Everything is going perfectly. The camel does not actually need any directives; however, both rider and steed are aware that something could happen any second that may cause a need for different instructions, perhaps evasive action.

Complete circle, release right leg, sit up straight and slightly back. Stop. Lean quickly forward and press left and right toes against camel. Full gallop to end of grounds. Release side pressure. Sit straight. Stop. Twist to the left. Turn around. Stop. Trot slowly for two, three, four, five. Move hands to neck and hold on. Squeeze both sides. Explode into a full race gallop straight down the grounds.

Stop. Turn around. Walk to the center of the grounds in front of troops. Turn right and face them. Stop. Lean back with legs slightly forward. Back up. Put right leg inward toward camel. Turn right while backing up.

The demonstration continues for another ten minutes. Veronica and Master Squishy-Lips end by doing a full gallop around the Training Grounds, ending where they had started. She then waits for the troops to be dismissed. Both she and her well-trained camel are pleased to have "shown the men how it is done."

Veronica sees movement among the Roman officers and thinks, *Something is different. Is something wrong?* The horns blare again, which send the sixteen cavalry troops from each side into the center. They form an arrow-straight line of horse and rider directly facing the troops.

This is interesting. Perhaps they are going to give a rank advancement. These things always take too long. I have 600 kilograms of sweaty camel under me, and I am also ready to get refreshed, Veronica thinks to herself.

She looks down at her camel to see how formally he is holding his head. *He has gone back to "attention" mode. This is odd.* She looks up to see that the horns had made their way to the center front of the horses and thinks, *Wow, they are serious about this!*

As Veronica is anxious to care for her camel, his standing at attention and the formal-looking activities intrigue her. She watches her senior trainer and the senior Roman officer walk to the center of the formation and reasons, *They are doing the formal march step, not casually walking. Why are all the troops looking in my direction? Did I mess something up? Are they going to take Mr. Squishy-Lips away?*

The senior trainer and senior Roman officer stop, make a rigid left turn, then look directly at her. Veronica's attention is piqued.

The trainer's right arm comes up and motions for Veronica to come forward. Her camel knows to walk as formally as a long-legged, squishy-lipped camel can and moves forward. Veronica notices some people coming over the Training Grounds rise. *That is Dinah! There is Daniel as well! What is going on?* She says to herself, *Focus, focus, focus,* as her camel takes the final few steps to be stationed directly in front of the two familiar Roman soldiers.

"Cush Cush." The camel kneels, Veronica lights off and stands at attention, hood up, in front of them.

"Please lower your hood, Veronica," her senior trainer requests.

As Veronica slowly reaches up with both hands to grasp her hood, her mind is racing, *I hope my hair is OK. What are my friends doing here? I do not like being the center of attention.*

Veronica pulls her hood down quickly with a bit of drama, which causes a gasp among the troops she had been training. The thought comes to mind, *Dinah said I would show the men how it is done. I hope she is pleased.*

A soldier from her right marches forward carrying something as another comes in from the left, also carrying something. They both stop. The senior Roman officer reaches over to take a ribbon from the first soldier. He raises it up to show the crowd and announces, "The Ninth Dromedarii Legion of his highness Caesar Augustus presents this medal of civilian honor to you for having achieved the level of Senior Master." He places the medal around Veronica's neck.

He then reaches over to take a crown of leaves with flowers from the other soldier and carefully places it on Veronica's head. The crowd cheers. Dinah and Daniel cry, while at the top of the rise, among his staff, the Jewish leader sheds tears of joy and sorrow. For the first time in her entire life, Veronica stands at attention, sobbing, and speechless.

She gathers courage, looks up at the Roman officer and says, "Thank you sir." She notes that his eyes have tears as well. She turns to the senior trainer and says, "You were so very patient with me. Thank you, my selfless mentor, my friend." His eyes are shedding so many tears that he can hardly see her. It certainly is a well-deserved moment of celebration for extraordinary accomplishments.

Soon after this glorious recognition, Veronica's life changes. Veronica has to find Dinah. She must break the law, which forbids women to be in public during their time of cleansing, of renewal. She is fraught with worry, her chest swelling with anxiety as she sits in the chair next to the old wooden door in her small home. Her mind exclaims, *It has been only five or six days long each cycle ever since I became a woman.*

She leans over against the cramping to put on her sandals and continues to reason in her mind, *It has now been eleven days. It needs to stop. I cannot keep asking Adina, Hannah, and Lila to take my place in the temple with my children. The trainer will be expecting me next week. Where will Dinah be at this time of day?* Veronica's shawl is in place as she opens the door and rushes out into the rain-wet morning air.

She continues to find reason in her pain. *In the past, running was so easy. What is going on? I must push myself to walk quickly.* Veronica rounds a corner and comes face-to-face with an old man looking at the ground. She tries to miss him as she lurches to the right but bumps his shoulder. He almost spills to the stone pathway as she manages to snatch him up. "Sir, I am so sorry! It was my fault. Are you OK?"

"Oh yes, I am fine. You are young and in a hurry. I am slow and have nothing left to do except pray morning and evening in the temple." He looks up into Veronica's eyes and advises, "You go along, you have important things to do. I am perfectly fine. Hurry, or you will be late." He smiles a gentle smile and returns on his way.

"Oh yes sir, thank you so very much and please have a good day. God is watching over you and is pleased," Veronica says passionately as she watches him shuffle away through the light rain for a moment.

Her plight is temporarily replaced by what this kind man had said. She thinks about it. *"I am slow and have nothing left to do except pray morning and evening in the temple." How could he feel as if praying in the temple was of little worth? I beg to be able to go back to the temple. My girls are so sweet and delightful. I have so many important skills to teach them.*

He also said, "You have important things to do" … Yes, I do have import-
ant things to do, and they involve teaching, training, and serving. I need
to get back to them. I am sure Dinah knows someone who can help. I am
sure I am not the only one who has had this happen … why am I so weak?
Veronica gathers her shawl up against her neck to have something stable to
hold on to as she forces her legs to move more quickly. She takes smaller
steps, so she does not fall over.

Peter's Apprentice

4

"OUCH! THAT IS TWICE THAT has happened this morning." Sitting on the not-so-comfortable fishing boat gunnel, Tobin's left foot has fallen asleep again. He stretches his leg, places his numb foot on a rock while he adjusts the fishing-net repair needle in his yet-to-be-firm grip. He had been trying to focus on the sequence so that it becomes part of his subconscious; "Over, around, snatch, twist, then—pull. Peter can do it effortlessly," he says as his foot starts tingling.

It is early morning in Capernaum where Peter's apprentice is focusing on repairing one of the many fishing nets they have responsibility to care for in support of Peter's family fishing business. The apprentice does not notice Andrew, Peter's younger brother, approaching. Andrew silently makes his way to the opposite side of the boat, grabs the gunnel with both hands, and starts shaking it … hard.

The apprentice loses his focus, looks up across the water, and as he does, Andrew yells, "Earthquake!" The apprentice instantly jumps to his feet, looking for a safe place to run, while Andrew begins laughing hysterically. His tingling foot is not helping matters as he almost falls on the rocky beach.

"How did you sneak up on me again? I hate it when you do that!" Tobin exclaims.

"Well, earthquakes happen frequently. You need to be prepared," responds Andrew, still chuckling.

"Andrew! Here is one for you! Fetch!" Peter yells as he tosses a rock into the Sea of Galilee. The water is quiet, so the rock hitting the surface makes a clear *kerplunk!* sound as ripples radiate outward.

"How fast can you fetch it little brother?" Peter says with a grin as he continues his energetic hike down the hill.

Walking over to the water's edge Andrew shouts back as Peter nears, "Ah yes, I remember falling for your little trick when I was six, Peter."

"Yes, six ... and seven ... and eight ... it was a wonderful pastime," Peter announces with a big grin, "and to tell you the truth, I felt bad that you fell for it so many times ... but it was still very entertaining ... and if I think about it, you are still entertaining occasionally."

Peter approaches Andrew and tries to bump him into the water. Andrew swirls to the left, catches Peter's sleeve, and sticks his foot out to trip Peter. Peter is heavier and does not move as quickly or as easily as Andrew hopes. "Aha!" says Peter as he catches hold of Andrew's leg, holds on to it, and stands straight up.

The sight of Peter holding Andrew's leg waist high while Andrew is trying to keep from losing balance and head for the water makes the apprentice yell, "Watch out, Andrew!"

Peter, now holding Andrew's leg by the ankle with both hands, says quietly, "So, Andrew my close friend, do you want me to lift it higher?" He lifts a tiny bit, to which Andrew yells laughing, "No!"

Knowing he has the best of Andrew, Peter cannot resist asking, "Twist this little leg to the right?"

"No! Not today!" Andrew is laughing nonstop.

"Well, OK, I'll release my prisoner." He lets go of Andrew's foot and it falls, making a splash. "But I will keep the prisoner's footwear as hostage!"

Peter holds up Andrew's sandal, Andrew lunges for it, and Peter tosses it to him and places his hands on his hips. His eyes are sparkling with delight, while grinning ear to ear, which can be seen, even behind his beard.

Andrew hops over to the water's edge and leans on the boat while putting his sandal back on. Peter says, "So ... now that we have established the pecking order around here," he glances over at Andrew and winks, "let us stop worrying about earthquakes and get some work done. We need to be prepared for the evening fishing. The Committee's spies will be on the alert to track who takes in the biggest fish haul, so we will be sure to make our report accurately and on time." Peter looks over at the apprentice. "That's your responsibility today, correct?"

"Yes Peter, I am prepared," Tobin responds.

The apprentice has been successfully learning to run the business, which Peter's family has been operating for several generations. With the increased trade in the fishing industry, Peter is expanding his capacity while ensuring his licensing requirements are being managed with the Israel Fishing Industry Advisory Committee in Jerusalem as well as with the local committee who manages the daily Sea of Galilee fishing reporting processes.

The local committee is responsible for the over fifty harbors, as well as the multiple packing facilities which support the 650 licensed fishing vessels, whose owners all pay fees and taxes.

The committee also manages what the fishers call "The Fishing Police," who keep an eye on individual boats, especially those known to "spread the catch" in order to not be fined for catching fish "over the limit." Everything about the fishing industry is regulated. The number of business licenses is restricted for both local sales transactions as well as for transactions made to international trade brokers.

Peter, Andrew, and Tobin all pitch in to prepare the boats, arranging the nets so they can be dropped into the Sea of Galilee easily. They launch for the day's work.

"WE HAD A GOOD HARVEST today! God is smiling down upon us," Peter announces to his wife, who meets them at the dock.

"Well, I am so happy for you!" she replies. She then looks at Andrew, who was on land with the ropes already and says, "Yes, I am happy for me as well … you know what he is like when things do not go so well." She smiles and takes one of the ropes from Andrew, pulls it over, and attaches it in place.

Peter looks at his apprentice. "Thank you, Tobin, for handling the reports. You are doing well. When you arrive in Jerusalem, make sure to see Joseph when you visit the Committee Office … tell him that his handsome friend from Capernaum, the one with the best fishing vessels, says hello to him as well as to his lovely wife. You will not forget, will you?"

"Of course not Peter; I cannot forget anything you ask me to do, especially to say hello to your ... let's see here, how many is that now? Hmmm...." Peter's apprentice is exaggerating his heavy task. "Yes, Caiaphas ... the man who cuts your hair, Levi ... the priest you give your sacrifices to, Benjamin ... our faithful net weaver, Dinah ... your mother-in-law's friend who does all things textile, Ephraim ... our international trade broker, and ... who was the last guy? ... Josephine! Right?" He grimaces.

"No, you know perfectly well it is Joseph. We have been doing business together for longer than you have been around my young apprentice. My father Jonah knew his father and our grandfathers did business together and so on. Never a problem, never a cross word. All gentlemen of honor and great integrity. Not like those you will see at the local committee, that's for sure," Peter, who enjoys having trustworthy friends remarks, then adds, "They are stable, even in the fiercest storms of life."

PETER'S APPRENTICE, TOBIN, FINDS JERUSALEM busier than it was the last few times he had traveled there. He knows the way to the office of the advisory committee, and they have already received Peter's business request to add to what Peter calls his "marvelous fleet," which has been supporting the international trade licenses he was granted several years ago.

Joseph knows the apprentice the moment he steps inside the ornate building, turns, and walks toward him with, "How are you my young friend? It has been some time since Peter has released you from his little fishing camp up north. How have you been? Good to see you!" He gives Tobin a grandfatherly hug.

Tobin starts to reply, "Yes sir, all is ..."

"Yes! I am so happy to see you have arrived here safely. Did your journey take longer than you expected, or was it calm and peaceful?"

Tobin knows Joseph is always in a hurry and so keeps his answer short, "Yes sir, it was fine, we ..."

"The documents arrived very well in time, and so I provided them, along with my notes, to the advisory committee, who are meeting this afternoon ... oh," He glances up at Tobin and continues, "Well they have started their session so let us go now. What are we waiting around here for? Come along," Joseph says as he makes a quick right turn and shuffles more quickly than usual down the hall to the meeting room. "Come along," he repeats again.

The apprentice knows how this works, so he moves down the hall behind, not next to, and certainly not in front of, Joseph. They make their entrance into the advisory committee room as an elderly gentleman is pleading his desire to entrust his five-vessel, local license to his grandson, who is eldest to his firstborn son.

His request is upheld without representation, voted on, and approved, for a fee, which is higher than it was when paid last year. This was ordinary, to see fees rise when licenses are transferred in ownership. The operating taxes, however, are regulated, so they stay the same, regardless of ownership privileges.

The committee recorder finalizes the decision with, "We have reviewed this request and hereby approve it. Let the records show the change as requested. Please present yourself to the treasurer to process the request and receive your documents."

"Next case for review?" The chairman asks. Joseph walks (he does not shuffle in the least) directly to the center and stands up straight as if he were only thirty years old. His presence before the advisory committee is impressive....

"Greetings to all from the requester Peter Bar Jonah of Capernaum, holder of fifteen licenses local and five licenses International Trade Consortium, Sea of Galilee. The request you have received for review two months ago is to increase International Trade Consortium licenses from five to ten. The requestor is as of records dating recent, in good standing both fees and taxes, with zero complaints and zero infractions."

Joseph takes one step back to indicate he has completed his representation of the requestor's bid.

The committee recorder sets the paper he is looking at down on the ornate desk and announces, "We have reviewed this request and hereby approve it. Let the records show the change as requested. Please present yourself to the treasurer to process the request and receive your documents."

So, as quick as that, Peter Bar Jonah receives his new licenses, allowing his business to expand, with Tobin likely to manage one side of the business. He is not sure if it would be the local or the international.

Tobin waits until they are back in the hallway and thanks Joseph formally, "Very well executed, Joseph. Peter Bar Jonah thanks you for your kind services. He …"

"Come along, come along," Joseph says as he shuffles along down the long hallway.

The treasury office attached to the advisory committee had outgrown its old office several years ago because the fishing industry grew substantially. They are now in a very nice office equal to the fishing industry's economic importance and kinder than the Agricultural Advisory Committee buildings.

Joseph stops, turns right, adds another fifteen shuffles, and says, "Martha! How are you? How is the family? I hope your husband still remembers his name, of course he does! Great to see you! Your hair looks wonderful today!"

Martha is delighted as she turns her head toward Tobin and winks, turns back to Joseph, and says with enthusiasm, "Yes, Aaron! So good to see you! Your mother was such a wonderful woman!" She glances over and winks at the apprentice again.

"I am not Aaron! I am Joseph! Why do you always keep calling me Aaron?" Joseph retorts with a grin. He turns to Tobin and gives an exaggerated wink, then looks back at Martha.

"I have been calling you Aaron since the day your mother told me she lost Joseph and his fancy jacket when he went on a trip with his eleven brothers. That is who you are, even if you deny it, Aaron!"

"I have told you 127 times … your mother is wrong! I am Joseph! I do not have eleven brothers, I only have one sister, whom my mother wanted to name Ruth, but that name was already taken, so they dug to the bottom and produced the name Martha … that is how you got your name … sister!"

"Well, yes, I am your older sister and deserve more respect than you give me my little brother Joseph-the-Bewildered," Martha confirms as she approaches Joseph and gives him a hug.

Joseph and Martha both chuckle as Tobin watches with a grin on his face.

"Yes, we got him you think?" Martha asks Joseph quietly.

"Oh my, you were stellar, you were," is Joseph's reply, patting Martha's soft folded hands.

"Oh, that was good, so refreshing to tease you until you get mad," Joseph says to Marta with a grin and slight nod of his head.

"I've told you over and over, I never get mad; I only get justice," Martha returns as she moves to retrieve papers, which she then presents to Tobin slowly, with both hands.

"Keep these safe and do … not … flaunt … them; they can be stolen." She reaches over and places her hand on top of Tobin's, confiding, "You have a very good business owner. We trust him as well as his brother Andrew, and we have known his mother-in-law, Muriel, for many decades. We hope his business continues to thrive and grow. He deserves it, and so do you."

Tobin is touched, nods his head saying quietly, "Thank you. Peter has great regard for both you and Joseph and wishes you well. Thank you once again."

Joseph closes his visit with, "Yes, well, come along Tobin. Thank you, Martha, for helping us get the paperwork together so quickly. You are a blessing to your mother's name, a curse to your intelligent, handsome brother, but you do well toward your mother each day God lets you stay." He smiles at Martha and shuffles out of the office and back down the hallway.

The apprentice thinks as he follows Joseph, *Now that was interesting. Joseph would have probably kept talking all afternoon if he felt like it. I always love visiting. Seems like family everywhere I go. Of course,*

*everyone knows everyone else around here and most of them are related,
and they will tell you so. I cannot wait to get back to Capernaum; there
are many tasks to accomplish.*

"WELL DONE! WELL DONE INDEED! We are going to sup together in celebration! Is that OK with you? You look famished. Come along, come along," Peter says, mimicking Joseph, ending with a Joseph-style shuffle as he guides Tobin and his guests toward his home.

After everyone is washed, placed, and comfortably eating, Peter looks at Tobin and says, "So, you have obtained the licenses for the future we will all build together. This is very good, and I thank you for braving the wild city of Jerusalem for the good of the business. How about the more important part of your sojourn? What have you to report?" Peter is smiling with anticipation, eager to hear the news.

"Yes, well, everyone is fine, and they all say hello to you, and you and you and you!" Tobin reports as he looks at everyone gathered around. He then looks down at his lap as if to pretend he had given the report, but he cannot keep the grin off his face.

Peter jumps in with a joke of his own, "What? And exactly why would Caiaphas want to say hello to my darling wife and her sweet mother?" Peter is on stage now. "And why, perchance, would Levi and Ephraim be doing the same?"

He grabs a small bite of food, places it in his mouth, and chews it quickly like a hungry goat while looking down and saying, "Hmmmmm ... and so, I understand why Dinah would offer her kind hello as well as her sincere condolences to my intelligent mother-in-law for her suffering while being held in captivity in such a backwards family as this."

Peter reaches for more food and closes his drama by saying in an acquiescent voice, "So that is it, OK. Thank you." He turns to his wife and mother-in-law, who are about to burst out in laughter and adds, "This is great food. Thank you for creating it to celebrate our hero of the day." He stops for an instant and then adds, cocking his head to the side, "When is he going to arrive so we can celebrate with him? Did he get swallowed up into a sand hole from which there is no return?" Peter leans over so far, he almost loses balance and utters, "Humph?"

There is a tiny moment of tension, and nobody moves a hair. They are all ready to explode and have repressed grins across their faces. They start looking around at each other to see if it is OK to laugh. Peter finally breaks the tension and starts his deep belly laugh, which releases all the pent-up energy in the room, with everyone following along.

After several moments of raucous laughter, Peter looks at Tobin, nods his head, and says, "That was a perfect setup. Thank you for giving me the straight line so I could deliver the punch line ... that was good." He looks straight at Tobin at as if to say, "What is the real report on everyone?" The room grows quiet again to hear the response.

"What? That was it. That is all." Tobin cannot not hold it in and starts laughing because Peter is looking him in the eyes, and he cannot keep a straight face. Tobin looks up and begins his report, "It was a marvelous expedition into the wilds of the southern territories...." There has not been such joyful laughter in the household for quite a while. Everyone is truly happy to be together and excited to hear news from Jerusalem.

The next few weeks and months are spent implementing plans for the growth of the family fishing business. The apprentice has earned his position of managing the international side, while Andrew is dealing very well with the growth of the local trade.

A Quiet Time Together

H ER SOFT FACE IS CALM, while her clear, blue eyes seem intent on something far away, yet so close. It seems she wishes to reach out and touch, yet she remains motionless while the warm water is poured over her long, gray hair.

Dinah's mother Lidia has been ill for a long time, and while she allows only her daughter to wash her hair during her weekly visits, she has been partially dependent on others to provide daily care. She is beginning to take short walks near her home and visits with those who frequent the area, including three age-old friends who are priests with whom she has served in the temple for so many years. As Dinah gently wraps the towel around her mother's brow, she asks, "Mother, have you heard the amazing stories about the Rabbi from Galilee?" There is no immediate answer.

DINAH IS A VERY NOBLE, gracious, and caring woman, with family ties to temple service which extend many years. Zacharias the high priest is her mother's uncle. Dinah began serving in the temple with her mother and learned as she participated in support of the Sons of Aaron with ordinances of animal sacrifices, and years later, she advanced to support the high priests in their duties.

Dinah began her textile career as an apprentice doing carding and loom weaving. Over the years, she has become the go-to expert, ensuring that nothing but the most perfect products are offered to service in the temple. She is business-minded, but in the beginning, most all her business was related to temple activities.

The stringent organizational and production skills Dinah developed supporting temple leadership became the basis for her business career. She has become the primary supplier of all things textile for not only the temple but for most of the major buildings and institutions within Jerusalem. Her business also supplies the interior decorating textiles for many of the noble Roman and Jewish leaders whose summer and winter homes lie outside of Jerusalem.

"WHAT ARE YOU LOOKING AT, mother?" Dinah gently asks Lidia.

"I am not 'looking' at anything at all; it is what I 'see' that amazes me. Still after all these years I have memories that are ever-present. Do you ever smell your memories, Dinah?" Lidia responds matter-of-factly.

"Yes, mother, I sometimes smell the small, sweet cakes you often made with anise seed. I can smell them right now speaking about them."

"Ah, those are simple yet marvelous little cakes. You used to smell them before taking a bite, sometimes for almost a whole minute!" Lidia says while giggling.

Dinah remembers an idea and says, "We will need to take some time to make some together. I would enjoy doing that. Get away from the business for an afternoon." She then thinks, *I wonder how many times I have said something like that?*

"Yes, well, I am here waiting. Any time you schedule yourself an entire afternoon away from your 'business' I will be available." Lidia then interjects, "Of course, I am now taking walks a couple of times a week and doing quite well, I have to admit. So, if I am gone, retrieve me from up on the hill, where Elias, Jacob, and Gabriel are always talking nonstop. I can hardly get away once I get to talking with them."

"Oh, they are so sweet! How are they doing these days? Do their wives still 'encourage' them to go out of the house so they can get something done?" Dinah asks, thinking kindly of them training her as a young girl many years ago.

Dinah reminisces, *When I was being trained in the temple by them with my friends, they were very kind and tender and paid close attention to details. But it was a different thing altogether when they were all together ... like a theatrical presentation ... and certainly a comedy.*

Lidia laughs, "Ha! You still say aloud what you are thinking. You are correct in what you think, er, say, but you need to practice being quiet or your brain is going to get your mouth in trouble! I remember once when you were almost six-sophisticated-years-old, and I took you to a temple planning meeting when construction was beginning … Hee Hee. I still think it is funny.”

Dinah asks, “What was so funny? I cannot remember that far back. Tell me how clever I was!”

“Oh Dinah, see? I can think of entire paragraphs in an instant, and none of it comes out of my mouth. A very nice arrangement I have studied, or ‘I have carefully practiced’ with my brain and mouth since I made a fool of myself when I was a very mature twelve-year-old at my bat mitzvah.”

Dinah tried to bring Lidia back to the topic, “And so, how did my cleverness cause you great difficulty? I hope you were not reprimanded for toting me along.”

“No, I expected you to make drawings of wonderful designs you have always had inside your ‘clever’ little head, but you were distracted.”

“How was I distracted? You know that is difficult while I am drawing.”

“Oh yes, I know. Well, we were speaking about what would be needed for temple operations support. We had started to speak about incense and how the incense suppliers would be chosen and how we would determine, very carefully, if their incense was worthy of the temple.”

“Yes. Did I offer my opinion?”

“Yes, but not at that moment. One of the gentlemen had brought some incense to show us, and his servant set fire to his sample—the aromatic smoke began drifting up, and the smell was wonderful.”

“I am sure I had something to say, or announce, about that, didn’t I?”

“Well, yes, you looked up, and your eyes were as round as could be. You looked up at me and said in a whisper, ‘Mother, that is a very special smell. Does God like it too?’ I patted your little hand and said that I was sure that God loved the smell just as you did.”

“So?”

“We had a very large, old gentleman named Asher with us, and he was very kind and thoughtful. He did not interrupt the ladies when they spoke. Well, he was allergic to that incense. He later said it was because of the ‘filler’ the supplier placed in the sample incense.”

“What happened? Did he pass out?”

"No, the opposite. He sneezed, and you had something to say about that."

"A sneeze? I said something about a simple sneeze?"

"Well, it was not a *simple* sneeze, but rather a huge sneeze that seemed to start in his feet and get louder as it made its way through his torso, grew in his chest, and by the time it came out, we were all shocked by the force if it. We put our hands over our mouths for fear of laughing at his sneeze and embarrassing him. Everyone became quiet, except one little six-year-old girl next to me, kneeling with her art supplies."

"Oh no! I laughed, didn't I?"

"No, actually, you did not laugh at all. You made an observation and posed an innocent question."

"Oh boy, what happened?"

"You had jumped to your feet and were standing straight; your eyes were wide open with your arm pointed to the poor gentleman. With your index finger stretched out to be perfectly precise whom you were talking about, you exclaimed, 'Mother, is his father a camel? He sure sounded like a camel sneezing!'" Lidia recounts as she tries to repress a laugh but fails.

"Oh no! I am so sorry!"

"No, it is what you next did that people are still talking about. It gave everyone there a clear view of your kind and gracious soul."

"Tell me. I really do not remember, I am sorry to say," Dinah asked.

"As the tension of the room was about to explode, you walked up to Asher, placed your hand on his knee, looked with your sweet face right into his eyes and spoke. 'I am so sorry. That must have hurt. Please, is there anything I can do to help you feel better?' Asher glanced over at the burning incense and back to you. You understood the problem and, at six-years-old, took charge of helping someone in need as you said looking at the servant with the burning incense, 'Thank you kind sir. We all appreciate your assistance, now, if you would be kind enough to remove the sample from the room so our friend will be able to breathe without difficulty.'

Your straightforward-yet-peaceful request was carried out. The meeting was distracted back into some order, and we quietly completed our business ... and you became famous, instantly."

Dinah is speechless and reflects, *I have failed to build upon that moment and am too absorbed in 'the business'.*

Lidia responds, "No, you have not failed at all my dearest daughter, and the hushed tones spoken about you since that day are of parents saying about their children, 'Oh, if this child would but seek to learn charity and love as we all see in Lidia's daughter Dinah. She is such an example; everyone hopes to have her teach their children how to serve in the temple with reverence and thanksgiving.' You are an example, and you are busy because you try to serve everyone you come in contact with. Do not forget that God is pleased with you. Speaking of serving, how is little Veronica doing?"

Dinah is not allowed to regress into herself for the moment.

"Oh yes," Dinah says as she is pulled out of the past and into the same room, "Veronica is an absolute delight, and although I do not know about her background, she is attentive, on time, and learns very quickly."

"Is she part of your training group at the temple?"

"No, she is now with Suzanne's group with her friends Hannah, Lila, and Adina, whom I am sure you know."

"Yes, their parents are all kind, so I expect their children are as well…. Veronica will do well."

"Do well? Do well? I will have nothing of the sort spoken about my fledglings…. They will excel!" Dinah laughs and adds, "You forget who you are speaking with, dear mother."

"Yes," Lidia chuckles, "I do forget, and I know very well that when I forget, there is always someone to remind me." She then adds softly, "I am not able to speak about Veronica's background but have heard things… so sad." She wraps the small kerchief she had been holding around her hand and looks out the window."

Dinah knows her mother was holding back something she had buried long ago and wonders, *Should I press her for more information? Do I need to know what she is heard? More importantly, should I know what she knows? With mother, it is always hard to tell, but, in the end, she knows what I should be aware of and what would distract me needlessly. Being a mother and having that wrestle takes strength, wisdom, and patience.*

Lidia does not say if she heard Dinah's thoughts this time, and Dinah is happy, even if she had heard them; the thoughts were honorable and respectful.

TRANSITIONS

A LTHOUGH VERONICA HAD ALWAYS HAD a propensity to talk to herself, mostly in run-on sentences, she uses it to punctuate the silence, trying to remain sane in her seemingly endless time alone. Looking at the heavy door of her home, she begins quietly....

Reflecting on my desperate flight to Dinah many years ago, it seems appropriate that it was raining. The rain was not heavy, it was constant, as if every angel in heaven was watching me and crying tears of grief. It was that very day when after consoling me, Dinah revealed her joyful news that she and her kind husband Aaron were expecting a child and expected it to be born in the springtime. I tried to be happy for her but was numb with worry and doubt.

Now, after a year since, I am still not healed and have been banished from serving in the temple with no expectation to return. Adina drops by from time to time, but she cannot stay too long. I think it is difficult for her sensitive soul, and she cannot find the words to make everything better, so she gives up.

She does not give up on me. She gives up on herself. It must be difficult for her. For the first few months she would say "How are you feeling today?" and "I am here if you wish to talk." She does not know how strengthening those visits were. I am worn out talking about it, and how I feel never changes.

It is like a slow path from Hebron—down, down, down to the bottom of the Dead Sea. I am not talking about the shoreline; I am headed for the bottom of the deep, dark sea itself ... and it is hard to see anything from

*down here. I have not had a hug or touched any human or even an animal
for more than seventy weeks.*

*I suppose that last part is not exactly true. I remember a tiny bright mo-
ment of sunshine that took place when I snuck out to the Training Grounds
about six months ago. To avoid those who are prone to yell and curse at
me when I leave my home against the well-understood rules, I slipped out
the back way.*

*I arrived in the late afternoon on a Sabbath eve to return when everyone
had their heads down, scurrying to be home before six. This hour of arrival
was good timing, as informal training was taking place and there were a
few soldiers practicing. Flavius, my senior trainer was arranging gear in the
storage area. I walked right up to him, trying to show I still have strength
and vitality. I wobbled a bit, but at least I was smiling.”* Veronica is brought
back to that time with clarity....

“WELL! HELLO THERE MISS VERONICA. We thought we had frightened you
away but then learned what happened to you. It must be a heavy burden
to carry. We are most sorry that you are quarantined inside your home.
Knowing how active you were, it must be very difficult. Please understand
that if you can make it here, you are welcome to visit any time,” Flavius
says with a warm smile, filling me with strength and hope.

“Yes, thank you. I enjoy it here and would desperately love to visit as
often as possible. Do you believe it would be possible for me to ride Mr.
Squishy-Lips for a moment or two ... please, if it is not any trouble?”

Flavius notes that Veronica looks like an angel with broken wings
and replies with enthusiasm, “Of course! I told you! You can come
any time you wish. Your ‘Squishy-Lips’ companion may be engaged,
but there are plenty of camels available, and with you in command,
any one of them would be better off learning from you, no matter how
little time you can spare for their benefit. Squishy-Lips will be right over
there if he is not out with a rider. Let us go look.” Flavius reaches out his
hand, takes Veronica by the hand, and motions toward the ready stalls.

They slowly walk over and make it around the barricade when one of the Roman infantry scout dogs comes walking by in the opposite direction. Veronica thinks, *This is odd. They always have the scout dogs with their masters.*

She forms the question and is about to ask, "Why is it loose?" when she sees the dog leading five very young puppies. Her heart jumps with joy as she instinctively kneels to greet them. They all scamper to her outstretched hands, sniffing and licking.

Veronica cannot control her emotions and begins crying with immense joy. The experience is overwhelming as she looks up at Flavius with tear-filled eyes and exclaims, "This is the most wonderful moment in my life. I love these puppies! I can tell they will be strong and well trained ... and loyal." The mother of the pups walks over, bends her head down in the center of action and nudges a couple of her brood as if to say, "OK little ones, it's time to explore some more places before it gets dark."

The black-furred mother turns to led them away, and one by one they follow her; however, the little gray puppy with black spots plops down right on top of Veronica's foot.

Flavius chuckles and observes, "Ah. Looks like you have a little friend there. He is either sensitive to your condition, or he is a bit tired of running around with his siblings."

Veronica responds, "Or maybe a bit of both. Animals can be very sensitive," as she reaches down with both hands and picks the little furball up, nuzzles him with her nose and tells him, walking toward the mother, "OK. It was great to meet you. Mother is ready to show you more interesting things before you go to sleep tonight, so get moving."

Veronica is smitten and does not want to set him down as she says to herself, *His fur is so soft,* but she bends over and gently places him on the ground and after he gains a steady foothold, she pats him on the rump and stands back up.

Veronica glances over at Flavius while wiping her eyes with her shawl. He grins back with kindness.

THE WEEKS OF VERONICA'S ILLNESS stretch on and on. She reflects once again in solitude....

I am not sure if I am tormented more by the physical pain or the emotional anguish. Sleep, when it comes, is the only moment of solace when I am free of what started twelve long years ago. Prior to that time, I was living the dream of every Israelite young woman ... sacred service in the temple.

Although it was under construction for as long as I can remember, even with the commotion all around, the Jerusalem Temple remained solemn and eternal in nature. The lights around the perimeter acted as beacons of truth and love—there for all to see.

I started temple service by invitation of Dinah, who had served there many years and whose mother, Lidia, had also served for decades. Lidia has shared with me many marvelous stories of miracles she witnessed inside the sturdy walls of the temple.

I learned many things and was advancing in my level of modest responsibilities when it all ended one dark and rainy day. I had completed my monthly woman's time away in solitude when, on the day I was assigned to return to service, the bleeding did not stop as normal. I was fraught with anger. "How inconvenient this is to keep me away longer than normal!" I thought. Frustrated, I tried to keep myself busy, waiting to return to normal health, assured that it would soon be over.

It continued from that point for a week longer, and when it still did not stop, my frustration turned to anger which turned to fear. Was I going to die? I asked myself. I do not want to die! I have my entire life ahead of me!

Darkness was enveloping my mind; friends were afraid to visit me, and I was declared unclean. Dinah visited from time to time, for which I was very grateful.

As the ailment's tenure turned from days into months, I was confused more than afraid, and although I had been taken by Dinah to several physicians, they offered no beneficial results ... at all. I cannot speak of what they did to me.

One bleak day, as I was sitting, or maybe lying, alone, staring at the wall next to the door, looking at the designs in the ancient plaster, aimlessly staring, there was a knock on the door. I heard it, and yet my mind was not inclined to make any move whatsoever to go open it. I did not care about what was on the other side. I was alone, the way it seemed it was supposed to be.

I stared at the door. The knocking sound came again so I thought about the sound and how it was made. It seemed to be created by something soft, like knuckles; otherwise, it would have a sound with a higher pitch, like a wooden cane. Now that would have made a different sound. I wondered what noise a stone would make. A small stone. A large stone.

I continued gazing at the door and the memory of the noise faded away as if it had never happened, and I had no care about the fact that I was incoherent, not connected to any item or any-one as if floating. Am I dying? Who will care? I guess no one because I remember no one and I am no one. So, this is the way it hap-pens ... nothing ... at ... all ... There was a creak that only happens when the door is opened very, very slowly....

"Veronica? Veronica? Are you well Veronica? Are you awake? May I come in? This is Rabbi Abraham, Veronica. I need to speak with you. I am coming in."

The sounds seemed friendly, although I did not know what they were. There was a cane coming into the room, a foot, a leg.... Oh ... a person is standing there looking at me. He looks familiar. He has a traditional hat. He is standing there looking at me. He is making noises again. He looks kind.

"Veronica. I am Abraham, your rabbi. You look very pale. If you per-mit, I will get you something to drink. Do not move."

He is making noise again. Oh. He is getting something over there. He is back. This is fascinating, yes, thank you, I will drink. Hmmm, that is cold.

"Do not drink too much at one time. I will hold the cup for you."

I felt the cold reach down inside me. I do not remember having other feelings, except the cramps, the dull pain deep down. This feeling was kinder. I felt a sensation on my face. It is warm but something is, oh ... he opened a shade and there is air coming in. Yes, I would like to drink some more. Thank you.

"Here, drink some more. Yes, color is coming back to your face. You are going to be feeling better Veronica. I am so glad I found you in time."

His eyes are so kind. I heard what he said. Where was I if he found me? I thought. I felt as though I must be polite, so I said....

"You are my rabbi. Your name is Abraham. Thank you for coming to visit. They are all so mean to me. Please tell them to stop yelling at me. I have not harmed them in any way. Could I have a small, sweet cake please? I believe I keep them over on the small table. Yes. Thank you." Being polite was exhausting. I almost passed out.

"Here you are, take very small bites. Do you remember when you ate last?"

"No. I am not sure about anything at the moment." All I could see was Rabbi Abraham's eyes looking at me with the care of a grandfather. I thought, "Are you my grandfather? I would love to have a grandfather."

"Let us get you stronger. We will talk about how to help others later but let us make sure we take care of you first. You need to be strong to help others," Abraham counseled.

"Yes, thank you ... that seems to make sense," I whispered.

Abraham was trying to bring me back little by little. After a bit more food, I fell asleep. He sat next to me, praying for my welfare, and hoping for the best recovery possible. I slept soundly for a couple of hours, and then I stirred.

"Hello Veronica, you look like you are feeling better," the rabbi said in a cheerful voice.

"What? uhm, yes, I do feel better. Thank you. Where was I?"

"You were in a very dark and lonely place. You had lost hope, my dear. God does not want any of His children to lose hope. He has great plans for you Veronica. You may feel alone, but God is always there. He never sleeps. He loves you and will guide you, even when you are not sure what to do or where to go. Take a moment to chat with Him and you will see. So, tell me about what you have learned at the temple," Rabbi Abraham counseled in kindness, suggesting I focus on the only

steadfast experience I have had ... the temple ... the foundation of my faith, my hopes, and my life.

I have learned many sacred things in God's Holy Sanctuary....

Veronica is mostly back to herself and is experiencing, for the first time in what seems a very long time, an audience who is truly interested in each and every portion of her many temple-related stories. Rabbi Abraham's eyes light up as Veronica articulately shares the experiences she had with the temple workers, the animals, the visitors, and the processes, as well as with the sacred covenants.

Veronica is filled with light as she completes her energetic tutorial. She is a bit embarrassed for being so enthusiastic as she looks at Abraham the rabbi and says, "I am sorry for taking up your valuable time." She reaches for her cup and takes a small sip while grinning.

Her kind and patient rabbi smiles back at her and says, "I wish to thank you for spending your valuable time helping me understand how the temple can be the centerpiece of faith and good works for God's children, Veronica. I appreciate every single word you shared. If I could, I would ask you to teach those who are not so kind to you. I am sure they would be the better for it."

"Thank you, Rabbi. I wish they had something good to think about instead of yelling at me," Veronica observes as she sits up, looking at the floor.

Abraham asks, "What do you think we could do to help them?"

"Maybe if they knew that I know my situation, they would not feel so eager to remind me," Veronica says while seeking the right answer.

"Something visual, so when you must go out, when they see you, it will tell them that you are aware and that you have permission to be where you are. Is that what you are saying?"

"Yes, and they can be aware and keep their distance," Veronica responds.

"And they can keep their mouths shut," adds Abraham.

"So," Veronica shares her newly formed idea, "what if I wore a shawl that was a certain color that was unusual enough to let them know?"

"Yes, that could be useful. What color?"

"Red. Solid red stripes, one on each side. It would look lovely and present a message."

"What is the message, Veronica?"

"You ... do not know my story. God knows it, and He loves me, so that is the only thing that we, His children, need to be concerned with. I have suffered God's will, and you need not be concerned. Nod and be on the path God wants you to be on."

Veronica looks up as if to retrieve closure, pauses, looks her rabbi in the eyes, and says, "Let the color of what covers my bowed head remind you of the blood being sacrificed on your behalf ... and think of that covenant as you walk humbly in your path."

Abraham's tears and the smile on his aged face bring comfort to Veronica. He nods and offers, "Veronica. Thank you for teaching this old rabbi many truths this day. I am a better man for having been taught by you."

"You are so very welcome Rabbi Abraham. It is I who owe you so much. Thank you for saving my life and my soul today," Veronica responds with humility.

"Well, yes, you needed some assistance, I would agree. Do not forget to eat again. I will let the local seamstress know you will be quickly visiting to discuss how she can help you with your new shawl."

"Rabbi, you need not worry about the seamstress. I will craft my own shawl. I do not want to be a burden to anyone." Veronica looks at Abraham's eyes and adds, "I will do fine with it. Thank you for your kind offer."

The rabbi looks up at Veronica, who is now standing, and says, "Of course, I forgot. Yes, you will certainly do a superb job on that." He reaches out his hand and pats Veronica on the hand saying, "Be at peace my daughter. Be at peace."

"Thank you, Rabbi Abraham. I am full of peace. Goodbye."

"Oh, I have had an important scripture come to mind that I must share with you," the rabbi says as he looks back into Veronica's eyes.

"Yes, please. What is it?" Veronica replies with enthusiasm.

Abraham softly says, "Position both your imperfect body as well as your soul to approach God and always remember ... Exodus 20:21:

'In every place that you mention My name, I will come to you and bless you.'" He smiles a calming smile.

"Oh, Rabbi, please visit again should your busy schedule allow. Thank you!" Veronica expresses in sincere appreciation.

Rabbi Abraham shuffles to the door and leaves, having been uplifted and strengthened by someone who had seemed to have given up. He gives thanks for having acted on the impressions he had received as he greeted the overcast day many hours prior. He smiles and slowly makes his way home down the stone-covered street in Jerusalem.

ABRAHAM THE RABBI'S WORDS TOUCH Veronica's heart deeply as she stands for a moment in front of the closed door. She then seeks a place to sit and ponder…. *I love what he said at the end. I feel the words of my soul coming to my uplifted mind. "Get something to write with before they are gone, Veronica."*

Veronica then writes the words as they arrive, trying not to miss anything….

Thou hast given me life and saved me to do
thy work and serve thy people.

Oh, Eternal God, I kneel before thee to accept thy will.

I am lonely and seek to join with and partner
with a worthy son of Abraham.

I have seen under thy care happy children
who have mothers who love them.

Please bless them and keep them from harm.

I yearn to speak softly to my child as I cradle it in my arms.

Please strengthen my heart that I may
bear the burdens I have received.

Thou God art the center of my soul, my life, and my eternity.

Let thy strength be my strength
as I seek to accomplish thy will.

Prepare my heart to welcome a child
and be worthy of their love and soft voice.

Watch over the mothers who need thy strength.

Please bless all mothers and their children with thy love.

I stand alone and desire a companion to share my life with.

Eternal One above the earth I pray
my heart will accept thy divine guidance.

That I may show gratitude for thy love and receive strength
to serve thy children as long as I have life.

AMEN

THE PEACE VERONICA RECEIVES DURING her visit Rabbi Abraham provides lasting strength, with inner peace. She reflects while sitting in her home, *Frankincense is burning which brings some amount of relief. The oil Dinah brings helps more during the night to help me sleep. It has been almost two and a half years now.* She takes a slow, deep breath, holds it in, and then breathes out slowly.

She continues her thoughts, *It is quiet outside this afternoon. I wonder why. Perhaps …*

She is interrupted by a very rare knock at the door—firm, three knocks in a row. She stands carefully so as to not lose balance, walks over as straight as she can manage, firmly grasps the door, swings it open … and is stunned at what is right there in front of her.

Standing purposefully is a man with a dog, who is sitting at attention next to him. The man's eyes look familiar, but his hair is golden, which she does not remember seeing before. His eyes are looking straight at hers while she tries to steady both her mind and weakened body … *Yes,* she thinks … "Flavius? Is that you? Without a helmet?"

"Why yes, it is. So good to see you, Miss Veronica. We all hope you are managing as well as possible?" He is still standing almost at attention and has a pleasant smile. The dog looks to be the gray dog with black and gray spots she had seen as a puppy. The dog has a friendly countenance and is attentive to even the slightest of Veronica's movements.

Veronica is still taking in information about this unexpected visit as she replies, "Yes, I am doing, 'as well as possible.' Thank you for asking." She gains some composure. "I hope you understand, I would love to invite you in to sit down, but ..."

"No, no, I fully understand. Please do not feel bad." He looks at the ground momentarily, looks back up, and announces, "As you are aware, Roman soldiers are under twenty-year contracts."

Veronica's heart skips a beat as her brain screams, *No! Do not leave me! You are one of my most trusted friends! Please!* Her grip on the door tightens as she prepares for what he is going to say.

"I served ten years in assignments prior being assigned here as your trainer, er, the Senior Ninth Dromedarii Regiment Camel Operations Trainer...."

Yes, she thinks, *We started when I was sixteen, so it has been ...*

"Which will complete ten years in a month. I will then be honorably discharged...." His tears are flowing, "from my ... I am sorry, this is difficult for me, please forgive me ... from my duties as your trainer." Time stops.

He regains his composure, but the emotion in his voice is palpable as he offers, "It has been an honor to be your senior trainer. You have taught me well, and I—we—wish you the very best in your life."

Veronica does not know if she can stand any longer. Her grip on the door is slipping, and the tears are flowing nonstop as she responds, "Oh, my goodness, this is surprising, but, you know, it is the right thing to do. You have served so well and are a master teacher, which I have tried to emulate each day of my life, and I thank you for everything. You made me better than I could ever have dreamed of being. So, can I come by for a visit a couple of times before you must leave? Perhaps three times, please?"

Those same angel eyes are once again looking through his soul. Her request gives both of them time to adjust to the coming change. He looks down at the canine still sitting at attention and then back to Veronica, makes a huge smile, and says, "Yes, I am so very glad you asked! Your visits will give us all a chance to see how you are doing with Ognir, your new scout dog!"

Veronica looks down at the dog and discovers that he is no longer next to Flavius the senior trainer, but has positioned himself sitting, at attention, not five centimeters from her right side.

"What?" she exclaims as her hand reaches to touch Ognir's head. He instinctively turns his head and licks her hand once. "Really? Ognir can be my scout dog? And stay with me?" It is almost too amazing to take in.

"Yes, of course. He is yours, and you are already familiar with the commands and what he can do. His food will be provided, so never worry about that. You have been given the Civilian Medal of Honor, which entitles you to more than you realize. Plus, the Ninth has adopted you as their own 'Master Camel Attaché,' so if you ever need anything, anything at all, you let someone know. Do you understand Veronica, the 'Ninth Dromederii Regiment Camel Operations Master Camel Attaché'?"

"Yes, my senior trainer, sir, I fully understand, and I will comply. I will see you next week. Be prepared. I will be observant." Veronica shares a friendly grin in front of the formal orders and response. It is needed to relieve the emotional tension of the moment. Life has changed once more.

Flavius steps back, waves goodbye, turns, and is gone out of sight quickly. Veronica stands motionless, looking into space. Ognir stands up, turns, bumps her hand, and takes one sideways step with his front paw into her home.

His coaxing is needed; otherwise, Veronica would probably never leave her stunned position. She lets loose of the door and turns to go inside. Ognir leads the way.

VERONICA BEGINS CHATTING WITH HER new companion, "Well, my new friend, Ognir, we need to get acquainted now, don't we?"

Ognir is still standing, looking at her in a relaxed way, breathing with his mouth slightly open and his tongue falling slightly out of the right-hand side of his mouth. He looks intently at her as she quietly gives voice commands in rapid succession.

"Sit." Ognir's rear hits the floor before the "t."

His mouth is closed, his eyes intent on her commands. He has been through this process many times.

"Down." Ognir's front paws both lift up simultaneously, move forward, and land on the floor twenty centimeters in front of where they had been. Nothing else moves.

"Lie right." Ognir lies to the right, and his four paws extend straight out and hit the floor instantly.

"Sit." It is as if he was already sitting. Veronica hardly sees a half second of shuffling and repositioning. All she knows is Ognir is sitting in a flash.

"Stay." Veronica steps back four steps. Ognir is motionless and looks as if he is enjoying himself.

"Come." As soon as the word is out of her mouth, Ognir is already finishing sitting down right in front of her, looking up.

"Heel." Ognir stands up and walks to Veronica's left side, continues around behind her, and sits on her right side where he had positioned himself outside minutes before.

"Good boy, Ognir." Veronica says as she reaches down and pats his head. He puts his nose in the air as if to say, "I like you, Veronica. We will get along together fine."

"Done." She says as she walks away to tend to some chores. Ognir immediately relaxes and begins the slow, detailed sniffing routine he will repeat each time he enters his new abode. Once he takes inventory and is aware of his surroundings, he walks to the door and lies down off center so he can sniff under the door, hear what is outside, and lie his head down facing wherever Veronica is at any time, day, or night. "Done" or not, Ognir is his new master's guard and companion and is never really "off duty."

Veronica mentally reviews the checklist in her mind, "sit, heel, stay, come, attack, down, jump, growl, teeth, drop it, back up, crawl, side, fetch."

During the next few days, Veronica and Ognir begin sneaking out the back into the adjacent cartier, where she will be less likely to be shamed or harassed into retreating back into her home. Her walks must be short, but she has worked out the least-traveled routes with the least number of people.

Veronica has received a new purpose in life.

"Let us go Ognir. Are you ready?" Veronica askes as she approaches. Ognir is sitting at attention at the door, almost smiling. "Ognir is always ready, aren't you boy?" Veronica says as she opens the door and walks out. Ognir is at her side, sniffing the air as he walks (in formation) next to Veronica.

They proceed along the narrow pathway and come to the clay-stamped road moving off to the right and upward. As Veronica looks up the hill, she selects a window to watch, giving her focus as she tries to not lose momentum and make it to the top without slowing down. She thinks, *I can make this hill and I am going to move quickly all the way up.*

As they make their way, an old woman appears from the right and turns to go the same direction. *OK, I can catch up to her and pass her. That is my next goal. She seems to be moving slowly enough,* Veronica reasons as she focuses on a successful triumph. They approach the slow-walking woman and easily pass her to the left.

Something is different.

Veronica is shocked to find Ognir missing from her side. She stops to look back, and there he is, walking at the pace of the old woman ... right next to her. Veronica thinks, *What? The woman is looking at me, smiling. I better go back down. Maybe she needs help.* Veronica walks carefully back down the hill holding her left hand so she can touch the wall as she descends. Ognir looks up, grins, and then looks at the woman and back at Veronica as if to say, "Hey, I found you a new friend! Come and meet her!"

Out of breath from her efforts to get up the hill, Veronica greets the old woman, "Well, hello! My name is Veronica, and I am so very sorry that I passed you without saying hello or asking if I could be of some assistance. I see my companion Ognir has already made your acquaintance."

The new acquaintance replies, "Why yes, he has. He is a very handsome dog and well behaved. 'Ognir' you said?"

"Yes ma'am, Ognir. I have only had him a few days, and yes, he is handsome, and intelligent, loyal, and true" Veronica offers with a kind smile.

"Ah, yes that is wonderful. My name is Lidia, and I am glad to meet you both. Being old is a lonely profession on occasion, and it is comforting to have a bit of company." She looks down at Ognir and says with a smile, "You, sir, are a gentleman to escort me along this mountain that we are ascending with skill and grace." Her smile turns to Veronica, who feels as if she had met a long-lost relative. The feeling is mutual. It has been many years since they had last met.

They slowly walk together and eventually make the summit, sit together on a welcome bench, and exchange stories from the past. While Veronica explains her personal journey, Lidia nods her head in an understanding and comforting way as if she has knowledge of everything Veronica is explaining.

Lidia then says, "You are exceptional and of great worth to God and your fellow travelers here on earth. You must become once again a woman with purpose; do not lose your focus. Find a way to serve. Do what you can. God loves you, and there is good for you to do now and in the future."

"Yes Lidia, thank you. You are so kind and loving. I appreciate our conversation and hope we will be blessed to meet again. Thank you for sharing your time with us." Veronica looks down at Ognir, who has stationed himself to have a grand view all around.

The accidental meeting ends with both parties going on to their preplanned destinations, Veronica and Ognir retreating back down the hill to achieve safety in their home before there are too many people out and about. The meeting brings strength to Veronica, with Ognir enjoying being of assistance.

Veronica's smile warms as she thinks, *Seeing and spending time with Lidia has been very good. She has so many interesting stories, but most of all, she is there, she is strong, and she—I believe—loves me. What a great blessing.*

A WEEK GOES BY, AND Veronica finds herself on another covert adventure, speaking aloud to her new companion. "Ognir, you and I are going to visit your old home today! How does that sound? Do you know that we were both trained on the very same training field? I rode a camel, and one day you will ride one as well if you want of course. It is very enjoyable, and I only fell off once after I forgot to be polite. Well, maybe I fell twice actually.

"It was not actually my fault … well maybe it was. Squishy-Lips and I were trotting, well, I was on his back, and he was trotting, which he is very good at doing. I turned around in the saddle to see where something was—I do not even remember what it was. So, we were trotting along very gracefully, showing the men how it is done with grace and style.

"Wait a minute, Lidia used that phrase, well … I was twisted around looking—in the wrong direction mind you—when I was swiftly launched in the air. I saw the ground come up to my face very quickly—you never think about things like that you know. The ground coming at you instead of you going to the ground.

"It happened so quickly, and I was next being picked up by Flavius and his aid. I saw someone grabbing Squishy and walking him away and another person walking away with … listen very carefully Ognir, this could save your life … they were walking away with a snake!"

Ognir is listening carefully, taking it all in with rapt attention as his mistress continues, "So, my young friend, watch out for snakes. I am sure your mother will agree. So, if we can leave, we may get to see her. Come along."

They follow the same path they took when they met Lidia. The uphill climb is as dreadful as before, but Lidia is not around. It would have been nice to sit on the bench at the top, but there are three old, very old, gentlemen occupying that space, so Veronica and Ognir continue down the other side. As they progress, Veronica hears some enticing noises coming from further down; the sound of children playing.

Veronica focuses on the noises, *Yes, girls. Younger than twelve years old, older than eight. This is bringing back memories. What has it been?*

Ten years? I wonder how Hannah and Adina are. Oh, how I love my girls. She finds herself next to the narrow passageway from where the energetic sound is coming.

Veronica stops and asks herself, *Keep walking or go in? Keep walking or go in? Run away or face the past? What if I faint and stumble or fall?*

These questions are still cascading in her mind when she notices Ognir's eyes, looking back at her from three steps in toward the sound. Without realizing it, she moves forward while focusing on Ognir and finds herself next to him. His tail begins wagging as he looks toward the source of noise and escorts Veronica into the wide courtyard. She stands transfixed on the girls and tries to absorb their energy, their joy, and their youth as she declares to herself, *I have died and gone to heaven. I love these girls.*

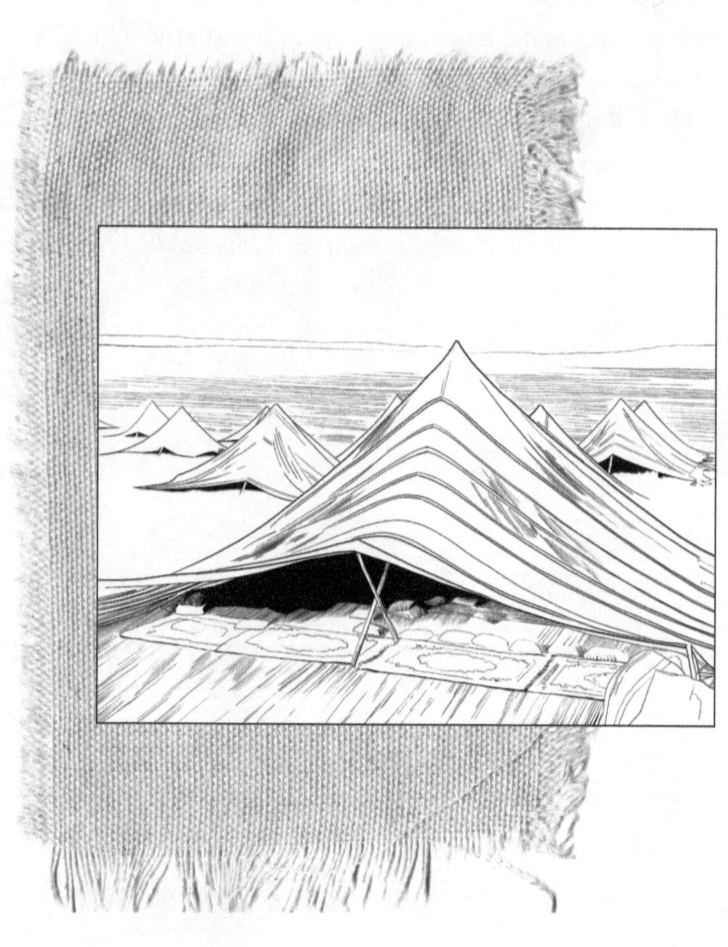

Travels to Jerusalem

Joshua, whom his friend and traveling companion the Camel Herder calls 'the Young Merchant' verifies everything is in order to leave, join the appointed caravan and begin the long trek south. A brief introduction by Joshua may be helpful if you have never been on a camel caravan of several hundred kilometers….

The first three days in an arranged private caravan are a remarkable sight. With anywhere from twelve to twenty groups taking part, a caravan can have as many as two hundred camels. Although most caravans try to keep between fifty and seventy-five camels, our caravan is headed to Jerusalem to stock the entire city with goods to sell at Passover. It is the largest caravan of the year and purportedly includes 160 camels.

One may think that keeping that many camels in a straight line would be an enormous task. To be sure, camels are not like cats or chickens; those who are in a caravan are trained professionals in the strictest sense. The terrain and path of this trip is not new to most of them. They have been here before, and they remember. They also only need to "follow the guy in front of them" … which is not an idea to dwell on.

Once a camel has trekked over a long trail or even from city to city, and especially from water well to water well, they know exactly where they are; they know where they are walking in relation to the next source of water, and they can smell it many kilometers away. They stay in line, and even though the camel herder may be bewildered, the camels are never, ever, bewildered.

The largest challenge of dealing with 160 camels is that when they arrive at a well, it cannot be a hole in the ground with a tiny bucket to haul minuscule amounts of water from. Fortunately on major trade routes, there will be at least one very efficient watering station with mechanical water delivery systems.

Keep in mind that each camel, especially after a multi-day trek across dry terrain, will drink up to 150 liters of water in only fifteen minutes. They do not mess around. This means that our caravan's host of 160 camels will have an intake of about 25,000 liters or over 25,000 kilograms of water … all happening generally in less than an hour. Never get in the way.

WITH MOSTLY MERCHANTS DELIVERING GOODS, the traveling team's caravan's daily start and stop times can vary slightly if camels are difficult or if packing loads does not go smoothly. For the most part Joshua expects a fairly good trip, as in this season's caravan there are many very experienced camel herders as well as merchants.

Joshua is one of the youngest merchants but has been learning from his grandfather for about twenty years, having been allowed (expected) to join the family business at the age of twelve. This trip will allow him to complete a total of sixty thousand kilometers, only five years away from seventy thousand … a huge event for a land-based merchant in this part of the world.

Unlike commercial caravans, which are managed and controlled by large enterprises, private caravans gather groups as best they can and always allow family groups to come along. There is one thing, however, which is always true: the caravan leader is always in charge, and purposeful disobedience of any of his instructions will bring swift and sure punishment.

Over the years, Joshua has heard of terrible outcomes for groups or individuals who try to get away with disobedience. The caravan leader has eyes everywhere, and even if you think you can get away with something, you are wrong. This is why leaders make absolutely sure each participant understands the rules to have an uneventful trip and agrees to have a good spirit about assisting in the caravan's success.

This caravan's leader is Boaz, who has been in the cargo transportation business for more than forty years. Joshua's grandfather has a great amount of respect for Boaz, having teamed up with him on countless journeys through good times and bad.

He is a man of honor, and although he needs to press everyone to be diligent in their tasks and ofttimes (always) seems hard-headed, Joshua's grandfather often relates stories in which Boaz risks his life to save someone who was in the wrong place at the wrong time.

Joshua once saw a weary Boaz shed tears of great sorrow when he had to bury a very young child who had died from illness while the child's young parents were traveling in one of his caravans. No one was aware, but Joshua personally saw him rocking the child all night in an attempt to persuade God to spare her. That one act he witnessed changed his heart forever. Joshua will never look at Boaz or any other seemingly hard soul the same way again. Everyone has some amount of compassion, no matter how deep it is buried.

AFTER THREE DAYS' TRAVEL, THE caravan gains its cadence. The camels know exactly where they are going, how long it will take to get there, and where the water is going to be. They are calmed down and are about their business, one step at a time.

Because the caravan is traveling to Jerusalem ahead of Passover, it includes several families joining the caravan on their way to be with family and in some cases, to present twelve-year-old boys to God at the temple, a very important rite of passage.

One of those boys is Gabriel, who has connected with the Camel Herder. The boy seeks him out when not doing chores and has been asking him questions nonstop. Joshua would have already been annoyed, but his good friend takes it all in stride and has been teaching Gabriel with patience and clarity.

The Camel Herder also has an affinity for entertaining the children on the caravan. Each evening he says a few poems, provides entertainment with stick puppets, and performs with the most talented and entertaining partner one could ever enlist: Revolk the camel.

It is a refreshing experience, and when the children laugh, they can be heard clearly across the camp. The pure joy exhibited by the little ones while with him lightens the mood of everyone in camp, except for the Greek lead guard, Theseus, who is always observant of happenings inside and outside the camp.

THE PATHWAY OUR CARAVAN IS following has been used for thousands of years. Although many hundreds of kilometers pass over ever-shifting sand dunes, a larger portion of the trade route trail is through areas with vegetation, springs and rivers, and along coastlines. There are treacherous passages through high mountains and barren plateaus. As I said, the camels know it all … every inch; they even know where they have been attacked in the past and get nervous when revisiting those areas.

As the caravan approaches a city, interesting things happen, no matter what city, anywhere along the route. The first thing is that there are rarely any marauding bands who attack. They are afraid of the populated areas where locals will not put up with their thievery. The second thing is visitors.

The caravan comes through a village or small hamlet intent on taking goods to the market. Artisans and farmers from as far away as one hundred kilometers from a large city (a five days' journey) see the caravan as a selling opportunity for their handmade crafts, potions, crops, and even animals.

There are also the beggars who follow caravans in search of scraps of food. These poor people try to take the place of the birds, which follow the caravan from the first step. When the beggars arrive, the birds have competition and the battle that ensues is saddening and sometimes frightful. It is not uncommon for a bird to be too slow, which enables their competition to grasp, pluck, cook, and eat them.

"YOU HAVE THAT LOOK ON your face. Is it imminent?" the Camel Herder says to Joshua quietly.

"We are being watched by thieves. Boaz sees them, and he is taking precautions. This set of thieves is professional, unlike the few boys who tried to steal a few weeks ago," Joshua responds. "This time we will use the sacrificial lambs on the perimeter, each with a tiny bell on a collar around its neck."

"Yes, I remember. The guard dogs know and recognize the sound of distress. They sneak up on the thieves while one dog warns the caravan master. I hope they deter the attack," the Camel Herder adds.

"Yes. This time they are not going to come mounted because they fear losing their animals and they are also too sure of themselves," Joshua remarks.

They have both seen this before, but it does not make them any more reassured. Bloodshed is a common occurrence in these situations.

The warning of the pending attack spreads, bringing fear and trepidation to the camp, especially to the children old enough to know what is happening.

The Camel Herder has a bag he carries everywhere. He calls it his "bag of wonders." He opens it, and the first item he pulls out is a very small flute. He walks out through the tent door; wipes it off on his smock; places it up to his lips; takes a long, calm breath; and starts playing a whimsical tune.

The camp's children abandon their fears and come running. They surround the Camel Herder and sit down, and his little friends focus long enough to bring back their innocence and pure, gentle smiles. They have come for entertainment many times before and feel safe.

As the Camel Herder begins his engaging stories, poems, and sing-along activities, Revolk, his personal camel, roused by the familiar musical tune, comes slowly into the circle, gently kicks the Camel Herder to move over, takes his place, and plops down with a big thump.

The children are speechless and wide-eyed. They do not dare move or make a sound. Revolk looks at them one by one and then places his gaze on the Camel Herder. Revolk holds his gaze for several moments and lets out a huge BURP! The children become hysterical, laughing and screaming with delight.

The Camel Herder raises both arms in the air; makes a *shhhhhh* noise to quiet the children down; and as their noise softens, he slowly lowers both arms and places his index fingers on his lips, signaling to be quiet and listen ... he now has their full attention. Revolk is quietly chewing.

And so, the Camel Herder begins, "There is a camel who lives on the outskirts of *your* village. You have never heard of him and have never EVER heard his name spoken by anyone. He is ... the ... 'Camel Without a Name,' and his story goes like this ... so listen very carefully and see if you know who he is and try to remember if you have ever seen him."

The Camel Herder smiles while raising his eyebrows to enhance the suspense. He begins repeating the poem he learned from his grandfather years ago. The children jump when he starts the poem with a loud exclamation ...

There is an un-named camel in my tent!
He looks clean, but sure has a nasty scent.
He is gobbling up my mother's fig cakes.
He will not stop, and it is a big mistake!
I should not have said how tasty they are.
And should not have ever opened the jar.
The camel sniffed and tasted and thought they were GREAT.
And I could not count how many he ate!

"How many cookies can you eat?" the Camel Herder asks the children, looking at them as he moves his head from left to right. Multiple answers squeak out. He continues ...

The jar was now empty, and I do not know how
I will explain this to mom.... She is coming home NOW!
I wander around and try to stay calm.
He will not leave so I slap him with my palm.
With a start he jumps and runs out the door.
When he left, he knocked the jar on the floor.

The Camel Herder gives the children a look of resignation and an inquisitive look as if to solicit advice from his audience ... who have worried looks on their faces. In a slow pace he continues with a lowered and hushed voice...

Mom set her package down as gentle as can be.
She took off her shawl, turned, and looked straight at me!
Her face was kind looking, but her eyes were stern.
I tried to seem innocent, but my heart started to burn.
I mustered the courage to tell her the deed
Caused by the nameless camel, the haphazard steed.
I told her the story, and she did not even shout,
But she firmly scolded me, and I tried not to pout.
The jar was not broken, so I arranged it back right.
Mom made me clean up the mess which took nearly all night!
It has been a few days, and the camel stayed gone.
I started to miss him. He has been away too long!
I pondered and thought and came up with a plan.
The camel, I said, came from the tribe of Dan.
They like to eat cakes! I grinned with a smirk.
Yes, this plan is fine and will surely work!
So, I told mom my plan as plain as I could.
She thought and she pondered and still she stood ...
"Yes, he can have some, and they will be free,
But the most he can eat will only be three."
I thought in my five-year-old-brain, "Well there.
Mother has spoken, and her plan sounds fair."
I will now go outside and with a loud voice exclaim ...
I am urgently looking for 'The Camel with No Name!'

"So, there you have it! The entire story that comes all the way to us from long, long ago." The children look pleased, and the Camel Herder notices that they are not moving around so much, which is a sign to end.

Long shadows have formed, and darkness is beginning to fall over the camp. The Camel Herder ends the delightful evening by picking up his tiny flute and playing a soft and peaceful lullaby, which is Revolk's signal to lie his giant camel head right on the Camel Herder's lap and begin to make snoring sounds. The gathered adults covered their mouths in surprise, and several have to turn their heads to keep from laughing aloud.

The children know it is time for bed, and even if they want to laugh aloud at what they have witnessed, they do not want to disturb the sleeping camel who is now their friend as well. Their parents came to the circle and are ready to peacefully take children to their tents and place them in bed. The first child gets up, carefully walks over to Revolk on tippy toes, pets him, and silently walks to her parents standing nearby. Each of the children does the same. It is magical.

As the last child is gently picked up by his mother, Revolk briskly opens one eye, looks at the Camel Herder, who shakes his head "No." The camel closes his eye and waits until his master makes three quiet clicks with his mouth.

At that signal, Revolk opens his eye again and receives a "Yes" nod. He lifts up, looks around, and makes a low grunt as he stands up. He then looks over to where his two camel companions are chewing, casually walks over, and joins them, lying down with another thump, as if he were going home after a long day's work. A camel grunt is heard, but it is impossible to know who is greeting who. The sounds of the night watch setting up their stations are heard as darkness sets in.

The Camel Herder picks up his bag, looks around to make sure he has not forgotten anything, closes the bag, and walks over to his tent, being careful not to trip over a tent line on his way.

"So, did you get them quieted down after you made them crazy with your funny stories?" Joshua asks as he looks up from studying sales records.

"Yes, it is Revolk who leads the show. Whenever I become boring and the children start getting distracted and start touching each other or try to wander away, he does something only a camel can do and get away with it. He brings them right back. He was well trained by my grandfather and still recognizes each flute tune and remembers what he is supposed to do when he hears it. I am not sure who has more fun, the children or Revolk."

Theseus appears at the tent entrance and without pleasantries declares, "We are contained, the guards are in place. There will be no wandering. May God be with you."

Theseus is the senior caravan guard who has worked for the caravan leader, Boaz, for about twenty-five years. He never chats, he distrusts everyone on the planet, and he holds grudges—and a lot of them, because he remembers everything.

There are those who say he even remembers his birth and can describe how he pushed his way past his brother to be born first so as to receive the Greek birthright.

Theseus can be trusted with any confidence and any task and will defeat any foe. You do not take his word lightly, and it is best if you obey his instructions with exactness, without fail. As soon as Theseus's instructions are delivered, he instantly disappears … silently.

The moonless nights three days north of Nazareth at this time of the year are brisk, and because there is no moon, the horizon's edge is almost invisible, especially when there is cloud cover. Luckily, the night is clear, and even without a moon, the star band above allows the horizon to be clearly seen by the well-placed guards encircling the caravan encampment.

There have been intermittent attacks on caravans in this area for the past two years. In most cases, they were led by mercenary thieves acting as solo entrepreneurs, unattached to any larger organization, which was not an intelligent way to enjoy a career as a vagabond thief as 1) leaving an existing illicit organization places you on their hit list and 2) you cannot, in general, know how a particular caravan is managed and defended unless you have someone on the inside, and most solo bands do not have the patience to approach their targets this intelligently. The wait begins.

THE DAY SOPHIE MEETS VERONICA

LIDIA ALMOST MAKES IT UP the hill to the bench before Veronica, whose stamina is fading. Veronica looks ahead and remarks, "Someone moved the bench; there are two! I am so glad. I need to sit for a moment."

Ognir is surveying the situation while he stays on the right side of Veronica. As they approach, he sniffs and recognizes the scents of the three old gentlemen sitting on one of the benches.

Lidia responds to Veronica, who is out of breath, and says, "Yes, the committee agreed to move the benches where there is more room so that people can sit and chat instead of sit and observe those passing by." Lidia then greets the trio, "Hello, my friends, don't you like this new arrangement?"

The middle man, Elias, responds, "Yes, we like what they have done. How long has it been like this? A couple of years?"

The man on the left, Jacob, says, "Elias, they changed it two weeks ago, but they purchased the new bench three months ago from a craftsman from Nazareth, who charged a fair price I hear. He delivered it with his son, who seemed like a nice lad. Very helpful."

The man on the right, Gabriel, turns to look past Elias and asks, "Jacob, what are you going to Nazareth for? It is a waste of time. Anyway, you will get lost. I remember when you got lost on the way to the Mount of Olives when you wanted to get a good deal on raw oil, when that was all the rage. Heeheehee … you ended up buying a year's worth and it went sour before you could guzzle it down … 'three tablespoons before going to bed … every night.' All it gave you was gas. Humph."

Jacob replies, "Gabriel I did not get lost on the way there, I got lost on the way back, because it took that olive oil vendor way too long to reduce his price to an acceptable level. And I am not going to Nazareth tomorrow or any other day. Do you know how busy it is up there? Especially now. The merchants with all their commotion will soon be coming through. I do not know why they hold celebrations up there anyway … it would give me a headache."

Veronica and Lidia sit across from the three gentlemen. Lidia reaches over and pats Veronica on the knee, "They are always like this, or have been, at least for the last twenty years or so."

Veronica asks, "We," glancing down at Ognir, "have seen you gentlemen up here before. Do you come here often?"

Lidia interjects before their response, "Yes, their sweet wives kick them out because they talk nonstop."

"Yes," says Elias, "and mine says I always mumble, which is not at all true. She mumbles, and she does it all the time, even when she sleeps. Wakes me up and then I cannot go back to sleep. Do you know what it is like to not sleep? It makes you old-looking like Jacob here."

Veronica knows exactly what it feels like to not sleep, but she holds it to herself.

Gabriel adds, "My wife of sixty-five years, or seventy-five … not sure. She was always the one talking to someone about someone else. I already know too much about them, their family, and their grandparents back six generations … did you know that Jacob went to Nazareth to build this fine bench for us? He delivered it last year but did not tell us.

"My wife would have found out what he was up to. She always kept me up to date on what was going on. She should have stayed around longer; now I have to listen to these guys' stories, and they do not have a clue what is going on outside their heads, and they only know part of what is going on inside them. She left too soon." Gabriel stares at the ground; tears gently wet his cheeks.

Veronica is touched by this kind man's tears and now knows why he had not joked about his departed wife…. "*So sad,*" she thinks. Her right hand is on Ognir's head, caressing him softly. Ognir is looking at the man who has tears in his eyes while at attention in front of Veronica. She slowly pulls her hand away, places it on her lap and very quietly says, "Done."

In one fluid motion, Ognir stands up, and while still looking at Gabriel's face walks over to the old man, sits down in front of him, and places his head on Gabriel's lap. A broad smile brakes Gabriel's sadness as he places his hand on Ognir's head and quietly utters, "You, my friend, are a remarkable creature. Thank you."

Not another word is said. Ognir stays in place while Veronica thinks, *I may not be able to help people as I would like to, but my loyal companion takes my love and spreads it around simply fine. We need to get moving soon.*

WHILE WALKING A FEW MINUTES later, they are approaching the place where Lidia takes a right turn. Before they part ways, Veronica asks Lidia, "So, who is Zacharias, and why were the gentlemen laughing about his wife having a baby?" Lidia slows down and explains how God allowed Elisabeth to conceive at a very old age and took away Zacharias's speech for unbelief. Lidia concluded, "I have heard that their son, John, has been preaching in the desert, saying the Savior is coming soon."

"Is he?" Veronica inquires with a joyful tone.

"I am not so sure. We have seen others profess the same thing for centuries, most of the time with declarations that they themselves are 'The Anointed One.' When you have time, we can chat more. You have to get over to your Training Grounds. Please give my regards to Squishy-Lips, and do not overdo it if you think you are strong enough to ride." With that, she squeezes Veronica's hands while looking into her eyes, smiles, then turns and walks away.

As Veronica makes her way to the Training Grounds, she ponders what she had learned, *This is so very interesting. I wonder if Dinah has heard what is going on. I am sure she probably knew Zacharias, maybe not. How long ago was it? Thirty years or so? Not sure. There is a lot of activity on the Training Grounds of the Ninth Brigade.*

Veronica leans on the gate and watches. There are three groups in training; one is loading cargo on four camels; one is being taught how to groom and saddle six camels, and the other with ... eight camels is practicing advanced field maneuvers. *Oh, how I would love to be out there* she muses. Ognir on her right is wagging his tail. Its bounce on the ground catches her attention as she wonders, *Where is my trainer? He should be right there in the middle of his program.*

"Veronica, so glad you could come for a moment," says a deep voice a few feet behind her right shoulder.

She instantly recognizes Flavius's voice as she turns with a grin while having a thought flash into her mind, *It is a different voice from what he used as the senior trainer, which demanded attention, comprehension, and obedience on the field. This is the voice he uses with peers and perhaps loved ones.*

"Yes, hello! I see you have a full schedule today, and I do not wish to interrupt, but I promised I would come to visit a bit," Veronica responds.

Flavius notes Veronica's frailty. Her drawn facial features, pale complexion, and the way she leans on the fence as she speaks to him. She is not relaxing against it; she seems to need its support to remain upright. His heart aches for her as he offers, "Here, I brought you some fresh water and a small bite to eat. Have a seat, tell me what you have been up to."

They only spend ten minutes chatting, but the time with the senior trainer, a respected friend of perhaps eighteen years, is invigorating not only to Veronica's mind but her heart as well.

Flavius smiles and says, "I would keep you here all afternoon, but I know you have things to do, places to go, and people to see." He offers his hand as he stands and helps Veronica up. "I will not make you promise, but if you are in the area again, please quickly visit to say goodbye. If not, I wish you all the happiness possible. I am sure we will see each other again. Perhaps you will visit Gaul where I hope to retire with my wife." He reaches out with both arms in invitation for her to receive a formal hug and say goodbye. He fears she will not be able to come again.

"Oh yes, I will most certainly try to get back, but ..." she looks at his eyes, "in case ... Thank you once again for all you have done for me. Please pass my regards to Squishy-Lips of course." Veronica hugs Flavius and adds, "Goodbye my friend. I will search you out in Gaul and look forward to meeting your wife. I must thank her as well."

THIS PARTING IS PAINFUL FOR both of them. As Ognir and Veronica walk toward Dinah's workshop, she has so many ideas happening all at once that it is difficult to focus on one at a time. It seems she arrives in no time at all.

Veronica finds Dinah standing in her usual place, the design table. After customary greetings Dinah seems engrossed with solving a problem. She picks two pieces of fabric up and holds them together focusing intently. Dinah grins and says, "Yes! That is it! Excellent! That took too long." She looks at Veronica and offers, "I am sorry, but I was compelled to complete that step before I could take another breath. So good to see you and thank you for all the tunics you have been completing. You must be exhausted." Dinah had noticed that Veronica's energy has been slowly decreasing month after month.

Veronica shakes her head, "Yes, I am a bit tired but doing the best I can, given the circumstances of course." She changes the subject, "So, I saw Lidia today. She seems to be doing very well. She is so very kind."

Dinah looks straight at Veronica and says "That is so nice you can see each other. Mother thinks the world of you, Veronica. She loves your companionship, and since I cannot get away often enough, you provide her with happiness. Thank you for taking the time for her." Dinah glances toward the adjacent room and offers, "I have the right thing for you, some anise cakes and drink. I will be right back. Stay put." Dinah scurries away, leaving a smile as she passes Veronica.

As Dinah is away, Veronica ponders, *I remember spending time working in the temple as a young twelve-year-old assistant to Dinah, who had responsibilities involving the high priests' activities, their ceremonial robes, the fabric used in all parts of the temple. I loved being dutiful and focusing on the importance of my role until I was twenty, when my entire world changed. I need to focus on the good. I must focus on serving others ... with purpose.*

It helps Veronica somehow to recite the tragic story. Her previously once-a-month time away from the temple and other social activities is now permanent. She never stops bleeding. She has felt so much, and so deeply—grief, disbelief, anger, self-incrimination—as she tried to come to grips with the deterioration of her health, the destruction of her life. Resigned to her condition, Veronica tells no one of her suffering. She has become a woman who tolerates pain and endures her deprivation in solitude.

DINAH WALKS BACK IN WITH a pitcher of fresh water, and surprisingly, a young girl walks in right behind her carrying cups and a basket of small bread cakes.

"Veronica please meet my daughter, Sophie. Sophie, please meet my able assistant, Veronica!"

No one makes a sound; no one moves an inch. Both Veronica and Sophie gaze at each other for the longest time. Dinah interjects, "So! I will place this on the table." Still, no one speaks as she pours three cups of drink.

Sophie finally asks, "Are you the lady with the ghost-dog that is outside? We saw you in the courtyard at the bottom of the hill. My friends have spoken about the day you both walked by, when the ghost-dog began wagging his tail, we knew you were kind. But after that, you were gone! I told my friends, 'I saw her eyes and they are very kind. Maybe she is a spirit angel watching out for and guarding us.' They all agreed, and Lorna said that she felt better when you visited. She also named your dog 'the ghost dog' because his colors are unusual and he is perfectly obedient, and, of course, we did not know if you were real, of course. Was that you? It had to be you. Was it?"

"Yes, that certainly was me, and I recognized your beautiful eyes when I was there, although I could not place where I had seen them before. Seeing you with your mother puts everything in place. I am so very honored to meet you, Miss Sophie. You look like your gracious mother's twin. Would you like me to pull your hair up in a bun?"

"Thank you!" Sophie said lightly with a tiny curtsy, "Nice to meet you in person! I would not so much enjoy a bun but would rather for you, if you wish, to braid my hair, like you have yours done. Would that be possible if you do not mind, if you have the time? Please?"

Nothing could have thrilled Veronica more. "Yes, I would be once again honored, Miss Sophie. Let me take a drink and we will get right to work!"

Veronica reflects as she takes a sip of her favorite licorice drink, *A new friendship has arrived. I already love this young girl as if she were my own. I wish life had allowed me to meet her sooner than this; nonetheless, I appreciate her coming at this time and place ... especially today.*

"Sit right here, my young friend," Veronica says as she pulls her dress up slightly to get closer to Sophie. As they form a friendship, Dinah is focused on a project at the design table.

Dinah thinks, *Oh, I am so glad Veronica arrived at the right moment. Sophie has been upset at something one of her friends said, so engaging with Veronica is good.... Perhaps they will be good for each other for a very long time.* She feels joy watching what is happening so naturally and considers, *I wish I were able to have more free time to spend with Sophie. I will see if Veronica would like her own personal assistant.... Yes, this will do fine.* Dinah places an engineering drawing down and turns facing the two, now giggling, young women in her life and says in a very motherly fashion, "When you two ladies are done with your very important project, I have a proposal that will concern you both."

They do not stop chatting, but at least they respond, at the same instant, "Yes ma'am!" which makes them both burst out laughing.

Dinah says to herself, *This is going to be wonderful to watch. I hope they do not go out of control.* She smiles and continues with her valance project.

Veronica and Sophie are now standing with small mirrors looking at Sophie's new braids. Veronica explains, "So, if you want your hair to have waves in the morning, moisten your braids ... don't make them drip ... and then, in the morning when you take the braids out, your hair will look like the ocean waves."

"Blue?" teases Sophie.

"Yes, as blue as you wish. You can add your own seaweed to make it look real if you desire."

"Yes, with a small fish from the Sea of Galilee—an old, dry one. I do not wish to smell like a fish!" Sophie says with sophistication, then laughs with glee.

"Yes. That is a point to be considered, Miss Sophie," Veronica responds, trying to be serious as she looks to see if Dinah is ready to make her proposal. She thinks, *The word 'proposal' is a formal business term, so we must behave ourselves.* She looks at Sophie, puts her forefinger to her lips, and motions her to sit quietly. Sophie follows along but lets a tiny laugh out with a squeaky noise. She turns pink trying to hold it all in.

Veronica tells herself, *As much as I want to, I better not giggle or we'll both explode and ruin everything.* She takes a slow, deep breath and lets it out carefully without even a tiny squeak. The workshop now seems professional enough for Dinah's proposal.

Dinah steps over from the worktable to be in front while she slowly paces like a schoolteacher in front of them. She articulates her proposal, stopping from time to time to make a critical point. She begins....

"We are approaching Passover, as you are aware. This means that our two sets of government clients, the Jewish Sanhedrin, and the Romans, will be increasing their orders far beyond what's customary. Our private 'elite' clients will be placing last-minute orders, and we have increased the number of agreements with local vendors and distributors this year by fifteen percent." Dinah looks at Veronica and Sophie as she pauses to let this sink in.

"To be successful, we will need to expand our staff and reorganize."

Veronica gets a sudden, tense pang in her gut as her mind exclaims, *Oh no! She is going to let me go. I will not let her do that because it will hurt her. I will dismiss myself. I will be OK; she needs competent people. People who can get the job done. OK, that will work.* She gulps and refocuses her eyes on Dinah, who is looking directly at her.

Dinah turns her head and looks directly at Sophie and says, "Sophie, Veronica is my senior assistant...."

Veronica's mind is rattled, *What? I am her senior assistant? When did that happen? I guess right now,* but she manages to look back at Dinah as she sees Sophie nod "Yes" out of the corner of her eye.

"... and she knows the business, she is trusted by all our clients, and she has a passion for excellence...." Dinah is saying.

Veronica feels like crying and jumping up to hug Dinah but thinks, *Better not do that.... She is so very generous.*

Dinah continues, "... and she will need an assistant to help her get important projects completed. Someone who is willing to learn the business, who can be trusted, and who shares a passion for excellence." Dinah glances back at Veronica, and the look on her face is asking if this sounds OK. Veronica gulps again, smiles back and mouths the response, "Yes!" Veronica's eyes are beaming.

"Sophie, are you willing and able to become Veronica's assistant and begin working with her ... tomorrow?"

Sophie is still ready to explode with delight and responds, "Uhm, yes, I would be honored to become Veronica's assistant and look forward to learning excellence from her and how to become an amazing seamstress as well. Yes, I will accept."

"Thank you both. We have a lot of work to do. Sophie?"

"Yes."

"Veronica needs to retire to her home." She glances at Veronica with a smile and winks with one eye. That gesture communicates more than could ever be written. "Please escort her to the door. Thank you, Veronica for coming to our assistance today; we appreciate all you have done."

Veronica is floating with joy as she carefully stands up. She says good-bye and walks outside with Sophie. Ognir is already at Veronica's side the instant she comes out. Both Veronica and Sophie hold their excitement in as they ensure the door is completely closed.

An instant later, they both exclaim their joy and hug each other while Ognir wags his tail in approval.

"Sophie, I am so happy to spend time with you. I am excited to teach you as many important skills as possible. Of course, the teaching will need to facilitate the workload, not be instead of it."

"Yes Veronica, I am so thrilled to be your assistant. I hope I do not slow you down, and I especially do not want to make mistakes and make you look bad."

"You will do fine. Mistakes are part of learning. I should know, I have made a million of them. I do, however, know the speediest way to correct most of them." She gives a giant grin to Sophie.

"OK, what do you want me to do? When do we start? I can come to your place if you wish?"

"We can start tomorrow if that is not too soon. I will expect you in the late morning, and we, together, will look at what we need to accomplish, and you can help me make the correct decisions how to move forward. Does this meet with your approval, Assistant Sophie?"

"Oh yes! I will be prompt. Goodbye Mister Ghost-Dog-named-Ognir. I will see you both tomorrow." Sophie gives Veronica a hug and pets Ognir on the head, to which he replies with a quick lick of her hand.

Ognir approves. He then escorts Veronica home.

I AM LIVING IN A *dream,* Veronica ponders while walking home. *How can I be slowly dying, one drip at a time and suffer the loss of my entire life's pursuits by banishment from the temple and the devastating loss of strength to ride, to instruct my girls in the temple and the soldiers of the Ninth? How can everything be disappearing on one side, and at the same time God is taking away, I am receiving on the other side ... even gifts unbearably delightful and amazing!*

In the same day, my heart is wounded and healed. My mind experiences both despair and optimism. My hands are left holding onto a fence post to steady my frail body while they then braid a beautiful young girl's hair. The girl who spent years in my mind as a reflection of someone I could not identify ... and now there she is, my personal assistant. How can all this be?

I am certainly not worthy to receive such enormous blessings only God could arrange. Not only is MY life playing out a Greek tragedy they taught us in school, but the world around me is also playing on the same stage, with actors both heroic and fearsome, angels singing and devils screaming, yet the night is drawing near as it did yesterday and the day before, and the sun will rise in the morning, and as far as I know, the next day as well. Lidia told me to serve as best I could, so tomorrow is my new morning, my new day, and my new hope.

Am I ready to teach Sophie? Where are my textiles? Yes, I have at least learned to have a proper system to give some order and consistency in my life; the only thing I have any control over. Everything in its place. It will do me well midmorning when Sophie appears. Like a light bursting through the darkness, she will bring strength and enthusiasm.

Ognir, of course will wag his tail and guard the door. What would I ever do without him? Flavius has no idea how he has blessed my life. Regardless of the reason that he and the other members of the Ninth are here, he is kind, generous and deserves to retire to Gaul. So ...

Ognir is lying against the door watching Veronica who has made it home and is arranging her small design table so all will be ready in the morning. She hopes she will have enough energy. She makes her way to her bed where sleep overtakes her quickly.

SOPHIE IS SO EXCITED SHE can hardly stand still, in fact, she wakes prior to the Roman neighbor's rooster she named Gallus-Gever and thinks, *I sure would love to sneak up to him and scream "Good! Morning! Gallus-Gever!" to him, right in his ears ... which roosters do not actually have, so, well, exactly how do they hear things? Next time I pluck a chicken, which is against the law here I will look to see. No, gross, I have never plucked a chicken and have never cleaned a fish. Hmmm, I am lacking in two primary housekeeping skills. I will put them on my list to ask Veronica about. Maybe not. I will have two lists. One for textile and one for housekeeping. Another for how to greet famous people and another for how to sit*

and how to ask polite questions to get interesting answers. Another list for places around the world, which I have only heard about. Lina said her uncle knows someone who met a merchant who had actually been to Rome. I wish the sun would come up so I can watch the shadow move across the walkway to where Gallus-Gever the rooster lives so I know when to go to Veronica's. I cannot be late.

VERONICA FEELS WARM WIND ON her face while half asleep and dreams she is next to the Jordan River. The breeze happens for only one second with a brief pause in between. Her brain starts working on this odd situation; she opens her eyes and finds Ognir's nose only one inch from hers, and his eyes are staring right at her. His tail starts wagging the moment her eyes look into his. She speaks to him, "I guess it is time to get up, Ognir. Thank you. Did I dream yesterday, or did it actually happen? It is hard to tell these days. I push so hard to do even the simplest things. I guess we will see what happens.

"Hmmm, my sewing tools are all set in a row on the design table, arranged as if I am about to do a demonstration. What is her name? Her hair is fine, soft, and shiny and I really liked braiding it. Did that happen? What did Lidia say about Zacharias and his wife Elisabeth? Is the 'Anointed One' actually coming soon? Where is Flavius going to retire, Gaul?

"I am sure all this was a dream. Why are my alteration tools out? I need to stop dreaming. Ognir, you are standing by the door, and I do know what that means. Well, Ognir, am I ignoring you? I am very sorry; I have a lot on my mind. Here, let us go out for a bit."

When they return, Veronica has her wits about her, prepares something to eat, and is ready for Sophie to arrive. Ognir smells her under the door, and his tail starts wagging. Sophie knocks on the door briskly, and Ognir jumps up as if someone were arriving to take him out to play fetch ... he loves playing fetch.

Veronica looks at the design table again as she walks over and opens the door to welcome her guest, one of the few who has come by in many years. Veronica wants to cry with joy when she sees Sophie curtsy and say, "Senior Assistant Veronica, I am your assistant, Sophie, and I am ready to assist you in any way possible. So pleased to be at your service."

"Welcome, Assistant Sophie. I am happy you are eager to assist; we have many projects to attend to. Please come into my design studio!" Their eyes meet, they giggle, and within a few minutes they are discussing business.

THE COMMITTEE

THE FISHING INDUSTRY IN THIS area has continued to flourish serving the expanding local population. The Sea of Galilee has become even more productive, so the international trade prospects have also increased. The fish processing industry is one of the largest export markets for Israel.

Peter and Andrew are upright citizens, honest businessmen, and fair in all their dealings with their community. They are also very religious and pious in their faithful observance of the law.

"This day will yield another bounteous harvest if God so wills, Tobin," Peter announces as they prepare the boats for early morning launch into a calm Sea of Galilee. Peter is not saying those words casually; his faith has grown to understand that all man receives which is good is delivered by God and in God's timetable.

Tobin replies with a grin, "Yes, of course, and you will now tell me in very precise words precisely what my responsibilities are, and as I do them with exactness, for fifteen hours or so, you will allow me to receive additional instructions...."

Andrew interjects, looking at Peter, his older brother. "That is if you do not fall asleep and fall into the deep because all you are doing is talking and taking charge, watching your poor enslaved employees do all the work!"

Peter looks up at Andrew, who is arranging several nets on board and grins as he is preparing his reply.... "Yes, you are both exactly correct. My throat is already becoming dry from needing to tell you everything each time you forget, so ... I will close my mouth and let God himself tell you what to do. Keep your ears attached and listen carefully because I will be silent starting ... now!" Peter concludes with a confirming nod of his head.

Andrew takes Peter's declaration seriously. He had seen Peter make decisions and nod his head in a comparable manner many times before and knows better than to continue to tease him as he announces, "Tobin, take us out to the south and keep close to the shore. I feel we are going to have a great harvest this fine day."

Peter sits in his appointed place in the boat between Andrew and Tobin, watching carefully while seemingly enjoying keeping his mouth shut as Tobin expertly maneuvers the craft for several minutes.

Tobin, whom Peter calls his "intern" looks up and asks, "There you are! Does this spot look favorable to you gentlemen?"

Andrew looks at Peter for a response, but Peter smiles and looks back, waiting for Andrew to respond to Tobin's question.

Andrew stands up and says, "Yes, Tobin. Thank you." He looks at his older brother and says, "Peter, let's cast the first net on the shore side."

Andrew notices someone approaching the shore and adds, "Make sure you don't fall in, and cast well, because it seems we have someone watching us on shore."

Peter stands in confirmation, and while he and Andrew arrange the net and cast it out as they have done for many years, they hear the stranger from the shore call softly to them with purpose and clarity, "Come. Follow me, and I will make you fishers of men."

"THEY LEFT, AND YOU WERE alone in the boat ... in only one short moment?" Muriel asks after hearing Tobin's explanation.

"I believe the man was the Rabbi from Nazareth, the person everyone has been talking about," Tobin offers. He then adds, "I heard that the Rabbi also went straight to Zebedee's boat and called James and John as well."

"What did they do?"

"They both left with the Rabbi ... and Peter and Andrew."

"Tobin, you keep focus on the business. You will do very well. Do not worry about anything," Muriel says and then looks at Tobin directly and adds, "We are blessed to be living now and will see wondrous things. I am sure Peter will stay connected. You need to know he trusts you."

Tobin replies, "Yes, I think he does."

"No, he trusts you completely. He brags about you all the time. You know how he is; he would not want to make you too proud by saying what he does about you in front of you," Muriel confides.

She places her hand on his and adds, "Tobin, Peter knows you can run the business while he is working with the Rabbi. Peter, my headstrong son-in-law also knows that God will instruct you better than he can, so we will do our best and ask God to assist." Muriel pauses and then adds with a smile, "I will be there with you, and we will do well together. Thank you for your loyalty, your goodness, and your expert knowledge of the fishing industry."

Tobin smiles back and responds, "Thank you. I am sure we will be successful enough for Peter and Andrew to notice some improvements when they are able to visit."

"Yes, I am sure you are correct about that, Tobin!"

BECAUSE OF THE LIKELIHOOD OF graft and corruption in the ever-increasing and lucrative fishing industry, a committee was initiated to ensure fair trade and to levy taxes to support the Jewish as well as the Roman governments.

Peter had received his license to fish as well as to sell fish locally and to export brokers.

When Peter left, word spread, and multiple buyers pressed the committee for purchase of Peter's licenses.

When licenses are issued, they are property of the family and cannot be rescinded if someone in the family is actively using them and adding to the economy.

The committee assumed that Peter's licenses would no longer be used and felt there would be a profit to be made (for the government and personally). They waited for the right moment, which they rushed into quickly.

Tobin sees them coming in the distance. He knows instantly and thinks, *Here they come. Always three. Always with two as old as trees and another younger committee member, often smarter and more educated, sometimes easy to work with and other times as sharp as a cracking whip.*

He hefts the last net out of the boat, walks over to the end of the old, wooden hanging rack and begins carefully placing it up to dry. As he does so, he inspects the hundreds of knots which form the net, looking at the pattern he has memorized. He takes his time, wondering what the inevitable committee experience is going to be like. It takes them a while to make the final descent to the dock. The younger member respectfully walks behind.

"So!" the senior committee member says with the minimal energy he has left after making the long walk, "We see that you continue to work without your master being around. That is commendable. You are a skilled fisherman. What is your name son?"

Tobin notices the man is leaning on his long staff so as to keep balance, and the thought goes through his mind, *I hope he does not die here on the spot. They will probably blame me.*

Tobin looks at the committee representative and responds, "Hello dear sir! A pleasure to meet you. My name is Tobin, and your name, dear sir, is—?" Tobin quickly wipes his right hand off on his pants and sticks it out toward the aged visitor while taking a step forward so that his hand almost touches him.

"Yes," the committee member replies as he takes a small, frail step back, looking at Tobin's outstretched hand. "Tobin, we have heard your name spoken of with praise. You are respected by the members of the Sea of Galilee Fishing Industry Inspectors Guild. They say they have been keeping a careful eye on your operations."

"They are fine gentlemen," Tobin replies. He then, in the same breath, asks, "Please tell me sir, does the committee care for and take responsibility for the lives of those they employ as inspectors to ensure the Sea of Galilee fishing industry continues to be a growing economic concern?"

"Why yes," the voice of the committee responds as he glances at the other two members.

Tobin leaves no silence and responds, "I am happy to hear that." He looks down at the shoreline then turns his attention immediately back up to his visitors with, "When will the committee ensure that these excellent inspectors know how to sail their expensive boats *before* they are launched into dangerous waters? Please tell me how I can support you in your important responsibility in this regard."

All three committee members stare back at Tobin, who knew he was on the right track to keep them off balance as he softens their resolve to complete their assigned task.

"Do you review the reports your stalwart inspectors carefully create for your committee?" Tobin asks in a softer tone.

"Yes, we are sure those reports are reviewed by someone on the subcommittee. Of course, they are," the committee member replies while gaining concurrence from his companions, who nod their heads in agreement.

"This is a fine process you have created, and I appreciate the support the committee gives. Since the inspector's reports are carefully examined in the subcommittee, I am sure you are aware of the multiple occasions each season where the active fishermen you are supporting on the Sea of Galilee have, at their own peril, rescued your inspectors and saved their lives. Do you know this? Are you aware we have saved them from certain death?"

Tobin only lets that statement sink in for a moment, then offers, "I am *sure* you know and am sure you will investigate these two important items when you meet next as a full committee. Am I correct in this belief gentlemen?"

Each of the three committee members shakes his head "Yes," so Tobin continues, "You are men of sound resolve and you have strength of character. Please know that we common fishermen appreciate your endeavors on our behalf. I have only one more request," Tobin says. He then looks again at the pebbles on the shore and completes his thought by saying, again in a calm, pleading voice, "a simple request from us simple fishermen." He then looks up and says, "Please ... please teach your supportive inspectors what fish actually look like."

He continues, "They have absolutely no idea what is being brought up by our nets. I will tell you something … once word gets out that certain inspectors know *nothing* about the actual fish they are supposed to be inspecting, fun-loving fishermen will be sending them on wild goose chases, looking for imaginary catches at the other end of the Sea of Galilee."

Tobin sees confusion in the faces of his visitors and decides to let them down carefully, "We are here, I am here … to support your honorable committee's valiant efforts to ensure the success of this industry. We all want you to be rewarded for your efforts. Do you not believe the lack of inspector training and proper certification is wasting the resources you have put in place, and do you feel obligated to see to it that your subcommittee makes a full accounting of these three important items as judiciously as possible? I know you feel this way and on behalf of the several fishing consortium organizations, I wish to thank you for your efforts on our behalf. Please accept our best regards and please have a pleasant evening."

Tobin concludes his remarks and turns away hoping his visitors will naturally retreat. He takes a few steps toward the other end of the net-drying rack, looking at and touching the nets as he passes. He hears the committee members start to walk away, but they begin to make noise as if they are upset with the outcome. Tobin keeps walking but can hear one set of footsteps coming back his way. *Those steps are of the younger man, who will surely pass me the communication they came to deliver in the first place,* Tobin thinks as he prepares for the confrontation.

Peter's mother-in-law Muriel—'fragrance of God.' It must also mean wrath of God.

She knows where they meet, she knows it is tonight, and she knows their meetings are not any more than a reason to overeat, over-drink, and make rash decisions. The only person who remains sober is the Roman records keeper, spy, influencer.

Muriel waits patiently outside until they are ready to negotiate, then barges into the meeting, and takes over … completely.…

The Roman records keeper receives a glance from her, and he quickly obeys and pulls his record book out, dropping his piece of meat in flatbread on the floor as he does so.

"So, you believe you have pulled a fast one on my family ... in direct conflict with the Roman law established to keep you from being disrespectful to the citizens of this department!" Muriel says in the tone of voice only women can use and which all men instantly obey.

They are stunned. Those who are still coherent gaze at each other in disbelief. They have known her for many decades and also know her parents and grandparents. She has always been a woman to be reckoned with and this evening she is on a verbal rampage, denouncing them in front of the Roman, who will take the minutes of this official committee meeting back to headquarters before the sun comes up.

She glances at the Roman recorder again to make sure he is capturing everything. He nods he is ready, so she begins, "According to law, you did not even have the right to discuss taking away our fishing licenses for any reason, especially when the business is alive and operating, paying taxes as required." She makes sure this point is taken down.

She continues her presentation for another ten minutes, including the names of witnesses she will be calling to the following meeting, which are among Capernaum's strongest fishing families, rulers, and judges.

They could all lose their well-paid positions by noon tomorrow. She lets the import of what she is delivering sink in as she prepares the final, closing argument. The room is silent, and several attendees start looking at the exits.

Muriel looks at the two doorkeepers and nods her head. At that signal, they bar the doors and stand in front of them. She still has the attention of the Roman record keeper and as she looks at each individual in the room, she announces their full family names pausing long enough for each of them to be written.

Muriel prepares for the conclusion, "Everyone will know what evil deeds you have been up to." She looks again at the record keeper, who glances at her in accordance, "The reputations of your families will be sullied, and this deed will be known and talked about for generations.

"Your children and grandchildren will live looking downward and will never be able to earn respect or positions of influence because of what you have done." She lets that also rest on their hearts a moment.

Every coherent eye is still fastened on her as she moves to be in the center of the room and states, "It is proposed that the decision to rescind Peter's operating licenses be revoked and a regulatory notice be issued that the same licenses are not for sale and the moneys already received as deposits to obtain said licenses be returned double-fold, all in favor!" She raises her hand in the air, and everyone follows along.

Muriel looks at the Roman recorder, who is astonished, and says, "The decision is unanimous. So, it has been decided. So let it be recorded. The clerk will make note and arrange for proper payment."

"Thank you, gentlemen, there is still wine available. Enjoy your meeting," she says as she gives the doorkeepers the cue to open the doors as she leaves the meeting. Silence only lasts a moment before she hears from several paces away a voice declare, "Yes! Wine! Bring us the best wine reserved for those who can hold it!"

One committee member, Zebulon, remarks to Levi, sitting next to him, "Well, it was worth a try. Too bad ... at least she is still to this day highly entertaining when she is angry."

THE FIRST DAY IN JERUSALEM

JOSHUA IS PLEASED TO HAVE arrived in Jerusalem and ponders as he walks to his appointed office where he will attend to important paperwork before visiting his merchants. *Every time I have come to this city, I am dumbfounded by the absence of any flat pathways anywhere. When I was twelve, my grandfather Nehemiah told me that the collection of hills Jerusalem is built on are sacred and have a long history. I responded to him that my legs did not like to visit here, and they were complaining and wanted a rest. His quick response back was that if I told my legs to get stronger by moving quickly, every hill would make that happen. I am still waiting.*

At the top of this hill is the esteemed Office of the Commerce Committee, which will be very busy this afternoon. Every visiting merchant must have documents of authority prior to any commercial transaction in Jerusalem. I have my grandfather's documents which, although our family has used them for hundreds of years, need to be renewed each year.

I hope Nathaniel is on duty this morning, the Young Merchant says to himself as he enters the formal reception chamber where there are already several merchants engaged with commerce agents.

He scans across the room and notes to himself, *Ah, there is Nathaniel. It looks like he is finishing with the fur traders. They were part of my caravan. Nice fellows, even though I cannot remember nor pronounce their names. They have traveled far.*

The Young Merchant steps forward into Nathaniel's view and sees him thank the fur traders while pointing down the hallway toward the Registrar's

Office, where they will pay their fees and receive their trade documents. Nathaniel turns his head from where the fur traders are headed over to the Young Merchant.

"Well, young man! I am so glad to see you have arrived safely. You are safe, aren't you?" Nathaniel says cheerfully as he gives a hug to the Young Merchant.

"Nathaniel! Yes, I am safe, or I was safe until you embraced me. You still have the strength of an ox. I hope your dear wife is doing well and keeping you out of trouble. Is this true?"

"Oh, you will learn my young friend. A man's teaching by the woman he marries is never over. It is a steady uphill battle that never ends. The man who surrenders quickest is the man who is happier longer ... if he keeps his mouth shut," Nathaniel responds as he places his right hand on the Young Merchant's shoulder and looks into his eyes, "especially when such a man has something he believes is very clever to say. Ha! There you have it. The key to success! Keep your mouth shut!" He concludes with a smile and a snort of a laugh.

"Thank you! Thank you! Thank you, Nathaniel. I will keep those words close to my heart in the event I fall head over heels off my camel and land at the feet of some needy soul of the female type!" Joshua responds with a chuckle.

Nathaniel laughs aloud responding, "Yes, sound advice, but more often than not ignored. Let us get you settled and on your way. I am sure there is a daughter of a shopkeeper who is sitting by, waiting for you to arrive." He ends with a happy snicker and a mischievous grin.

I wonder how many times he has offered that sage piece of advice to those who have been trapped into getting married for one strange reason or another? the Young Merchant wonders as he reaches into his bag.

Nathaniel notices what the Young Merchant is reaching for and interrupts with, "No ... no, no, no, I have seen your papers at least forty," he looks up at the ceiling, "no, fifty-seven times ... I know your merchant rights as well as my own address, which I cannot remember at the moment, but you have ..." he holds up his index finger and declares, "One—exclusive rights to deal with the government project manager's textile needs, as well as Two—the right to engage with small shopkeepers, not conglomerates, correct?" He looks up at the Young Merchant's attentive eyes.

"Why yes, that is absolutely correct! You are amazing, Nathaniel!"

"I knew you were coming and have already prepared your papers ... here," Nathaniel announces, handing the Young Merchant a certificate and saying, "You know what to do with this, but I must first share with you all the news since last you were here...."

"Yes, thank you. I would love all the news. Let us go and sit together over where it will be more comfortable," the Young Merchant says as he points with his outstretched hand to the long bench with cushions against the south wall, where they spend the rest of the morning.

ARMED WITH MORE NEWS THAN he could ever remember, the Young Merchant begins selling, hoping to complete his rounds prior to the caravan leaving for southern Israel and Egypt.

In between shop visits, during the time all shops are closed for midday meal, the Young Merchant waits in the shade of a busy square. While watching people pass through the small plaza, his attention is caught by someone who is not passing through but is stationary.

Who is that short, thin fellow over there, the one with the small delivery cart ... which he is taking exactly ... nowhere at all? he thinks as he observes, *He is trying to sink into the wall he is leaning against and is almost succeeding if he stands motionless. How does he do that? He has piercing eyes that are never still, darting back and forth.*

The Young Merchant concludes, *It is strange that when the man with the cart turns his head to the right, his eyes are peering to the extreme left, so you never really know what he is looking at. I had better get moving myself ... why would someone like that wear what looks to be brand new, very expensive sandals? Every large city has similar characters. I wonder what this one is up to.*

The following day at her workshop, Dinah is visiting with the Jewish leader's senior assistant and project manager, Daniel. They invite the Young Merchant over to Dinah's workshop to discuss the drapery needs and to formalize the Young Merchant's commission to get exclusive fabric from Egypt. The Jewish leader's senior assistant and the Young Merchant get along well and agree to have lunch later that day.

As the Young Merchant and Daniel are chatting, Dinah slips away to speak with a visitor. The Young Merchant notices that she is speaking with a younger woman, and although he cannot fully understand what they are talking about, he is struck by her voice and, at the end of the conversation, while he is looking in her direction, the younger woman glances in his direction and their eyes meet for an instant.... The Young Merchant is smitten.

Waiting in the square for lunch with the Jewish leader's senior assistant, the Young Merchant sees the man with the cart once again, and as he is watching him speak with someone, he sees that the items on the cart are the exact same items in the same exact position as they were previously. The man with the cart's eyes meet the Young Merchant's gaze, he starts, grasps the cart handles, and rushes out of view.

He did that move more quickly than he should be able to pull a cart of that size, the Young Merchant thinks watching the cart lunge forward in a burst of speed.

There is air under one of the wheels as the cart bounces over the cobblestone ... it actually comes off the ground ... the parcels, baskets, and wrapped packages on the cart are empty!

This guy is certainly a spy. With that yellow-colored blanket with blue markings on each end draped over his shoulders, I would recognize him anywhere. He still has the new footwear as well.

SOON AFTER, DANIEL ARRIVES, AND takes Joshua to a small café where they chat. "So, Daniel, tell me truly, how is your boss Reuben treating you?" the Young Merchant inquires, while he lifts his cup up to his mouth.

"He is the same as he was last you came through. He says he is relieved Herod is gone, along with his zeal for starting construction projects, but complains that Pontius Pilate does too little." He looks at the Young Merchant and shakes his head while adding, "It's all a grand circle, that never ends ... until you die."

"Yes, I agree. But you have an increasing demand for interior projects I see, at least based on the orders of fabric I have been transporting to you."

"You mean you carry, or your camels carry. Yes, the new leadership is very interested in one-upmanship, or at least their wives are, and also, the Romans have been using Dinah for their high-end decorating binges."

"Yes, I brought several distinct types of fabric and specialty textiles for Dinah on this trip. They are definitely not what the shopkeepers order," the Young Merchant affirms. He then looks down at his plate, looks back at Daniel, and asks "There was a younger woman visiting Dinah today. Do you know her?"

Daniel grins and offers, "Yes, I saw you blush like a schoolboy."

"I didn't blush!" the Young Merchant protests.

"Call it what you want, but when you and 'that woman' looked at each other, there was a clap of lightening and the gods of Zeus sang a crescendo, all at the same time my friend."

"It was that obvious? I need to be more discreet."

"You need no discretion. She is beautiful. She is intelligent, and she is very accomplished."

"Really? What is her name?"

"She has a name, or the Romans have a name for her...."

"What? The Romans? Is she a slave?"

"Oh, no. Not at all."

"What do they call her?"

"The Ninth Division of Light Camel Dromedarii call her 'Master Camel Trainer.' She is well known and has trained many Roman soldiers in the fine art of battle. She is a legend."

"What?" the Young Merchant responds with wonder.

"You heard me right. She began training with them when she was only sixteen years old.... She did so well, they kept training her, and after they ran out of things to train her with, they asked her to become a trainer herself. You would be amazed at what she can do while riding a camel. She and her camel are one. She does not even need to use her reins. Some people believe that she thinks commands, and the camel knows and does whatever she has in her mind."

"So why was she exchanging completed projects and picking up new fabrics from Dinah today?" the Young Merchant asks while trying to learn more.

"She does that as well. She is also an expert designer and formidable seamstress. She is no match for a lowly, camel-riding merchant like you," Daniel offers with a smile, then adds, "Your friend the Camel Herder, now he would probably be a good match for the Master Camel Trainer," Daniel advises and then asks with amusement, "What's he been up to lately?" He looks at the Young Merchant who seems to be preoccupied thinking about something else.

"What?"

"The Camel Herder? Did his brothers agree to allow him to travel with you? Alone? Without adult supervision for the first time?" Daniel chides.

"Oh, yes. He is traveling with me. A great companion. He knows his camels as well. We leased them from the same camel vendor up in Byzantium, whose children are growing, and they are all doing well. Thanks for asking."

"I did not ask about the camel vendor. You need to get your head out of the clouds so you can get on to business. You do remember why you are here, right?"

THE YOUNG MERCHANT HAS A spring in his step as he arrives at the camel stables. "My friend the Camel Herder! How have you been doing? Daniel says hello and wants you to know he has arranged a marriage for you, but you cannot see *this* prize until after you have completed your first solo trip with the excellent Young Merchant!" The Young Merchant barges in on the Camel Herder's conversation with the stable owner, who laughs at his good news and then exclaims, "This man? Married? Without even meeting his lucky spouse? She must not know him; otherwise she would not agree to such an arrangement."

The Young Merchant looks at them both and continues, "Why yes! This type of arrangement is made these days, you know. It is for the benefit of both families, who, in this case, made agreement right after we left." He looks at the Camel Herder and asks, "Your brothers? They did not tell you what they were doing on your behalf? Why did they suggest you bring along an extra camel for your bride-to-be?"

The Camel Herder does not have any of this and retorts, "The 'bride's camel' was my idea, not theirs. What are you talking about? What did you and Daniel have to drink at lunch? It was not water, that is for sure!" He turns to the stable owner and shrugs his shoulders.

There is silence for a moment while the Young Merchant is thinking of the Master Camel Trainer and the Camel Herder is sorting out where this new proposal came from when it hits him....

"You are the one who produced this little plan! It was not at all Daniel's plan, and the reason you cleverly invented it is because you saw someone you want to marry, so you decided to produce a distraction to get your mind off of her! It was her wonderous eyes, wasn't it? Tell us the truth my Young Merchant! That was it, was it not?"

I have lost control. This is not good. Daniel was right. People can see right through me. Time to come clean, the Young Merchant thinks as he looks down at the straw-strewn stable floor and ponders in tense silence.

The Camel Herder looks over at the stable owner, winks, and says in a reconciling tone, "We are all friends here; you can confess your juvenile sins. We forgive you. You must forgive yourself," he nods at the stable owner and completes with, "and you must tell us all the details. Who is she and when is the wedding celebration?"

The Young Merchant is without escape as his mind searches for a respectable and calm response. *Do I tell them? How can I tell them when I know almost nothing? Only one … short … glance.* He takes a breath, looks at his companions, and divulges his secret.

The Young Merchant offers the most concise explanation he can conjure up while the Camel Herder and the stable owner sit down and listen compassionately, never interrupting.

When the Young Merchant finishes, they both sit motionless, knowing silence will intensify the Young Merchant's isolation. They are very satisfied they have placed "this poor soul" in a fine position and are elated to cause him a bit of humorous "pain." They slowly turn toward each other and shake their heads, and while looking sorrowfully at each other, say in one voice, "He has been lost. He is hopeless."

The stable owner, hoping to save his reputation as a wise and thoughtful coach in life's inconvenient situations, asks the Camel Herder, "So, should we help him?" to which the answer instantly comes, "No, he is beyond help."

Both men burst out laughing, and the Camel Herder falls sideways into a pile of hay, gasping for air between bouts of laughter. He is so delighted in himself. The stable owner feels sorry, so he stands up and steps over to offer his condolences to the young, smitten merchant.

THAT WAS MISERABLE. THEY WERE *ruthless, but I am glad they had a good laugh,* the Young Merchant reasons. *I am glad the Camel Herder had the*

camel loaded and ready for the Roman armorer. His delivery is always heavy. He moves through the crowded street toward the armory, taking care to negotiate the narrow passageways so the load does not catch on to anything. The Roman armorer is waiting for him when he arrives.

"It took you less time from the stables than it took you last time!" Jari exclaims.

How does he do that? I did not see any spies on the way, the Young Merchant questions but does not dare ask and responds, "Well, your team cleared the way for me and made sure I was not challenged by any of the guard. That is how I traveled here so quickly, and I wish to thank you. You have a fine delivery of everything you ordered, as well as some unique items from the iron smiths. They send you their greetings by the way."

"Good to see you! How is your grandfather? I have known him for many years, and we have raised a toast in many places together. Is he well?" Jari, the Roman armorer, says as he stands with arms extended.

"Grandfather is fine and has decided that he would like to spend more time at home. He sends his best regards. He has also sent your standard supplies: several heavy brass plates, heavy polished metal plates, the smaller thin brass, and steel sheets."

"Yes, yes, all is good. I see you have some substantial pieces here as well," Jari comments as he points to the larger bundles being placed on the table by his staff.

"Of course. He knows how you love forging and smithing, and even though you rarely get the free time you hope for, he sent you several iron rods and at least twenty-two lengths of the latest steel, which makes the finest bows and sword blades to be found anywhere," explains the Young Merchant as he uncovers a sample of each item delivered.

"Thank you!" the Roman armorer exclaims as he walks over to the camel and touches the nearest bundle with his weathered hand. He looks over at his assistants and shakes his head yes. Except for one package, what had taken the Camel Herder an hour to load, is unloaded, inspected, recorded, and stowed in only five minutes.

THE ROMAN ARMORER REPRESENTS THE sectarian world that is mechanical in its pursuit of domination and perfection of efficient processes, the industrial approach to feeding troops and making effective weapons, sometimes customized for specific purposes.

The Roman Machine is exactly that. In the same way the traditions of Israelite society have shaped daily life, the Roman military is about process-driven order. It is manifest at the height of process perfection from exactly how each helmet is made, worn, and cared for, down to the process to tie battle shoes to prevent any mishap during a city confrontation or field battle.

The Roman Machine is built and maintained by those who observe, analyze, plan and act. They observe everything, everyone, and every process, which is distilled down to the absolute basics of how something goes from idea to design to fabrication to manufacturing on a massive scale. The creation of Standard Operating Procedures exists for the manufacture and maintenance of everything from cleaning Roman robes to making footwear to spear sharpening ... everything.

A culture which develops and standardizes efficient processes is a culture that can dominate. At this period, the Romans are not only the best, but they are also the only culture who drove processes to full acceptance at home and abroad. Understanding this concept is key to understanding the Roman mind and actions.

Transportation includes movement of supplies and finished goods including food, equipment, animals, and armament. These are basic to Roman domination.

The transportation of raw materials such as metals, hardwoods, leathers, fabrics, and chemicals is carefully planned and orchestrated.

Inventory is carefully managed so that only enough and not too much flows through the supply chain to the deployed troop activities. Those who carry this responsibility are looked up to and hold senior rank.

The production of all supplies is carefully observed and controlled by standard steps, checklists, and placement of each component of any assembly. Whether it is corn cakes or helmets, sandals, or shields, it is well documented, then checked and rechecked.

Production of armament is Jari's specialty. He has studied, performed, and taught each part of every known piece of equipment that exists. He has also invented and produced items of war which were later adopted by the general Roman Armory Quartermasters. Of course, Jari provided the step-by-step Standard Operating Procedure as an integral part of the new and improved items.

When Jari is about to make or repair something, he refers to the process and carefully orchestrates the approved system which minimizes movement, waiting, overproduction and overprocessing. When he is successful with all these components of his process, he avoids defects. He regularly presents perfect equipment to well-trained Roman soldiers and officers.

Jari had served his mandatory twenty years; however, when the assignment to Jerusalem was offered, he took it. The Roman Army has a proven process for the pay of its soldiers which includes a skills hierarchy driving its pay hierarchy. Perhaps complex, but always the same and very efficient.

"YOU DO NOT KNOW HOW I appreciate you bringing these supplies. What I receive from the dispensary planning department is adequate for common armor and chariot repair parts, but these days, the officers' equipment is getting more elaborate and ornate than it needs to be … in my humble opinion," Jari says, following up with a grin.

The Young Merchant hoists the remaining package, brings it over to the worktable and sets it down. He looks at the senior armorer and says, "Here it is, your gift from your longtime friends at the foundry. They call it, 'the finest steel ever made.' All they ask is that you do not waste it on making nails for convicts." He unwraps the package and lays out its contents.

Jari reaches over to the new steel on the table and as he takes a bar out of its wrapper, comments, "I see that your sources still take pride in their workmanship. Receiving materials which were uncared for and carried across the salt water always end up pitted and rusted." He rubs his index finger against his thumb and says, "They still oil their work and ship it in oiled paper covered with protective cloth."

"Look how clean it is," the armorer says as he inspects one of the five bars, each fifty centimeters in length and as wide as his palm. "It feels a bit lighter. I cannot wait to heat it up and test its malleability." He looks at a member of his team and says, "Take these to the secure storage and make sure you cover them completely with the oil cloth." His request is completed immediately.

Jari looks again at the Young Merchant and observes, "You certainly don't see that pride or this craftsmanship anymore. Thank you. Thank you for your care and vigilance making sure this has been hidden from those who love to pillage caravans. Hmph … I have seen my share. Thank you again."

"Thank you, sir. I will pass your kind remarks to grandfather. He will appreciate them. He has a very high regard for you … and your wife. He passes this to you to give to her with warm regards. He also asked me to make sure she has not kicked you out of the house yet, and if she has, I am to forebear giving it to you," the Young Merchant says jokingly as he passes the small gift to Jari.

Jari expresses a friendly grin and replies, "Ah, yes. I am still allowed to return home most days. You will see my young friend … you will see. I will gladly pass your kind regards to my wife who has been following me around the empire for so many years. Thank you!"

"Thank you for that bit of wisdom you offered earlier. I do not plan to get married for many years. There are too many things to accomplish and cities to open for business. Places to explore," the Young Merchant replies with confidence only a young person can aspire to.

Jari glances up from looking again at the gift and replies, "Yes, sounds entertaining.... You will see soon enough though, and nothing you plan or do will prepare you for it when it happens.... Did you bring any smithing coal? The stuff they bring us is made to cook with, not for heating steel."

"Yes, the coal will be delivered in the morning with three camels, straight from the stable. It burns hot and clean."

Jari turns to the Young Merchant and says, "Thank you once again. We will be ready for it. You be sure to come for a visit before you leave south so I can show you what this steel can do. I have some ideas in mind already, and although I make what I am told to make, it will not be nails. Not with this." He places his hand on the Young Merchant's shoulder saying, "Thank you again. When you come by, I will provide you with a list of what I need from our friends in Cairo."

"You are very welcome. I need to get this camel where it belongs and make a couple of visits for my grandfather before it gets dark. I will see you before we head south," the Young Merchant replies as he completes tying the load rack securely again on the camel. With a friendly nod, he leads the camel to the left, then, turning to where he had arrived from, is gone. He wonders about the blind widow he has plans to meet. *I think I will pass by Rebecca's on the way back. I hope she is well.*

CAMELS ARE LIKE HORSES WHEN *it comes to knowing that they are headed toward their stables. Even if they are temporarily stabled somewhere, they remember where they spent the last night and most especially, they remember where they last were fed,* the Young Merchant thinks as he notices the camel picking up the pace as they near the stable.

Unlike horses, camels show very little of what they are thinking. They always look bored and disinterested. Their ears stay the same, even when they are angry. Horses' ears at least give you warning when they lie down straight. Not so with camels.

"We should be getting close my friend, and I do not want you getting cross with me. We will not be long. I promise that we will get you fed soon after our visit," the Young Merchant says to the camel as he prepares to veer off the direct-to-stable course.

It is interesting to note that the Young Merchant, the Camel Herder, the Camel Vendor, the Stable Owner, and nearly anyone who spends their careers with camels, tend to chat with their camels as if they were close friends. Camels, by the way, are more loyal to humans than dogs are. Perhaps that is why they are not to be trifled with.

"OK, here we go. To the right. Third door to the left." The camel moves smoothly but makes a small snorting noise. "Behave yourself, we are here. Oh, she is sitting outside."

As they advance the last several steps, the Young Merchant thinks, *I wonder if she will remember me. How should I introduce myself? I hope her hearing is still good.* He is interrupted by a confident and somewhat loud greeting....

"Hello! How are you? Please come over and sit. Your camel is already unloaded, so she can lie down and have some water I have prepared. Please tell me how your grandfather Nehemiah is doing and Ruth. Please, come over. Sit!" Rebecca says with enthusiasm.

"Yes, we are coming! Thank you!" Joshua responds and wonders, *How did she know? How could she know about the camel?* He is surprised, yet it brings back memories of previous visits. He settles the camel and sits down near Rebecca as the afternoon shadows start to lengthen.

"I bring greetings from grandfather and grandmother. Grandfather remembers well the many times he was able to spend time with your good husband Levi. They send you this gift and hope it will make you happy and provide comfort."

The Young Merchant takes the soft blanket, which was folded in a square, unfolds it and places it on Rebecca's lap. She feels it being placed there and touches it with both hands, her face lighting up as she exclaims, "Oh how wonderful! This is the softest blanket I have ever felt. You should not have gone to so much trouble." She reaches up to wipe a tear away from her eye and adds, "You are so kind. Thank you. Please thank dear Nehemiah and Ruth for me next you see them." With both hands, she pulls the blanket up to her smiling face and holds it close.

The Young Merchant is touched and considers how lonely she must be without her husband and without her sight. He softly says, "Tell me how you have been, how you are, and if there is anything I can do for you, Rebecca." The disinterested camel chews in the background.

THE SALES ROUTE

I T IS EARLY IN THE morning at the camel stables, and steam is coming out of the camels' nostrils with each breath. Pitching another bale of hay, the Camel Herder notices the Young Merchant is about to arrive, so he calls over to the stable owner, "You better get ready now! He will be here in a minute, and you know he is allergic to camel dander. Did you spray perfume, so he does not get upset? You know he is interested in perfume these days … or so I have heard! I think …"

The Young Merchant is standing next to him, so his next reminder is cut short. "Oh, hello. You are here early. What kept you? I hope you find the stable accommodating," he says with a smile. The stable owner comes over and asks, "Do you gentlemen need anything? I am going into the market area this morning."

The Young Merchant looks at the Camel Herder and says, "We need to work together as a team. The only reason you are giving me such a challenging time about the girl I met …"

"You didn't meet her."

"Well, you are jealous because I have a relationship…."

"You don't even know her name."

The stable owner watches long enough and interrupts by saying, "I am out of here. You both sound like schoolboys. Stop it, or I will tell your mothers." He turns to leave.

At that, they both jerk their heads around and look at him, so he adds, "And don't think I won't." As he walks out, they look back at each other and agree he is right. They spend several minutes going over what they had learned their first days in Jerusalem and what they need to accomplish that day. The Young Merchant then makes his way to the palace, where he looks forward to meeting with the Jewish leader's senior assistant, Daniel, and Dinah. He is relieved the tension is gone.

THE YOUNG MERCHANT SETTLES HIS camel, Bindi, and while he is unloading the two cargo camels at the back entrance to the palace, he murmurs under his breath, "Getting past all those guards around this place takes too long. You would think they would be able to tell each other I was cleared, but, of course, each of them only really wants a small bribe, and could care less about their actual guard responsibilities."

Daniel, the Jewish leader's senior assistant had approached from the palace and says with a surprise, "Why are you muttering out here by yourself … or are you sharing your woes with your camel employees?"

"Hah! If they would only listen to my woes, I would be a better man for it. Good morning, Daniel, senior assistant to the Jewish leader of all things construction and modernization in the little village of Jerusalem and beyond."

The not-so-hidden sarcasm is appreciated by Daniel who thinks, *It is nice to work with people who are normal and not always on the make for swindles and deals and power.* He then replies, "You have obviously spent far too much time in the Mediterranean deserts with your camels, my friend. Let us get these fabrics in place before Dinah arrives. You know how she hates to waste time because someone is unprepared."

WALKING FROM ONE SIDE OF the room to the other, Dinah details her observations: "The light, of course, will hit differently, but since the walls and ceiling are all uniform in color, the effect will be similar. Look how the blues in this fabric highlight the vases on this wall, and the shelving will not have the shadows you see now but will be illuminated directly from that window at formal reception time." She looks at Daniel and asks, "You see?"

"I see what you are seeing, but we need to be careful of the draperies that will be hanging on either side of these windows, so they do not block sunlight," replies Daniel.

The Young Merchant is looking at the ancient vases Dinah mentioned. They are ancient, intricate, and beautiful. He walks over to get a closer look.

Dinah continues, "So, the light will directly enter the west windows." She walks over to the east windows, looks out, places her hands on her hips, and exclaims soberly, "We have a problem."

"What's wrong?" Daniel asks as he makes his way over and looks out. He cannot see what the problem might be.

Morning light is shining in their faces, "Don't you see it? It is obvious Daniel!"

"Do not start talking like the king's wife. What is it?" Daniel looks up and to both sides.

"Daniel, we are talking about light."

"Yes."

"Light bounces."

"Yes, off water, off snow, off glass, off silver ..." He is reaching for the answer.

Dinah is well ahead and declares the solution, "You will build a bare trellis twenty feet from this east window that is forty feet long and twelve feet high."

"OK, and it will serve what purpose, may I ask?"

"The sun will be coming in the west window, correct?"

"Yes."

"It will also be hitting the building that is outside of the window on the east. The light coming from the west will bounce off the building and come through the east window. Is that correct Daniel?"

"Well, yes...."

"What color is that building? Do you want that color to come streaming inside your interior, washing everything in the room with a dull brown that looks like dirt?" Dinah declares, then says, "Thank you gentlemen, we will be fine, unless she changes her mind again." She looks at Daniel as she moves across the room and adds, "I have an appointment to get to, please engage the suppliers to start work as soon as you can. If that is not immediately, let me know and I'll do it myself." She looks at them both, grins and walks out. They know she will.

THE SHOPKEEPER ON THE SOUTH side sets down his load of merchandise, glances over as the Young Merchant walks in, nods his head as he looks to ensure his load is placed neatly. He is thinking about what he is going to say to the new visitor, how he was going to let him know who is in charge and all the important business history he knows.

He turns toward the Young Merchant, shuffles up to him with a bit more energy than he has displayed in a long time and announces, "Oh yes, I see you have the same pouch with secret writings in it." He is looking at the well-worn document pouch, again slowly nodding his head. His steel-blue eyes have a glint from the past.

"I am here with your very well-chosen order. Where would you like me to place it sir?" the Young Merchant offers in his usual upbeat and attentive conversational voice.

Ezra the shopkeeper continues with his instructional approach, looking from the pouch to the Young Merchant's face, "I have known your grandfather and his father who carried it. I told your grandfather that those who know these things say that when your family gained its powerful position in international trade, one of your ancestors used the secret writings ... it drove him nuts and the whole family disappeared overnight ... everyone, never to be seen again. He had evidently spent time with the prophet Jeremiah, who was also crazy." He pauses to take a breath and continues as his gaze is now fixed on the Young Merchant's eyes.

"They believe, and I believe it to be the truth as well, that the family was taken by force by those hired by the judges, and they were all murdered south of the city. Your grandfather did not believe me, but I know people who have said they know people, close people, who have actually seen pieces of your ancestor's blue, silver, and gold vases sitting out in the open right inside Herod's palace ... to this day they are still there I tell you," Ezra emphasizes as he reaches out with his wrinkled and slightly shaking hand and places it gently on the Young Merchant's forearm.

His head stops nodding when he finishes, but he stands there motionless, with his hand giving quiet assurances to the Young Merchant that the message he has delivered is true. He pats the Young Merchant's arm a couple of times as if to declare that he is finished.

There is no doubt Ezra feels that he alone is the proper and informed messenger of this important tale which must be passed on to my family ... again, Joshua thinks. Joshua had never heard of such an event, but his customer seems to feel satisfaction in telling so it he replies, "Thank you for your concern. I appreciate this information more than you could ever know."

At the same moment, another old man who had been coming in the shop while Ezra was finishing his historical essay walks right over and declares, "Ezra, are you telling stories again? Well, at least your facts stay the same. I have to give you credit for that."

Looking at the Young Merchant, the new arrival advises, "Quit wasting your time listening to this old man. I have to get merchandise ready for Passover, and if I let you stay here, it will come and go with no money being made and my reputation will suffer."

"Josiah! You never had a reputation from the day you sold Sarah fabric which melted in the washtub!" Ezra snaps back with a wry smile.

"Well, Ezra, she is your wife, and I try to keep you happy by selling her what she picks out!" retorts Josiah.

"Well yes, Josiah, she is also your sister, and you should have educated her before you put her up for marriage!"

Joshua is beginning to worry they will start throwing things at each other when they both chuckle, grin ear to ear, start laughing while simultaneously looking at the Young Merchant, still trying to gain their composure.

Ezra gains his breath first and exclaims, "We got you! We bet you did not read that piece of jovial theater in your grandfather's sales notes, did you?" He and Josiah start chuckling again. Joshua feels like he has known them for years, and says, "Yes, I have been had. That was a good one."

Josiah then turns to Ezra and exclaims, "Well! I never offered my bossy sister up for marriage! If I had exercised that power, I would have sold her to the Egyptians like your grandfathers did to my grandfather, Joseph!"

"Watch what you say my old friend, she may be listening again, like the time we planned to take over the business from his," pointing to the Young Merchant, "grandfather and escape with only a couple of camels, no troubles, and too much freedom," he offers in a hushed tone, ending with both hands up in the air as he says the word "freedom."

Josiah turns to Joshua and says matter-of-factly, "So when you are done with this cranky old fellow, come over with my goods, and I will not offer you any more old and dusty gossip." He turns for the exit and without breaking his stride, tells Ezra, "Take care of yourself, have a good evening, and I will see you at readings."

And then he is gone.

Ezra walks, slowly this time, over near the back wall and as Josiah had done, speaking without an apparent audience and without changing his gait or gaze, "Yes, he is a very old friend and has had a very rough life, but he takes the time to visit which is a good thing for the both of us. Your sales records may show volume of merchandise, profits, and losses, but it does not hold what is in the hearts and souls of those you visit."

They conclude their business and as Joshua leaves for Josiah's place, he can only think, *He has no idea what secrets the pouch contains … no idea at all.*

LEANING AGAINST THE WALL, THE Young Merchant is observing the man with a cart engage with two publicans who seem uninterested in the gossip he is peddling.

"What you are thinking is only the beginning," says a seemingly friendly voice, interrupting the Young Merchant's thoughts, whose observation remains focused. The Young Merchant does not move.

The voice continues with a Roman accent, "He fancies himself as the only holder of truth, the primary resource of knowledge of anything that is happening in this city."

The Young Merchant keeps his eyes on the subject while interrogating the source of the voice, "Why are you so interested in Jerusalem's foremost busybody, being a Roman as you are? I suppose you purchase his product to save time, right?"

"I am most interested in locating healthy men who wish to become part of the most powerful army that exists anywhere, those who are capable of becoming officers. I am also authorized to gather helpful information and assist citizens in their work and pleasure-seeking aspirations."

"That sounds like the freest of any Roman occupations I have ever heard of. How could you be of any use to anyone who already knows what they are doing and who is successful in their own right?"

"I know that when you finally entered the palace, you had taken too long and were, let us say, 'lighter' than you had expected, maneuvering through the guards. You passed how many? Four? Five?"

"You already know I passed six. Each a bit more expensive than the previous. It is the way business is done in this city and in many others."

"Here, take this token my friend."

The Young Merchant is forced to turn and see his new "friend," who is holding something like a coin in his left hand at the waist level, to hide the transaction from those around.

The Roman continues, "Next time you must pass by those who are gatekeepers, guards, or access monitors, you show them the token. You will be admitted immediately, and in some cases, will be offered other services, free of charge."

"Why should I do business with a Roman, who also sides as recruiter and operative?"

"I assist honest people who do honest work and make honest profit. I never charge the least amount, ever."

"Why do all these 'protectors of the elite' recognize this token and react in favorable ways? They are obviously on your payroll."

"You are a successful businessman, so you will understand. You all pay license fees, like you did with Nathaniel, to obtain the right to do business in Jerusalem; you also pay import taxes and then, when you go to, in your case Cairo and Alexandria, you pay export taxes, correct?"

The Young Merchant is trying to keep his eyes on the man with the cart but is now being distracted and thinks, *How does he know everything about me? Did he know all this about my grandfather as well? Why did grandfather not teach me about how complex this all could become?* He thinks there could be some advantages here and replies "You already know the answers to every question you are asking, so stop wasting my time."

"I do this as a favor between you and me. The 'protectors' as you call them are indeed on our payroll, which is handsome."

"Yes, and the retribution for failure to perform well is, let me guess, 'debilitating and perhaps fatal.' Right?"

"There is a reason why I knew you will be a good Roman officer. What else do you wish to know?"

Veronica Teaches Sophie

WORDS CANNOT EXPRESS THE JOY Veronica feels each time Sophie arrives with enthusiasm and a freshness that is fortifying. Veronica's sorties are fewer and fewer as her health declines, yet she gains strength by teaching Sophie how to serve others by achieving excellence in her chosen craft. It is a delicate balance, difficult to maintain, that fails on occasion.

Veronica awakes with Ognir in her face, but her attention is caught by a dreadful realization, "Oh no! He is gone! I missed Flavius and will never see him again! I am a failure! I ignore my friends and they disappear! How could I have done this to him?" The sobbing begins as she sits up in bed with tears streaming, her breath heaving in and out as her lament overtakes her.

"Ooo-nooo...." The sobbing continues and shakes her frame as she bows her head thinking, *I am useless. I have no purpose. I have failed again.* Veronica looks up, and the world is a blurry mess of confusion, which intensifies the sobbing. She exclaims out loud, *Why am I even here? Why does God not throw me in the Gehenna trash heap and burn my useless body to hide its shame? I am worthless and have been dying for so many years.... I am soooo tired.* She falls back asleep with Ognir's head on her lap. She does not even notice.

"Ver-on-i-ca ... Ver-on-i-ca ... Hello Ver-on-i-ca.... It is Sophie.... I am here to take care of you." The dream seems as if it is from another world. The sound is distant yet familiar. It comes again a bit closer.... "Ver-on-i-ca ... Ver-on-i-ca ... Hello Ver-on-i-ca.... It is Sophie.... I am here to take care of you."

Veronica does not want to wake up. Her soul seems to say, "No, thank you anyway. I do not want to wake up. Sleep is the only peace I find, thank you, I am at peace, I am sleeping."

"Ver-on-i-ca … Ver-on-i-ca … Hello Ver-on-i-ca…. It is Sophie…. I am here to take care of you." Sophie so very gently moves a lock of Veronica's hair from her face. Her angelic and patient smile is ready for Veronica to open her eyes. Ognir is looking at Sophie from right next to Veronica's bed, being perhaps the most patient, as he had not been out yet and it is midmorning.

Everything is quiet. Sophie places her warm hand on Veronica's forearm and holds it there. Veronica's eyes slowly open and are able to focus on Sophie's kind face. Sophie welcomes Veronica back to reality, "Hello sleepyhead. Ognir and I are so happy to greet you on this sunny day. Do not move a muscle. We have made you some peppermint infusion which you can sip a little at a time. It will steady your nerves and let you wake up slowly. It looks like you had a dreadful night. Keep quiet and do not say anything. We are here to help, aren't we, Ognir?"

Veronica is slow to come around and is not exactly sure if she is still asleep. She feels empty and abandoned by hope. Optimism, her constant companion in times past feels like a distant memory, if she had ever known it at all. She can feel the peppermint travel into her body … warm … relaxing. Its smell is soothing and familiar.

"Do you mind if I work a bit while you are resting? I will be very quiet." Veronica nods her head, "yes, go ahead."

"I took Ognir out, so he is fine."

It is still like a dream for Veronica as she begins to think about Sophie and their time together. None of her thoughts venture outside the walls of her home. Ognir again places his head on her lap. The warmth he gives her is as comforting as a child's favorite blanket, though she could not drag Ognir around as he has four legs and would not appreciate it.

Sophie keeps an eye on Veronica while she works. Once Veronica has a bite to eat and seems to have more clarity in her eyes and color in her cheeks, Sophie starts telling her what she is up to.

Veronica remains still while quiet thoughts roam through her head. *This assistant of mine is telling me exactly what she is doing as if she is teaching me the craft. She is quite good at this and has a wonderful career ahead of her. She lets her compassion show more than her mother does. I am so very lucky to have her and her mother in my life, both Sophie and Dinah. She has not abandoned me the way I abandoned my senior trainer, who is gone and now far away. I wish him well. I need to visit Lidia and see how she is doing. I wonder if I can walk. I should try to stand up.*

Veronica pats Ognir on the head and keeps her hand there as she sits up slowly and places her feet flat on the floor. She looks down at them to make sure they are straight. She tightens her upper legs and leverages her upward movement on Ognir's head. Now standing, she remains motionless until she feels more stable and releases her hand, which is Ognir's signal to be at her right side, a little closer than normal so that she can lean on him if needed.

Veronica straightens up, takes a breath, and looks at Sophie, who is poised and ready to jump to her rescue in case of imbalance. A few tentative steps are managed without difficulty, and within a few minutes, the two are talking business, matching patterns, and planning for the needed sewing steps ahead. The stormy thoughts and weakness seem to have passed into the distance and over the horizon; Veronica's strength and stamina return to the work at hand.

The next few days see the completion of ten tunics, three custom drapery sets with valances and cords, along with two bedding sets. Veronica thinks, *Sophie is not only good at her craft, but she is fast as well. Passover season will be arriving, and I believe we will be ready. I wonder how my temple girls are doing and expect that some of them may be married already. The outfit Sophie made for Ognir is hilarious. We had a good laugh together. I needed that. I am sure he is the only dog in the world with a custom-made outfit. I wonder if he would like to show it to the troops of the Ninth?... Hee Hee.*

BOTH ORGANIZATION AND COOPERATION ALLOW Jerusalem to thrive. The movement of food, clothing, and other necessities into and around the

city requires a massive effort. Animals are everywhere, with donkeys and camels as the primary means of transportation. Small carts are also used by people to cart bulky items or loads of many items. Keeping the streets clear of dung is a monumental task.

At the local level, and most particularly in Jerusalem, the street cleaners are at the bottom of the transportation-trade tier. They gather refuse and animal dung from every corner of the city. As the city population expands at Passover season, their work intensifies, with additional workers being added to cover additional shifts. Although this is seen as demeaning work by some, it is critically important to safeguard the health and safety of the populace.

The hierarchy of positions in the transportation industry is very clear. At the top are the families with expansive influence in providing cargo services for international trade, transporting goods on the well-known trade routes from Rome to Alexandria. They serve in a cooperative relationship with the powerful families who buy and sell merchandise.

The next layer down are the small cart owners, then the donkey owners, then the donkey owners who own carts. It is hard to know where the cargo camel owners fit in, but a camel can carry up to five hundred kilograms of cargo. They do not drop dung very often, but when they drop it, it must be gathered.

To make the system work, communication is key. Stepping out your door and yelling, "Donkey please!" or "One cargo camel needed here at noon!" would only attract stares from neighbors. Flags do not work, and since everyone uses fire to cook, smoke signals would get lost in the haze. That is where runners come in.

They are everywhere and do anyone's bidding. Found easily at any neighborhood market and in certain areas where businesses thrive, they are on almost any street corner. When engaged, they will take a verbal or written message and will also fetch any type of transportation, including arranging rides from place to place. Most people who use a runner on a regular basis know them and often prearrange to have their needs met, as Veronica and Sophie do to tote their completed textiles to Dinah's shop.

Veronica and Sophie arrive at Dinah's shop in the late morning, noticing the merchant traffic is beginning to rise in preparation for merchants to gather inventory for Passover sales.

"MOTHER, WE ARE HERE! I cannot wait to show you what we designed!" Sophie announces exuberantly. "Oops! I am so sorry to have disturbed your conversation." She looks over at Veronica, smirks, and covers her mouth.

Dinah does not look over but keeps her attention on what the younger man standing in front of her is saying. By his accent Veronica can tell he is from the Galilee region. Based on his clothing, he is a tradesman, probably in the fishing trade. His hands are not calloused, so he is not a stoneworker from Nazareth but probably from one of the many fishing communities established all around the Sea of Galilee.

It is amazing how we quickly we have become a major player in the international trade industry with smelly fish, Veronica thinks as she listens.

The fisherman concludes, "Yes, thank you. I will be back down in four weeks and can pick it up. Will that accommodate your needs?"

"Yes of course. I appreciate that you made a special trip from so far, and I will ensure that your request will be attended to with promptness as well as careful attention. Please extend my heartfelt greetings to Muriel for me, Tobin. Tell her I hope to come up after the Passover season so we can catch up."

"Yes," Tobin says, smiling in his big-grin sort of way. "Thank you once again, goodbye." He turns and walks out.

As Dinah turns to Sophie she realizes, *Tobin is twice the size as when I last saw him before when his parents were killed during one of the frequent uprisings. His face shows he has been out on the water far too many times. The Sea of Galilee is sometimes a fearsome place and has taken far too many down to its depths in sudden storms.* She looks over at Sophie, smiles, and says, "Well hello! How is the assistant to the Professional Designer and Project Manager Veronica?"

"Well, Mother, she is fine," Sophie says as she curtsies as a princess before the queen. "We have something amazing to show you!" She quickly looks over to Veronica, who is sitting down.

Veronica smiles and nods toward the bundle Sophie is referring to, "Don't talk about it, Sophie, show the business owner what you've designed." She thinks, *Sophie has bloomed into a very well-established designer and deserves credit for this project.* She then has a question come to mind, *Did Dinah say, "Professional Designer and Project Manager Veronica?" I have done nothing of any great import. It is my student who is progressing and has earned recognition, not me.*

Sophie pulls the bundle apart, lays it on the large design table exclaiming, "Behold what we have created! Over here you will see how the center of the valence hangs, showing off these primary designs while the curtains on either side have matching design points here, here, and here, while the best part is how the patterns all match at this point, this point and rise up to match right here and ... here," she says in a thoroughly professional presentation style.

Dinah looks again at each of the details shown by Sophie and is visibly touched by the craftsmanship. Looking up at Sophie with a warm smile of appreciation and love, she exclaims, "Well done, Sophie, very ... well ... done!" She takes a step over and gives Sophie a hug that lasts several seconds. "It's beautiful!" Turning to Veronica, she adds, "Veronica, I thank you. You do not know how much your kindness has meant to me. I appreciate your willingness to be such a great instructor and mentor. You are absolutely amazing!"

Veronica wants to jump up and hug Dinah but is too tired from the walk over, so she holds her arms out to embrace them both. Soon all three join in a warm hug. Veronica is feeling emotionally stable for the moment and wants to stay and enjoy the feelings which overcome her.

"So!" says Dinah. "We have additional orders coming in which include the special tunic for the gentleman you saw when you arrived. He was sent by Muriel from up north. Of course, every tunic you make is special, and I am sure she will be pleased. Two additional draperies without valences, three table runners, and, best of all, twenty-four horizontally hanging flags for the west gate!"

Sophie stands straight up, places her hands on her hips and asks with earnestness, "And you believe we have enough free time to do all that? We can do twice that and then some!" They all laugh and begin looking at the details. Dinah shows them the engineering drawings indicating where the flags are to be placed, while Veronica looks at the drapery sketches, happy that, with all the merchants coming to town, finding textiles will be easy. Choosing which ones to use will be the challenge.

VERONICA IS ONCE AGAIN OPTIMISTIC while she ponders, *Ognir seems to remember I told him last night that we would try to see if we could go for a short walk and perhaps see Lidia today.... It was probably the word "walk" that got his attention. Every time I say it, his ears go to attention, and he gets a dog-smile on his handsome face.*

I know that all our tunics are "special," but I think I remember hearing him say the word "special" as we were walking up. I will need to see what we can do for this kind, honest-looking fellow. He is handsome and it seems like he is about my age, although I look older. He would never be interested. I will be dead soon; I am sure about that. Why do I even try?

Ognir is once again so close to Veronica's side that she can lean on him as they walk the "nobody-knows-me" route hoping to see Lidia as she continues to think, *I need some comfort. Sophie has been working solo for two weeks and has the remaining open projects well in hand. I am ready to complete the hem on the special tunic. Perhaps Lidia will have an idea or two. I personally am thinking that adding a simple embroidery of a distinct color will make this tunic remarkable in a subtle, regal way.*

THIS BENCH IS MORE WELCOME than ever, Veronica says to herself as she sits down at the bottom of the hill to gain the strength needed to start the upward trek, one step at a time. *They say it is impossible for hills in Jerusalem to grow over time, but I have proof otherwise. It used to be 150 paces to*

reach the top. It now takes 240 paces to get to the benches waiting for me. Eventually the grade of this ascent will be so strenuous I will need a rope to make it. I will ask Lidia; I am sure she will have a clever response.

Veronica looks around as she sits waiting. *I wish I did not have to wear this cloak. It will not let me turn my head and see anything, I have to grab and turn it. I wish I had my riding cloak. Where did it go? I love seeing the birds start moving around. Late winter is full of miraculous transitions, mostly with the small, deep purple crocus that are showing their regal ...* She stares at the flowers on the side of the road and wonders, *Are those real? They are amazing ... that is the correct color I need for the hem....* She slowly leans over to look more closely.

After several moments a kind voice floats into the silence, "Yes, I agree, they are the perfect color for that special tunic you have been working on."

Veronica starts. "Oh!" she blurts as she adjusts her cloak to see.

"I heard every word you said. This color will be amazing."

"You heard me thinking?" Veronica asks in disbelief.

"Well, I am not sure. Possibly, but I feel what you are feeling. These flowers caught my attention the moment I came around the corner. I also knew it was you sitting there before you showed your lovely face, my young friend. I am glad you are able to find the time to visit with me today. You are sunshine in my life, even though it is overcast today. Shall we?"

Veronica stands up carefully, "Yes, of course. It is a pleasure to see you again, Lidia. How have you been?"

"Well enough. Thank you for coming along. You must be very busy. Passover is arriving quickly. There is excitement in the air, and everyone is busy these days. They need to remember to schedule themselves the time to stop and remember why we celebrate the day of Passover. Take time to think about God's dealings with Israel in the past and His promised blessings of the future." She looks at Veronica to her right, who is staying as close to the wall as she can with Ognir at her side.

"And you, my dear, are a blessing to so many around you. You need to remember that and step up with strength."

"My steps are getting shorter, and my body is getting weaker."

"That may be so; however, you still have your sight, and you are able to create items of beauty for the benefit of mankind, and womankind," Lidia giggles. "The men pay for it, but the women enjoy what you create for them. Creation for others' benefit. Think about that. You bring joy to people's hearts. You help them feel glad they are still around."

"Yes, I suppose, but I rarely meet the 'mankind' I serve. I wish I could at least feel who they are."

"Well, my dear, one of them is climbing this mountain right next to you!" Ognir turns his head in Lidia's direction as if to agree.

Smiling, Veronica chuckles, "Yes, Lidia I am so glad we have met. Can we stop a moment?"

"Yes, of course. You know, we met several times long ago ... yes, we did."

"We did? Where?"

"At the temple, when you were only twelve years old and were a brand-new temple girl."

"What? You knew me way back then? I do not remember meeting you; I am so very sorry. Oh, that would have been wonderful to do my chores and assignments with you!"

"Well yes, I am sure I would have learned from you."

"No, I would have learned from you!" Veronica protests as she begins walking again.

"Veronica, you were and still are an exceptional woman. I met your entire class of beginners. They were so bright-eyed, and you had very high expectations for yourself."

"I was trying to be who I should be while serving God in his sanctuary. I was honored to be allowed to even move one step inside those magnificent walls."

"Yes, I watched those walls as they were constructed, as well as the more recent cloisters on the east side. I also witnessed many wondrous happenings inside those 'magnificent walls.'"

"Zacharias! Is that where you saw him? Did you talk to him? What was he like? Was he tall or short? Did you know his wife, who had a baby when she was too old? If he could not talk, could he hear? Where did it happen?

Was there lightning and fire like in olden times? I am sorry; I talk too much, but when my brain starts asking questions, it goes crazy."

Having arrived at the summit, they both sit on the bench facing west, as they have arrived only moments before the three gentlemen. Lidia holds her finger to her lips so as to not start her reply before the gentlemen arrange themselves. It is customary to allow the men to settle in and have their say … it calms the air, so to speak.

"Well! I see the women have beat us to the best seats today!" Elias declares as he shuffles to the center of the open bench.

"The best seats, Elias? There is only one seat left, so do not take up all the room. And do not lie down like you did last week. Here, move over a bit," Jacob says as he sits, as always, to Elias's right side.

"What are you two arguing about this time? Next thing you know you will be sitting over there with them and trying to get a hug," Gabriel offers with a huge grin as he sits while looking at Lidia and Veronica.

"Why do you want us to sit over there? We are in the wrong place anyway; we cannot see anything except the building behind them. Where are we? Gabriel, did you get us lost again? Why can't I see anything?" Elias inquires.

"Be quiet; we are not lost, we're looking east instead of west. See, the morning sun is shining on our faces and coming from behind them." Jacob says, trying to get Elias to settle down. "Besides, you can smile back at her and because you are in the shadow, she won't think you are flirting with her."

"You two are both certainly hopeful young lads today. If you still know how to smile nicely at a woman, they cannot see anything even if the sun is shining. Your beards cover everything except your eyes and your ears, and neither of those can do their jobs very well these days, can they?" Gabriel says as he looks at his companions, who decide to be quiet for the moment.

Veronica thinks they are very entertaining, and she has her enchanting smile on, despite how she feels inside. Lidia takes advantage of the pause, "Yes, thank you gentlemen for your kind and courteous greetings. We extend to you our loyal gratitude as well," she remarks with a kind but slightly forced smile.

Elias's attention is roused, "What did she say? I did not get all that. Did she say there was a platitude in the well?" He looks at Lidia. "Lidia, sweetheart, please speak clearly so we can hear properly."

Jacob explains, "Elias, we are all fine, she was telling us that we ignored the women, marched in and interrupted them without even noticing or acknowledging their presence."

Elias is quiet but cannot hold back the opportunity, he giggles then says meekly, "Gifts? Lidia brought us gifts? What did we get Gabriel?"

Gabriel responds in an overly peaceful reproving tone, "Yes, Lidia did bring us delicious cakes, and I 'accidentally' ate yours...." changing his tone again he continues, "of course not, she meant 'presence,' not presents."

Elias nods and giggles again, "Yes, that is what I thought all along, I could not help myself.

Gabriel mutters under his breath, "Behave, or you will wet yourself ... again."

Veronica is always delighted to witness the three gentlemen banter. Though from time to time, it turns a bit coarse for her. "So," she says, moving the discussion to a more civil subject she feels will bring out the best in them, "Who among you have had the privilege of working in the temple?" She raises her hand as if she is their school instructor.

Their responses are instant. Jacob raises his hand and keeps it up, Gabriel raises his hand and keeps it up, while Elias raises both his hands and keeps them up, as shaky as they are. "Very nice. Thank you. Elias, why do you have both your hands up?"

"I have both my hands up because for forty-two years, I worked to support both the morning and evening prayer assemblies. It was the best time of my lonely life," Elias says while Jacob and Gabriel roll their eyes. As soon as temple discussion topic came up, they are sober and, in this case, have to admit that Elias's dedication was extraordinary.

"Forty-two years? That is a lot of service. I thank you all for your service," Veronica says, looking more alert than earlier in the morning. Ognir is watching the men, alert for tears while keeping his eyes in surveillance mode around their small gathering.

She asks, "Do any of you remember Zacharias, who was struck dumb? Was he a priest? What duties did he have?" Veronica knows his situation had been brought up in jest before but wanted to frame the subject with sacred responsibilities rather than creating babies and being dumb.

It works to her delight. They are talking about the solemn duties they all had given their lives to, during the temple reconstruction period which Herod the Great had spent time and money championing and which Herod Antipas continues to this very day.

"Yes, that is what I remember. It has been a time of great renewal and magnificent growth, regardless of being repressed by the Romans, and it happens when we focus on God and do not get distracted," Jacob says as he looks around.

"I agree but let us not forget that the Romans brought new engineering methods and were the source of many projects which would not have happened had they stayed away. Think about the sewer system and water system to name only two," Elias says.

Gabriel pipes in, diverting the discussion to experiences Lidia has had while working in the temple. "Ask Lidia there, we used to call her the 'Temple Matriarch' back in the day." He chuckles, "There was not a formal position called that, but since Lidia served with all her heart and loved being there to assist people from all over the world, she became widely known and accepted as a foremost authority of behind-the-scenes temple service operations, and they were operations, large operations. Go ahead, ask her." Jacob and Gabriel lean forward slightly. Elias leans forward and turns his right ear (the best ear) toward Lidia.

Lidia begins softly and a is a bit sarcastic, "The only reason I came to that situation is because I was not afraid to say, 'I do not know, but let's go find out together.' I learned because I was curious and never stopped asking questions." She bumps Veronica with her elbow.

"I was able to help people because if something needed to be done, and no one wanted to do it, I stepped up, did it, and gained knowledge in the process. It was pretty simple, and I am sitting next to someone who has a reputation for doing the same thing. She is still spoken about in temple operations. Though she had to retire about ten years ago, her former students remark, 'Now this is the best way to "complete this process with excellence, as our instructor Veronica says.'"

Veronica blushes, "They say that about me? I want to cry. I miss and adore them."

"As I told you earlier, when you lose yourself in the service of others, you are helping them recognize God in their lives, and thus, you are serving God." Lidia lets that settle for a moment.

Lidia then continues, "I remember what happened about six months after Zacharias's wife had her baby and he regained his speech, Simeon and Anna both took Joseph and Mary's tiny baby in their arms and declared he was the promised Messiah, the Holy One of Israel." She pauses and looks into the air as if remembering the day the little baby's parents brought him to the temple.

"I was walking behind the assigned priest that day, and although I was not very close, I remember seeing both of them making the incredible announcement, right there in the open. Right in front of everyone who was there at the time."

The three men are nodding their heads while Veronica wonders if they were there as well as she says, "How wonderful," as she scoots forward in the bench, looks at the ground, and remarks, "So first, the baby who was to prepare the way for the Savior was presented, then a few months later, the *Anointed One* was brought by Mary and Joseph ... and both happened in the temple. I had never heard that this was happening ... right now. So, where are they? John is preaching outside the city, right? Where is the other baby, er, adult? Is he preaching, or is he raising an army? Is he going to call fire down from the sky? Exactly how will this work itself out?" Veronica turns slowly to look first at Lidia, then at the three gentlemen.

"I have heard rumors that there is a rabbi who has been preaching in Nazareth, Capernaum, and sometimes in Jerusalem for some time now. We will need to get together again to chat," Lidia says as she stands, giving Veronica the distinct impression that such a discussion is a private one, as the rabbi's activities are of questionable report in the general population, including among the three gentlemen.

The three gentlemen are agreeable to say kind goodbyes. Before Lidia and Veronica are twenty paces away, the three brethren switch benches and are looking out over the western horizon, bantering as they do so well.

The Sample

AFTER A BRIEF TIME IN the city, the Young Merchant considers the numerous rumors in Jerusalem; more than usual. *The rabbi from Nazareth has a large number of followers. He spends most of his time up north in Galilee teaching what city dwellers believe to be naive to uneducated fishermen. Some around Jerusalem seem interested but refuse to take the time to go inquire for themselves, mostly because they are too busy making money.*

Early afternoon is not a suitable time to make sales calls. Most every vendor is asleep or having a noon meal with the family. The Young Merchant decides to see how the Camel Herder has been doing and is not surprised by what he finds; he has gathered an audience.

The Young Merchant walks carefully up and stands behind three elderly gentlemen who are sitting on a bench near the camel stables watching a young, Egyptian-looking man in his spotless white robe and distinctive headgear. He watches his Egyptian friend, the Camel Herder, entertain several young women who hang on his every word; the three older men observing.

The fancy turban the Camel Herder is wearing catches the Young Merchant's eye who says to himself, *Very colorful and only worn by the very rich. I hate it.* He stays to listen to the Camel Herder's tale and watches them all.

The Camel Herder stands still and in a quiet tone summarizes his story with, "... The next time the Sultan saw me, he embraced me as his son, thanked me for saving his daughter from the thieves, and invited me and my companions to the feast he was throwing in our honor."

The young women are paying close attention. A couple of the youngest are doing the winsome "hop-up-and-down, folding-hands-under-the-chin-because-I-am-happy" dance. Two others look at each other in delight, imagining they are going to the celebration as well.

The young Camel Herder has set the stage well. He is about to infer the proposal he makes at the end. "Well, we accepted with gratitude his kind invitation and we were very happy to be fed, very well, that evening."

The Camel Herder then brings the story to the present tense to gather the girls into his personal circle of friends, "I expect the Sultan will present his fair daughter to be my wife." He lets that thought hang.

Some of the girls seem happy about that point, while others seem to not like the idea at all. "So!" he exclaims as he looks into each of their faces one by one, "What ... do you suggest I wear to the celebration?"

All the girls offer their advice, and he agrees with each one of them. It quiets down a bit, and he asks them a personal question. "Now," he completes the question in a soft, personal voice, "what would *you* like to wear to attend this evening with me?" He looks once again at each member of his fan club.

The aged man on the bench cannot stand it any longer. He looks at the fellow to his right and says quietly, "This guy has a unique way of hunting his prey. Look at those biscuits and bread cakes the girls brought him. He will not have to cook for a month."

"Yes, he looks like Ichabod from the sand country. The sun is hot, and the shade is moving; we will have to move soon," another of the elderly gentlemen replies.

"No, not at all, he does not look at all like Shorty-Snorty. He is too tall." He stands up and comes around to the back side of the bench, looks at the Young Merchant, and says, "My toes were getting hot, do you mind?"

The Young Merchant shuffles over and replies, "No sir, I do not mind at all. I know this man. He is from an influential cargo family in Cairo. He has five older brothers. They do business all over the world, even up in Gaul."

"Ah, yes, he does well with the girls also. I never had women courting me with tasty food to eat."

One of the remaining men on the bench turns around to confirm, "He is perfectly correct; no women courted him at all. He spent five years gathering a dowry, and then the first three fathers refused. I told him to not start at the top of the ladder, but he never listens to reason."

"I didn't want to marry your sister, Elias."

"How did you get back there?" Elias says, then continues, "I thought you went home to take a nap. I am getting hot and need to find some shade." With that, he gets up, using his cane for leverage, and joins the others behind the bench.

"He is going to need some help to get those cakes down. He will make himself sick if he eats them all," observes the last patriarch on the bench.

The Young Merchant offers, "Yes, they usually are very good cakes. He has shared some with me on occasion. I call him the Camel Herder to tease him. He takes the cakes into the desert on his long caravan trips. He eats some; however, he passes most of the cakes out to the children when he entertains them. He is very noble, kind, and charitable."

"You know this guy? We need to leave but would be very grateful if you could see if he could part with perhaps three of his cakes," the man still on the bench suggests.

"Let us see what we can do. Excuse me please," the Young Merchant replies as he slides around the bench. The seated man gets up and takes the now vacant place.

The Young Merchant walks over to the Camel Herder, and whispers, "That turban you are wearing makes you look ridiculous. Do not ever wear it on the trade route; they will kill you." The Camel Herder grins ear to ear and asks, "What do you want?"

"Can you ask your girlfriends to offer a cake or two to these three gentlemen standing in the shade behind the bench?"

The Camel herder leans over and motions the girls to approach him. He whispers loud enough so they can hear and points to the three older men. They all turn, smile, snatch one of their various cakes, and run giggling with glee to present their treasures to the three now wide-awake gentlemen.

The girls each look their man in the eye, hand him their gift, lean over, and plant a kiss on his cheek, give a big smile, turn, and go back to the Camel Herder in the turban. The men are very lucky they are standing behind a bench with a back, so they have something to hang on to while being kissed by several young girls.

"Let's take our cakes and go up on the hill and watch the sunset," one of the men proposes as he moves from behind the bench.

"You are imagining things! It is not sunset yet. We need to stay here to make sure the girls are safe. They may need saving from the Sultan. When does the party start? Stop walking so fast. Are we going to meet Ichabod? Someone said he was here today," another of the gentlemen rambles while being escorted away.

The original speaker replies, "Elias, by the time we get to the benches on the hill, it will indeed be sunset because you walk so slow. Come along or we will not arrive until the morning. You dropped a cake, here, I will get it for you."

"Why are you reaching in my pocket? Are you taking my cakes because you already ate yours? My granddaughter visited me today and gave me a kiss. She brought her friends, and they kissed me too. I am glad she picks nice friends. I need to go back and tell them thank you," Elias rambles again.

"You already said thank you. Come along Elias," the third man says in a kind tone.

"Thank you? Why did you tell me thank you? I never did anything for you, except that time when you slipped on ice when it snowed late in the year, and you were showing off in front of the girls. You hit the stones hard. I thought you were dead. We almost missed our service at the temple because you almost died. Where are we going? Stop walking so fast," Elias protests as he expertly uses his cane to keep balance.

And so off they go to the next bench while the Young Merchant watches and thinks, *It is a real miracle they ever arrive at their intended destinations. Maybe they get help along the way. Who knows.*

ALWAYS THINKING TO ENHANCE HIS relationships of trust with his clients, the Young Merchant reviews, *My first shopkeeper visit this afternoon is on the West side. I am so very glad none of those men died on the spot when they were kissed by the girls. I know what happens to my heart when I even look at a pretty girl and cannot imagine having two or three girls approach me, hand me a cake, and then actually kiss me. I am so glad they did not die.*

It must be a common trait of humans around the world, especially with old men, to gather in groups of three, find a bench, sit down, and observe the world passing by. Is it one of the seasons of life? Do you watch life go by when you can no longer have children, raise them, see them get married, and then have grandchildren visit from time to time? Hard to tell.

I like to let my older clients tell stories. It makes them happy, and I appreciate them trusting me to receive their stories, which ofttimes recount tragedies, other times romantic ballads. I suppose they certainly deserve to have a good opinion of themselves. I wonder where the man with the cart is today; I have not run across him. I would like to see Ichabod. He is probably allergic to dust, and that would be a horrible thing as far away from the sea as we are. He would never survive in a caravan. Hmmm, my client looks to be busy but available. That is always a good thing. Joshua steps inside the shop.

"I have been hoping you would come by today. I have two questions and need to place a quick order. Do you have contacts like your grandfather did? Never mind, I see you do," The merchant says glancing down to the leather pouch on the Young Merchant's left side.

He continues as the Young Merchant spreads his order on the table. "What have you brought this time? You have been to Byzantium? Good. Come here. Let you and I do some business together. I have a deep respect for your grandfather. You do not know half the good things he has done for the community around here. Let us look closely at what you have brought me from far away."

As the elderly merchant inspects the merchandise delivery to ensure it meets his expectations, the Young Merchant is thinking, *He talked about my grandfather for two reasons: first, he was a fair trader and very honorable and second, based on grandfather's sales notes, I know that this shopkeeper has always been involved in local charity work. His most recent (the last seventeen years) interest has been helping a boarding school that serves abandoned children, of which there are many these days. I have an excellent surprise for them.*

The transaction goes well, additional items are ordered, stories of the past are related, and the Young Merchant offers a blessing to the merchant, his family and all his current and future clients.

PASSING THROUGH A SQUARE ON the eastern side of Jerusalem, the Young Merchant's eye catches something familiar, *Well, there he is again. I suppose he works in all parts of the city, each with a different persona. He has no cart, but he brought his blanket. He needs to find a shadow. I need to find one as well so when I stop to look at him, he does not see me.*

My neck would hurt if I moved it around like he does. He has a code name, I am sure. I wonder if he has a real name. The one his mother used to call him by when he got into mischief.

The voice of the Roman spy, the Young Merchant's "new friend," arrives again without a sound and answers the question, "His name is Mordechai. He will next arrange his viewing and listening post with his blanket."

"You need to learn to warn your 'friends' when you pop into existence right behind them," the Young Merchant says as he is thinking, *He has the blanket down and is sitting on it, but his sandals stand out like bright colored tassels on a camel.*

"He will next take off his left sandal, then his right, nest them together, and place the pair behind him."

As Mordechai does that, the Roman spy adds, "He will now look around again and take some dust from between the street pavers, sprinkle it on his feet, and rub some on his face."

"You waste a lot of time watching this fellow, don't you?"

"Your observation lesson is not complete. He now lies his head on his right shoulder as if it is broken so he can watch who will be coming through the south entrance. He will personally know each one of them and will take note of whom they are walking with and whom they are speaking with. Every exchange of money is also noted," the Roman spy instructs, followed by an interesting summary. "All quite amazing when you think of it. This guy is a genius."

THE YOUNG MERCHANT LATER VISITS a shop and completes his delivery with the shopkeeper's wife. As he returns to the front of the shop, he sees a woman asking for a special embroidery thread of a certain color. The shopkeeper reprimands the woman and sends her out. When she turns to leave, she must pass the Young Merchant. She looks up at him briefly, looks out the door, and quickly leaves.

This is the Master Camel Trainer! the Young Merchant realizes as he is again smitten by her voice and again by her eyes. He quickly concludes his business and chases after her.

As he is running, he reaches in his pouch. *I need it right now. There it is. Good. I hope this will work,* he thinks as he snatches and pulls the embroidery thread he had been keeping. *I never knew why I kept this until this very moment,* he thinks to himself, *There she is, now slow down and act like a gentleman. Do not trip or bump into her.*

"Excuse me. Miss, please stop. I have what you are looking for. It is a gift to you." He comes to a stop at the same instant she stops, turns around, and looks back at him.

She has a worried look in her eyes and her face is drawn. He holds up the small skein of embroidery thread so she can see it clearly in the sunlight.

"They call it Tyrian Purple. I am not sure if it will be enough for what you need, but I hope it will be sufficient, and maybe it is the right color," he says, trying to catch his breath.

She looks at it. It draws her full attention. Her eyes begin to tear up as her hand slowly reaches out to touch it gently. "Yes," she says as she looks into his eyes. The Young Merchant looks back and becomes speechless for the first time in his life. Time stops for both of them.

Veronica jerks her hand back quickly and says, "I am sorry. I cannot purchase this. It is from Tyre and must cost a fortune. This is meant for the palace, not for me."

She looks back at the deep purple fibers glistening in the afternoon sun. "It is so very beautiful sir. It is made with priceless craftsmanship. Even if it is a gift, I cannot pay in any way for this. I cannot owe you or any other merchant what I do not have to give." She looks into his eyes again and then down to the ground, anticipating retreat once more.

I have to keep her from running away, he thinks, scrambling for a plan, and says softly, "I understand. I have one question for you if you do not mind." She looks back at him again with a "Yes, what is your question?" look on her face.

He begins, "The only people who know exactly what they are looking for and will only settle for that specific item are professional artists as you must be.... What project is this thread intended to be used for?" He holds the purple gift up with it sitting across both his palms. He looks down at the proposed gift and then looks into (and is lost in) her tearful eyes. He waits for a response.

"This," she looks into his outstretched hands, "is 'intended' ... to be used in the final hem design of a special tunic I have been preparing. It will be the last component of the project." She reaches out to caress the gift once more without looking up.

His hands move up to place it in her grasp. As soon as she gently and tentatively picks it up ever so slightly, he pushes his palms further up so she will grasp it, then pulls them away quickly, leaving the gift in her slender hands as he says, "Good, that is perfect. I present you this gift free of cost if you promise to fulfill the agreement to use it only on the special tunic you have been working so diligently on."

She is astonished as her regard moves from the gift to him to the gift once more then back to the Young Merchant. "Thank you, sir. You do not know how very much this means to me. This gift will be prized, and I cannot thank you enough. I must be going as I have work to do." She looks in the direction she intends to travel as Ognir observes her every movement.

"You are so very welcome. Please give me the honor to be your escort back home. I will be dismissed when you are safely within reach of your destination." He takes a step in the direction she is looking to see if his proposal is not too forward.

Veronica says, "Yes, this will be appreciated, come along."

As the Young Merchant sees her turn quickly and begin walking with purpose, he notices that she seems a bit frail, as if she were not feeling very well.

He is fully cognizant of her guard dog, which looks as though he could rip someone's leg off in one bite. He makes absolutely sure he does not get too close and makes only slow, nonthreatening moves.

As they settle into a comfortable pace, the Young Merchant makes sure he walks so the dog is between him and her as they progress. It is clear that the dog is walking her home and that he is lucky the dog is allowing him to tag along.

"I saw you at Dinah's earlier today. Were you delivering merchandise?" Veronica asks in an upbeat tone.

"Yes, she had ordered Roman textiles for some draperies, and while—"

Veronica interrupts, "You bought drapery fabric? I have to see it! Is it the blue and silver pattern with some diamonds of brocade?"

"Yes, it is, and it survived the long trip with no damage at all. I am glad there were no sandstorms along the way ... thieves attacked us twice but other than that ..."

"Oh no! That would have been horrible!" she exclaims, once again interrupting.

"Yes, the thieves were—" he is again interrupted.

She explains as a professional teaching a course, "You know what sandstorms can do. Sand takes the sheen out of everything. The cords! Did you bring the cords? They did not get stolen, did they? The shiny cords with finials at the end, from Rome? Are they OK? If they are ruined from the sandstorm, we will have to redesign the lay of the cornice and use, maybe silver buckles … with broad diamonds to match the brocade on the fabric, not too broad or it will distract from the way the light from the west window will reflect as guests are entering the room. Guests, you know, from all over the world will be arriving. I cannot tell you who, but I am assured they are all very important, and the palace must look amazing, which, of course it will, because you brought the perfect fabric … and you must be aware …" She continues all the way home, releases the Young Merchant, and goes about her business.

The Young Merchant, on the other hand, is dazed as he tries to sort out what is going on in his mind…. *I cannot believe what happened to me. That woman is amazing, wondrous, and smart and her eyes … her eyes absorb me … her stride is confident, as well as her knowledge…. Oh no, I cannot tell the Camel Herder one word about this. Maybe I will never see her again. I have to see her again. This is totally unexpected.*

I wonder if she is afraid of camels … no, she is the Master Camel Trainer. Was the Roman officer telling me the truth? She probably is afraid, like most city women. I will need to introduce her to Bindi. That will be the thing to do. The Young Merchant has been struck and his mind rattles all the way to the square he travels to in the city.

How did I get here so fast? the Young Merchant wonders as he approaches the busy square and looks around … thinking, *There is Mordechai, but he does not have his cart again. Why is he walking to a shadow and setting a yellow blanket down on the ground in this square? He is taking his high-priced sandals off and hiding them behind his back as he did before.* The Young Merchant observes how the bright blue corners of the blanket get folded under so as to not be visible.

The now-seated man settles down a moment and retrieves some dust as before. As he starts his routine, his eyes notice and fixate on the Young Merchant, which produces a jolt of adrenaline through the Young Merchant's veins.

The Young Merchant asks himself as he stares right back, *Exactly who is this person named Mordechai? He is clearly up to no good.*

A group of people obstruct the stare down momentarily, and when they have passed, Mordechai is no longer there.

THE TAX COLLECTOR

"HE DOES THAT," THE FAMILIAR voice states in a matter-of-fact way.

"What?" the Young Merchant asks, again irritated by being snuck up on and surprised at every turn.

"He is very good at that ... escaping in an instant when he feels threatened. You should stop threatening him the way you do."

"It is surely his problem, not mine that he feels so insecure when someone knows what he is up to."

"You are observant, but you have no idea what he is up to. You will see in a few minutes if you stick around."

"Should I?"

"What?"

"Stick around."

"You can do what you want, but when he returns, it will not be pleasant. Entertaining, perhaps, but not pleasant."

"Entertaining?"

"Yes, when you tell your troops about it several years from now as an officer and commander in the Roman Army."

"Ha! Or when I tell my children when they are teenagers who love to sit around and listen to all my grand adventures and stories I suppose as well. Right?"

"I have something I would like to show you and your friends. I would like to invite you all to come up to the Training Grounds for an afternoon. I think you will like it, and I know that Veronica will love it."

"Veronica?"

"Yes, the camel master you are interested in. That is her name if you have not been able to weasel it out of anyone yet," the Roman spy says with a sly grin.

"Well, you are a source of valuable and interesting information. Thank you. Yes, when would you like our little adventure to take place?"

"Tomorrow afternoon. Veronica knows exactly where it is. Ognir also knows. Bring Bindi, Revolk, and Miskah."

The Young Merchant turns around to ask how he knows the camels' names, but the Roman spy has vanished. Turning back to look across the square, his eyes rivet on Mordechai's outstretched arm pointing right at him while he is saying something to a seemingly well-dressed person of some report.

The colorfully robed man struts straight to the Young Merchant with an air of superiority. He stops too close and says in a condescending voice, "You are in this city selling undocumented merchandise to unauthorized shopkeepers, and neither your camel tender nor you have the correct papers to perform such transactions. You will pay me forthwith a fine as well as taxes on each of your sales. So, we will settle this matter before I call the authorities. Show me your papers, or there will be further fines." He then adds, "By the way, I am the authority in these matters."

The Young Merchant is not pleased to have to deal with this tax collector, yet he was not surprised and replies, "I understand kind sir, that you have important business to attend to and can assure you of my full and complete cooperation. So that I may pay proper respect, please help me understand … exactly which government office do you represent in your important duties and to which regulatory committee will we pass a report of our transaction to this fine day, if I may ask, in order to fulfill all regulatory requirements of course?"

"You have no papers, and you have no respect speaking to me in such a way," the tax collector says, glancing back at Mordechai with a worried look on his bearded face. "I tell you that you must pay me now so that we may be on our separate ways. You know you have no right to be here as a salesperson."

"Yes, I have full right as granted by the Commerce Committee. You, sir, have not answered my question, which I also have a right, and a duty, to ask." The Young Merchant stops as he looks directly into the tax collector's nervous eyes.

Seeing that he has the upper hand, the Young Merchant adds, "To whom do I make my fraudulent taxes report? Who is your superior, or should I report in person to the full committee next they meet? When do they meet? Is it once a week as we are approaching Passover and there are so many commerce affairs happening? Please tell me, so that I may be in accordance with the law, kind sir."

The tax collector begins to shake with rage. "I have never seen such insubordination coming from a common merchant bent on skirting the law. I tell you that you have not seen the least of the power I yield in Jerusalem!"

The Young Merchant sees Daniel traversing the square, and Daniel sees Mordechai looking attentively at the confrontation happening. Daniel changes his plans and comes directly behind the Tax Collector and listens in for a moment. He then says in a calm, authoritative voice, "Yes, I agree with you fully, Jeremiah. I will take charge of this merchant, and you will be on your way … now!" Daniel slips something into Jeremiah's hand as he shifts to face him.

Jeremiah looks from Daniel to the Young Merchant and back. He seems to decide that he has lost the game and abruptly leaves. Daniel moves so he can see both the retreating tax collector and Mordechai, who both then retreat out of the square, clearly not pleased with their failed extortion attempt. Daniel faces the Young Merchant and offers, "I am surprised they have not tried that ploy sooner. You must look formidable."

"Yes, well, I was holding my own. It was not as bad as it could have been. Thank you for interceding. How much did you pay them as a dispatch fee?"

"Oh, not a lot. It was more of a message that we have caught them extorting one of our esteemed and most beloved merchants."

"Oh good, so that chapter is closed, right?" the Young Merchant asks in jest, knowing full well that such activity will never fully stop. It will only change form.

"They will be more discreet next time." Daniel replies with a grin.

"Ognir! I am so happy to see you!" the Young Merchant says as he approaches Veronica's door, still about twenty feet away. Ognir is already standing in front of the door at attention. His tail wags slowly, giving permission to approach the perimeter safely.

The Young Merchant turns his head to look back and passes the message along to the Camel Herder, "It's OK, bring the camels."

Bindi's head comes around the corner before anyone else. She knows what is in store, as she and Veronica have a relationship from previous visits.

The Young Merchant waits for the entourage to settle down before he knocks at the door, which opens before he has finished his customary knock. "Well hello all my friends! You look so very splendid today!" Veronica says with enthusiasm. She walks out a few steps, closes the door, reaches out, and caresses Bindi behind the ears adding, "Are we going on an adventure today?"

"Why yes, we are. Are you ready Veronica?" the Young Merchant says.

"I have been ready for a while, so let us go! Which camel should I ride?" Veronica asks, sweeping her hand through the air pointing to the three choices.

"I believe my friend the Camel Herder has the right camel for you, and his name is Miskah. A very loyal camel to be sure. Is this correct?" the Young Merchant says as he looks over at the Camel Herder.

The Camel Herder smiles and adds, "Not only is he loyal, but he is also comfortable and offers a smooth ride. He does not spit, if you are going to ask."

"That sounds like an excellent choice, and I thank you, 'the Camel Herder,' very kindly for your attention to my traveling needs. We shall do marvelously, don't you think, Miskah?" Veronica says as she walks over and scratches Miskah's head and looks him in the eyes. "You certainly have lovely eyelashes on today. Let us get going," Veronica adds as she easily climbs up and takes her seat.

The Young Merchant watches Veronica climb up on Miskah, turns to Bindi, and attempts to get on, but she moves her head into his path. He stands straight up, looks at her and says, "What? Did I forget something? I will check your rigging." He walks to her other side while explaining, "She is very sensitive to how her harnesses fit, and that's a good thing."

Tugging and adjusting all the way around, he arrives on the mounting side again and reports to Bindi, "OK, we should be fine. Thank you for asking me to double-check." The Young Merchant steps up to mount and is almost knocked down by Bindi's head. She opens her mouth, grabs his pant leg with her front teeth, and pulls him around so he is now in front of Bindi.

The Young Merchant has never seen such a reaction from Bindi. He raises his arms and shrugs his shoulders while looking at the Camel Herder and Veronica, who are looking quite amused.

"I believe my friend, that Bindi does not want to take you aboard this fine day. What have you done to deserve such treatment?" the Camel Herder asks in a convincing tone, with a huge smile on his face. "Perhaps you should consider asking Veronica if she would like to ride Bindi. Veronica?"

"Why, yes, we could see if that helps Bindi's temperament. Look, she is looking at me. Perhaps I can help," Veronica says as she dismounts, walks over to Bindi, and says, "Hello Bindi. Would you allow me to ride with you today?"

Bindi turns her head back straight ahead again, and in an instant, Veronica is in place and says, "Huph Huph," at which Bindi immediately stands and is looking very pleased with herself.

The Young Merchant is the only one left standing on the ground. His face is flush with embarrassment as he walks over to Miskah, who is looking disinterested while chewing as usual.

"So Miskah, it looks like we will be traveling partners today. Are you OK with that?" he says as he starts to mount and then adds, "I hope so." Miskah is amenable and acts as if he is unaware of what has transpired.

Bindi, Ognir, Miskah, and Revolk make their way to their destination north of Jerusalem while the Camel Herder giggles as he describes many times how happy he is that his "Future Bride's Camel" finally has a bride.

AS THE GROUP GETS CLOSER to the training area, Ognir's senses are on higher alert, and his step becomes more formal, with ears raised up and nose searching and interpreting the air.

There are soldiers at the gate, which they open to welcome the visitors. "Welcome! We are glad to greet you all today!" After the cadre of guests pass through, one of the guards says to the other, "Ognir is here. That means she is here. She must be in front. That would be right. They better have her camel ready. She always has lofty expectations."

Walking out into the pathway, the Roman spy, dressed more formally than usual, raises his right arm in a welcoming gesture and says, "I see you have the Master Camel Trainer in front with her guard dog, Ognir! Welcome to you all! Please, dismount and take some refreshments."

"Thank you, kind sir," Veronica says as she dismounts. She reaches down to her right, touches Ognir's head, and says "Done." Ognir races ahead, makes a turn to the right, and is gone.

"Thank you for your kind invitation," the Young Merchant says as he walks up to the Roman Spy with a smile.

"Yes, thank you," the Camel Herder adds.

"We have a good meal and plenty of water for your camels," the Roman Spy announces as he looks over to his left and motions to where three camel tenders are waiting. They come over and look at the Camel Herder for permission to take Bindi, Revolk, and Miskah, to which he acknowledges approval.

"With your permission Master Camel Trainer, we have prepared your camel should you wish to take him out for a leisurely ride," the Roman spy offers to Veronica with an inviting smile.

"Why this is a pleasant surprise. Yes, of course, I would love to see how Master Squishy-Lips has been doing," Veronica responds looking over to where her camel is standing a few yards away with his saddle already mounted and a soldier holding his reins. "You gentlemen tend to your little show. When you are ready, I will show you how it is done with style and grace." She glances at the Young Merchant and adds, "and speed." With a smile, Veronica walks in the direction of where her camel is now waiting and looking straight back at her.

"Mister Squishy Lips, you are looking very good these days, I am so sorry I have not been here to see you as much as I would like. You are a bit thinner, but your eyelashes are looking great. I hope I do not get too tired to ride. There you are my companion and friend," Veronica says kindly as she approaches and begins scratching behind his ears. The master camel looks as pleased as a camel can get. "Now, let us see how we do together. Please be gentle; I have become a bit weak since we were last together. Ok?" Veronica offers as she mounts, this time using the soldier's assistance. "Huph Huph."

As the Roman officer's stallion comes into view, the Young Merchant almost loses his breath. It is marvelous and stunning. Each step makes a definitive sound in the freshly raked sand of the training ground. Each step announces intention, authority, and strength. The Roman spy/army recruiter watches the black horse be led forward and takes the reins, places them over the neck, steps into the stirrup, and swings up, saying, "Let's see what an officer's mount can do." He looks at the Young Merchant and adds, "Pay attention. You will someday be doing this on the horse which will be issued to you."

As the horse moves to the center of the training area, the Young Merchant watches for a moment, then looks over to where Veronica is riding and thinks, *She looks so regal, sitting straight up and so much in charge. She is amazing. I hope her strength lasts through the day.*

The Camel Herder nudges him with his right elbow as if to say, "Pay attention." The Young Merchant focuses on the intricate paces the horse is performing and tries to imagine himself doing the same while he thinks, *Yes, I believe I would look stunning up there. Maybe I should reconsider. Look at that gait. Look at the muscles on that horse.*

"Well, you perhaps would indeed look 'stunning' on that skinny horse, but for me, you look better suited to be riding through the desert on your new riding partner, Revolk. All you need is a bride's veil, with some new sandals perhaps," the Camel Herder observes wryly, not taking his eyes off the equestrian demonstration.

"You will probably get mysteriously lost in the desert between here and Alexandria if you keep talking like that. Look, he is coming in," the Young Merchant warns, and he steps forward to meet the Roman spy and offers, "Excellent show of valor and prowess my friend! You have great skill. We thank you for your impressive demonstration."

"Well, if you don't keep getting distracted my young friend," he looks in Veronica's direction, "you will become a fine officer in the Roman Army.

You will have prestige and honor, and everyone will respect," he looks back in Veronica's direction, "and admire you. Now," he then says, "it's your turn … up you go!" as he hands the Young Merchant the reins.

Surprising would be an understatement. The Young Merchant is not expecting this but takes the reins and easily mounts the shiny, black horse. He looks to the center of the training grounds, takes the horse there, and spends the next several minutes riding the magnificent animal, thinking, *Now this is something incredible to ride! The saddle is tight against the horse's back, and I can feel its muscles move. More of an experience to be remembered than sitting up on a slowly plodding camel. I suppose I should not spend too much time out here. I better get back.*

The Roman officer is ready with an encouraging reaction to his potential conscript, "Well done! I can see it is not the first time you have been on a well-trained horse. You will spend many hours learning from the finest Roman trainers as soon as you decide." His eyes meet with the Young Merchant's, hold them for a moment, and with no instant reply, he turns his attention to the Camel Herder and announces, "It is now your turn my friend … you have some horse experience, do you not? Do not worry, my horse can sense when riders are inexperienced and will take loving care of you … would you like to experience a fine ride?"

"I do not like to ride horses; they mostly have attitude problems, along with their riders and owners," the Camel Herder responds. He then adds, "But for you my commander, I will see what this sweaty animal can do." He grins, takes the reins and with feigned apprehension says, "Horses are not polite like camels and will not kneel down. Please help me up." The host obliges.

Veronica is keeping track of what is going on with the recruiting efforts and is fascinated to see the Young Merchant do so well with the officer's well-trained horse. She is now watching The Camel Herder and thinks, *He took the reins as someone who has extensive experience with horses, and then, he actually asked for help up? What theater is he staging over there? I can tell he is trying to make it seem as if he has never been on a horse, but I can see his legs are telling the horse what to do. This is going to be very entertaining to watch.* She leads Mister Squishy Lips over to where the Young Merchant and the Roman officer are standing.

Veronica and Mister Squishy Lips are standing directly behind the other observers as she thinks again, *This Camel Herder is expertly guiding the horse with his legs to go one direction while leaning in the opposite direction. He is hilarious.*

The demonstration horse comes to an abrupt stop which catches everyone's attention. The horse backs up a bit, bends its rear legs and as the rider leans forward, he ever-so-slightly nudges the horse with his heels, and it explodes into a full racing canter, the rider in full control.

"Woah!" the Young Merchant exclaims.

"His family has instructed this man well. Let us observe and learn from him. He is one with the horse after the show of inexperience he tried to give. Watch carefully. He is a master. Maybe we have two future Roman Army officers," the Roman Spy says as he watches carefully.

Veronica is delighted. *This man has some stories to tell. He pretends to be a lowly camel herder, but he must be so much more.* The camel under her twitches as if he wants to get out with the horse and race around.

"I bring back your esteemed horse and apologize if I have taught him a couple of new moves. You know, he learns quickly. Thank you for allowing me the pleasure of spending a bit of time with him. It was an honor," the Camel Herder announces as he rides up, dismounts, and hands over the reins.

"The pleasure was truly mine, sir! You have taught us all many things equestrian, and we thank you," the Roman spy says with enthusiasm as he looks at the Camel Herder then at the Young Merchant. He notices Veronica's arrival, and as he looks at her, he offers, "Would you like to ride as well, or show us something with your steed? What is your desire, Master Camel Trainer?"

"I cannot do better than what our friend the Camel Herder has been so kind as to have shown us, but I believe it would be interesting to have a little race. Is your fine horse up with racing my steed, or is he in need of a nap? Hummm?" Veronica asks, cocking her head to the right with the question.

The Roman grins ear to ear and looks around the Training Ground's perimeter then back to Veronica, offering an enthusiastic response. "If you request, so shall it be done, Master Camel Trainer. What course do you prefer?"

"I know your horse is a bit tired, so I suggest that we start on the far north side and end at the middle stations. Will your horse be OK with that?"

"My horse will fall asleep from boredom if he is asked to only warm up at that distance. He would like me to request of your excellent camel to start at the south end, race to the north end, and then return to the point of departure ... if you are willing and if your fine camel is able."

"Mister Squishy Lips, what do you think about this audacious challenge? Are you up to it?" Veronica asks her camel, who snorts in response as he begins to walk to the starting point. Veronica looks at the Roman horse and says "Well, it looks like *he is in*. You'd better hurry up or you will be left in the dust." The Roman Officer mounts and is at Veronica's side instantly.

Oh no, what has she gotten herself into? I hope she has the strength to hang on. I know how fast camels can run when motivated, the Young Merchant thinks as he and the Camel Herder walk quickly after the competitors.

The Roman officer considers his options, *I cannot win the race by too much or I would bring dishonor to the Master Camel Trainer. Probably should not be too kind, because I have seen her in action before and her reputation is that she takes no prisoners in competition.*

Veronica silently speaks with plans of her own, *OK Mister Camel, I am going to launch you into this race and let you do what you want to do. Please do not make the shiny, black horse look too bad. I will hang on tight but will not rein you in. Are we together on this?* Squishy responds with a happy snort. He then looks over to the horse and then to the tall wooden pole at the north end of the Training Grounds.

There is tension in the air as both animals and riders are readied at the starting point. The animals snort as if to communicate superiority. It becomes quiet, then "GO!"

Dirt is kicked up and spatters into the Camel Herder and the Young Merchant as the race begins. "We should have stood somewhere else. Look at them go!" the Young Merchant exclaims. He then yells, "That camel has not lost an inch. Watch him run!"

It is hard to see from their vantage point, so they are not sure who is in the lead, but a few moments later, they are thrilled to see the camel make the turn around the pole first. In fact, the camel had made it around the pole with enough space to pass by the horse going the other way. The camel looks at the horse and seems to slow down to let him catch up.

"Did you see that?" the Young Merchant says as he grabs the Camel Herder's arm.

Veronica is also surprised, more by Squishy slowing down than by his speed. *What are you doing my friend?* she thinks as he slows down and turns to look at the horse and his determined rider. *They are catching up to us! What is your plan?* She thinks as if she is witnessing the race almost as a bystander…. *Trust, trust, trust,* she tells herself as she sees the horse pull aside. She looks at the Roman Officer, who seems a bit frantic yet relieved that he had "captured" his prey.

OK, let us show them what we are really made of, my friend, Veronica thinks as she gives a squeeze of confidence with her knees. In response, she feels the camel start the race anew, as if he had been relaxing, toying with "this frail horse who is trotting next to me."

Master Squishy bolts ahead and gains one full length, then two, then three entire camel lengths, with a fourth added before he victoriously gains the end of the course. He comes to a stop next to the Young Merchant, who is expectantly watching to see how Veronica is faring.

"Oh no, she is going to fall off!" the Young Merchant realizes as Veronica catches his eye with a pleading "please catch me!" look in her eyes. As she slides off into his arms, her attention turns to the second-place competitor.

She welcomes her competitors to the finish with grace and style. Placing her feet squarely on the ground and standing as straight as possible while holding the Young Merchant's right arm tightly with her left, she is ready as the vanquished Roman officer dismounts and turns toward her.

Veronica is kind and regal as she exclaims cheerfully, "I am happy to have been invited to race with you and your gallant steed. I feel we have sealed a strong friendship and want to thank you for inviting us to be your companions this fine day, sir."

Tax Collector's Revenge

I AM SO GLAD THAT VERONICA *did not fall off her camel yesterday ... she could have been killed. She was, once again, in control, and after making the Roman officer eat dust—a lot of dust—she was as kind as I have ever seen any winning competitor ... amazing. I need to visit her before we leave for Egypt. Maybe I should stay and not leave at all. Perhaps I should become a Roman soldier and remember to never race her in public,* the Young Merchant ponders as he makes his way to the storekeeper he had read about the night before after taking Veronica home and having made dinner for her.

He arrives at the shop where Michael has more than a few words to say, "Well yes, you are here! I heard you were making your rounds, my friend. Exactly why did you visit me last, before you pack to leave for the land southward ... and why were you out galivanting around with a Roman Army officer? You know the only reason they want to talk to you is greed. They want to enthrall you with stories of glory and amaze you with promises of horses. They have shown you a magical horse, haven't they? Well, if they have yet to play that trick on you, they will.

"What about women? Or did they throw prestige and honor and whatever else they are selling today? Do not listen to them; they have been nothing but trouble since they arrived with their chariots many years ago. Have you seen what those steel-wheeled chariots have done to our painstakingly constructed roads? The road to Joppa? The road to Bethlehem? They are a mess, with ruts in them; Jonas had his donkey actually break his leg trying to traverse one … absolutely disgusting it is, I have to tell you, absolutely.

"So, what did you bring me, after making me wait so long? Is my order delivered in full? Or did you get robbed, like your grandfather was only thirty-eight years ago, when you were not even dreamed about yet. Let us get moving; I have no time to waste chatting with you all day. Did you hear? You probably did, but I will give it to you straight, Jonathan's mother has been buying frankincense and lots of other oils from a different merchant."

"Yes, from Jehoshaphat, I buy them from him as well," the Young Merchant returns politely.

"Well, yes, Jehoshaphat, that is his name. Why did you bring him up? Let us get our business done. I have no time to spare chatting with you all day—what do we have here?" The shopkeeper, Michael, points to the bundles the Young Merchant had carried in.

"These, my kind Michael, are exactly what you ordered, and I have a little something for your very kind wife. She has not kicked you out of the house yet, has she?" the Young Merchant says as he pulls the bundles apart and lays them out for inspection.

"Yes, this is correct, and this one," Michael says as he lifts the fabric up to look at through the light coming into the shop, "is double woven with what they call the Persian Weave. I have no idea how they do this, but it is very popular, and it lasts a very long time."

Each piece in each bundle is similarly inspected in detail, with a full commentary that Michael is well known for. The Young Merchant is as patient as Job was with his friends many years ago. Michael has yet to answer the Young Merchant's question about his wife, so when an opportune moment of silence arrives, he asks again.

"So, I perhaps did not hear your response; How is your wife? She is well I hope?" the Young Merchant tries asking in a separate way.

Michael responds directly and very loudly, "My sweet wife? She is very well and treats me with too much love and attention! I love her and try always to keep her happy!" He then leans over and very quietly advises,

"She is most certainly listening to every word we say. Be careful…. I love her from here to eternity."

The Young Merchant smiles, nods his head, and sees Ruth walk in the room and hold her finger in front of her lips as she silently approaches.

The Young Merchant agrees with, "Ah yes! Love like that is hard to find anywhere!" He waves his arm through the air for the word "anywhere" and catches her eye as he kicks Michael under the table to place him on alert.

Michael responds by leaning toward his visitor and says, "I hope, my young friend, that you find a woman as wonderful as I have found and that you marry her and not marry her sister as I did so many years ago."

"I don't have a sister!" Ruth exclaims.

"What?" Michael exclaims back, "You are here? How did you sneak in here when I am doing business with this fine merchant from afar?"

"It is so good to see you, my young friend! How is your overly generous grandfather? He is well, I suppose?" Ruth says as she walks over and gives the Young Merchant a motherly hug.

"Yes, thank you! He is fine, and he sends his warm regards, along with this vase from Ethiopia. He hopes you will like it and have the perfect place to put it on display, if Michael has not placed merchandise in the way."

"The merchandise stays out here, and yes, I do have the right place for this, where both the morning and evening light will shine on it and radiate love throughout our humble home. You are so very kind. Please tell me what adventures you have been up to these days. Are you married yet?"

"WHAT ARE YOU TWO UP TO? You look like you have been in some mischief," the Young Merchant says as he arrives back at the camel stables, only to see the Camel Herder and the stable supervisor in an animated conversation that must have been very funny.

"You tell him!" the Camel Herder says to the stable supervisor.

"No, you tell him. They are your camels, except for Bindi, who was really the key player in all that happened," returns the stable supervisor.

The Young Merchant begins asking questions before the owner of the tale has been decided. "What? What happened to Bindi?"

The Camel Herder smiles at the Young Merchant and replies, "If I remember correctly, Bindi is not so keen on letting you ride her. You look better on Miskah," looking over at the stable supervisor for confirmation.

"I am not getting involved in that." He looks at the Young Merchant and says, "I came back to the stables late this morning and saw that someone had tried to steal your camels and the remaining merchandise."

"What?" the Young Merchant replies, looking around to see what had been done.

"Yes, they must have had a look out and as soon as I left this morning to go in town, they snuck in here and tried to snatch Bindi, Revolk, and Miskah, along with several bundles."

"So, the camels are over there chewing as if nothing happened."

"Well yes, as far as we can tell, they came in and started their dirty business, but the camels did not want any part of it. The camels took care of everything in a very efficient and appropriate way we'd say." The stable supervisor looks at the Camel Herder for confirmation, who nods yes and says, "Go ahead, tell him what you found when you got back!"

"I do not know in what order things transpired, but when I returned, I found Bindi out of place; she was lying on top of someone, pinning him to the ground. She almost killed him, as he could barely breathe. She was chewing as normal, with somebody's legs sticking out from under her belly. The fellow's eyes were bulging, and he wanted to be saved in the worst way."

"I then looked over near the fountain and deep-water trough and found two others in the water up to their chests, being held hostage by Revolk and Miskah. Their teeth were chattering like musical instruments. It was hilarious I tell you, entertaining in so many ways." The camel stable supervisor then adds, "I hailed the constables who had a good laugh as well" and concluded with, "They hauled the guy out from under Bindi and helped the two camel prisoners get out of the freezing water and took them in for questioning. From what I heard them say as they were being rescued, er, arrested, I suspect that the tax collector had put them up to it." He looks at the Young Merchant and says, "So now, you know the whole sordid story. Are you happy with your camels and did you have an altercation with the tax collector?"

SOPHIE SAVED BY OGNIR

"Veronica," Sophie says in a soft and tender voice, "I never knew I could get so weary while doing so many interesting things. I am happy and exhausted at the same time."

"Ah yes," Veronica replies, "You will get used to it. You need to make sure that you are not only occupied, but you are busy doing the right thing for the right reason. If you get tired working that way, you will always want to return to your work, and your clients can tell by what you deliver in which way you were busy." She looks from her work over to Sophie, smiles, and then adds, "It is about time to stop anyway. You do not want to work on that type of detail without enough light. It will strain your eyes."

"I am not sure I want to stop, but I suppose you are correct. I believe Ognir agrees as well. He looks ready for a little trip outside," Sophie says in agreement, her focus going from Veronica to Ognir and back to Veronica. She then adds, "You notice I did not use the 'w' word, so he does not get too excited to go out."

"Yes, that is right," Veronica says as she giggles. She looks at Ognir and observes, "He does understand certain words. He also understands emotions and, when on duty, is aware of intent ... a very perceptive animal we have here." Veronica looks up at Sophie and offers, "If you would like to take him out, you probably should go now. That will give you enough time to get home before darkness arrives."

"Ognir! We are going on a walk! Does that sound interesting to you, boy?" Sophie exclaims as she jumps to her feet and dashes to the door, simultaneously realizing that she has used the "w" word. Ognir beats her to the door, his tail hitting her multiple times as she manages to get around him and take hold of the door without falling down.

"Put him on duty before you leave, Sophie," Veronica reminds, to which Sophie responds with a smile and an affirmative nod.

"Ognir, sit." He sits instantly.

"Come," Sophie says while pointing to the floor with her right hand at her side. Ognir moves into position and Sophie smiles at Ognir and then looks at Veronica with a sophisticated look on her face and says, "We will be back shortly. We will not be long."

"Thank you Sophie," Veronica says as she places her work on the table. "I think I will also stop for the day and sit down for a rest. See you soon."

Sophie and Ognir leave as Veronica is stretching after she sits down. She tries to not fall asleep.

The brisk air of the late afternoon gives both Sophie and Ognir a much-needed recharge of energy as they walk along the road. They then turn to the right to follow their normal path, away from the busy crowds who are overly interested in Ognir, which today would be cumbersome as they need to make this walk a quick one.

"I don't hear Gallus-Gever crowing today like normal," Sophie thinks as she reaches down to touch Ognir. She looks down at him and notices his ears are up and he is sniffing the air, looking to understand something.

"Hmmm. Maybe a stray animal ate him, feathers and all, and Ognir can smell the battle. I hope not."

They continue on their way while Sophie begins thinking about the several projects she and Veronica are working on. Time passes quickly until the moment it stops.

Sophie also stops as she realizes, "Oh no, I don't know where we are." She kneels to be closer to Ognir, who would normally sit at this point but who remains standing on high alert.

"Ognir, I need your help. I need you to take us home," Sophie says in a soft, but urgent tone.

Ognir senses danger and whips around to look behind them. His defensive stance is apparent to Sophie, so she looks to discover what is there and is frightened by the voice that arrives out of a dark corner. "We will take you home. You need not worry about anything. Come along quietly."

Sophie knows it is time to flee and as she tries to turn around, she feels someone grasp both her arms tightly above the elbows. At the same moment, the scene is enveloped in a chaotic cacophony of growls, screams, and voices yelling.

Ognir whips back around to attack the man who grasped Sophie and savagely bites his ankle, which causes the assailant to release Sophie as he screams and falls on the ground.

Sophie takes that instant of freedom to turn away from the voice, jump around the man screaming in pain, and sprint away while commanding Ognir to come. Ognir is occupied with the voice for only a moment. He then joins Sophie in her escape.

Sophie looks down at Ognir, who moves in front of her to guide the way. A few moments later he slows, then stops, and as Sophie looks at him, he raises his head to show her the sandal he had removed from the owner of the voice.

"What is this boy?" Sophie says as she removes the sandal he has in his mouth. "Oh, I am so glad you didn't bring his foot along as well."

The moment Sophie takes possession of the evidence, Ognir again moves ahead and looks back as if to say, "OK, let's keep moving."

"I am with you," Sophie says as she stands and follows her guardian. Sophie thinks of nothing except keeping focused on Ognir's path; trying to keep up with him is not too difficult, as he can sense where she is and slows as needed to ensure Sophie's safety.

VERONICA IS JOLTED AWAKE BY the loud noise of the door opening with Sophie and Ognir arriving with a heightened sense of energy. Sophie has a distressed look on her face, and Veronica knows there has been serious trouble when Sophie bolts the door.

Veronica is still in shock from such a rude awakening but manages to say, "What happened? Is someone chasing you? Are you OK?"

Sophie takes her shawl off and as she is walking to the nearest seat, looks at Veronica and puts her finger in the air to communicate that she will answer the questions but must sit first. Ognir is standing at attention squarely at the door, ears collecting information.

Veronica tries to be patient. Sophie starts to explain, "It is all my fault. I was not paying attention. We were walking, and I got us lost, but of course, Ognir knew where we were, but I didn't, and when I stopped day-dreaming, I told him—Ognir, not the man in the darkness—that I needed his help, and so there was a voice in the darkness who said he would take us home, but I couldn't see him, and I was terribly frightened and wanted to run, and then Ognir was angry at the voice, and then I was grabbed from behind, and it hurt terribly, so Ognir saved me by taking a bite out of him, so I ran, and Ognir brought me home safe, and I am so very thankful, and Ognir is a hero, and I am starting to shake and don't feel so well. It is all my fault, and I am so sorry, and I feel like crying."

Veronica has made it to Sophie's side to comfort her. "It is fine for you to cry. Here, put your feet up and put this under your head and try to relax. I will get you something to sip on. Take slow deep breaths. Think about breathing very slowly, Sophie. Everything will be fine. You are safe. Breathe slowly. Focus on the air you are breathing. In and out."

"Yes. I will try," Sophie says as she starts to tremble.

Veronica caresses Sophie's hair and holds the back of her right hand against Sophie's cheek while she pats her shoulder with her left. She reassuringly tells Sophie, "Do not feel bad about shaking. It is natural after an exhilarating battle." It takes a while for Sophie to calm down and fall into a relaxing sleep. Veronica adjusts the coverings, stands up, takes a deep breath, and looks at Ognir.

"My dear friend, Ognir, you are so very marvelous. Thank you for saving our dear companion today." Veronica walks over to the door and quietly unbolts it, saying, "Ognir, we are expecting a friendly visitor soon. I am going to ask you to step outside and greet him when he comes. Can you do that for me?" Ognir understands perfectly and takes his assigned post.

HEARING A SOFT KNOCK AT the door, Veronica opens it up very slowly and places her index finger over her lips to indicate silence is needed. As the Young Merchant steps in, Veronica tiptoes back in and points to Sophie.

She leads her polite gentleman visitor to the far side of the worktable and explains what has happened. She then says, "That is what Ognir retrieved from the abductor she calls 'The Voice from Darkness,'" pointing to the sandal.

"I know exactly who that belongs to...." the Young Merchant affirms. He then looks at Veronica and adds, "It belongs to Mordechai, the 'evil lord of knowledge.'"

Veronica looks back at the Young Merchant and can only shake her head in recognition of what all that could mean. "We will need to get Sophie home soon," she announces.

"Yes, I agree. How can I help?" he responds.

"Take that," Veronica says as she passes him and points at the sandal on her way to where Sophie is sleeping.

LOOKING STRAIGHT AT THE YOUNG Merchant, the Roman spy authoritatively remarks, "Passover is prime season for human trafficking. The crowds of entire villages come from everywhere. They let their children loose and do not keep close track of them. In addition to the observation posts next to the temple, we have dispatched over five hundred troops to keep an eye out."

"That is a lot of resources."

"Yes, and still, there are a dozen or so families who lose someone to this activity every year. Those seeking to gain a slave or a wife are many, and they sneak them out while everyone else is leaving."

"I never knew this was going on."

"The real shame is that the 'brokers' who live right here in Jerusalem or close by are the ones who kidnap based on an order, and deposit, placed well prior to Passover. Our Proctorate Agreement prevents us from rounding them up and taking them to the justice they deserve." He looks around the corner and surveys the crowd. "He should be here in his peaceful-sitting-pose location today, unless he changed his schedule."

He begins walking slowly. "There he is. Remember, you 'gently' hand his sandal back to him. I will trail behind and pass along his 'new instructions.'"

The Young Merchant pulls the sandal out and holds it ready in his right hand, waits until Mordechai is distracted by something on his left, walks past him, and as he does, takes the sandal, and launches it briskly at Mordechai's face. The force knocks his head against the wall.

The Young Merchant keeps walking even though he wants to take physical retribution out on the scrawny little creature.

A moment later, the Roman spy walks up next to Mordechai and does not say a word but holds his dagger right in front of Mordechai's face, its shiny blade ready to make an impression.

As Mordechai looks away from the Young Merchant, he is again startled to see the blade, held by someone staring into his eyes. He takes a fearful breath, as he and the Roman spy have crossed paths before.

With the tone of the Angel of Death itself, Mordechai is slowly and carefully informed, "We know who you are, we know where you live, we know everyone you work for…. If you ever look like you are even thinking of making trouble again … there will be an unfortunate accident in the least expected moment." The Roman spy does not release his visual grip on the eyes of his terrified prey. Then, in an instant, he is no longer there.

The Roman spy catches up to and surprises the Young Merchant by walking right next to and in step with him without saying a word. Without looking to his side, the Young Merchant asks, "So, did you kill him for me?"

"Of course not; you almost killed him when you tossed his sandal 'gently' … but I did place the fear of God in him. He was sweating and almost passed out. I love doing that to criminals I cannot arrest, try, and place in a convenient, private, faraway Ergastulum. You will learn to do the same thing and will learn new and more effective techniques when you are appointed to Officer School."

The Young Merchant turns to reply but the "Angel of Death" is nowhere to be seen. *How does he do that? They will teach me that if I join? He must sleep with his knife in his hand.... I hope his nose never itches while he is sleeping. I wonder if he ever really sleeps. I need to get back to see Veronica.*

RETURN TO THE DESERT

WHILE THE CAMEL HERDER IS organizing the gear, food, and merchandise for the trip south, the Young Merchant is making his last sales rounds. He has one important thing he needs to tend to prior to leaving. He remembers his assignment....

I already said goodbye to Veronica, which was more difficult than I would have thought. I now need to visit Sariah. Several months ago, I promised my grandfather I would take her a gift from him, my grandmother, and my mother. They have been close friends for decades.

The morning I left for this trip, I saw my grandmother walk quickly out the door and hand my grandfather a small thin box. "Here it is dear," she said as she passed it to him with two hands and softly looked him in the eye as he took it from her and handed it to me. "Here you are. I know you will not forget to give it to her while in Jerusalem. Thank you."

Sariah is home and opens the door quickly. "I heard your camel snort and knew you would be coming, so I was ready. Welcome, please come in." She steps to the side as her right hand makes a sweeping welcoming motion. Joshua responds, "Thank you kindly. My grandparents send their love and well wishes."

"Please thank them for me. You certainly have grown since I saw you last. How is everyone in the family?" Sariah asks.

She has a very welcoming smile, and her voice is friendly and warm. It makes me feel as if I have heard it before, in pleasant circumstances, long ago, but try as I may, I cannot place it. She looks younger than it seemed to me she would be. Is she my grandmother's sister? No, I would have known that. There are so many mysteries. Joshua and Sariah spend a good amount of time together.

THE ROMAN SPY IS STANDING out in the open when Joshua arrives at the southern square. He is already looking in Joshua's direction as if he has been watching Joshua's movements and is waiting for him. He walks straight toward Joshua, glancing up and to the left as he walks, as if to make a signal to someone on the roof of one of the surrounding buildings.

"Good afternoon, Young Merchant!" the Roman officer says as he bows his head. "I know you are terribly busy getting ready to leave, what? Tomorrow morning? To Alexandria? Yes?"

He catches Joshua off guard with his knowledge that he and the Camel Herder are leaving and where they are going. Joshua asks himself, *What else does he know?* as he nods his head as if what he has said was common knowledge of every single person in Jerusalem. The way this city is, it is not a surprise one little bit. Joshua looks in the eyes of the Roman Spy and responds, "Yes, you are correct. I would like to thank you for your truly kind consideration of our needs and interests while we were here. I am sorry it has been only a short visit."

"Do not think anything of it. I believe you are amply aware of what you have been taught by me and are hopefully considering making a change in careers. Yes?"

Who can say no to that? Joshua thinks, then responds, "Yes, thank you once again, and I will certainly consider your overly generous offer to become an officer in the Roman Armed Service. I will think about it and look forward to meeting you when we get back after Passover."

The Roman takes a step forward and says with reassurance, "Now, I want to let you know exactly what my offer looks like." He nods his head and moves his eyes to tell Joshua to look behind him.

Joshua turns his head, and before he is fully looking in that direction, he sees the most handsome black stallion he has ever laid his eyes on. The amazing horse is adorned in full military parade gear of black and silver. The saddle looks as if it has never seen service. The black coat and mane, the tail, they are all so … perfect. Joshua is stunned and asks himself, *This would be mine?* Joshua looks back at the Roman officer, who is enjoying his reaction.

"Yes, imagine the regal uniform that accompanies this fine war horse. Your own tent, your own staff. People get out of your way when you ride through. It is amazing the honors you will receive, the privileges you will have at your disposal." He pauses to let Joshua absorb what he is offering, then continues …

"Yes, think about these things while you are away, but you will need to …" his head makes a slight motion to the handler, "make a decision quickly when you return. The next officer class will be closing soon after that."

Joshua looks back at the horse and is surprised that the handler has taken the war horse away while he was looking at the recruiting officer. Joshua then looks back to the officer; he too, has vanished.

Joshua is amused and thinks, *Very impressive sales offer closing tactic. I should develop something similar. Maybe I could paint Bindi black, braid her mane, and put bells on her neck … no, it would not be the same. That was an incredible horse though. They are very well trained. You think something, and the horse does it. I have heard they do the same thing with their scout dogs. Ognir is a perfect example. They probably also do it to eagles and perhaps snakes. I wonder how the Camel Herder is doing. I better get my rounds done.*

BACK AT THE STABLE, ALL is seemingly well. The gear, food, and merchandise are all ready and in order to load. The camels are being tended to in their usual fashion. Blankets are drying out on the line and harnesses are being cared for.

"So, I am almost ready here," the Camel Herder says as he adds more oil on a harness and begins rubbing it in.

"Let me help you with that," Joshua says as he picks up the last bridle hanging on the stall fence and places some oil on the leather to rub it in. He puts more than is needed and so has to glide the excess down on the leather, so it does not drip on the ground.

"Be gentle with the oil I always tell you, but, no, you slather it around as if it's water in one of the Roman bath houses," the Camel Herder says with a grin, speaking as if he is Joshua's mother.

"It was only one drop. Be quiet. Looks like you are ready to head out and make tracks in the sand. Thank you."

The Camel Herder nods in agreement. "So, did the guy who wants to make money by signing you up to be a handsome officer who gets whatever he wants find you?"

"He came by looking for me."

"Are you an idiot? He always knows where each and every one of his prospects are ... day and night. Of course not, he was probably waiting for you, wasn't he?" He tried to be serious, but his smirk was showing through.

"No, well, perhaps. He was standing in the square waiting for me."

"Yes, the trap! I bet the square was empty when he made his final sales pitch, wasn't it?"

"Uhm ... hmmm ... yes ... it ... was ... empty. How does he do that?"

"You are the salesman, and you were not prepared? You did not say yes, did you?"

"No, actually, I told him I'd think about it."

"I hope you will not think about it. It is all glorious and beautiful when they are doing the pitch. They even take you out and show you how romantic it all is ... horses, gear, slings, banners, shiny helmets ..." he lowers his voice, "women."

"No, none of that, well yes, some, and perhaps he did show me a horse ... again."

"Again?"

"Yes, well he showed me the horse that will be mine when, or if I join. It was amazing."

"What?" the Camel Herder is now serious and starts speaking as if he is Joshua's grandfather, with words of wisdom. "Let me make this perfectly clear to you, my young recruit. The horse he showed you has been displayed to at least ten or maybe fifteen of Mr. Officer Recruiter's prospects.

"When you become his catch and join, you will get a donkey, a left-hoofed donkey who will be blind in one eye and he will not see well out of the other. You will be sent somewhere stupid like Gaul and will be away for at least six years at a time, if you survive the bloody battles they will put you in. And do you know what? They place their 'handsome officers' in front, so you will probably not survive.

"And that is not even talking about those who report to you, that you have responsibility for. They are recruited from everywhere or conscripted from whomever they conquer that week. None of them speak the same language. OK, go ahead, join up, have an enjoyable time. Veronica and I will get married, have lots of children, and because she 'loves and adores you,'" he makes a dreamy smile at Joshua and bats his eyelashes, "we will have our children all write you love notes on your birthday. But be aware, my handsome-Roman-officer-on-a-donkey friend, the notes will take a full year to get to you, so we will change your age on the notes so you will not be disappointed." The Camel Herder closes his diatribe by looking down and feigning a sad whimper.

Joshua smiles and says, "You do have a point. I will wait until we get back to decide. Agreed?"

The Camel Herder quickly stands up, reaches over, and hangs his freshly oiled gear on the fence, looks at Joshua and declares with a smile, "Agreed." He points to the harness in Joshua's hand and adds, "You need to keep rubbing that oil in my friend, and don't add any more."

Joshua begins rubbing the oil into the harness as his mind goes right back where it was before he received a lecture, *I hope my Camel Herder friend feels better and that he, as he will tell the tale years from now, made a dramatic difference in my life. No matter, I will marry Veronica, and he will need to find himself someone for his lonely, future-bride's camel.*

They complete packing the camels early in the morning and join the prearranged southbound caravan before the sun gets too hot. It is the same caravan master, Boaz, and the same master of the guard. Joshua reflects, *I feel safer already. Bindi seems happy to get back to being useful on the trade route again. I can feel her relax and settle into a comfortable pace. This part of the trip should be at a calm and leisurely pace. There will be no bands of thieves. The Egyptians have an influence far beyond their declared borders and do not put up with caravans being molested.*

"SO, YOU LIKE MY TURBAN? You said it is absolutely ridiculous, but in your little mind, you are very jealous of my beautiful turban, and you wish you had one like it, well perhaps in gold and with a bit of trim … lots and lots of fringe, the color you gave Veronica! Yes!"

The Camel Herder sits tall and begins his feigned tale of Joshua's life, "He sat tall and proud in his saddle as he approached her with a marriage proposal, he had practiced hundreds of times, which he would say to her as he looked into her 'wondrous eyes.'

"As he was about to open his mouth, she held out her hand and firmly said, 'Stop right where you are! Exactly why are you riding on Bindi … my camel? You know you belong on the Camel Herder's camel. The one he is saving for his future wife with wondrous eyes, and I love the cute turban you are wearing.'"

Joshua thinks the Camel Herder had proven that he has been in the sun too long and advises him, "You need to drink some water because you are starting to hallucinate."

The Camel Herder retorts with whimsical sarcasm, "Perhaps you are correct about the water, but Veronica will think you will look adorable in your turban. And you are the one saying her name in your sleep. So exactly who is hallucinating my friend?"

Part of Joshua wants to knock him off his saddle, but he imagines, *The image of riding with a fancy turban is too funny to get mad about and I am very worried about Veronica's health and wish there were something I could do to help her. I feel so helpless.* The camels plod along, although Bindi turned her head toward him when the Camel Herder mentioned her name. Joshua wonders what she is thinking.

He pats her on the neck, "Good girl Bindi. I will not make fun of you." A question pops into Joshua's mind, *I said her name in my sleep? Wait a minute! He could not have heard me say anything. We have not been in the same tent since caravan!* He turns to the Camel Herder and says, "So, I have a very simple question for the Camel Herder."

"Yes, the Young Merchant. I have all answers instantly, in multiple categories—math, language, sciences, planetary movements. I even provide my close friends with well-tested advice for their romantic problems. What do you wish to ask me?"

Joshua thinks, *He for sure has been in the sun too long,* and asks, "I am glad I came to the right person. Exactly how did you hear me say Veronica's name in my sleep?"

The Camel Herder cannot contain himself and laughs hysterically. "Yes, you have confirmed that you have fallen hopelessly in love with the seamstress." He laughs again, "You should have asked that question when I made the assertion, but I can tell you one thing ..."

The Young Merchant interrupts, "I've been distracted...."

"Yes!" the Camel Herder interrupts, "This statement is absolutely true. I even heard you singing to her!" he says with laughing words.

Joshua notes to himself, *How he laughs with delight in his strange form of humor. I will tell his mother that he has gone nuts. She has always liked me more than him, and it has always irritated him every time I have said so for the last ... how long has it been? ... almost twenty-two years ... my, how quickly time moves these days.*

Bindi flexes her shoulder muscles to adjust how the saddle sits. She ignores all the laughing and continues on as if nothing else in the world is happening. Joshua wonders if she sometimes walks in her sleep.

ON THE FOURTH AND MIDDLE day, arrival at the water station comes earlier than normal on this leg of the journey. Other than the traveling flock of birds, there are very few outside interferences.

Once unloaded, the camels are watered, fed, and groomed to remove any trail debris, burrs, and other things which may have dire effects if not corrected. The camels are then allowed to roam, but they never wander far.

Of particular interest to the children of the caravan are the Camel Herder's camel, his "bride's" camel, and blue-eyed Bindi, the Young Merchant's camel, each of whom have entertaining characteristics that amuse the children.

The children are allowed to assist in caring for these camels while under supervision. By this time in the caravan, most of the children are well versed in their various chores, with the older boys carrying water and the older girls coaching the young ones on brushing. The camels love the attention ... when they are in the right mood.

The Camel Herder responds to a young girl asking a question, "Yes, you have permission to lie up against Revolk if you wish. The sounds you will hear are his stomach working on the food you gave him earlier."

"Thank you," she responds, then walks over, sits down on the ground, and leans against Revolk. Revolk does not seem to notice as he continues chewing. She lifts her arm up to scratch his fur and turns her head to place her cheek against his warm side. She falls asleep quickly.

Bindi ends up with four children napping against her, while Miskah relaxes as best as possible with three boys. The boys are not interested in taking naps, but rather are inspecting every inch of Miskah.

"You boys may wish to stop bothering Miskah so he can get some rest," the Camel Herder says.

They ignore his suggestion and move to Miskah's face, ears, and nose. Their fascination ends up centered on Miskah's nose and lips, which they find very entertaining. Miskah pretends the prodding does not bother him ... until his throat starts quivering; the Camel Herder notices and warns ...

"Run! He is going to spit!"

The boys scatter in all directions and barely evade a disgusting reward for pushing an otherwise calm camel over the edge of tolerance.

The Camel Herder grins as he walks over to Miskah and says, "That was a very good move, my friend," as he pats him on the head. In response Miskah says, "Burp!"

THE CALM AND PEACEFUL AFTERNOON is about to be shattered by something every desert caravan fears … a sandstorm from the east. Sandstorms from the west are inconvenient and messy. Sandstorms coming across the barren deserts of the east are fearsome, destructive, and often deadly.

Boaz stops what he is doing, looks up, and walks outside his tent. Standing still, he places all his senses on alert to feel what is happening. He suspects the wind is picking up slightly, so he leaves his tent and walks several yards to a higher point from which he can see the horizon and stops again. He gazes to the east interpreting the intangible changes he suspects may be happening in the desert around him. He looks down at the sand to confirm what he is feeling, then looks up and moves quickly with purpose.

Khamsin! Boaz realizes. *It is early, but it will happen without regard to man's reasoning. Time to prepare … now!* he thinks as he rushes to tell his captain of the guard.

The captain of the guard does not ask Boaz if he has actually seen the dust clouds on the northeastern horizon; he knows Boaz is able to know the impossible, as he has shown this power many times before. He quickly passes instructions through his guard who all rush out to spread the word.

The Camel Herder sees the running and commotion in the distance and knows what it is. He acts instantly, grabbing his sack of sweetcakes and waking the few children who are still with the camels, saying, 'I have more cakes for you, and we are going to have a race back to your parents. They will be so happy to see you. Come, let us have some fun and surprise them.'

The children are obliging and jump at the chance for a surprise followed by a cake. The Camel Herder takes care to ensure the children are protected from the fear which will arrive soon. As he drops each set of children off with their parents he instructs, "OK, here are your cakes. We are going to stay in our tents to eat our cakes and there will be a lot of dust. Tell your mom and dad that it will be OK, especially when it gets noisy. Can you do that for me?"

The children all nod yes, and the Camel Herder thanks them, saying, "You are going to be brave! Thank you, and we will see you later," as he smiles as broadly as possible.

He then sprints back while pulling his plan together, *OK, they are now as safe as possible. I have to get to my friend the Young Merchant and help him secure the leased camel team. I cannot lose any or it will be bad for many years. We will bring our camels in our tent and ride it out.*

The Young Merchant yells as the winds begin to pick up, "The camels are settled down and in place!"

"Good! Thank you! I will get Revolk and Miskah!" the Camel Herder responds as he turns urgently, holding his arm up over his eyes as the sand is now being blown with the strengthening wind.

Leaning forward to keep his balance, the Young Merchant responds, "I know where Bindi was! I will get her!" The Camel Herder is already out of sight, and the noises of the camp are overtaken by Khamsin's now raging sound.

'Khamsin' means fifty, the number of days during which sandstorms are common in Egypt, beginning mid-March and blowing from the northeast to the southwest, causing destruction and death along their paths. Time seems to stop as the two travelers attempt to gather Bindi, Revolk, and Miskah. The Young Merchant arrives back first.

As the wind whips the tent flaps fiercely, Bindi enters the tent easily and kneels down while the Young Merchant thinks, *Where is he? He better not get lost out there. I need to look.* He then grasps the door with both hands and carefully allows it to open and peers out into the intensifying sandstorm.

The amount of dust has increased to the point that nothing even close to the tent is visible. The Young Merchant stands with his coat pulled over his face leaving only a slit to see through. *Where are you, my friend?* He tries to will the Camel Herder back into the relative safety of the tent. As he peers through the dust, he perceives a shadow he estimates is some thirty feet away. "Come here! We are here!" Over here!" he screams, each breath now coming in with painful grains of sand.

"I've got to go get him!" the Young Merchant says as he tries to step out of the tent into the now deadly Khamsin.

He is pushed back by a camel's snout and almost falls over, "Here's Revolk!" a voice says. "I'll be right back!"

"Stop! Do not go! Your camel will be OK! Come back!" the Young Merchant screams as he regains his balance and stands motionless and in disbelief at what is happening. "Why did he go?" he asks himself aloud, "Why is this happening to us? I cannot lose him."

His wandering mind is brought back to the present with a strong nudge by Revolk, who wants to be shown where to lie down. Revolk would also prefer to have a bite to munch on while the storm passes. Joshua gathers straw and places it in front of both Bindi and Revolk.

Camels are built to weather sandstorms, with ears, eyes, and noses equipped with sandstorm-proof layers of protective closures and filtering membranes with tough skin. Miskah will most certainly survive this storm, but the Camel Herder will most certainly not. The Young Merchant settles Revolk down and then kneels to plead with God for the safety of his lifelong friend. When he looks back up, Revolk is looking through the dusty air right at him and seems to share his anxiety. The Camel Herder does not return.

KHAMSIN LASTS LONGER THAN NORMAL. The silence of its passing with the dim light of dawn wakes the Young Merchant up with a start. He opens his eyes and for a moment is not sure where he is or what has transpired. Once he gathers his thoughts, he springs to his feet, looking frantically around for his companion.

Not finding the Camel Herder inside, the Young Merchant makes his way around the camels and opens the tent door with urgency. Looking out, he sees nothing except the nearest tent, which has a side lying in the sand, with emptiness to the horizon. He turns back into his tent to gather provisions for the search.

"Where is Revolk? Where did he go?" His eyes survey the lower portion of the circular tent. They stop at a deep furrow, large enough for a frantic and determined camel to crawl out of the tent.

What? Where did he go? the Young Merchant is overwhelmed to see what had happened. He suddenly feels entirely empty, until Bindi turns her head to look at him. The look on her face seems to say, "Well, there is nothing we can do inside this dusty tent. Let us go look!" The Young Merchant nods back and reaches over for the camel brush, picks it up, and knocks the dust out of it on his thigh.

The camp is silent as Bindi is led out, ready to begin the search. Her master mounts without asking her to kneel and begins thinking about how to proceed with the search and rescue mission at hand.

"I have water, I have food. I need to watch my direction so I know where to return; no, Bindi will return if needed. I should let her choose. She will find them faster than I. OK, I will make a slow circle around the camp and let her decide where to go from there." He begins the slow route, praying for the best.

Moving his eyes in a rhythmic pattern across the horizon, the Young Merchant has memories come to him of his amazing adventures with the Camel Herder. "We need to find them Bindi" he says aloud. He sees some movement in the camp out of the corner of his eye and looks over to his right and reflects, *It looks like there was not significant damage to the tents last night. Oh no! I forgot to look at the leased camels! They may all be gone! I hope Revolk did not rouse them to escape with him. Maybe not. Revolk cannot untie knots, as far as I can tell.... I hope.* His attention is diverted when Bindi turns her head to the left as if she sees something. He loosens up on the reins, so she knows she is free to make her own decisions.

"What are you seeing, girl?" the Young Merchant asks. Bindi plods along, still keeping her head turned to the left. Her nostrils look to be zeroing in on something. She continues this way for some time until she lifts her head to sniff several centimeters higher. Her anxious rider peers at the horizon without seeing what he is searching for.

Without warning, Bindi makes an abrupt turn to her left and heads out away from the camp. The Young Merchant's heart skips a beat. He wants her to run, but she continues plodding steadily forward, edging to the left or right only occasionally. The sun has breached the horizon to the east, casting a long camel-with-rider shadow to the west.

Please go faster! Please find them. Please, find him alive, is his silent plea to his trusted companion. They walk up a slight rise, raising his hopes, but to no avail. Bindi snorts on the north slope of the rise, but her cadence remains unchanged: slow and steady. The Young Merchant feels like he is going to go mad.

Why did she snort? I am sure it was to clear her nostrils of the sand from last night. He tries to focus on the horizon ahead and is shocked to see a spot, a distinct color in one tiny area ahead. *Yes! Is that them? Bindi, hurry! Let us get there now! Stop moving so slow!* Joshua rises up as best he can to focus on what he is staring at. As they approach, the spot of color in the sand turns into a bump, rising up beyond the horizon into the sky, ever so slightly.

The combination of joy, expectation, and hope overcomes the Young Merchant, and he begins calling, "OMARI! We are coming. Please hold on!" They plod along, the bump in the sand develops into a camel, then a camel with someone lying next to it. "There they are! Bindi, run! Run!" he screams, rocking forward trying to persuade Bindi. He knew better than to kick Bindi into a run; that would launch him into the air, followed by a rude faceplant in the sand.

He is not moving. I need to get to him. He needs help. Why is his camel not looking at us? Are they both dead? No! His mind is racing as his impatience increases beyond his ability to control. He leaps off Bindi into the sand with the intent to run the final twenty yards.

His intent is met with a light and fluffy layer of sand which only allows him to sink and scramble almost on his stomach the rest of the way. Bindi keeps up her steady pace, arrives at the stranded pair, then stands calmly, waiting for him to arrive.

At that point, Revolk raises his head to look at Bindi, sand falling off his muzzle as he does. The Young Merchant arrives, nearly reverently kneels next to his friend, reaches over to pull the fabric slowly away from his face, worried about what he will find. He dusts the sand away from the opening, speaking softly as if he is waking a newborn.

The motionless Camel Herder's eyes are swollen and closed, sand lodged in every crevice and wrinkle. "Oh, please be alive my friend. Please come back from the dark," the Young Merchant coaxes gently. It seems he is breathing. "It is time to wake up. We are here for you." The Camel Herder's face muscles twitch. They move again only slightly, indicating he is trying to open his eyes. "Take your time my friend. When you are ready, we have water. Revolk came to you last night and saved your life."

Hearing his name, Revolk snorts and looks at the Young Merchant with an "Of course I did, what else was I going to do? He is my master. I will do anything for him" look on his dusty face.

"Thank you Revolk, you are an honorable companion," the Young Merchant exclaims.

"Miskah, did Miskah come in?" the Camel Herder asks coarsely.

"You are alive! Welcome back!" the Young Merchant says exuberantly.

The Camel Herder clears his throat, "Miskah?"

"No, he has not returned yet, do not be alarmed, he did fine last night. We need to get you back to the camp and clean you up. The children will be expecting you," the Young Merchant says, hoping what he said is true.

THE SWELLING SUBSIDES FAIRLY QUICKLY as the Camel Herder's eyes are washed in clean water several times throughout the day. Children arrive to check up on him as well. He feels as though he will be shaking dust out of his clothes and body for weeks to come.

The Young Merchant comes into the tent with a visitor and says, "My friend from the sands, you have a young lady visitor who has brought you a gift."

"Oh, yes, Anna! I know you! We have traveled thousands of days in the desert together, haven't we?"

The young girl steps forward holding her hands behind her back. "Yes, we have. I hope you are feeling better. I brought you a surprise," she says in a confident tone as she stands still.

"Oh! And what do you have for me?"

"You have to guess."

He looks back at Anna and rubs his chin, then exclaims with a swollen smile, "A crocodile from the Nile!"

She grins and responds, "No! Silly. I brought you flowers!" She then brings her hands forward and displays with pride a full bouquet of straw, in all its glory.

"How sweet of you! Did you gather all these all by yourself?"

"Of course not! My friends helped, and they sent me to deliver them to you. They hope you feel better. Where is the Camel with No Name? Did he blow away or is he hiding because he is scared?"

"Well, his name is Miskah, but in the poem he is 'the Camel with No Name' and he is out there somewhere, and we are sure he will come back when he is ready," the Camel Herder responds, glancing over at the Young Merchant.

Anna understands and takes the lead, "Well, we talked about him, and we decided that you need to play him the song!"

"The song? What song do you think will work?"

"The song you play to get Revolk to come over and play games when we all have a fun gathering. You know!"

"Well, I am not sure he knows what to do like Revolk when I play the song, and my little instrument is probably broken from the sand."

The little girl, probably five years old, places her hands on her hips and takes charge, "Oh, so here is the plan: you get up and find your music maker and clean it up, and I will gather all the children, except the very little ones, and we will come and keep you company while you play the 'Come Home' song. Miskah will come right along, we are sure … got it?"

Before the Camel Herder can answer, Anna exclaims, "Good! Get ready. We will be right back!" She turns around and walks with purpose out of the tent.

"She is way too young for you, but perhaps she has an older aunt who has as much enthusiasm for making you do what is correct. Think 'obedience to women with authority,' my friend. I will help you find your noisemaker," the Young Merchant offers in a convincing manner. It is obvious he was holding in a glorious burst of laughter.

WITH PASSOVER ARRIVING SOON, THE city of Jerusalem, far to the north, is focused on sacred happenings with holy purpose, except in certain shadowy corners, where evil is being planned.

THE STORM ON THE SEA

A S WITH MOST BUSINESSES IN Israel, the fishing industry is supported by the prosperous efforts of licensed, family-centered, commercial enterprises. The seafaring business on the Sea of Galilee also includes cargo transport and paid-for-hire passenger voyages to cities and villages around its fifty-three kilometers of coastline.

Although it is known as the Sea, the ancient lake is fed by multiple springs. Its main water source is the Jordan River, and the 'Sea' lies low in the Great Rift Valley. Surrounded by hills, locals know it to be susceptible to quickly rising, violent storms, risking life and property not only on the shores, but particularly in the passageways across the waters. These hills resemble cliffs, an average two hundred meters above sea level with the tallest cliffs three hundred meters above sea level. It is eleven kilometers wide and twenty-one kilometers long with sixteen harbors. Fishing boats made of cedar and oak are up to ten meters long and over two meters wide, capable of holding a working crew of up to fifteen men.

The peaceful calm of the Sea of Galilee can quickly become transformed by violent storms. Winds funnel through the east-west-aligned Galilee hill country and stir up the waters quickly. More violent are the winds that come off the hills to the Golan Heights to the east. Trapped in the basin, the winds are sometimes deadly to fishers and travelers alike.

"Tobin," says Muriel, as she approaches early in the day while he is repairing a net, "I heard from Zebulon's wife that 'The Fish Police' approached two of Zebulon's boats last night."

Tobin responds, "Yes, I was there. They approach our vessels often, inspecting, spying, causing mischief. I do not blame them. They do not have anything else to do out there. They must be bored out of their minds. I could not do that every day, although I do wonder what Manasseh and his crooked crew are up to from time to time."

"Tobin, this is serious. Ever since I 'surprised' the esteemed committee I have wondered how they would react. Well, they have engaged the 'bored' inspectors to start focusing on our fleet, and they are collecting information about us from other fishing crews. It is disgusting; I will not have this happening right in front of our faces." Muriel is agitated as she completes her report.

"Yes, I know all that. Zebulon and I are having quite a game with them. They always ask about other families' business dealings when they inspect our catch and verify our records."

"Exactly what do you mean 'game'? I hope you will not be fined for what you two are up to."

"Ha ... no fines. The catch of invisible fish and other fish which fly out of our nets are not listed in the 'regulated species' register. In fact, triple-footed blues are not listed either."

"What?"

"Zebulon, I, and other 'esteemed fishermen' from our local docks sometimes tell them tall tales. They are eager to take notes and go investigate. We usually tell them stories about crews on the other end of the lake, and they spend all night going to investigate."

"Don't those crews get upset with you for doing that?'

"Of course not; they tell them even bigger tales about what we have caught," Tobin explains.

"I have been part of fishing on this lake for several decades and had no idea you fine gentlemen were pulling pranks like this."

"It has only been happening over the past couple of seasons. Before that, there was not an abundance of regulations, police, or active boats." Tobin then looks at Muriel and adds, "You need to remember, in the old days, the regulations were self-imposed by the fishers themselves to keep things even. With the amount of fishing happening these days, we actually need outside 'help.' Even though they have overdone it, it is not a terrible thing to have them inspecting and asking questions."

"So how do you all get away with your foolery?"

"Oh, that is easy. They cannot get an honest fisher to take a job as an inspector. They would go nuts. They hire inspectors from the administrative schools, teach them some sail management, toss them into a boat, and toss the boat into the water ... they are not fishermen, have never seen a live fish, and have no clue if what we are telling them is true or not!" Tobin says with a smile.

"Why don't they 'catch' on? Pun intended." Muriel asks.

"Ah, yes. Well, they get bored, and spending time on a boat as an investigator is only temporary ... maximum of one season. The turnover of these guys is remarkably high. They also die often, so they are replaced, along with the boats they sink."

"Die?"

"Yes, well, some think they die from boredom, but many of them cannot swim and fall overboard or get tossed over the side. The boats get lost along with their crew during storms ... flash storms. It is not really their fault. So, there you have it."

"Oh yes, I have known families who have lost their entire crews in a storm ... so sad. Well, you know more than the wives who waste time trading what they think are 'secrets.' Nice to know. Thank you," Muriel says. As she is about to step away, Tobin offers some additional information.

"The mother-in-law of Peter Bar Jonah caused a ruckus at a committee meeting a while back. Do you know her?" Tobin says with a sly grin while looking at Muriel.

"Of course. I know her all too well. She did an excellent job rectifying what they were trying to do," Muriel responds with a grin.

"Well ... ever since she completed her 'fine job,' they have been *very* nice to me. Their wives have even baked fine breads and cakes which their apologetic husbands deliver to us with smiles on their faces," Tobin explains, ending with a huge, sneaky-looking grin on his face.

"Yes, I do not doubt that, but do not get too cocky. I know where they purchase those lovely breads and cakes, and you can be sure they are only nice because the Romans watch them closely. They will not stand for those who engage in coercion and fraud ... especially at the same time," Muriel advises with a wry look on her face. She wishes Tobin well and quickly strides back up the bank.

He looks back at the net he had been mending, adjusts the needles, and begins where he had stopped. His mind wanders to other times, recent times, which changed his life, *Peter's wife has been gone with him a couple of times as he follows Jesus on ministering trips. I wonder where they are now. The stories we hear of His teachings are very new and sometimes hard to understand. Did he really feed all those people with so little bread and a couple of fishes? I saw them come back one time, but I have not heard Him teach. Maybe someday. I am so glad my foot does not fall asleep anymore.*

Tobin leans to the right and adjusts the small blanket he is sitting on. The water laps softly on the rocks as he completes the net repair and his mind focuses on work, *I need to make sure I have everything stowed properly for tonight's catch. I hope God will be generous.*

LABAN THE YOUNG CHIEF INSPECTOR reviews in his mind, *Registered fishing boats are easily inspected. Records are quickly examined. This assignment is among the least difficult I have had in my two years at administrator school. If it was not so boring, I might like to do this my entire career. Those who died out here were stupid. There is a process to everything. The Greeks perfected it, and the Romans took that and added scale and control. It is all process management. You can control any system and chart any sequence of movements: mathematics, construction, coordination, fluid flow dynamics ... everything.* He adjusts the rudder while his companion swings the sail to tack to the north.

They are the night inspectors with an organized list of crafts they plan to inspect. Laban, a brilliant student and talented in all the learned sciences, is in charge. He has sailed multiple times and through study and practice is an excellent sailboat skipper. He "follows the book," and while he is well studied in many things, he is somehow unable to establish successful processes or relationships with humans. Although he is not (yet) despised, he is avoided.

Out on the water in the early evening, Tobin sees the red-flagged vessel tacking his direction. He makes no moves to avoid the meeting and wonders what the inspectors are thinking to be bothering his boat so early in the shift. "They are doing very well tacking, don't you think? The last police boat we encountered took almost all night to reach us. They were hilarious!" he says to his crew of four, who turn to focus on the small boat with only two occupants: one in the back on the rudder and the other midship, taking control of the sails.

"Good day gentlemen!" Tobin calls Laban and his companion. "It is so good to see you on such a fair and delightful day! You are doing well we suppose?"

"Yes, we are inspecting tonight and warn you to allow us access to inspect your daily catch following regulations: one-seven-three, point seven, process three and process five; Common Fishing Vessel Inspection and Fishing Daily Catch Limit Verification."

Oh, my goodness. What do we have here? I could have some fun with this fellow. I have heard stories about him. Let us see what he has in mind, Tobin thinks after hearing such an overly formal greeting. He responds, "Yes. Absolutely. Welcome to our vessel. Pull aside and pass your tie rope. We will secure you for your prompt inspection. We are happy to oblige!"

The second inspector and one of Tobin's crew members secure the boats together while Tobin watches Laban hastily review his process and prepare notes. Laban then launches his extensive and well-documented interrogation.

"I see you have hidden your daily catch. Show it to us so that we may inspect it, sir."

"We have received zero fish from God and have nothing hidden, kind sir. Please inspect the gunwales; there are no nets holding fish."

"Are you assuming I am not aware of the many methods local fishermen use to hide their catches from authorized inspectors, sir?"

What is this guy talking about? Tobin is thinking. He then responds as politely as possible, "Please, inspect anything you wish, inside my boat and all around it. This day's fishing starts at the tail end of dusk, which, you will notice, will be coming on us in a little while. You will notice during your inspection that my highly trained crew is readying the dry nets we will toss into the sea. Nets are used to catch fish in this lake. Perhaps they use other methods in other lakes you have previously owned, er, had responsibility for, Inspector … sir."

"We have a responsibility we need to carry out. This is for the good of all fishers on this lake. We are sure you are aware how misdeeds are accomplished on a regular basis."

"I am not aware of any on this side of the lake kind sir, yet if you happen to visit, in your responsibilities, fishers on the southeast side of the lake, you could possibly hear of dark deeds. On this part of the lake? No … we have been fishing these waters for several generations and are honorable, but the new fishers on the side of darkness, they have only been fishing for two or three generations, they are upstarts and hide catches in secret places…. I hear … from good authority. If you wish to inspect our records, they are freely available, and we would be glad for you to ensure we have documented the processes well. We are easily located in Capernaum."

"We will be on our way. Be reminded to follow the regulations strictly. If you should require assistance or hear of infractions, we are available to complete proper inspections on boats, as well as on shore in each packing facility. You need to be aware," Laban advises as he tries unsuccessfully to stand at attention with his feet together in the center of the vessel. He almost does not get through his memorized statement.

The ties are removed, the authorized inspection vessel moves off for another encounter while Tobin's well-trained crew begins casting nets in the planned sequence. The night's work has begun.

"God has been generous but not too generous," observes Tobin. "We are pleased with this catch but not so pleased to have needed to chase the fish so far out," he adds.

As the inspector correctly observed, everything has a process. Tacking up and down the lake or across it is a mathematical equation, which, if you pay attention and your timing is precise, will get you anywhere you wish to go.

During certain celebrations, there are crews who race a complex course in the Sea of Galilee. They are experts in judging the steady winds, the sails, and the rudders. They control their navigation processes with exactness ... then, there are the variables: rain, waves and the most feared, the savage wind.

On this lake, the wind is able to go from absent to fearsome in only a few minutes. Rain can move from delightful sprinkles to torrential in the same amount of time, and when these two variables combine, the waves respond with relentless fury. Combined, these components form lightning and thunder, making for a drama of life and death with which no Greek tragedy or Roman theater can compare. Lives are taken, and families are ripped apart.

We need to move homeward. We need to do it now, Tobin instantly thinks as he feels an odd change in the wind. *This wind is dry and is coming in from the North. We are going to be in trouble if it builds. The signals are always the same. Either from the North or from the West, if the wind is dry, it is descending from the surrounding hills. When winds cool quickly, they start their own weather systems ... deadly weather systems, which do not follow a process any human would devise.*

"Turn the sail!" Tobin yells. "We must get home. Now!" The crew has sensed the danger as well and are ready to make the proper moves to speed homeward as quickly as possible.

"Light the emergency flare! Tie it fast!" Tobin instructs as he walks through the storm preparation checklist in his head; *Yes, empty jugs with secure plugs. Yes, ropes to secure the sail.* He reaches down to his side to feel the well-honed knife he always wears. *Yes—knife to cut the sail loose if needed ... and cut the catch away if things get bad. Four of us. Four bailing baskets. God, help us*, Tobin rehearses and pleads as the wind increases.

The raindrops begin with no warning at all. They come in heavy, powerful, and sideways. Smashing themselves against anything in their way, each drop feels like the sharp slap of a whip.

Navigation is impossible without visibility, Tobin thinks as he instructs, "We must stow the sail!" The two forward crew members jump to the mast, pull the release cords fastened to hold up the now soaked sail. It falls instantly, swinging to align with the bow-stern line of the boat, which the senior crew member strives to hold into the wind. The crew member on the right side ducks instinctively as the boom whips past. Tobin lunges to assist with the rudder, which he prays will not be cracked in the storm. It is the only tool with which they can fight against the storm and survive … perhaps.

I feel sorry for them having to take the waves like that, Tobin thinks as he and his crew take wave after wave right in the face. He can no longer see details but knows what has been happening. *They are doing well holding on up there. Holding on with one hand and bailing as fast as they can with the other. I pray they do not give out. They will certainly be washed over.* Tobin holds the rudder with his right arm while his senior crew member fights it with his left arm. It is a constant battle.

In such situations, it is almost impossible to breathe. Water coming at you from all directions makes it impossible to breathe in any air without inhaling water. You choke, you cough, and you feel overwhelmed with each attempt. It becomes a personal, seemingly endless battle. Living through a storm such as this is rare, and if there are survivors, they commonly suffer lung failure within a few months of being on land.

"We are getting nearer the shore!" the senior crew member yells, pointing to a faint light behind them.

Tobin turns around to look and after a moment yells, "Could be! But it is moving too much!"

They both look at each other, realizing at the same instant what the light most likely is. They know it is another boat and are helpless to do anything as it grows closer.

Why is it coming closer? it should be traveling the same speed and di-rection as we are, Tobin thinks. He then realizes, *On no! They are flooded! They are getting ready to sink! Oh God, bring us to their aid! Where is the rope? We will need to move fast. We are good at bailing. It is ahead of the water. How many will there be? We can leave them in the water with the jugs to keep them afloat if we need to … tie them to our boat. There they are.*

Tobin looks to his rudder companion who shakes his head yes. Reaching over for the rope as he stands up to brace his legs against the boat's erratic movement, Tobin throws the rope at the two men in the other boat. Through the lashing rain, he sees them open-mouthed, screaming silently, their voices rendered useless and their boat full of water.

They are as white as can be, Tobin sees as he commands, "Light the emergency flare! Tie it fast!" then realizes, *Oh no! It is the inspectors! They always arrive as white-faced city boys.* He throws the rope as he yells, "Grab the rope. Grab the rope!"

Tobin screams again, "Grab the rope! Tie yourself to it! Do it now!"

They stare at Tobin as if he is a ghost. Time stands still as the rain slackens for a few seconds. Tobin turns to his senior crew member and points down to the churning waves between the boats. "Stay here!" he shouts at him, grins, and launches himself into the water.

It only takes him a few minutes to transfer his new human cargo from one boat to the other. The rain and wind come to a complete stop while he makes the transfer. The two survivors are silent as the six rain-soaked men make their way, on calm seas, back home.

They have been blown five kilometers south of where they started, so it is a long morning, but the light winds are favorable. As is common after flash storms, a small crowd has gathered on the shore waiting for them. They are mostly silent as well.

MURIEL IS SITTING NEXT TO Laban, the inspector, when he awakes. The first thing he does is grasp his chest.

"What is wrong? Are you hurt?" Muriel asks calmly, watching his eyes. *Quite a nervous fellow, this one is,* she thinks.

Laban looks around as if he has been robbed of a treasure and is desperately searching for it.

Muriel helps him. "Your record book as well as your regulations manual are over near the fire, drying out. You may wish to eat them for dinner. That way you will always have them close by," she says with a resigned motherly tone. She adds, "You are lucky to be alive on this fine day. One of the fishers you feel are worthless and stupid and always up to breaking regulations saved your pitifully educated life last night … risking his own life for someone who despises him."

She stands, walks over, gathers the records book and manual, walks back, drops them on Laban's chest and suggests, "You may want to spend some time pondering the systems and processes that caused that, my young friend."

As Muriel is walking toward the door she adds, "I have important things to 　　　　　　　　　　　　　　　　　　　　 ɪ feel up to it."

THE JEWISH LEADER'S SECRETS

LOOKING BACK AT THE LIFE of Reuben, the Jewish leader, is a surprising journey, as it is when one looks at anyone's past. We all have aspirations with setbacks, triumphs followed by disasters, deep insights coupled with confusion. To judge a person only by what you see now discounts the entire journey. You cannot consider the defeats and victories of the past; neither can you guess at the plans and dreams of the future.

As a boy growing up with his twin brother, Gad, at his side, Reuben was most always ready for an adventure. In their small village south of Bethlehem, the rocky landscape was the perfect setting for young imaginations. Gad and Reuben fashioned imaginary forts, villages, and kingdoms. Building roads with bridges was Reuben's specialty while Gad loved to create outposts which overlooked their "territory."

They took turns ruling as they got older. Reuben tended to focus on local improvements while Gad's ideas more often than not enlarged the land they ruled. As they learned more about the world around them, these tendencies became more sophisticated. When they were taken by their father to local council meetings, Gad would leave with political insights and ideas while Reuben would walk away with a mind full of buildings with road construction plans and proposals.

This combination of natural interests and skills made the brothers an effective team in their teens; however, the political divergence which characterized the world of their late twenties became a wedge. Roman incursion was of particular interest to Gad, who felt something had to be done. Reuben did not like being subjected to Roman rule, but he marveled at their engineering prowess and their seemingly endless resources, with associated planning systems.

"You should pay more attention to what they are doing to our pure society, Reuben. They are taking us apart one tradition at a time, one family at a time."

"Gad, I have told you many times, pay attention to what they do well. Look at the aqueducts, the roads ... even the sewer systems are amazing improvements."

"I know a group of true followers of the Israel tradition. They know how to move against the Romans, retrieve power, become free once more."

"Yes. Do you know who else 'knows' this little group of yours? The Romans. They know everything. They are aware of all groups planning anything, large and small, in secret and in the open."

"No, you are mistaken, they have no idea what I have arranged, who I have contacts with. It is a net, and it spans from across the sands of Egypt to Mount Hermon."

"Have you not considered that there is a precise reason the Romans who you say know nothing have built their military barracks right next to the temple? They watch everything. The 'net' you say you are part of is actually a spider web."

"The Romans have no soul. We will take them down one column at a time. We know their delivery routes and how to disrupt them. We know they are growing weary of supporting their vast army presence. They are getting weak. Look at the way they have become casual in their watch over Jerusalem. They have parties all the time; they are getting fat."

"I tell you Gad; the Romans have surely seen your spider web, and they will ignore it for only a while. When you are least expecting it, their operatives will report that it is time, and they will dispatch their swift and ruthless spider-killing team."

"They will do no such thing. I have proof they are getting weak and lazy."

"No, you don't."

"I have. Tangible proof."

"Where?"

"To the north of Jerusalem, we are building a wall to extend the boundaries of Jerusalem. They do not care. See?"

"They have yet to place one stone on top of another up there. The request has been made over and over again with the approval now being granted. The plans will need to be completely revised, then, I am sure, revised again."

"It is happening, and we need to be ready."

"Yes. How ready have the many revolts been in the recent past? As ready as any of them thought they were … were sure they were, they were as a spider in the corner."

"We are different. They were not aware of Israel's hidden strengths as we are. God is with us. He is leading the way."

"Do not make foolish decisions. The best way is to learn from the Romans, is to incorporate their technology so that we are ready as a society when God will see fit to deliver us. Have you not noticed that as long as the Romans are here, we are not enticing to the kings of Persia, or Greece, or whoever else wants to become our rulers?"

"The foolish decisions have already been made … by our past and current leaders. We have infiltrated. We know. We will be successful this time. I can assure you. I will let you build as many bridges as possible, and roads, and buildings when it is all settled."

"The Romans will know every move the spider makes. They will move silently and quickly. The only thing people will see the next morning is a spider, like all the rest, smashed in the corner … or hanging on a cross for all other would-be spiders to see and marvel at as they say to themselves, 'This fellow got caught because he was stupid. Our plan will succeed. We know people.'"

REUBEN SCANS THE CROWD HE is giving a speech to, looking into the eyes of his audience, paying particular attention to the powerful who are nodding slightly as he comes to the closing he had practiced with his brother until the words came easily and with enthusiasm and confidence.

"Opportunities are everywhere. We have an excellent education system available to all who are interested. We need to increase funding for our children's future. I tell you, this building will be admired by every citizen and marveled at by pilgrims as they arrive by the thousands," Reuben, now a young Jewish leader, says as he completes his speech. The crowd seems to appreciate it. While they do not appreciate the new, "temporary" tax, they know the prestige their children will gain by attending and graduating from a state-sponsored institution. Reuben joins the crowd and begins "working" it.

"Well done, Reuben. We are happy to support this venture. Your last community-improvement project was a clear success," the older man observes. He then bends closer and whispers into Reuben's ear, "Even if you had to bribe a Roman or two to get it through."

Reuben leans back and quietly offers his reply, "Yes, and it cost less than the approved budget, and the 'consulting fees' were less than they have been in a long while."

The older man is a very influential politician who has taken a liking to Reuben and become his mentor, introducing him to those with similar power and influence. Acting together, they swayed the Roman financial ministers to spend their exorbitant taxes and levies and fees and license income on projects which strengthen the community and bolster their own riches in the process.

"You have been doing well, Reuben; we appreciate your enthusiasm as well as your skill," he remarks. "The planning, engineering, and execution you have demonstrated have earned you a seat on the Senior Committee, which will set you up for many years of service. You need to keep from going astray before all of us old guys die," he smiles while continuing, "one … at … a … time." He then quickly slaps Reuben's shoulder saying, "Hah!" as he turns to glad-hand others who are near, leaving Reuben alone with his thoughts.

This went well. The seat on the committee. Now that is the step I need. It is about time. I have more projects in mind than anyone could do in three lifetimes. Gad. I wonder how he is doing since he moved away. I pray he was distracted from the path he was on. It would not have ended well. Reuben is approached by another member of the Senior Committee who congratulates him as well while he realizes, *I never noticed it before, but yes, they all actually do have one foot in the grave. There will be a lot of funerals to attend.*

"... We are ready. We are connected. We shall be free!" is the cheer in the secret meeting. Gad leads the chant that follows, "Free Israel! Free Israel! Free Israel!"

This crowd is not interested in civic improvement. Their only object is disruption, and eventual overthrow, of all Roman rule.

They have each memorized an extensive list of evil done by the Romans, and when items on that list are no longer useful, they invent additional items. Gad has become an expert in engineering dissatisfaction. He feels he has perfected his message and has achieved his objectives through developing a common enemy; uniting many communities who had never before worked together.

Under a shared theme of resistance, Gad educates his followers about the evils of Roman occupation. The Roman spies report this as an insurrection.

"Yes sir. They are well networked, and their leader is declaring that they are ready."

"What is this group's leader's name again?"

"Gad."

"Oh yes. How many groups are attached to the central command?"

"They have mentioned twenty-seven, but we have only verified eighteen organized groups with identified leaders."

"Are they growing or shrinking?"

"This group has grown for the past five years. They stopped recruiting additional villages a year ago and have been training their leadership who, in turn, have been training local adherents."

"I understand. Do they have specific movements planned?"

"Yes sir. Covert action is planned against the stable in one week."

"Stealing horses or camels?'

"Horses, sir. They will then confirm their next action which they plan for the following week."

"Do we know what that action will be?"

"It is planned to be an armory raid, sir. We are verifying which one but believe it to be local to their leader's residence, on the coast, near our distribution center, Captain."

"Anything else?"

"No sir."

"Thank you. I will review this with the major. Do not leave. I will get back to you the standard way. Dismissed."

"Thank you, sir."

The tall, slender covert operations liaison departs, ready for action, thinking, *This will be good to stop before it gets out of hand. Gad has been incredibly careful and not as hasty as many other insurrectionists.*

"THIS WILL BE YOUR FIRST military expedition. Are you ready?"

"We are indeed ready. We will be in place tomorrow night."

"Are the transfer tents ready on the west?"

"Yes. The decoy camels are in place as well as the Egyptian handlers."

"You have four days' provisions at the tents?"

"Of course, we do. We have gone over every detail at least twenty times."

"I apologize. This is my first time sending anyone into obvious danger," he looks up, "and possible death."

"I understand. And you will pick up the horses?"

"Yes, with at least twenty-five local leaders who will each take horses with them, in different directions."

"Do you have the blankets to cover the Roman horses?"

Smiling, Gad says, "Of course we do. We have gone over every detail."

"Twenty-five? All leaders? It will be good to have our resources disbursed."

"Yes, one strand at a time."

"A net?"

"No. A spider web."

GAD IS WATCHING THE HORIZON. The full moon allows a clear, crisp view of the horizon, with the escape route on the right side. His leaders will start arriving in two days. In the meantime, Gad watches for Roman troops.

"They should be visible in the next hour," Gad says calmly.

"How can you seem so calm?" his watch partner asks.

"I have been patient for an exceedingly long time. There they are. The tent crew sees them as well."

"Why are they in lines?"

"Roman mounted battalion horses are not so easily 'acquired,' but they know how to stand in lines and follow the leader."

"Oh, I am glad we didn't go after the stupid camels."

"They may look stupid, but they are very clever and are nearly impossible to steal, and if you steal one, they will most likely escape and run, faster than a well-trained horse, back to their owner ... after they spit in your face. Here they come to the tents."

"Why are the tent-keepers throwing dirt?"

"Perfectly groomed Roman horses are easily spotted, even from a distance. These horses need to become dull, and they will place blankets on them, beads in their hair, and they will burn incense inside the tent to make them smell like the camels, and they will feed them calming herbs, so they don't even *act* like Roman horses ... now, we wait to see what happens."

"Really? Camel blankets? I hope one of them gets kicked into the air."

"That would be entertaining, but it will not happen. Watch for anyone coming in from the outside without Arab robes on."

"Yes sir."

"What have you seen, Gad?"

"We have watched for four days, and there's been no Roman movement on this road at all."

"That is good. They know they have lost their precious horses for good."

"No ... that is bad. Hanukkah is in three days. All the roads are busy. Busy roads equal Romans. These are the Ninth Battalion Mounted Cavalry Troop's horses. They have many other patrol horses which, in normal times, are seen on a regular schedule. No horses to be seen is not at all normal."

"So, they are busy elsewhere. I heard the group from east of the city was planning an uprising the day before the celebrations. We could go in tonight and remove the horses early."

"No ... it is a trap. We will pull out tonight.... Us.... Not the horses."

"What will happen to the horses?"

"The camel herders will get bored, approach the Romans watching them, sell the horses they haven't eaten to them, and be very happy for their week's work."

"They know where the Romans are hiding?"

"Of course they do. You do not survive in the desert for two thousand years without knowing everything that surrounds you both day and night. You will never catch any of them by surprise, ever.

Gad surmises, "It is a trap, as I thought. The culprit should have been caught at the Training Grounds. These horses are worth more than gold to the Ninth. Even if they got away with the horses, a thousand Roman troops would have descended on every inch of every escape route. It would have been over in only hours. The Egyptians manning tent operations are too calm. They have already spoken with the Romans. Time for the next plan the 'insider' knows nothing about. We will be victorious."

"THEY BROKE CAMP AND LEFT to the north, sir."

"Excellent. All of them?"

"Yes, sir."

"Have the cavalry unit retrieve the horses and pay the Egyptians. Make sure all twenty-five horses have the Ninth brand on them, and if any of the horses have been eaten, kill everyone and release their camels."

"Sir?"

"Repeat back to me what your instructions are, Corporal."

"Yes sir. Have the cavalry unit retrieve the horses and pay the Egyptians. Make sure all twenty-five horses have the Ninth brand on them, and if any of the horses have been eaten, kill everyone and release their camels."

"Correct. Dismissed."

The Corporal turns to leave. His face blushes.

"Corporal."

The Corporal spins around, "Yes sir."

"Those Egyptian gentlemen are friends of mine. Before you arrive with the cavalry to 'rescue' them, each horse will have been brushed and cleaned. They will shine for a parade ... even their hooves will glisten. Please say hello for me." He has helped the Corporal feel better about his mission and prepares to move his operations.

WHEN THE CORPORAL ARRIVES WITH the cavalry retraction team, he finds everything as he was told it would be. He pays the Egyptian leader and says hello as requested, at which point the Egyptian leader is very pleased and nods with enthusiasm at another camel team member behind him, who dashes to retrieve something large in a blanket. The bundle is presented to the corporal with some amount of impromptu ceremony.

The Corporal stands holding it, not exactly knowing what to do, so the Egyptian leader motions for him to unwrap it, which he does, only to discover he is holding a thighbone, which he instantly surmises is from a horse they have eaten. The room is silent.

The Corporal is staring at it confused, as he had personally counted the clean and shiny horses and they are all accounted for.

The Egyptian leader begins, "Horse." He pauses, then requests, "Please tell your leader, 'Thank you, sir.' We were very pleased today to eat his horse for him. He is exceedingly kind. Please thank him."

"How could you?" The stunned Corporal's tongue is tied as he stares back.

"We have eaten horse all day because we knew you would have to kill each one of us, so we now will die happy, with our bellies full. Thank you kindly. We are ready. Who would you like to kill first, or should I ask for volunteers?"

His team had lined up with hands held together submissively and provide solemn looks on their faces. The moment the word "volunteers" is said they all begin to jump up and down asking to be first.

"Me! I want to be first!"

"No, me, please pick me!"

"I deserve to die first; you were killed first last time!"

The Corporal is frozen, so the Egyptian leader walks up to him and says quietly, "You are the ranking soldier here so you must fulfill your responsibility and kill us all for eating your leader's horse. We ate every bit of it and deserve to die at your hand ... now ... or we will take down our brand-new tent and go home to our wives and children. I believe my wife is fixing young goat with red wine and couscous ... would you like to join us?"

The five cavalry troops, who have seen the same prank before, can hold it no longer and burst out laughing. The Egyptian leader grins while his team is hitting the ground laughing.

By the end of this long day, tender goat with red wine and couscous is the Corporal's favorite meal. The five-man cavalry team has already had it several times during their previous work with the Egyptians.

"Sir, the insurgents are camped south of the approach road in the trees. Our covert troops are positioned as planned."

"Good. They are not insurgents. They are only common thieves. They have gathered a formidable collection of manpower, yet they still lack the resources of war, which is why they are coming to 'visit.' They could not hold back lusting for the shiny armor we have been teasing them with. Gad loves shiny things. That is why he is a thief … at the moment … until he hefts his shiny broadsword. I will tell our Captains the spider is about to make a mistake."

Gad looks again at his heavy sword. He came upon it through a chance encounter. Fine craftsmanship and incredibly old. As he inspects it, he turns it slowly to see the fine edge he has placed on both sides of the blade and thinks, *How many Romans will you deliver to their grave tonight? It has been a long time for you, I know. We will move together as one. It is what we have been preparing for over a very long time.*

Someone approaches him from his right, stops, and nods yes, while someone from his left comes and makes the same signal. Gad is pleased and determines, *All is set. The spider will now make his move.*

Clutching his sword, Gad stands and takes confident steps into the clearing.

"The dark runner has already left. It may be the last run for both the horse and runner. If caught, they will both be killed, with no trace, by Herod's covert assassination unit," Reuben says. His face is drawn, his eyes are staring far away across the temple construction works to the southern hills covered with afternoon haze.

"Let us pray that he will get there before the 'Death Unit,'" Daniel says, trying to support Reuben's statement.

Daniel is a young apprentice. Reuben trusts him because he has an engineering mind with a valuable gift of establishing close relationships with almost everyone he meets. Not only does Reuben trust him, any person with an honest heart also trusts him. This combination allows Daniel to get more done in a given amount of time than almost anyone else.

"Well," Reuben adds, "She was warned to be ready to flee should Herod act. Her son Joshua is only about eighteen months old and is in mortal danger. Her baby girl, Veronica, is only four months old and should be in less danger, but you know how that group operates. They could take everyone, both male and female, regardless of what their orders are. You are not old enough to remember, Daniel, but it was very ugly."

Daniel has a great deal of compassion and feels for her. "Even if Mariah's husband Gad were still alive, he wouldn't be able to do anything...."

Reuben cuts him off, "My brother Gad should have not gone off on dangerous paths. I warned him for years! Now, my sister-in-law has been forced to move to Bethlehem to be where I can watch over them ... and now this happens!" he slowly exclaims, still looking south.

"The Dark Runner I sent will make it there in time ... if the soldiers did not send road-clearing scouts out before," Reuben states as he turns from the veranda and walks into the room. He sits heavily at his desk and picks up a small rock in the shape of a bridge and looks at it as if looking into the distant past.

Reuben sets the rock back down, stands up quickly, heads toward the door, and announces, "Let us go now. I do not want to be here when it happens."

MARIAH IS READY. SHE IS sitting at her table. Being alone had become common years ago, followed by permanence when Gad had not returned a few months ago. She thinks, *I have always feared having*

to flee, especially since Gad became the leader of his fanatical group. My bags are ready. The children are ready. I am ready. The feelings of my heart, however, are different this time. I do not have fear. I know. This time I may not survive. I probably will not survive. They will catch me and kill my baby boy in front of me. I will fight back with Gad's sword, the light one. They will need to take us both, but I will take as many of them before that as possible. Mariah reaches for her hot drink, picks it up slowly and takes a sip.

There is a quiet knock at the door. She carefully sets her drink down, glances over at her sleeping children, and thinks, *I love you more than my own life. All I want for you is love and peace. Veronica, you will be a treasure.* Mariah stands and calmly walks to the door with solemn elegance.

His eyes tell her all she needs to know. He is alone. He only breathes three words, "It is time."

Mariah nods she understands, whispers, "Wait here," turns, and walks purposefully back inside.

She returns with two bundles and as she is passing him says, "Hold her" as she hands the small bundle over. He carefully takes the bundle expecting to pass her back. Mariah briefly looks at her daughter in his arms, looks in his eyes, and instructs, "She will not survive what is going to happen. Take her straight to Reuben."

He is startled and stares back at her as she quickly walks away.

She turns back and says with hushed urgency, "Do it now!"

She disappears into the darkness in an instant.

THE DARK RUNNER KNOWS WHAT to do. He had smuggled children before, but those were during localized Roman incursions, which were violent events that destroyed entire populations, including livestock, crops, buildings, and water systems. He looks down at his new charge, Veronica, asleep in her blanket and turns to retrieve his horse.

Hebron Road is busy, but there are three sycamore groves and multiple buildings to provide cover, he plans as he unties his black stallion, checks the cinch, and mounts. His bundle is quiet and peaceful for the short trip.

The thirty-five minutes pass without incident. He silently maneuvers his horse through a narrow passageway, stops and dismounts. *I hope she doesn't get mad like she did last time,* he thinks as he carefully balances the bundle.

He silently ties the horse with one hand, turns, and walks a few steps to her door and knocks (his knock) carefully. There is quick movement inside.

"What are you doing here so late and what are you holding?" she asks.

He reaches out with the bundle and whispers, "Here, hold Veronica. I will be right back." He does not dare look at her face as he transfers his charge to his mother.

Veronica? she asks herself, *He better come back. Last time he passed me a smuggled baby, we almost got arrested. In this town, you do not show up in the market with a new baby ... people talk.*

He takes care of his horse and watches Hebron Road for an hour, then goes back in and tries to explain, "Mother, I cannot tell you why, but you will know in the morning. This baby needs to go to someone in Jerusalem, but it cannot be tonight, and it cannot be me who takes her there. Can you take care of her tonight?"

THE DARK RUNNER'S MOTHER, SUSANNE, had seen this before. She takes the baby bundle and looks at the angelic little face with wonder, *This child is wondrous to behold. Why is she here? Her swaddling looks new and is of fine weaving. Where is her mother? She must be feeling empty without her baby girl. I will need to leave early to locate ... whom? Where will I take this treasure? I hope they are loving. I hope they can*

give milk, although there are many nursemaids available. We both better get some sleep.

Susanne carefully lays Veronica down and positions herself so she can easily hear Veronica's breathing. She focuses on the rhythm of soft noises coming from the precious bundle.

Egypt

"So, when you shared with us the poem, *The Camel with No Name,* we decided you were talking about Miskah, the Future Bride's camel," young Anna says, standing in front of a large, colorful fabric being held up by other children. In their morning's preparation, they dressed Miskah with their favorite blankets, ribbons, scarves, and beads.

Anna continues, "We are going to have a celebration, and the Camel with No Name is ready." She gestures with her arm for the surprise to be unveiled.

"Oh, my goodness!" the Camel Herder says with joyous enthusiasm, "He is as handsome as the King of Babylon."

The Camel Herder is watching the children with delight as the Young Merchant approaches and asks, "Do their mothers know this is what their children had in mind when they 'escaped' with half their wardrobes?"

"Yeah," is the quiet response, indicating the question has not been heard.

"Well, lucky for you, Miskah is mostly clear of all the dust he has been snorting out since he came back from his solo adventure in the lonely desert. I am sure they miss playing with his glorious gobs of camel snot."

"Yeah."

"Your mother always liked me more than she liked you. Don't you agree?"

"Yeah."

He's useless today, thinks the Young Merchant as he turns to walk away.

"Where are you going? Don't you want to stay for the naming ceremony?"

"Hah! You knew I was here!"

"Of course. I was watching what my young friends are doing. They have planned a fine celebration. It is a wonderful way for them to say goodbye.

Do you know that we will probably never see any one of them again for the rest of our days? I want them to have good memories when they head east to Cairo tomorrow."

They watch together as Anna places several children to the east and instructs them to be the horn players. She then strides to the Camel Herder and announces, "We are ready to give our camel a new name so he will be happy, and your mom will let him stay at your house so he can have sweet cakes any time he wants. Are you ready? Let us do this ... now," Anna reaches out her right hand to escort the Camel Herder.

He jumps to his feet as he reaches for his small instrument. *Music is a must,* he thinks as Anna leads him to his appointed ceremonial position.

The Camel with No Name is pleased with his latest look ... and his 'new' name, Miskah. It is hard to tell if all the official ceremonial decorations make it back to their original owners.

As THE CARAVAN READIES FOR the next leg of the trip the following day, the Camel Herder is visited by several children, including Anna.

"We want to say goodbye and thank you for teaching us many lessons. The camel Miskah is very happy do not you think?" Anna asks.

"Thank you, Anna! You did an outstanding job yesterday. Miskah is very happy. You have permission to walk over and say hello if you wish," the Camel Herder replies with a grin.

"Yes, thank you!" Anna says as she smiles and runs over to the personal camels.

Though saddened to leave the caravan, the Camel Herder is looking forward to seeing his family.

SEVERAL HOURS INTO THE DAY'S trek, the Camel Herder's troop of camels leave the caravan and head to a small village near Alexandria. Revolk, Miskah and Bindi pick up the pace as they get within a few kilometers of their destination. As they get to the last mile, with still only desert sands visible, Revolk lifts his head and begins sniffing.

The Camel Herder can sense they are close as well and tells the Young Merchant that his grandfather will certainly tell him all about when he went to school with the patriarch Abraham. He points to Revolk sniffing, nods his head, sits back, and waits.

The silence is broken, and the horizon becomes filled with a band of camels, then horses, all charging over the sand dune toward them. The duo makes no efforts to evade the approaching storm of riders. It would not have been advisable.

FOR YEARS JOSHUA HAS INTRODUCED his long time Egyptian friend as "the Camel Herder" from a little remote village somewhere in Egypt. The truth is that the Camel Herder's remote village *is* his family, the entire village.

It turns out that this menacing band is not an attacking force of destruction, but rather the advance group of the family who are welcoming the youngest son home from his first longrange camel caravan expedition. His family is a leading international goods transportation enterprise with both land and sea operations throughout the Mediterranean.

Several of the lead horse riders split off the ambush brigade and ride over to place themselves in line with those approaching. They form a "V" with an opening big enough for one horse and rider to pass through. War horns sound and one of the well-dressed officers asks, "And what business do you have that allows you to trespass into our homelands and desecrate our pure sand with the ugly feet of your stinking camels?"

The Camel Herder is about to attempt an answer when he is challenged by another question. "Exactly where did you get the arrogance you carry around and flaunt peacock feathers, young one? What name do you carry and whose son are you?"

The Camel Herder takes his camel to the center, where he is only a spear's throw away from all those now posted in front of him. He sits up as straight and regal as anyone sitting on a sweaty camel can get and announces, "I am

Omari Shadek Zinhah, son of Micah Sharif Zinhah. I have six older brothers who are strong and beautiful in their newly cleaned outfits, but their horses are looking poorly maintained and in need of training."

There is a silence as a lone horseman slowly traverses the opening at the point of the V. He is a very old man but is clearly the powerful chief warrior in this mighty brigade. He raises his arm as if to call a deadly charge and exclaims, "Welcome home, Son! You left a boy and returned a man! Let us celebrate!"

At that point, the horns exclaim jubilee, and dozens of women and children in full party dress come streaming over the dunes and into the center, followed by the musicians, then those carrying celebration tents and cooking supplies. A remote village appears in minutes with over five hundred relatives and friends participating.

Omari's brothers dismount and take their turns embracing him and congratulating him on his rite of passage. The servants take the horses and camels in opposite directions to be cared for.

The Young Merchant enjoys the entire event and wonders how they knew of their approach and were able to be so prepared to celebrate their arrival. He is amazed and delighted.

The Camel Herder's mother, Naunet, comes and welcomes the Young Merchant, so he is not forgotten.

"You know," the Young Merchant tells the Camel Herder's mother, "I tell him on a regular basis that you have always liked me more than you liked him."

"Well, that is probably true more days than I could count. It may be needed after he is celebrated over the next ten days to come," she responds, passing a motherly smile back as they walk together toward the growing family crowd.

"You are going to have to get your fathers to carry me to my sleeping quarters. I have eaten enough for three days," the Young Merchant says to the Camel Herder's young nieces and nephews who always crowd around when he visits. "Let's all go out to look at the stars before you get sent to bed."

"How does he do that? I cannot get my children to settle down no matter how hard I try," the Camel Herder's sister asks Naunet as they look at the circle of twelve children lying on the ground, all with their heads toward the center. The Young Merchant has his arm up, pointing and explaining how the stars move in a great circle.

"You can go join them, and in five minutes, you will know the answer to your question," replies Naunet, smiling at her youngest daughter, who is watching her two little ones engage in the serious discussion, on the ground, while gazing up at the stars.

BINDI LOOKS UP AT THE Young Merchant and continues chewing. She knows where she is and is very content to relax and eat. One of the Camel Herder's brothers casually walks up and asks, "Are you going to join the races this morning? Last time you were here, Bindi did well and almost did not come in last!" He is grinning ear to ear, shaking his head in a positive, welcoming way.

"I appreciate the offer, but I think we'll be happy spectators this time around, thank you," the Young Merchant responds with a smile, adding, "You should ask my friend the Camel Herder to race his personal camel Miskah, who has not been ridden since I rode him once in Jerusalem. He is fresh, young, and energetic."

"He took two camels?"

"Yes, Revolk was the camel he rode each day and Miskah was along in case of a special need."

"In case of what? Revolk has not been ill."

"Didn't you know? I thought you put him up to it."

"Help me out here. Why did our little brother have two camels?"

The Young Merchant loves that he can instigate something and replies, "Your brother ... took an additional camel ... in case ... he found a future wife to bring home. Don't you think that is very kind of him to be so prepared?"

The Camel Herder's brother is stunned and stares back at the Young Merchant, who looks at Bindi to verify his story and says, "Tell him Bindi. Tell him what I said is true."

"Oh, this is good. You say he thought of this all by himself?" the brother asks in amazement, then adds, "I cannot wait to tell the others. We will have a great surprise. Tell you what I am going to do…. We will have your young Camel Herder friend race this 'Miskah' in the camel race later today. We will make sure he is ready. Thank you for this little bit of intelligence. It will be great fun."

THE FESTIVITIES BEGIN. WOMEN AND their daughters wear bright-colored clothing from head to toe. The camels with riders walk forward amid the cheers of family, employees, friends, and neighbors.

The race director walks in front of the tense line of camels, whose riders have mounted in final preparation for the race. He raises his hand and the crowd hushes, anticipating the start. He announces, "We are gathered here to see the great camel race, and today, in celebration of his successful return, we have a prestigious rider who will please dismount and present himself before the crowd to be recognized. Please come forward!"

The Young Merchant watches as the Camel Herder, Omari, dismounts, while a couple of his brothers help him with Revolk. Omari stands straight as he walks to the race director.

The Young Merchant thinks, *This is odd. They are taking Revolk away.* He watches carefully to see what is going to happen. *Oh … this will be good,* he says to himself as he sees other brothers bring Miskah forward, fully decorated as the camel of the bride. The crowd sees what is happening and stays quiet, holding in their enthusiastic support of the prank being set up. They lead fully-decorated Miskah forward and stop behind Omari as if no change has been made.

"For the next three days, we will celebrate the rise of Omari. We wish to welcome him home and express our love and appreciation for him," the race director says, looking at the crowd. He then raises his arms and exclaims, "Let us give him a cheer!"

As the crowd goes wild, the race director reaches out and takes the end of the reins from Omari's cousin, hands them to Omari, and turns to announce loudly, "Riders, are you ready?"

At the same time, Omari the Camel Herder takes the reins, turns, and sees that race-ready Revolk has been replaced by wedding-ready Miskah, in all his glorious colorful ribbons, capes, and beads. He throws up his hands and greets him, "Miskah!" The crown again cheers, accompanied by the musicians. Omari looks around and quickly vaults up … in time to hear, "Go! Go! Go!" The great camel race has begun.

Typical of village camel races, this race starts in the center of the family compound, travels east to the sand dunes, around the rock outcrop, and back to the starting point. Omari the Camel Herder manages at least to stay on Miskah, who had never been in or near a race in his lifetime. He is unsuccessful in trying to remove Omari several times during the trip. When they cross the finish line, not quite last in place, many of his ribbons and wedding adornments are dragging on the ground or scattered five meters behind him.

Omari is all grins on arrival. He hops off Miskah and to the great entertainment of the cheering crowd, gives Miskah a big hug around the neck and a kiss on the nose. Everyone is happy, especially his cousins, who surround him, grab him, and lift him up over their heads. The brother who had also heard the background story about Miskah yells, "Yes! We all know why you took Miskah to collect a wife! It is because your future wife will be as ugly as a camel, so it all makes sense! Well done, Omari!"

"YOU LOOKED BETTER ON MISKAH than you do in your crazy turban, my friend. You should consider riding him instead of Revolk. The girls you always entertain would like Miskah, and maybe, if you do not wear the turban, one of them will wish to ride on him … into the desert … with you … back here to get married with you … despite your shortcomings … you think?" Joshua calmly asks Omari who is looking the other direction.

Omari turns his head quickly, and with some amount of tension replies, "You put them up to it, didn't you?"

"I cannot take credit for your brothers' artistic expression … at your expense, but I did tell them about the extra camel you've been hauling around."

"And you should be happy I had Miskah, because otherwise, it would have been Veronica, Bindi, and myself who would have had our little visit to the Roman Training Grounds … without you."

"Ha! I have to admit that you have a point there … sad, but true."

"Yes, and do not forget how crucial I am to your continued success—your business success as well as your romantic success," Omari says with a smile, then adds, "I will keep Miskah and may let you ride him again should the need arise."

Shaking his head in the affirmative, Joshua responds, "I appreciate your kindness. What is on the agenda for tomorrow?"

Omari looks up into the cloudless sky to think. He takes longer than usual, then offers, "Tomorrow morning everyone will gather again, but it will be more formal than today's event. They will make the presentation tomorrow, and you will be amazed. I do not think you have seen it before, have you?"

"No, not the presentation. Not yet. Do I need to dress in special clothing?"

"No need. You are fine as an honored guest. They will dress me so that my handsomeness will reflect the sun's rays. They will do an excellent job. My brothers and cousins will be in full regalia as well. The women have been preparing for a long time for this. I am so glad Revolk saved me the night of the sandstorm."

JOSHUA ARRIVES EARLY TO THE outdoor event area and studies what is going on. *Even the children are being quiet, unlike when I saw them all up early to prepare the parade grounds. I was caught off guard when I noticed the teenage boys walking around with buckets of water, which were dripping*

steadily out the bottom. I am so glad I did not jump up and tell them they had holes in their buckets. The children had a grand time walking all over the wet-down area so dust would be avoided. Even Uncle Omari was out there with them, until his mother informed him that he "had to be prepared ... now!" It was a great piece of theater.

I have never seen so many people gathered in such silence. Even the livestock are unusually peaceful this morning, the Young Merchant reflects again as he takes his place to view the morning's event with Omari's extended family, friends, and community members.

The Young Merchant looks to his right and notices what seem to be visitors from far away and determines, *These fine-looking people must be the families' business associates, government officials, and trading partners.*

Over the next few minutes, runners can be seen checking on details and passing messages. The expected riders will stay out of sight until their moment arrives. The band, however, is sitting quietly to the side in anticipation of a grand beginning to happen any minute. Their leader steps up and gathers their attention.

Like a lightning bolt of sound, the music ignites the air as a dozen women arrive, twirling their colorful skirts in a rainbow of joy.

The spectacle is captivating with the crowd cheering with delight, every spectator wishing the dancing would last all day. It stops after several minutes as suddenly as it had started. The dancers disappear, and the band is silent. The spectators hush as unseen drums start a slow cadence. The beat is soft at first; then it grows louder, heightening everyone's anticipation of what will happen next.

The riders arrive from the far left side of the dignitary section of the assembly, a perfectly straight line of ebony-black horses with riders dressed in formal robes and splendid turbans. The horses move straight forward, then do a precision pivot to the right and proceed until they stop directly in front of the patriarch, Omari's great-grandfather.

They then double pivot, so they became a straight line facing him in honor, with four horses on his left, then a space, and four horses on his right side, forming a perfect line four meters in front of him. The drumbeat stops the instant the line of horses stops. There is not a sound as the silver trim on the rider's turbans sparkles in the morning light.

The entire assembly is watching the horses as if they know what will happen next. With no noise, except the sounds of eight motionless horses breathing, there comes from the far left side, a single, riderless horse, led by a small boy. As it slowly makes its way in front of the line of horses, it is apparent that the perfectly black horse had been carefully groomed with oil so that it reflects the early morning sun's rays. It is more beautiful than a dream.

The new horse snorts and shakes its head a bit, causing the young boy to look at it with a surprised face. From the right, two men arrive, walking as slowly as did the shiny black horse. One of the men is Omari's father, clothed in traditional robes. The other is Omari, dressed in the same way as his eight mounted brothers. As he predicted, he is as handsome as ever, with the sun reflecting off his shiny black hair as well as his uniform.

The two gentlemen continue walking, then turn to the left to face the presiding patriarch and present themselves. The anticipation is palpable. The horses' breath can now be seen in front of the line of black horses, whose riders have not moved an inch. Everything is in place for the advancement of the patriarch's great-grandson to a formal position of authority and responsibility in the family.

Omari do not faint, the Young Merchant pleads to himself as he watches in awe at the magnificent spectacle before him. It is simple but profoundly moving.

The patriarch stands. A moment later, Omari's great-grandmother is on his left, standing as regal as a queen, holding a magnificent turban with silver trim in her hands. The patriarch turns to her, nods, takes the turban with both hands, and in one fluid movement, places it on Omari's head and slowly nods at him. Omari takes one step back and bows in respect and gratitude, to which the patriarch raises both his arms up in the air to announce what has been done. The crowd bursts out in cheers.

The cheers last but a brief moment and stop the moment the patriarch reaches out one arm with outstretched hand and nods to the young boy who then leads the amazing black horse to Omari's side. Omari turns to look at the incredible steed, takes the reins, slowly bows once again to his great-grandfather, after which he seems to fly as he launches himself up on the horse, rides to the opening between the two sets of four horses, and takes his place of honor in the family.

Those watching again cheer with abandon as the horses turn to their right and proceed in unison out of the open area. The music then once again explodes, and the dancers, now including their young daughters and sons, come out with unrestrained fanfare. Within minutes everyone is up and dancing, the food carts are wheeled in, and the final celebration has begun. It does not end before midnight.

INSIDE THE LARGE GATHERING TENT, the International Transportation Consortium leaders have completed an early breakfast, held their annual meeting, and break into smaller groups to discuss specific projects and transactions.

The Young Merchant is invited to Omari's group. Prior to beginning their discussion about eastern Mediterranean ground transportation, a runner approaches Omari's cousin—his team captain—and whispers something into his ear. He looks impassive as he listens, then looks at Omari, nodding yes.

"The goods we brought have arrived in Alexandria and Cairo and have reached their customers. The materials we wished to buy will arrive this afternoon, along with new orders, so … we remain in business, my friends," Omari announces calmly, with his usual upbeat tone. He then looks back to the team leader, who begins discussions concerning the growing Roman needs for both textiles and hard goods. Plans to accommodate this new workload are confirmed as well as the new levels of needed security and risk mitigation. The meetings last until mid-afternoon.

THE MEDITERRANEAN'S WAVES ARE GENTLE as the Young Merchant and his "adopted" mother, Nautel, walk casually along the beach at sunrise.

"So, you have all your supplies, gear, and merchandise ready to load up and be on your way tomorrow?" Nautel asks.

"Yes, thank you for asking. Thank you also for allowing me to participate in your family celebrations this week. They were marvelous, and I almost felt like I was intruding. Thank you."

Nautel places her arm on his shoulder and gives him a motherly hug with the admonition, "You are already a member of our family. It would not be right for you to miss such an important event. We are so happy you could spend this time with us."

"You are too kind. My heart is touched to hear you say that. I always look forward to coming, and I always hate to leave. Seeing Omari receive his turban and horse was amazing. Everyone seemed happier than he could possibly have been at that moment."

"Yes, I agree. You know, he has received a great amount of responsibility with that turban. He will increase both his capacity as well as his territory. I need you to keep an eye on him for me, will you?" Nautel says as she looks over with a question in her eyes.

"Yes, of course. You know I will. Sometimes he gets enthusiastic, so I temper that with blatant disregard, or, if needed, direct skepticism, unless sarcasm or powerful cynicism is the best tool of the moment," he replies looking at Nautel with a sly grin.

She laughs and observes with her version of a sly smile, "You two were made for each other … a fearsome duo who both at the same time know all there is to know about any topic and who have no clue about anything on any topic. I am sure your adversaries are conquered with instant confusion and quickly retreat in search of sanity."

"Yes, something like that," is his response as he picks up a small stone and tosses it into the water.

"Omari told me the highly entertaining story about your new flame, the woman you have some feelings for in Jerusalem."

"Yes, well, she is confusing."

Nautel stops to absorb that comment, motions that they should start back, and as she begins walking, says, "Tell me about her. She sounds amazing."

The Young Merchant spends most of the return walk explaining the various how, what, when, and where pieces of his relationship but cannot at all even begin to explore the why.

"I understand," Nautel mentions, looking down at the sand. "Do not be hasty in this or any other relationship and know that all will work out for the best. You will end up happier than you could ever imagine if you take that approach. You can oversee and control your emotions, even if you think she is confusing."

"Thank you. I will be as calm and peaceful as a dove in twilight."

"Do not relax too much while you are up there, or you will fall on the ground my young son. You should, however, make haste in your return to Jerusalem. I have the feeling she misses you."

"She misses me?" the Young Merchant thinks aloud.

"Yes," Nautel affirms as they arrive at the steps which bring them up to the village. They are greeted by many children's voices calling, "Ninnaa! Ninnaa!"

The Young Merchant turns his head and says with a smile, "It looks like your responsibilities have increased exponentially as well, Nautel.

"Yes, but with twenty grandchildren, my capacity has not increased," she responds with a grin. She bends over with outstretched arms to greet her energetic throng.

I disagree. This woman's capacity to love and nurture has increased in orders of magnitude, the grateful Young Merchant thinks as he observes the love manifesting right there in front of him.

THE RABBI FROM GALILEE

If I make the decision, I will need to go out the front door and walk through the area where people know me, Veronica thinks as she reasons through the plan she had yet to commit to. She reflects on the harsh treatment she receives every time she heads out through her front door.... *"Get out of here!" "Get thee hence!" "Hide your uncleanliness!" "Go back in your hole!" "Unclean!*

As the wave of memories of being attacked sweeps over her, Veronica reasons once again, for the thousandth time, *It is not my fault. You should pray for me and not despise me. I will not hurt you. Please ... leave ... me ... alone.* She feels something pulling her down into despair again and is not sure how to stop the slide.

Focus. Be aware of your surroundings. Sit up straight. Hold the reins loosely. Know where your knees are and keep your toes up. Veronica holds tight to the process of overcoming fear in a heated battle.

The seething hate and the familiar dust they have kicked in her direction for more than twelve years is the badge of disgrace she wears each time she musters courage to walk out the front door; but today is different.... It has to be done.... She makes up her mind.... This time she will find Him.

Veronica notices Ognir's ears move up; he sniffs under the door without moving his head and receives confirmation. He raises his head, turns to his left, and looks at Veronica. "It is Sophie. She is here," is his message.

Veronica realizes, *The decision is made. Ognir is always correct.*

"It is so cold outside. Are you feeling well enough to be out in this?" Sophie asks once inside and settled.

"Yes. It is my personal responsibility and my mission to approach Him and beg for a new life."

"I understand," Sophie says, following up with something she hopes will lighten the mood a little, "You used the words responsibility and mission. You realize that you will not be riding Mr. Squishy Lips through the frozen streets of Jerusalem this morning, right?"

Veronica laughs, "Yes. He is probably taking the day off anyway ... camels need rest. They have a lot of chewing to do."

Sophie responds, "Yes, I am so glad we don't have to chew everything twice like camels."

"I have thought about that. You know, if you really like, perhaps anise cakes, you could eat them twice each time ... maybe not," Veronica says as she makes a frown and then asks, "So, what news do you hear?"

"I understand that they will be coming from the northwest side and will probably head toward the temple as they did last time they were here," Sophie reports. She does not add that things could change at any moment.

"How will we know when?" Veronica asks.

"Dinah hired a runner. They are terribly busy when the Rabbi visits. More so each time. The runner will let us know as soon as he passes the gate."

"So, it will take a while to get there. We need to be ready and not waste any time," Veronica urges as she is planning the route in her mind. She does this even though she has no clue which way the Rabbi will go. It is a camel-master habit to keep one's mind busy on practical things and not think about the impending destruction of battle.

Sophie asks, "Have you already eaten? Do you have some food to eat on the way?"

"Of course. Yes, on both counts." Veronica turns to place her shawl and cloak on. Ognir stands up, looking at her.

"Do not get in a hurry. You will overheat in here and will catch a chill when you go out. It may start to snow," Sophie warns.

"Yes, I will set it all here, so it is ready." Veronica takes off both items, places them on the table, and pats them with her hand. She sits down, takes a deep breath, holds it, and then lets it out slowly. She becomes still as she focuses on something that is elsewhere and asks, "Sophie, do you think I am ridiculous? Do you believe I will be healed?"

Sophie looks up and replies instantly, "What do you think? What do you believe inside your heart? That will be your answer my dear friend, Veronica."

Veronica does not have time to consider a response as there is a knock at the door, quick and professional. Veronica tells Ognir to sit with a hand signal as she stands, composes herself, moves to the door, and opens it. She is standing straight up as if on the battlefield. "Yes?"

The messenger is direct, "He has arrived and is coming. None of us know where he is headed. We have runners everywhere. Do you want me to return with more news?"

"No thank you. Well done. Thank you again," is Veronica's response.

The runner leaves quickly for his next assignment as Veronica calmly closes the door, walks peacefully to the table, places her shawl over her head, and ties it in the front. She slides her heavy cloak on, approaches the door with purpose, and signals Ognir that it is time to leave.

"Sophie, thank you for accompanying me today. You brought strength to me," Veronica says as she stops next to Sophie, seeking affirmation and courage from her best friend.

The three of them walk out the door into a light snowfall. Sophie feels for the three sweet biscuits she has placed in her pocket in case with one hand as she closes the door with the other. Ognir sniffs the newly fallen snow to make sure it is safe and is right next to Veronica as she carefully but confidently moves along. Veronica's head is held high with dignity and poise.

As Sophie catches up to Veronica and Ognir, Sophie thinks, *I am sure glad it is snowing. That will keep most everyone inside except the children.*

Veronica is thinking the same thing.

THE WAY TO CROSS THE path of the Rabbi from Nazareth continues quietly.

Veronica reaches for her shawl and pulls it closer to her neck. *Luckily, it is calm and there is no wind,* she thinks as she looks down at Ognir, who is sniffing the snow as they get to the first turn to the right.

"How are you feeling?" asks Sophie.

"I am feeling stronger than I expected but more apprehensive than I had planned."

"Well, you prayed about it and received an answer. Right?"

"Oh yes … to both points. I am having worries that we will miss Him, and I am worried about asking Him to heal me."

"Why worry about that? You have been given the assignment to seek this blessing, correct Master Camel Rider?"

"Yes. Where are we?" Veronica asks in an anxious voice.

"We turn right then left."

They squeak along carefully in the quarter inch of snow, seeing very few people, but those they do see are rushing silently this way and that. They make the planned left turn and are surprised to see the three gentlemen Jacob, Elias, and Gabriel sitting on a bench right in front of them. Ognir recognizes them and looks up at Veronica to ask permission to say hello to his friends.

"Ognir, stop. Done." says Veronica softly.

Ognir steps up to receive a pet from each of the gentlemen and quickly returns to Veronica's side.

"He can be found in this direction," Jacob says, pointing to the left.

Gabriel points the same way. Elias looks at them, sees where they were pointing, looks at Veronica and Sophie, points the opposite direction, and gives a great big grin, asking, "Why are we pointing?"

"Elias, we are telling these ladies where the guy from Nazareth is, the one who did such a good job clearing the temple of thieves a while back … all by himself."

"Well, I hope he does it again and this time calls down fire from heaven, like Moses did to kill all the frogs," says Elias.

Gabriel leans over and corrects Elias saying, "Elijah called down the fire, Moses parted the waters."

"Thank you kindly, we will be moving along," Veronica says, looking in the direction they had pointed; well that at least two of them had pointed.

I should have asked them how they were doing. How could I walk away like that? Veronica tells herself after she takes a few steps.

"Sophie?" Veronica says as she quickly turns around, afraid she has lost her. Her mind is elsewhere, and her body is weakening with the intense physical effort and emotional strain.

"I am right here Veronica. Do not you worry. I am not leaving you. Do you need to eat something?"

Veronica offers a quick response, "Oh goodness. Yes, you are there. I am so thankful. No, I do not need to eat. Let us hurry."

Sophie steps closer to Veronica and holds her hand out, "Let me hold your hand. You will have Ognir on your right and me on your left. We will keep track of you for sure."

"Good idea Sophie. You are very smart, like your kind mother." She squeezes Sophie's hand, and Sophie returns the warm squeeze.

Veronica is surprised by what this gesture means to her, thinking, *I do not remember ever holding someone's hand before. Sophie's hand is warm. At the moment, I never want to let go. My legs are feeling cold. I am losing control. I need to focus, be aware of my surroundings. Focus. Remember and execute my mission.*

The two pilgrims continue their search, each feeling they are about to encounter the one who once called himself "I Am," the highest name, even God. They enter a small square with multiple passageways leading in all directions. The only people in the square are a young boy playing with perhaps his old grandfather.

Oh no! We are lost! We should have passed them by now, Veronica tells herself as she squeezes Sophie's hand and stops.

"What's wrong Veronica?" Sophie asks as Veronica turns to look at her, and Sophie has a rush of thoughts descend on her consciousness, *Oh, she is petrified. She cannot move. This cannot happen. I have to do something. We cannot give up. I have no clue where to go!*

Sophie's greatest fear is to not be successful in making sure Veronica is successful in her quest, the greatest quest of her life. She turns to look at the passageways with no path looking correct. Fear begins to rise from deep within her soul. She adjusts her grip on Veronica's hand to assure her that she is still there.

"How may I assist you miss?" a kind voice asks.

Sophie looks to her left and sees the older man standing calmly with a warm smile and clear blue eyes. The little boy is next to him looking up with an innocent, angelic face.

Instead of being surprised, Sophie feels as if she knows the man and is instantly at peace.

"Dear sir, my friend and I," she glances at Veronica, who is still in a frightening place, "are seeking ..."

The man interjects, "Yes, I understand. You are there." He looks at Veronica, reaches out past Sophie, and places his hand on Veronica's arm, looking into her eyes saying, "Everything is going to be fine. It will all work out. You will find what you are seeking by going through there. May God bless you both, as well as your loyal companion." He looks at the correct passageway, nods, and waves his hand as if to say, "Move along now, my children."

Sophie looks at Veronica's eyes, which have gained some clarity, so she moves her head as if to say, "Are you ready?" Veronica nods, "Yes" and begins moving to the way pointed out by the kind old man. Sophie follows quickly, but as she is entering the passageway she realizes, *I did not say thank you!* She quickly turns around to offer her heartfelt gratitude and gazes into the square where the snow is softly drifting down.

Sophie is startled, *They are not there! They are gone. How could they be gone?* She looks at the ground covered with snow. *I clearly see our tracks in the snow, but not their tracks. They left no tracks.*

Veronica squeezes her hand; Sophie turns to continue with her as she squeezes back. *How could this be?* She focuses on getting Veronica through the final passageway as they begin to hear the cries of a crowd.

"I HEAR PEOPLE," VERONICA SAYS with a fearful tone. "Too many people. They will hate me. They will send me away." She pulls her hand out of Sophie's, brings it up to meet her right hand grasping her shawl at her neck. She stops, staring ahead with fear. Ognir is in heightened alert mode, sensing Veronica's fear as well as hearing the voices of a crowd.

"Veronica," Sophie says in a soft, motherly tone.

Veronica responds, "Yes, I am here. I am sorry I let go of your hand, Sophie."

She knows my name, so we are good. She has avoided being around anyone beyond our small circle of friends for more than ten years. We can work through this, but I need to act now, Sophie reasons.

"Veronica, do you remember when the kind man said, 'Everything will work out'?"

"Yes. He was truly kind. I never said thank you to him. I am heartless and do not deserve a blessing. Too many people ..."

Sophie interjects, "Do you remember your training on how to focus when in battle?"

"Yes, focus ... follow effective, trained steps of action."

"Yes, action. Do you remember when you learned and prayed about the man they call Jesus?"

"Yes, it was a wonderful light coming into my dark soul. I remember."

"You showed faith, right?"

"Yes, faith."

"So, faith is an action word, correct? Something you do not only keep on a shelf. You do something with it, right?"

"Yes ... action," Veronica responds with more certainty.

"So, let us act and move forward and focus. Can you do that Veronica, take action?"

"Yes ... let's go."

Sophie reaches up, takes Veronica's left hand, looks at Ognir, and says to him, "Let's go Ognir, Veronica has something important to do." Ognir prods Veronica's right knee and starts walking.

The battle line is ahead. Sit up straight, hold the reins loosely in left hand. Keep your right hand ready to reach for your spear. Keep both knees evenly against Mr. Squishy Lips's sides and move into the fray. Veronica's tactical maneuver training is a needed crutch as they come upon, and fully into, the scene.

The crush of the crowd sweeps by. The noise is overwhelming Veronica's senses, Ognir becomes instantly on high alert as he holds himself against Veronica, who releases her hold, looks at Sophie, and says with courage and determination, "Sophie, this is it. I need to go now. Ognir, stay." She turns her head in the direction the crowd is moving and launches forward.

Sophie's heart feels simultaneously joyful and worried, as if watching her child take the path into the unprotected world for the first time. Her heart shouts, *Go forth with faith, daughter of God!*

Focus and be steady, Veronica reviews as she tries to look above the crowd for Him.

I need to get in front of him and plead my case, Veronica says to herself and is determined as she manages to pass two fellow seekers.

I am not going fast enough. Who am I to get in front of others who have similar desires? I am trained and am on a mission.... Focus and keep moving forward, Veronica's mind is racing as she makes more progress.

I am getting closer. Those three people there are looking at one person. It must be Him. Push through that hole! Now! Veronica makes it almost in front of Him, when her world comes crashing down.

She slips on ice and as she is falling, her view becomes exquisitely sharp. She sees in slow motion something which is so familiar that she knows it in great detail. Each thread and stitch of the tunic she had created months ago; it is here right in front of her, and she knows who is wearing it. The special tunic, the colored embroidery. She reaches out in hopes of touching it before it vanishes. *That's all I need do,* she realizes.

The hand keeps at ready on the right side while the left hand that holds the reins is extended as trained, and, while the world rushes onward, that trained hand achieves its goal and touches the tunic. Time stops. *I know what my fingers are feeling has been held before. I remember the softness of the gift I was given. I took care to create it with love....* Veronica hits the ground. *I have failed. The feeling I had when I touched his ...*

"Who touched me?" The question pierces Veronica's heart.

Oh God, I've done something wrong, Veronica pleads as she tries to disappear. She looks up and sees Him right in front of her, looking down as if she were the only person present. There is no sound.

Veronica's soul reacts to what happened, *His face is kind; His eyes see right through me. I have to explain what I did and why. No one else knows what I have been through and why I need His blessing. My body, it is glowing. It feels different; it feels whole ... what happened to me? Am I passing out? Focus. He is still there right in front of me. I feel His endless and eternal love. Am I going to die? Is this what it is?*

Veronica feels alone with Him and tries to explain, "I am so very sorry. I only wanted to speak with you but could not reach my goal and failed. I am so deeply sorry. I have been trying to get well so I could return to the temple and instruct the children whom I had to abandon when they would not let me back. The doctors tried to help me, but it only became worse. You would not believe the pain they caused, but it did not work, so they tried again, and again, and again, and I am so afraid I abandoned my children, my students at the temple, and I told Flavius I would come back but did not go back. I am utterly ashamed. It never stops; my failures never stop, and the kind man who helped today, I never said thank you...." Veronica stops to take a breath, looking like a little child into eyes of a man, the man she knows understood every word and felt every pain she had thrown at Him. His peaceful face melts all fear, all pain and all self doubt.

Her soul reacts with eternal peace, *He is so peaceful. He looks at me in a way that I have never experienced before. I love this man. He has made me whole again. I never want this moment to end.*

"My daughter, thy faith hath made thee whole."

Staring back into His eyes Veronica feels a thousand emotions, *The world has stopped. I feel clean. I feel new. Please do not go. His eyes are telling me He must go to complete His mission, which he will do with unwavering focus and excellence. I understand you must go. Thank you for what you have done for me. Thank you.*

He slowly stands, smiles, pets Ognir on the head, and is gone.

Veronica reviews what she has learned, *His smile. His smile is eternal and everlasting. He showed appreciation to me. He told me he loved me for every good thing I have ever done. He never mentioned all the poor decisions I have made and how I have abandoned so many people. He knows my faith, not my fear. How could He know? Of course, He knows. I have to tell the Young Merchant who it is that is wearing his gift. I have to thank Sophie. Where is she? Where is Sophie?*

"Veronica, I am right here. I saw everything and everything you said about him is true. I felt it ... everywhere. You were marvelous. I am so happy for you. We need to take you home so you can rest. Can you get up? Never mind, here, eat this. Relax a bit. Here Ognir, I have something for you as well." It has stopped snowing, and the sun is now hitting the buildings around them.

As is customary, news of Veronica's healing by the Rabbi from Nazareth is spread by those who believe, as well as those who have become professional observers and critics. Sophie and Ognir escort Veronica home, where she rests.

"How long has she been asleep?" Lidia asks.

"She took a drink and had a small meal when we returned yesterday. She said that although she felt better, she was tired, and then she lay down and has been sleeping like a baby ever since," Sophie replies.

"Has she had that smile on her face the whole time?" Lidia inquires.

"Yes, isn't it cute?"

"You used to sleep like that, Sophie, and you were cute as well … until you turned twelve and decided you were sophisticated."

Lidia giggles as she kneels down to brush Veronica's hair off her face. "This one has been through many trials for so long; she deserves a nice long rest. I can see the color coming back into her face. She is so beautiful." Lidia's eyes tear up as she looks back up at Sophie.

"Now Sophie, you get home before it gets dark. You have been such a kind senior assistant. You need some rest as well. We will see you tomorrow," Lidia directs.

Sophie bends down and gives Lidia a kiss on the cheek. "OK, I will be off then. You two do not go out and celebrate without me, hear?"

"Yes, we promise. Thank you, sweetheart."

Sophie is ready to leave. She stoops over and touches Ognir, who has not left Veronica's side, and says, "All things are well, my friend. Stay poised for action." She snickers, waves bye to Lidia, opens the door, and goes out.

DINAH AND LIDIA ARE CHATTING when Ognir meets Sophie at the door. He leads her to Veronica's side and looks back to Sophie as if to say, "Here she is, still sleeping with her smile."

Sophie looks over at her mother and grandmother and asks, "Has she woken at all?"

"No dear, she keeps sleeping, but look, her hands have a normal color, and they are warm again. She is regaining her strength. She breathes very well also. She could wake up any time now," Dinah offers.

"I trust you. I worry she will never wake up," Sophie offers back.

"If she does not wake up by tomorrow afternoon, we will coax her out of it. How does that sound?" Dinah proposes.

"Yes. That is a good plan. If she ever frowns tonight, I will 'coax her out of it.' I do not care what Ognir has to say about that," Sophie says as Ognir replies with a twitch of his ears in her direction.

After a while, Dinah and Lidia leave, with Sophie and Ognir having responsibility for Veronica's strengthening.

"I am so worried you won't wake up, Veronica," Sophie quietly says to her charge. "I am so thankful for your kindness to me when I was perhaps too difficult to teach. I am so happy you acted with your pure faith and were healed. I saw the embroidery on the hem, I recognized it, and I thought it was so beautiful when you crafted it. I watched you ask God what He wanted you to do with the gift the Young Merchant gave you. None of us could have dreamed who would be wearing it when you needed it most...." Sophie's one-way conversation continues on through the night.

Without Sophie realizing any passage of time, Ognir is up and at the door greeting Dinah and Lidia. "Good morning, Sophie. It does not look like you have moved an inch since we left you last night," Lidia observes with a friendly greeting.

"What? You are here so soon? Wow, how quickly time can move. Good morning!"

"How is sweet Veronica doing?"

"I am doing fine. Please ask Sophie to relax. She has been talking non-stop since it got light," Veronica says kindly, then offers a warm smile as she raises her arms and stretches from head to toe.

"You are awake!" Sophie cries, "Oh! How are you feeling?"

"I am feeling better. I have no pain at all. I feel refreshed. I feel pure and clean," Veronica says as she raises her hand. "I learned and experienced many valuable lessons last night. I had dreams which were amazing. I went places and beheld marvelous things. I cannot wait to tell you all about it. What a great sleep I had last night. I would say the best rest I've had in ten years!"

"Who's going to tell her?" Sophie looks around and asks.

Lidia steps forward and shares, "Veronica, you have been sleeping for three days. This is the morning of the third day. We are so happy you have rested peacefully. Welcome back!"

"Three days? Really? Three ... days. I learned something about three days," Veronica responds while looking in the air. "I am so hungry I could eat a camel, er, well, not a camel. I am saying I could eat a lot. How are you all doing? I am so sorry for keeping you here for three days. I will make it up to you, I promise. Dinah, I have some great ideas about the projects we have for after Passover. I am sure you will adore them as soon as I confer with my senior assistant," Veronica says as she looks at Sophie and winks with a smile.

The Jewish Leader
and the Roman Commander

R EUBEN ARISES EARLY TO ENSURE that all is ready for Felix, the Roman
Commander, when he visits. Reuben is apprehensive that this year's
Passover will be more troublesome than usual. His staff has done well, and
everything seems to be in proper order. Felix is demanding. "While many
avoid contact with him," Reuben has said, "Felix is a difficult customer;
regardless, I appreciate that he is consistent in his mannerisms."

"DO YOU DOUBT OUR ABILITY to maintain control of your many
rabble-rousers?" Felix asks, then, to put Reuben in his place, he states, "You
know, it seems your 'peace-loving' society reproduces troublemakers in the
dark of night who are released into the public square on a regular … and
frequent basis. Hmmm?"

"No. No doubts at all. We know your troops are well trained and well
disciplined," Reuben replies, trying to soften the meeting's tone.

"Yes. It is your people who are not disciplined at all. We will, as usual,
keep the peace during your immensely popular celebration. We will even
try to stop the fairer part of your population from being sold, by your own
people, to those foreign visitors 'collecting specimens of delight' … like
they do every year."

Reuben waits a moment and decides to talk details, "And then, we have
more specific visitor-control arrangements to be talked about. There is one
individual who is apt to cause riots, possible insurrections, and the like.

We will handle getting him arrested under Jewish law. Then, you will need to get involved."

"You want us to get involved? That only means one thing you know, Reuben."

"It will not be complicated. Our lawyers have reviewed his crimes and have made determinations," Reuben begins as he explains the Jewish Sanhedrin's desire to stop the Rabbi from Nazareth from gaining unstoppable power and causing major disruption in their religious and political systems. "He must be stopped." Reuben declares, then continues on for another while as they eat.

"That is a large sum of money," Felix says as he adjusts himself in the lounge chair, reaches over to select another date, turns his head toward Reuben, and asks with skepticism, "So, how are you going to pull off this complicated little entrapment?"

"It will all come together. We know his plans."

"Ah, yes, you need to have an insider. It needs to be away from the city," Felix observes, still not convinced such a plan will be successful without military engagement; something the Romans will not do to stifle insignificant, internal Jewish problems. He does not look at Reuben to see his reaction. He does not care. He wants to see the northern wall and verify if the Roman temple project is being cared for properly.

"The trial and sentencing will happen. I declare to you as a servant of the Almighty."

"Zeus?" Felix asks with a smirk. Still not looking.

"No, Adonai, Elah," Reuben corrects, looking at Felix with a calm, yet commanding tone.

They feast until midmorning while Reuben's guard readies the horses for the inspection tour.

Felix takes his cloth napkin, wipes his face, and stands. The servant attending to his needs steps forward with an ornate bowl of water and a woven Egyptian cotton towel. Felix dips his hands in the water, dries them, drapes the towel over the servant's arm, and begins to walk to the door saying, "Let us go to the north and see what you have to show. Let us see what your 'highly trained' Israeli engineers have crafted with their ancient tools." He grins to himself and keeps walking.

Reuben is also standing and nods at the messenger, who knows to bring the horses around the front ... the Roman Commander's horse first. They mount and are escorted by three camel-mounted Roman soldiers up to view the northern wall stonework.

I KNOW THIS RIDER, OR *I know of her. She was honored by the Ninth several years ago. She looks older, more mature than I would have thought,* Felix thinks as he recognizes a Roman battle camel in the distance. The other part of his brain corrects himself, *Yes, you idiot. It has been probably more than ten years. If you think she is getting older, you should be aware that you have gray hair, not to mention the strained focus it takes you to get into the saddle these days.* He pauses for a moment, then continues his inner dialogue, *I hate when that happens. I must be getting old. How long before I can retire? You should have retired years ago.* He continues to argue with himself as they approach the Senior Project Manager and the Senior Trainer Attaché.

Reuben begins the introductions, "Felix, let me have the honor of introducing you to ..."

"Introductions? I know these two. Perhaps by reputation only, yet I know they are esteemed by those who count on them to accomplish excellence in all they do," Felix says. He then sits up straight as if in front of his battalion. "If I am not mistaken," he moves his horse two steps forward, "We have the pleasure to meet Senior Project Manager Daniel and Senior Trainer Attaché Veronica. Is that not correct?"

Both Daniel and Veronica, who are by then sitting especially straight, smile and bow their heads in acknowledgement while saying, "Yes sir. Nice to meet you sir," in unison.

Reuben is less than pleased as he says to himself, *This contemptuous, smoothed-tongued hypocrite. I wish the Rabbi would have raised the battle cry months ago. Why did he choose to not fight? He should have called fire down and destroyed the invader Romans. He will now be taken, tried, and crucified in front of his followers … like …* His thoughts are interrupted.

Felix bows his head in response, "On behalf of the citizens of Rome, I personally thank you both for the marvelous amount of good works you have accomplished. Your names are known and spoken of with praise both here as well as in Rome." He quickly turns his head to look out over the northern wall construction activity and shifts his horse's attention to the northwest. "Tell me what we are looking at Daniel, thank you."

That's my cue, Daniel says to himself as he steps his horse forward to be next to the Roman Commander as he thinks, *I do not like this man, but he is the one who agreed to allow the project to be financed and to move forward, prioritized equally with the temple restoration, yet behind the construction of the temple for the Romans. He must be respected, regardless.*

Reuben had moved his horse to the left side of Felix and lets Daniel take the lead by staying silent yet smiling a politician's smile all the while they are conversing.

Veronica stays where she is, not wanting to distract their serious conversation. Her mind wanders to places she has never allowed it to travel, *Exactly who is this man, the Jewish leader called Reuben? Why does he seem familiar, yet such a stranger?* Veronica's thoughts are distracted by Daniel standing up in his stirrups and pointing to the northernmost point of construction.

She is also distracted by the three mounted guards stationed four paces behind the Roman commander. They are conversing, and she glances over to her left at them. They notice her move, stop talking, and sit straight again.

I know these soldiers. They were my trainees in the last session prior to my falling ill. They look older, but there is no mistake. I am going to have some fun with them. Their commander likes me, so I can get away with it, Veronica thinks while trying not to smile.

She looks over to where Daniel, the tour guide, is talking, and from his countenance, knows he will be a while. She then does something these soldiers have never seen a camel do before. She recalls the precise routine, *Left leg away from side, right foot turned toward side, touch side with toe.*

The camel stays looking straight ahead and steps slowly sideways to the left, nothing moving except the long, large-kneed legs.

Left knee bent, push rear to the right with foot while right foot is brought forward, pressing the neck to the left, sit slightly forward. The camel turns around from standing next to the three camels to standing exactly in front of the center camel, nose to nose, only two feet away.

Veronica, the Senior Trainer Attaché, looks at them individually and all together as only an experienced military officer can, and quietly says, "Hello mounted troops of the Ninth. It is exceptionally good to see each of you has continued with favorable duties since last I saw you. Well done."

Although they hold their heads perfectly straight, their eyes look at the others as if to say, "See? I told you so. It is her!"

The center soldier responds quietly yet formally, "Yes, ma'am. Thank you, ma'am. It is an honor to say hello, ma'am. We continue to serve with excellence as we were taught, ma'am. Thank you."

"Very well, mounted troops of The Ninth. Continue serving well. I am sure we will see each other again ... soon," Veronica charges them. She then does something even more surprising—*bring nose harness back, lean slightly back.*

The camel steps directly backwards two steps and stops. The mounted troop's eyes become wide. They look at the camel then directly at Veronica. She allows a smirk to display on her face, winks at them, moves her camel forward and to the left, turns around, and stops exactly where she had started.

The three mounted troops of the Ninth are impressed once more. The respect they had previously gained for their trainer remains and has now increased. They all think, *She did all those impossible moves without moving her hands at all.*

Veronica's mind debates with itself, *Stop showing off. I wasn't showing off. Yes, you were. No, actually ... I already know what you are going to say. "Showing men how it is supposed to be done, with elegance and style" ... is showing off.*

Perhaps, but I was so thrilled to see them, I couldn't stop myself. You are lucky your camel is Mrs. Smooshy-lips....

That would be Mister Squishy Lips if you please.

Whatever. You are lucky he trusts you. That is all I have to say, Veronica thinks, and then her mind adds, *You need to stop arguing with yourself. One day you will lose the argument ... or get stuck there.*

Veronica looks over the countryside and the construction activities and is delighted she has finally arrived there to visit as she thinks, *I wish I could go down to the actual wall. The plans showed a remarkably engineered method of connecting the corners, rendering the stability of the wall very strong.*

The tour party completes this visit and is soon at the Roman temple, where the Roman commander dismounts to look at every part of the project. He invites everyone to join him.

As she takes in the majesty of the building Veronica recalls, *Roman architecture is magnificent, even when done in what they would call "small-scale" projects.* She does not remember seeing the design plans at Daniel's office studio and asks, "Who is doing the design for this project?" looking at Daniel.

"The Roman Engineering Team designed the site layout with the labor being provided by us," Daniel responds.

Reuben adds, "We are financing this project as a tribute to our Roman guests."

Felix adds "Yes, guests, who own the keys to the doors," as he bends over to look at the exquisitely installed mosaic tiles on the floor.

Veronica ignores the political jousting and asks, "And the columns? And the layout? Who is involved and where did they go to school? It is all so remarkably beautiful...."

Reuben shoots her a disapproving glance which she sees out of the corner of her eye which causes Veronica to add a tempering phrase, "... from an architectural standpoint of course. Look at the symmetry." Veronica feels she should probably manage her enthusiasm for asking questions.

Felix is the one who responds in a more relaxed manner than how he had responded to Reuben, "The Roman engineers are taught in Rome and use the classical Greek structural basics, site preparation, foundation footings, base alignment, and primary roofing fundamentals. They then add refined and perfected details in between, as well as meticulously crafted statuary, representing the finest gods available on the market today."

No one knows exactly how to respond to the last comment until Felix, himself, begins to chuckle.

Veronica keeps thinking without asking a question or opening her mouth, *He is joking about the myriad of gods the Romans worship as if they were exactly what they are, sculptures of stone, regardless of what their literature claims. His sense of humor comes out when he is not having to be cumbered with military and political pressures ... something nice to see. Maybe he will ask to learn to ride Mister Squishy Lips someday ... maybe not. I need to get Squishy Lips back to his stable before it gets too late.*

"Fine work. Substantial progress is being made," Felix compliments.

"Our craftsmen are paying particular attention to the details, so it meets your expectations," Reuben replies and joins next to Felix as they walk back to their horses.

Felix retorts as he places his arm on Reuben's shoulder, "Yes, you are right, our inspectors are doing a fine job keeping your craftsmen from trashing whatever they touch." He turns his head to Reuben, shakes his shoulder and starts laughing. He adds, "Yes, everyone is doing a superb job. It looks particularly good. Please offer my gratitude to your entire team, especially Daniel. Without him, nothing would ever be completed. Keep him close, Reuben. Let us head back. Thank you again. This was a good tour." He looks at Daniel and smiles again while nodding his head in appreciation.

Passover Preparations

"**W**ELL, SOPHIE, HOW ARE YOU doing with all your projects? Time is moving swiftly if you have not noticed," Dinah asks as Sophie is preparing to leave.

"Oh Mother, it is wondrous to not even notice time because we are so busy. The projects are all on schedule as I am sure Veronica has told you. So, Veronica … she is amazing! She has unending energy. When she is engaged in a project or in helping someone, you know she is always helping other people, so … Veronica is so energetic, did I tell you that? … She actually glows when she is focused on serving others. I am learning incredible skills, and even more than before, you know when she was healed. Oh, I cannot believe I was there to actually see that; it was amazing. He is so kind to everyone. How can someone have such a great love? I wonder if He will come in town for Passover; there will be so many people. I hope He does. So, Veronica, it seems like she never stops. So, it is all good. I still want to go up and see the northern wall. I have heard so many interesting details about it. How is Daniel doing? Now, what was your question?"

Dinah has the half-smile-half-grimace look on her face looking intently at Sophie. "Yes, that was a great answer. I know how you both love what you are doing, and it shows in the fine craftsmanship you produce. Your customers are thrilled at what you have done, especially your customers who are 'somewhat particular' about how their places look after installation … they want you to come back and do more."

"The king's kind wife, who knows what she wants and wants it yesterday?" Sophie semi-sarcastically but enthusiastically asks.

Dinah responds, "Uhm, not exactly, but she does like what you designed and installed, and that's a huge accomplishment, that's for sure," and then adds, "So … exactly why are you preparing to leave?"

"Why not? It is time to get over to Veronica's," Sophie responds with a quizzical look on her face.

"Well, perhaps because Veronica is coming over here," Dinah says, then adds in a hushed, secretive tone, "Remember? We are celebrating to-day … do not tell anyone." Dinah feigns that there is a crowd around and looks to the left and right with her finger over her lips.

"Oh yes!" Sophie blurts loudly.

"Shhhhhhh!" Dinah warns.

They both start laughing. Dinah steps to Sophie, looks her in the eyes, raises her arms to give a hug, and declares, "I love you, my Sophie. This cel-ebration is as much for you as it is for our Veronica. I am so proud of how you gave strength to Veronica."

The embrace is warm, tender, and long. Sophie absorbs it for a while and then says, "No. Actually, it was Veronica who helped me. I needed her so."

"Well, if the truth be known, you were good for each other; you needed to learn to trust again, and she needed to be strengthened by reaching out and teaching someone in need." Dinah then pauses and says what is in her heart. "The person who learned the most and who was strengthened the most was me. You both have gently and lovingly taught me about true charity and honest love." Dinah then squeezes Sophie hard enough to make her squeal.

"Argh! I cannot breathe!" Sophie pushes air out to say.

Dinah releases Sophie and happily suggests, "So, let's get ready!" She reaches to her right to snatch up a tablecloth, motions toward the table, and says, "Here, help me put this on."

Sophie takes the cloth to help open it. "This is very pretty! It looks special." She spreads the cloth and starts to lay it down as Dinah is do-ing the same.

"Yes," Dinah says, "And do you know what? It …"

Sophie realizes what they were holding and completed Dinah's sen-tence, "It is the same design as what Veronica created for the special tunic.

The one she recognized and reached for as she was falling ..." Sophie looks up into Dinah's face.

"Yes," Dinah affirms as she looks back at Sophie. "Her faith in the Master saved her, healed her ... even as she felt she had failed and was falling."

They lay the cloth down as if it is a symbol of a sacred trust and covenant. Sophie completes the thought she believes they both share, "I wish you could have seen His face. He listened very intently to her story, her pain, as if He understood every moment. He was so appreciative for her faith in Him. He smiled a smile from eternity. I wish you could have been there, Mother." Sophie sheds a tear, reaches up and wipes it, looks at the tear on her finger a moment, then back to her mother..

"Sophie, I was there." Dinah counters in a soft voice.

"What?" Sophie says in a surprised tone.

"Of course. When you and Veronica relate your tale, I hear it but most of all, I feel it. I feel the truth in my heart. It is as if I was right there, sitting next to you. Truth is warm. Truth is familiar. When your story, the story of Veronica's faith in action, will be told to those with honest hearts, they will need no more; they will believe as if they were there, with me, with you, with Veronica, reaching out, touching, and being healed themselves. It will be a beautiful thing, like a ripple in the water—truth, strength, light."

It is silent for a moment as they both are lost in time. They have shared what will become a sacred experience between mother and daughter.

"So," Sophie asks, "What are we going to eat?"

The remainder of the morning is occupied with culinary excellence, created for the grand celebration. Sophie wonders who will be arriving, *It cannot be too many people; we do not have room for everyone I would wish to invite.*

THE FIRST FIVE GUESTS ARRIVE. It had been almost thirteen years since they were Veronica's young students. Sophie is thrilled to quiz them about their experiences. Hannah, Adina, Kaleb, Lila, and Hiram are gathered around

Sophie chatting with energy about their shared experiences as pupils of their beloved teacher.

Jacob, Elias, and Gabriel arrive next. They say hello and head straight for the food. Dinah entertains them for a couple of minutes until her mother, Lidia, arrives, with a porter who has a bowl of early fruits from the south which are now coming to market. She looks at Dinah, holds a small packet up, and says, "I have it and am going to place it right over here with the textile samples."

Dinah smiles in approval as Daniel walks in. "Hello Daniel, you look very nice today," Dinah says.

"Why thank you, Dinah!" he responds with a smile.

"He is looking relaxed for a change; that's what he is looking, Dinah," Lidia says as she looks Daniel up and down, then asks pointedly, "Did you quit your stressful job?" She then looks at Dinah and offers, "I am sure that is what happened. Either that, or his boss died … not sure which." She returns her regard to Daniel, "So, which is it, Daniel?"

Dinah steps closer to ensure she will hear the answer. They now form a tight triangle.

"Yes, well …" Daniel begins, "I did not resign from my esteemed position," he says, then pauses with a smile. He places his left hand on Lidia's forearm and continues, looking at her, "I did not hear that my esteemed superior had passed from this sphere …" he pauses again for effect.

"Yesterday afternoon I was informed by the palace staff that 'Her Majesty, the king's wife, has accepted all her draperies and interior accessories.' Thrilled is the word, thrilled," he says with an accentuated smile.

Dinah is stunned, "Thrilled? She is thrilled you say?"

"No, well, yes, well no … she accepted; I am thrilled … I … am … thrilled. I do not need to deal with her for at least six full, happy, blissful months. I think I will sleep the entire time." He places his right hand on Dinah's arm and shows a happy, smug smile.

Dinah does not have the heart to mention that new orders for Rosh Hashanah and Yom Kippur are probably only three or four months away and says, "Oh Daniel, we are so happy about this. Congratulations for your release from the 'prison of changing expectations,' my friend."

Outside, Veronica is finishing the walk from her home and is excited to arrive in broad daylight, without fear. She is still not used to walking without being covered—her head, yes, but not her mouth or nose. Air seems to be so free that she feels a bit naked ... at least in that area. She feels liberated. She hears a horse's footsteps and also hears what she knows to be soldiers.

Most people would cower at such sounds, but because of her background, Veronica is pleased, so she turns around in time to see an officer come around the corner. What he says makes her heart jump.

"Well, it is good to see you Camel Master—Senior Trainer Attaché Veronica! I bring greetings from the Ninth, who are happy about your sudden recovery and who wish you well. They desire to send you a formal invitation to return to your post as Senior Trainer Attaché of the Ninth Brigade.

"You are welcome to come as you wish, but you need to be aware ... Mister Squishy Lips has made a specific request that you not delay your return. He has some new tricks to show you." He pauses for a moment, then adds, "Camel Master, Senior Trainer Attaché, Officer."

Veronica is so surprised she almost faints. She notices she is standing at attention and focused on her former Senior Training Officer. "Yes, sir! I am honored to receive such an incredible invitation and promotion. I will decide to be fit enough to return to my post as soon as possible. Please inform Mister Squishy Lips that I expect he will be ready to teach me well and that I expect to achieve excellence post haste, if you please ... Sir."

"I will gladly pass your message and instructions to the troops. We look forward to having you teach us how it is supposed to be done. I must execute your wishes ma'am. Good day!" the officer says, then turns his horse with the reins, sits straight, and places his heels against the horse's sides and is gone.

Veronica knows she is not dreaming. Her mind wonders how he had located her, but the thoughts of preparation to be strong enough to return have already taken over, *I need to practice. I need to gain strength. I need to go up the hill until I can run up it. I do not care if women should not run like that. I will start this afternoon. Where was I going? Oh, Dinah's. Sophie should be there, I hope. Only a minute away ... focus.*

In anticipation of Veronica's arrival Sophie is placed at the door. The rest of the guests are ready to turn their backs toward the door so Veronica cannot see their faces when she enters. Sophie opens the door, sticks her head outside and watches.

"Veronica! You are here!"

That's an unusual greeting, Veronica thinks as she smiles back and waves. She responds, "Sophie! You are there! Why is your head stuck in the door opening?" She laughs while thinking, *She is in a very sparkly mood this morning. Wait until I tell her what happened on the way.*

Veronica steps up to the door and Sophie opens it wide enough for the officer's horse to make it through and announces, "Welcome, Veronica! Come in!"

Dinah, Lidia, and Veronica all think, *What is Sophie up to? She does not do drama easily.*

Veronica steps in and is approached by both Dinah and Lidia, who block her view inside. Her trained mind asks, *What is going on here? Be prepared to escape.* Dinah and Lidia step aside and motion for Veronica to come in as the crowd of guests suddenly turn and say in unison, "Veronica, so glad to see you!" as they all throw their arms forward in warm salute.

Veronica is stunned and wonders, *These people, who are they? Oh, my!* She does not have time to work through who is who as she is engulfed in hugs and greetings from her closest friends and former students.

It takes an hour for Veronica's heart to settle down and not be overwhelmed. She sheds tears of joy the entire time and feels at full peace amid this, her world of love and understanding.

Veronica trades glances with Dinah, Lidia, and Sophie often during the gathering. Those glances speak of what true friendship and support means to each of them having survived the past several years. They feel whole. It is a wonderful reunion.

Time passes and as Veronica is preparing to leave, Dinah asks, "So, did you meet anyone on your way over?"

"HELLO GENTLEMEN. I MADE IT up the entire hill without needing to stop for rest," Veronica announces as she approaches her three older friends with a smile.

"We are so happy for you. You are looking healthier than last we saw you. Getting some meat on your bones," Elias smiles back as he offers praise ... and observations.

"I would race you up the hill, but now you would win the race and I would hate you for the rest of my life, so we would better not race today ... perhaps we will consider it tomorrow, Veronica. Let me know when you are ready for a real race. I will be here ... thinking about how I will help you feel better when I win," Jacob explains with more energy than usual.

Gabriel looks at Jacob and says, "Humph ... Jacob, you can barely stand up without help, even when you set your mind to it, so do not go around challenging people to races. Veronica will make you look like a toddler." He then looks at Veronica as if to report what he has observed and says, "Be kind to Jacob and make sure there is nobody watching when you show him how a race is won."

"Thank you, Gabriel," Veronica says quietly, "I'll keep that in mind." She looks at Elias and asks, "How is your sweet wife doing these days? I need to arrange a visit."

"Oh yes! She is as energetic as ever. She hurt her knee the other day ... overdoing it as usual.... I am sure you know all about that. You have been helping so many people all over the place ... you need to watch yourself."

"Thank you. Does Judith need someone to help? Can she still stand? What are you doing here? When can I drop by? I need to be going now. Thank you for letting me know!" Veronica questions all at once as she looks with a smile at Elias then down at Ognir.

She looks up and announces, "I will see you all later!" and nods her head at Jacob and Gabriel. "So good to see you, and I am so very glad you are all doing well."

She takes a step away, stops, turns, and says, "Elias, thank you again. I will tell Judith you will be back early this evening." Veronica flashes a smile at him, turns, and strides down the hill.

Elias sits motionless, staring back as Jacob reaches around him with his cane, pokes Gabriel, and says, "He did not stand a chance, did he? She is like my granddaughter down in Bethlehem; she is bossy, but in a kind way. You almost feel complimented when she tells you what to do … hee-hee."

"You are right. Having a younger woman say anything to you is like receiving a gift from heaven. Having them say anything at all tells you that they noticed you are there. A good sign I suppose, at any age," Gabriel says, then turns to Elias and calls, "Hey, she had you there! You had better get home early, but not too early. Let them finish talking and take some advice—never tell Veronica of anyone who needs some help. You will be better off … and so will she."

Elias retorts, "I was trapped. I do not know how, but she weasels the truth out of you without you ever knowing what is happening, then it is too late."

Gabriel explains, "They have always been like that. It started with Adam. It is a wonder he lasted nine hundred years … such a pity … none of us ever stood a chance. Eve instructed her daughters well. I think I will go home early with you today so I can make sure you do not get lost … again."

And there they sit, the three of them, looking west, not saying another word.

"THE CROWDS HAVE BEEN ARRIVING for the past couple of weeks. I am happy we managed to make our purchases before the prices went up," Dinah mentions to Sophie, then asks, "Are you and Veronica still planning to visit the temple while you still can?"

"Yes, I think she feels ready. She has been preparing since she woke up from her 'healing nap,' and I believe she is prepared physically and spiritually. She has not wanted to go for cleansing and sanctification until she is as fit as she was in her early twenties," Sophie responds.

"Is she?"

"Is she what?"

"Is she as fit as she was in her early twenties?"

"She thinks she is, so nothing else really matters, does it?"

"I suppose not. I am worried for her."

"Worried about her health?"

"No. I see that she has made great progress in that regard. She is probably the only person ever who was able to make a full recovery after what she has been through ... she probably regained the strength and stamina she had when she was twenty. I am worried that now that things have settled down and she has been preparing to go back to the temple, she will be strengthened even more, her spiritual side, which was so very closely tied to service at the temple."

"So, why does that worry you?"

"I fear that Veronica will want to launch herself into temple service again and it will not work out."

"Do you mean that she has so many things she is doing that she will get sick again?"

"Actually, no. Our Veronica would serve others every day of the week and would think it a blessing to not have to sleep if she could get away with it. She would probably even go without food.... I am worried that once she has presented herself to God once more in the temple and has been cleansed and sanctified through the sacred ordinances and has offered sacrifices, she will want to present herself to the priests for service ... and they will refuse to accept her. It will crush her soul."

"Uhm ... why would they do something like that? She was not kicked out of her teaching position. They still talk about how good she was, and dependable too."

"Yes, all that is true. She was a light of purity and would be of profound influence for good at the temple once more, but she has a problem they may not forgive her for." Dinah does not want the words to come out of her mouth.

"And?"

"They do not like the person who healed Veronica. In fact, they hate him and have been looking for a reason, any reason, to have him put to death. The rabbi from Nazareth is seen as a threat by them, as is anyone who has a close relationship with him."

"She has not seen Him since He healed her that day."

"Yes; however, she was healed in a very public way. News of what happened spread as everything does in this city, so the Priests may hold her accountable for their hatred, or along with their hatred for His actions, regardless of Veronica's true value to the temple and its reason for being rebuilt. I fear what a rejection like that will or could do to her soul."

"Thank you, Mother, for explaining that to me. I have heard that Jesus may come into Jerusalem for Passover. People are very excited for it, and some are preparing a welcome for him," Sophie responds.

"Yes, I have heard the same thing. He will need to be incredibly careful. There is a lot of tension and a lot of talk among the leadership. I believe the Romans are involved also," Dinah offers in reflection and then pauses, looking out the window. She hopes the day will go well, is glad Sophie is going with Veronica, while being happy to have Ognir spend the day while the girls are at the temple.

AFTER THE MIDDAY MEAL, SOPHIE and Veronica take Dinah's and Ognir's leave and walk to the temple, ready to participate in ordinances and stay for the evening prayer. They are both as excited as two twelve-year-olds going for the first time.

"Veronica, I cannot wait to get there; do you want to run?" Sophie asks.

As tempting as that invitation is, Veronica responds, "Yes, I want to run, but that would bring attention to how slow you are, and I would feel bad."

"Hah! We probably should not anyway. We are supposed to be 'dignified' and act accordingly, both inside and outside the temple," Sophie responds in a solemn and dignified tone.

Veronica looks at Sophie with a brilliant yet mischievous smile, turns her focus quickly ahead, and launches into a sprint, holding her robes up so as to avoid tripping.

Sophie squeals and follows suit. After only three strides Veronica stops running, turns to Sophie, and with a somber face confesses, "I am only kidding."

Sophie starts laughing, which makes Veronica laugh as well. They continue to the temple with as much dignity as they can muster. When they arrive at the south stairway rising high above them, they stop and look up.

So, I am back after all these years. How I have longed to be here, exactly where I am, clean and able, Veronica says to herself. She begins to tear up.

Sophie notices, grasps Veronica's hand, and says, "Let us take these twenty-four steps one at a time." She leans forward while looking to the top and takes the first step. Veronica is right next to her, all the way up.

"Through these massive doors, we enter the open court where we will see peoples from many lands. Look ... are they all not beautiful?" Veronica announces.

"God's children, becoming one in a sacred place," Sophie adds.

"Yes, look over there. People from far away. I wonder how long it took them to travel here, and I wonder how many years it took them to save for their travels." Veronica is in awe, and as she turns, someone familiar approaches.

"Veronica, Sophie! I have been watching out for you! We are so glad!" Hannah greets them with welcoming hugs, "I have so many holy spaces to show you ... well, people too, holy people, doing sacred ordinances, making covenants ... sorry, you already know." Hannah smiles broadly, turns while saying, "We are ready. Come with me."

The two "dignified" women are treated to an insiders' tour of the operational side of the temple. Veronica's memories awaken while Sophie is amazed at all that happens to allow each temple visitor a clear and purposeful experience.

All transpires well. Hannah is honored to be their guide. Both Sophie and Veronica choose doves for their offerings. Veronica is then blessed with both cleansing as well as sanctification ordinances. She feels at home once again and as evening prayer time arrives, Veronica and Sophie have been fully immersed in a wondrous day which will never be forgotten.

They hold hands as they make their way back down the stairway. As they take the last step, they both stop to look back up and see the throng behind them. They do not want to look away.

When Veronica and Sophie do finally look away and set their eyes on their path of return, Sophie looks at Veronica and says, "I'll race you back home!"

"Why are you two so flushed? Did you need to escape from thieves again?" Dinah asks as Veronica and Sophie walk inside. She changes her tone from a question into a recollection of what she had experienced many times before. "Never mind, I know what you were doing. Who won this time?"

Sophie and Veronica look at each other, shrug their shoulders, and look back at Dinah as if to say, "Dinah, we do not have any idea what you are talking about. We did not behave in an 'undignified manner,' not us." Their faces are attempting, unsuccessfully, to mimic a four-year-old's innocence.

"Yes, that's exactly what I thought."

My apron still fits—that is a good thing. I will not be wearing it as an adult; however, I am glad it still looks nice on me, Veronica observes as she is reminiscing about her prior temple service.

The visit to the temple with Sophie was refreshing. It brought back so many memories. Even the smells and the sounds have deeper meaning than I would have thought.

Covenants. Covenants with God. Promises. It is what holds us together ... so far apart ... living in so many separate places. I love them all. God's people, my people. If I understand correctly, He called me 'Daughter.' We are all His children. Why do they hate him? I hope he comes, perhaps I will see Him.

When I was twelve, I was presented before God at the temple and learned what I was required to do. I agreed and made covenants with God. Covenants to serve, which were never removed or revoked. I am still held accountable. I need to return. I need to be presented as clean and worthy again. This will need to be taken care of once Passover has been celebrated and the city and temple become serene once again. Yes. Focus.

Veronica sets aside some time to visit the Roman Training Grounds, where she spent a great deal of time in her youth. She gazes as she walks forward with anticipation, *The Training Grounds gate is closed. It is new. They painted all the buildings—looks nice. Looks like a normal day. Smells familiar ... not pleasant but familiar. Smells like they have brought in more horses,* Veronica thinks as she opens the gate, goes through with Ognir, and closes the gate, making sure it is fully locked before proceeding.

I do not see anyone I recognize. I wonder if I should come back another time, Veronica considers, but she does not break her stride. Something is drawing her closer to where the activity is.

She draws near and overhears a young soldier say on the other side of the animals who are being prepared for a training session, "It is her! I am sure of it. The Senior Trainer Attaché Officer is here!"

"Where?" another young voice asks.

"Right over there! She is here! We are not ready! Oh no. We have to look sharp."

"Quick! Get her camel!" the second voice instructs.

Veronica is taken aback by the ruckus but decides she should do something that a Senior Trainer Attaché Officer would do, so she steps to the side and stops, at attention, and waits for her trainees to sort out what they feel they need to do since she arrived early.

This is going to be fun, she reasons with a mischievous slant, striving to keep a smile off her face.

Veronica reaches over and takes the beads out of her bag and adjusts the shoulder strap. She hears someone calling with frustration, "Where is her camel?" as they are rushing to be prepared so as not to receive a scolding on the first day.

Veronica turns to her left and places the beads around Mister Squishy Lips's neck and stands, scratching behind his ears with her left hand while her right hand does the same with Ognir.

TEMPLE CRISIS

Returning from her mother's home, Dinah reflects on the commotion, the intense, sudden darkness, and the earthquake, *I am so glad I was able to be with Mother today. The last two days have been extraordinarily difficult, as if the entire world has come apart. I am pleased she seems to be feeling better.*

Rounding the corner, she encounters three agitated priests in heated discussion in the small front courtyard of her home. The oldest of them sees her first, abandons the other two and, coming close to her, leans to place his mouth near her right ear and announces in a low but noticeably clear and distinct tone, "The Veil of the Holy of Holies has been rent in two. It cannot be repaired and must be replaced. We need you now." He then backs away quickly, having delivered his message. The three priests stand together looking at Dinah in anxious anticipation for her response.

Dinah understands fully the import of what had happened during the terrible afternoon darkness and frightening earthquake. She stands still and observes to herself while looking at them, *I have assisted the high priests and priests for decades and have always marveled at how slowly decisions are made and the long time needed to implement even the most minor of projects; and they are now here, at my personal abode with an immediate and urgent request. The world has indeed changed in the most amazing ways.*

"Yes," Dinah announces with authority, "I will come with you now. I have what we need to move quickly ... immediately."

Her tone surprises herself as well as the priests, who respond, "Really? You are ready? Do you have what is needed? Are you sure?"

"Let us not waste time, and get to where we need to go. Follow me." With that announcement, Dinah marches past the three priests who look and react like three young boys being scolded by their mother who is on an important mission.

Dinah has made the trip so many times that she knows exactly how many paces it is from her home to the base of the southern steps. She rehearses in her mind what will happen, *It is exactly four hundred paces from the steps to the always-guarded, no-women-allowed passageway to the inner court which protects the Holy of Holies. Daniel will certainly be waiting for me at that point.* Considering her age, Dinah would be a formidable foe in a foot race. She leaves the three priests behind without consideration.

VERONICA KIDNAPPED

T HE DAY PRIOR TO THE earthquake, her night's rest has done Veronica good. She lies in bed comfortably and as is common for her, engages in a meandering monologue, *I am happy I was able to see Lidia and hope she heals quickly from her illness. She seemed to be on the mend, so I suppose we will all be together for Seder dinner. Too bad we cannot have everyone over. Ognir likes the attention, don't you boy?* Veronica watches Ognir lie by the door sleeping as she recognizes his immense value in her life.

He is so handsome when he is relaxed. I need to take him out for some exercise this afternoon. Should we go to the Training Grounds? Hmmm, perhaps visit with Lidia? What's Sophie up to? Those training troops sure were funny when we went for the first time in months. I cannot forget the looks on their faces when they found all three of us standing there, composed, and ready. I had to hold in a laugh when the youngest of them said, "The camel is over there, with the senior trainer attaché officer and her spirit dog!" But the best was when they mustered the courage to come over and report their readiness, all standing in a line, when Mister Squishy Lips—who was unimpressed and chewing as usual—turned his head and spat without saying a word. Priceless move, my fine camel steed! I am glad they did well when the trainees came. Veronica stops daydreaming and stands with a morning stretch.

Ognir's ears move from sleeping position, lying flat against his head, to casual "all-is-well" listening mode, slightly raised, like a gliding bird's wings. Veronica smiles, thinking, *I wonder if Ognir could fly with those ears like that?*

"Ognir, time to get up and go! We are going up the hill to catch the sunrise to the east. Did you know the sun comes up in the east? One of the few remaining things we know with certainty. The world is changing so quickly; who knows, perhaps tomorrow it will come up in the west? Come on, let us get going," Veronica announces, looking over at Ognir, who bounces up as if he had been waiting a long time to get on with a productive day.

So, out the door they head into the pre-dawn light. *Mmmm. I love this time of day, especially this time of year. It is still very quiet. Spring is so invigorating,* Veronica thinks as she makes her way to the bottom of the hill, where the streets come together.

She looks each way and notices how quiet it is as her self-directed conversation continues, *It is so very quiet this morning. I would have thought that the streets would be busy with Passover being tomorrow. Oh. It is still dark; I suppose everyone is taking a long snooze this morning. I wonder what Jesus is doing. He came to Jerusalem last week through the south gate. The crowd who greeted him was exceptionally large and enthusiastic, but it has been quiet since.*

I wonder when the Young Merchant will be back. I hope he did not forget me. I pray he has not been killed. Egypt is far away, but people go there all the time. They have beautiful buildings there, some of them ancient. So, twenty-one days straight to Alexandria, without sales stops he said. If he is going to arrive here two weeks after Passover, he is already on the way. I am glad his trip ends here, so he will not be out when it gets so ridiculously hot.

Trips to Egypt are as common as the various festivals scattered throughout the year. Lots of people go up to Nazareth as if it were next door. I have heard them say, "It's only five days or so." Then they always add a note about "the time my cousin made it there in only three days for his sister's wedding because he forgot about it and his mother would have killed him if he missed it." I am sure they took two good camels, riding camels, and switched back and forth. They are faster than horses. I do not care what they say. The camels did simply fine I am sure ... if he cared for them properly. Probably not.... Poor camels.

The benches! Good. We made it in time, Ognir! Have a seat! Veronica does not even notice trekking up the hill as she is preoccupied thinking. Lidia has counseled her to be aware when her mind starts thinking and cannot stop, especially when distressful thoughts take center stage. She sits on the east-facing bench and wonders about her three older gentlemen while waiting for the sun to make its stunning appearance. Veronica ponders, *It is still quiet. I love the quietness outside. I hope the sun makes its arrival before the noise starts.*

"So ... SHE IS CLEANSED. I WAS not so sure it was true until I saw her and that brat companion of hers walk, out in the open, right up the temple staircase as if they owned the place. Maybe she was never sick in the first place. She was probably having a crisis, like all women have. Hers was the 'extended version,'" Mordechai reasons in his twisted mind, which is always up to no good, trying to make others as miserable as himself, for his own perverted amusement.

Alone in the dark, Mordechai continues to talk to himself with evil purposes in mind, "Well, with that being true, my plan will work. I was not allowed, even as a powerful 'information broker' to touch an unclean woman, so I did not. I obey the sacred laws—most of them at least. Now, selling Veronica will be easy, especially during Passover. No one will even notice. Dinah and the brat Sophie will not know what to do, the Roman spy will be too busy, and the three old men (or is it two now?) will not even know where they are. I have it all planned out."

He switches topics, still talking out loud to himself, alone in what he calls his command center, "The Young Merchant you ask? He will not even be back in Jerusalem when it happens. The day after Passover she will be delivered. Everything will be ready. I am invincible; my plan is perfect. I need to get to the hiding place. It has worked so well for so many unsuspecting Roman soldiers who missed their mothers and 'needed, oh so much,' to desert the Ninth and escape home. It has been a steady source of income.

It too is perfect," he speaks smugly to himself, who is about the only person he is close to and the only person who takes him seriously.

Mordechai prepares the hideout location, ensuring it is still as solitary as ever. Out of the way. Dark, empty, secure. As he walks out and into the light, he continues talking to himself with self-willed confidence, oblivious to the world around him, "This is set. I will double check its security once more the afternoon of Passover when there will be no one around. It is the perfect place, here under the temple walls. It is unknown and is the perfect refuge for deserting Roman soldiers and hidden retribution. Yes, perfect for plans of the past, perfect for this plan, and perfect for plans in the future. God has helped me in so many ways. He has no idea how dearly I appreciate it.

"Everything is planned and prepared in advance, including a walk-through of each step—who will be there, who will be passing by, and what to do in case of a problem. All is well," Mordechai concludes as he walks away. His head, as usual, is darting in many directions as he continues. One challenge remains....

"The major worry is the dog who almost took my foot off ... it needs to be dealt with ... and quickly. My blanket, although it was given to me by someone high in the government, will do fine, yes, the yellow blanket with blue designs will be ... perfect."

MORDECHAI SPEAKS IN A CLEAR, confident tone as he is closing the sale with his buyer's representative.

"Yes, healthy."

"Yes, energetic."

"Yes, she can bear many children."

"Beautiful? Of course, her green eyes will take your breath away."

"I will have her available two days after Passover, while everyone is leaving."

"It will be best to have a midmorning delivery for you?"

"Of course. She will be fully covered and ready."

"I will pick you up and we will go do the collection together."

"The donation will be half."

"OK, that will do."

"I give you my pledge and my honor."

"See you then."

The deal he had never dreamed could happen is finally arranged, with a handsome down payment, enough to purchase whatever he wants, for a long time. He is smug and knows his hand-picked team will be ready.

I am glad he did not ask if she is obedient. Knowing her, she will probably escape. I hope not. I would then need to move to a different city. All we need to do now is take care of the dog problem…. I have an idea, Mordechai thinks as he returns to his hiding place only a few select partners know about. He grabs his beggar's blanket prop and hurries over to the team meeting place, well out of sight of anyone.

After pondering about the blanket, Mordechai's attention is brought to the four corners where the blue designs are. He has an idea which provides the perfect solution, "We'll tie rocks inside the corners so it will weigh down the blanket around the miserable dog."

Mordechai folds the blanket containing the rocks and again starts talking to himself, this time in a low mutter as his eyes dart back and forth while he makes his way through the city, "I have pondered, I have planned a masterful plan, and now, for the next four days, we will practice and perfect the ingenious retribution I have in mind for the arrogant, selfish, sneaky Young Merchant and his lazy sidekick…. I am patient, I am clever, I am in control. The arrival of the Rabbi is perfectly timed; His followers distracted everyone when he arrived, and he has been quiet this week, the Leadership and the Romans are both on edge, wondering what he is up to. My runners report that the Leadership is up to something, but it is not clear what they are planning. An arrest is certainly probable."

Jerusalem is anything but relaxed. Street cleaners, merchants, and runners are working eighteen-hour days while the Roman guard is fully dispatched. They are visible … everywhere.

"AND HOW IS YOUR KNEE feeling, Judith?" Veronica asks with a smile as she removes her shawl.

"It is better. Thank you for the frankincense oil. It was helpful and took the swelling down. I can get around pretty well now. Of course, I will not be racing you up the hill any time soon, that is for sure," Judith responds, cracking a smile when she mentions racing.

"And Elias? Is he behaving? Do I need to get after him for anything?"

"Ha. No. He and his friends are fine. He asked yesterday when the Young Merchant and his sidekick the Camel Herder are coming back into town."

Veronica affirms, "Yes, they planned to be back after Passover has settled down and the city has emptied a bit … and the prices have gone back down to their normal 'too-high' levels maybe two or three weeks from now."

Veronica wishes for the Young Merchant's return more than almost anything for which she had ever wished. It seems to her somewhat odd to have such feelings, as they are new to her, but they are real and become increasingly a part of her thoughts as the days pass.

"I heard from my cousin that the Rabbi is planning to arrive soon. There is wide speculation about what He will do when he gets here. Both the Leadership and the Romans seem to be prepared … lots of meetings behind closed doors and late at night," Judith reports.

"Yes, I understand there will be a grand welcome when my Rabbi arrives," Veronica adds. "Some feel he will overthrow the entire government and others have prepared—again—to toss out the Romans. Many believe He will lead us to victory with nothing but the raising of His hand. Not both arms as Moses did but a slight gesture of a single hand."

"What do you believe will happen, Veronica?" Judith asks in a peaceful voice.

Veronica looks up at the light coming in and follows the bright path as it highlights the tiny dust particles in the air. Her mind is reflecting on how He looked at her, how deep and eternal He was. She also reflects on the vivid memories gained during her three-day slumber after her healing. She ponders, *So many invisible particles no one ever sees until the light is exactly right and they pay attention. It all makes perfect sense.*

Judith watches her closely, and although she does not understand the depth of knowledge Veronica had received, she senses it is sacred and brought Veronica to an understanding few people ever achieve, even if they seek it their entire life.

"He brings peace. Peace only He can bring. There will be no public battle, no public victories gained with instruments of war," Veronica tells Judith looking calmly at her.

Veronica continues, "The battle will be a personal battle, between Him and the evils of all men and women. He will pay the price for their sins. The doves, the goats, the other sacrificial animals can then be made free. The sacrifice will be completed. It will be public. It will be the final sacrifice. The eternal victory will then be achieved three days later. The final victory." Veronica's gaze drifts from Judith back to the particles being illuminated.

Veronica wipes her eyes, looks up at Judith, and says, "Miracles of victory will happen, but they will be personal and will happen only to those, for those, who surrender their hearts to Him, after He is gone."

She is trying to absorb all I said. I am not sure what I said, as I am also still trying to absorb what I saw, what I learned is to be in the next few days, Veronica again reflects as she gazes at Judith, who has a peaceful look on her weathered face. *She served so many years in the temple with her kind and faithful husband. She deserves to understand the import of what she is witnessing these days.* The moments pass.

Taking in a deep breath, Veronica claps her hands on her knees and announces, "I need to stop bothering you and let you get back to what you were doing. Thank you for allowing me to pop in to say hello. If I see Elias today, I will be sure to tell him we chatted and will confess to him that you told me how much you love him and that your eyes sparkled when you remarked that, 'Elias has, as far as I can tell, reached perfection.' I am sure he will love that," Veronica adds with a grin as she hugs Judith.

"Oh, he may well have done that, but be sure not to tell him. It will go to his head and will make Gabriel feel bad. We all miss our kind friend Jacob and wish he had not left so quickly. I am sure he is remarkably busy and keeping the angels in line," Judith responds with a kind smile.

Both women realize at the same moment that Gabriel would not feel bad. A statement like that would give him a great laugh and an opportunity to tease Elias for years to come. They look at each other and convey the joke without a word.

Judith smiles and offers, "Veronica, thank you for coming to visit an old woman in need of companionship. Your visits are so welcome, and they make me feel younger. Be sure to bring Sophie on your next visit! I will teach her some crochet!"

"Yes, I will do that! Be prepared for energy in a bottle!" Veronica responds as she carefully steps out.

VERONICA LIES DOWN, BUT SLEEP does not come. Her mind normally looks forward with hope and optimism; however, on this night, it is relentlessly examining the destruction, *The world changed yesterday afternoon. It will never be the same. The Leadership and the Romans have had their way. He is gone. They killed Him with nails, like a criminal. In response, the very earth groaned and ruptured in darkness. Sophie said they came for Dinah because there was a crisis at the temple. The very heart of the temple was torn with grief. She is probably still there, where I long to be. I left Sophie well and comfortable. I hope she sleeps all night. It is good to be home. There is an amazing silence this evening as Passover ends ... so quiet ... so mournful. On the third day something marvelous will happen according to my dream ... I need to rest.*

I should have visited Lidia is Veronica's last thought before she and Ognir find sleep in the dark silence.

MORDECHAI'S EYES ARE SQUINTING. WITH intense concentration he conjures up his thoughts of evil plans. "No dramatic diversion except that the city is alive with people preparing to leave and leaving ... it will quiet down as soon as the sun sets ... my buyer is leaving tomorrow, so no diversion is needed, but the time is right, or it will be too late. They got rid of the troublemaker rabbi, so the Romans are not as edgy. Runners have reported that the Leadership is also more at ease and has protected the burial tomb with guards ... good thing, as the followers would have certainly stolen his body," Mordechai reasons out loud to himself as he makes his way to the holding room.

"All is well," He announces as he slowly looks around and appreciates that it is quieter than he had imagined it would be. He looks up at the roof lines, inspects the surrounding doorways, then departs, reasoning, *The moment has come. The plan will be acted on with precise measure. The dog with teeth will not be a problem; my blanket is ready with fist-sized stones tied into each corner. The trap and containment have been practiced on a goat ... with horns. My team is ready and in place. Now to capture the prize.*

The thieves watch the temple guards pass. The next step is to see the priests who light the lamps one by one and then pass to their appointed places as night approaches. They move quickly and silently as darkness envelopes their evil deed.

Veronica's door is closed. They approach and call out.... "Help! Lidia needs you! Lidia needs you! Help now!"

Ognir is already standing at the door, his ears in alert mode as Veronica opens it. Instantly the well-rehearsed plea for help is repeated with alarm, and Lidia's near-death situation is exclaimed.

They pull Veronica out the door.... "She needs you now! Hurry! I will take care of the dog, go quickly. Lidia is calling your name!"

They seem sincere and are probably Lidia's neighbors, Veronica thinks as she frets about her friend and hopes she will arrive on time as she scurries out the door in a panic. Ognir bares his teeth in full attack mode as he is enveloped in the blanket; the door is closed, and the thief slips back out to go to his predetermined position.

Into the darkness they all flee, with Veronica being mostly carried by the men grasping under her arms. *Oh Lidia!* Veronica worries, *You should not be left alone any longer. I pray you will be well, and I can arrive on time. I should have spoken with you earlier today. What was I doing that was so important? Where is Dinah? I hope she is coming as well. She is probably running. I can only be carried I am so pathetic.* Veronica's mind continues spinning with fear for Lidia for several moments. That fear changes.

Where are we? We are *headed toward the temple! Why would Lidia be needed at the temple at this hour? She has no responsibilities there any longer. Why are these men being quiet? They are not Lidia's neighbors. They are wearing strange clothing from outside here. Where did they come from and why are they taking me to Lidia this way?* Veronica is desperately searching for answers, *Where is Ognir?*

Veronica feels a deep fear quickly course through her veins. "Focus" is her trained response…. *Focus on staying stable and as in control as you can be. Be aware of your surroundings. Know your strengths and be ready to use them. It is a trap!* She screams with all her soul, "Stop!" Her captors hesitate only an instant.

"Who are you and where are you taking me?" They grasp her more tightly and begin to move faster. One of them says, "Right here!" in an urgent, hushed tone.

"Stop I tell you!" Veronica tries to kick the man on the right side but since she is now being carried it is useless.

"Open the door," one of them says to the other.

"Bring her in quickly. Sit her down. Let us go. Be quiet. Hurry." The door closes quickly; the bolt lock is engaged and … there is silence.

Veronica tries to look around. It is so dark she cannot even see her hand right in front of her face. *Focus. Focus. Focus. Why did they do that? Did they kill Lidia? How did they know that I am Lidia's friend? I have done nothing to anyone to deserve this. I hate no one, so no one should hate me … except the fellow who tried to take Sophie away.*

If I am to survive, I must focus … take inventory …

Head—my brain is not stable yet, but I feel no apparent injuries.

Neck and shoulders—the neck seems tense, and shoulders are fine, but under my arms is very sore.

Chest and torso—the constant pain I had felt for years is gone, for which I am so very grateful. Oh, He is gone. Oh, there is no one to rescue me. They have crucified Him like a dirty criminal…. The Man who healed me, oh, where could He be? She is lost, racing in the possibilities.

Immediate fear is replaced with a deeper dread. Veronica begins shaking, *I remember being taught that this shivering happens after a battle, but I didn't know what it felt like.* Weariness begins to seep over Veronica. Uncontrollable dread begins taking her down.

This cannot happen. I have to have a plan. What is around me? Can I get out?" She is able to focus again and examines every inch of the room with her fingertips. On her hands and knees, Veronica finds a wall and feels each dimple in the plaster from the floor to as high as she can reach. She moves from one wall to the next, slowly, examining, inspecting the pitch black and dank odor.

Her senses are acutely aware as she feels the door—wooden, with iron slats and bolts and a heavy tread. *This room is made to obscure any light from coming in or getting out. There is not even the slightest drift of air movement. There is no way out. What is my plan now? Wait. Be still. They will be back, and I will destroy them.* Time disappears as the hours pass.

Veronica feels she is falling into a dark abyss and cannot help it. She feels herself stand and reach out….

She says aloud, "Hello Mr. Squishy Lips. I hope you are well this evening. We are about to take a journey never before attempted by anyone. You are the best camel steed in the Ninth, and our mission is secret. Let us check if we are ready.

1. Are you properly groomed? YES.
2. Are your blankets and pads on straight? YES.
3. Is your bridle adjusted? YES.
4. Feet clean? YES."

Veronica is hesitant to ask the last question. She looks down, takes a deep breath by inhaling slowly, holding it for a moment, and then letting it out very carefully. She is about to burst into uncontrollable sobbing.

5. "Are … you … calm? Yes…. No."

"What is wrong? Oh no! 6. The beads, I forgot the beads! I am so sorry. Here they are, where you like them. Thank you for telling me, I would have felt horrible."

Veronica looks down at Mr. Squishy Lips's imaginary eyes and says "Huph Huph." She then stands for hours as if she is on the Training Grounds. She rehearses every visit she has ever made, including the surprising training session which turned into an embarrassing medal presentation with so many friends attending.

"I am so happy Dinah came and Daniel and Reuben ... why did he come? Is he in charge of public relations with the Ninth? ... Probably." Veronica keeps standing, trying to maintain control. Trying to focus.

"I am getting weary and need to sit. Where is that chair? I wish I could see. It is so dark in here," Veronica says aloud as she is shuffling around to locate what she had been placed on when they shoved her inside this small dark place. She bumps up against the chair, reaches for it, and adjusts so it is beneath her as her strength to stand gives out, landing her in the chair. *Unconsciousness feels so good. I am sure I am dreaming.*

Where am I? Why is it so quiet? How did I get down here on the floor? I am so thirsty ... water ... I thirst for some water ... the Young Merchant's water. He is so kind. Did I actually meet him? Dinah likes him, and he is very capable, has a good network, and his camel, Bindi, and I get along simply fine. His water was incredibly good when he gave it to me that day. Am I dreaming? It was very funny when I was riding Bindi and the Young Merchant was forced to ride the Camel Herder's camel, Miskah ... the bride's camel ... the bride's lonely camel ... so funny. Veronica passes out once more and is tormented by dreams of becoming "unclean" again. The cramps in her abdomen surging again wake her.

Oooh, oooh ... why is this happening? ... I was dreaming ... was my entire life a dream? Am I dead? Am I dying? I am so thirsty. I am blind and cannot see. I must be dead, but my side hurts, so I can feel things. I hurt again. Why could that be? I am thirsty? Where is the Young Merchant?

He is still in Egypt, and I will be gone when he arrives, if he decides to come back. Will he? Veronica passes out once more but does not have nightmares. She is traveling somewhere.

"Veronica, Veronica, Veronica, Veronica" is the soft, peaceful, and inviting call of her name. It is calling her into another place. A wonderful place.

"Yes," she responds, unaware if she has said it or has communicated it without saying anything.

"Veronica, please stand. I have something to tell you." The voice sounds familiar. It is calming, like a trusted, old friend.

"Yes. Thank you for waking me. I want to come with you."

"Veronica, I have been asked to come and tell you that all will be resolved. Your Young Merchant will arrive soon and will have water for you to drink. He is an honorable man. Your heart is in the right place. Be at peace. All will be well. Have faith once again; it will make you whole."

"Jacob? You are here!" Veronica's fear vanishes; she feels strength, jumps up, and throws her arms around her visitor. "I am so happy to see you. You look younger!"

"Yes, many of us were resurrected after the Master. We have errands to complete. I am happy for you Veronica. You have been blessed and will be strong and bear children. I must go. Be of good cheer."

"I want to come with you," Veronica begs.

"You have many things to do here. You will teach and care for your own children as you have done for others so lovingly for so many years. Be at peace. God is aware of you at every moment." The messenger then leaves, still smiling.

Oh.... You are gone Jacob. You looked so strong. I am trying to be at peace. I am trying to have faith. I ... Veronica hears someone outside, and a small amount of light has entered the holding chamber where she had been thrown.

Focus. Focus. Be ... perfectly ... still. Reserve your strength to attack if they come inside that door. Focus. A healthy scream will surprise them. Veronica sits, reaches down, and grasps the leg of the chair so she can use it as a weapon the instant they come in. *Hold tight. Wait. Be ready to jump then pivot-swing. Be, very, still. Focus....*

Rescue at Daylight

As Ognir works his way along the scent trail, moving back and forth with assuredness and resolve, he turns right and heads down a narrow pathway. Eran the Roman Officer suspects he knows where Ognir is going. Ognir then walks past a passage to the left, stops, turns around, makes a right turn, and then gains speed. Eran knows exactly where he is going.

"I'll meet you there," he informs the Young Merchant in a hushed tone as he veers to the left and runs, then turns so he is quickly out of sight. Everything is quiet as the sun begins hitting the towering pillars which stand as sentinels high above the temple walls, with radiant beams of light streaming down from between them.

Eran knows the place. It is where he captured the Roman soldiers who were betrayed by Mordechai on five separate occasions. Eran readies his knife and unlatches his sword as he approaches the escape route. At that moment there is the sound of a dog attacking, vicious growling, a yelp, and someone who screams, "Run!"

Eran is ready for the capture. He pulls a passage gate closed, pins it, and listens for the hurried footsteps to get nearer … one … two … three. He steps out from the edge of the building and confronts two petrified men who almost knock each other down as they try to stop. They almost faint from fear, which overcomes them as they gain some small amount of stability. They start shaking with adrenaline overdose as Eran says in a strangely quiet voice that causes immediate obedience, "Get down on your bellies and do not move."

They instantly dive for the ground but cannot stop shaking. Eran says, "Hold still. Now!" as he pulls his sword out of the heavy leather and steel scabbard, which gives a sliding ring, starting at a low pitch and ascending to a high one as it becomes free. The man on the right wets himself, and the one on the left holds his breath, his right hand grasping his left against the ground to hold it still … he then faints from fear of being skewered in the next moment.

Eran takes his leather horse straps out from under his belt and hobbles his new prisoners. It is not the first time he had frightened liquid out of a foe.

The Young Merchant has come upon the two guards standing outside the improvised cell. Ognir wastes no time at all in a full engagement, which sends the hireling guards scampering away with little trouble.

Ognir is anxiously sniffing side to side the slot under a door. *Here.* thinks the Young Merchant, *I pray that Veronica is unharmed.* He quickly opens the door, walks into the passageway darkness, and begins to slowly feel the walls on each side for an opening.

Ognir has already located the familiar scent he was looking for and is sitting, with ears straight up, focused on the lower portion of the door. No sound can be heard as the Young Merchant carefully slides the bar lock, opens the door carefully, and peers in. He too, can smell the scent of the oils he had offered Veronica when they met at the shop several weeks earlier. His head fully inside the small temple storage room, he can see the faint silhouette of someone sitting in a chair.

He hears footsteps behind him but does not turn to see who it is.

The silhouette moves. "It's you!" Veronica exclaims as she arranges her dress so she can get up without falling. In one fluid motion she flies through the ten feet of space between them, throws her arms around him, and quietly exclaims, "I love you. Please do not leave me again."

Before he has a chance to evaluate what she has announced and consider the request, the owner of the steps he had heard is standing in the doorway. The Young Merchant does not know who this shadow might be, but it reminds him of the man with the cart who was also a shadow, even in the light of day.

The Young Merchant gently moves Veronica away and turns to fully protect her by facing the shadow, who breaks the silence with a shrill, strained voice. "So, you have found your prize. You believe you will rescue her from her new owner. She fetched a very handsome price and will be a fine addition to his collection now that she is healed."

The Young Merchant's mind races at that last phrase. Before he can process anything, he realizes that Ognir has not come into the room but has vanished. That realization is replaced with the view of another shadow approaching from behind the small shadow with the shrill voice.

The second shadow moves in silence, raises its arms, and brings them down around the small one and takes him to the ground. All that can be heard is a faint squeak.

The light is now showing a bit more detail as Eran takes his new prisoner and carries him out as he informs, "It is Mordechai's senior assistant, almost looks like him. I will transfer them all to the guard. You are both safe now."

Ognir growls as Eran carries his package past where he is sitting. He then looks into the room; his tail starts wagging, and he lies down at the door on the lookout as he has done so many times before. His mission was successfully accomplished.

The Young Merchant is speechless as he motions Veronica to sit down. When she is settled, the Young Merchant kneels and, looking into her eyes asks, "You are healed?"

"Yes" is Veronica's response, in a tone that could lift boulders to float off the ground. She looks into his eyes and tells him of her decision to act on her faith, the search, the crowd, the desperate lunge to touch something, anything, and of the instant cleansing she had felt, as if her body had been transformed into that of an eternal being, as when Moses was translated.

She explains the way He had looked at her, which allowed her to let the pain and suffering escape her soul as well; of His declaration; His blessing; and His farewell as He continued his journey through the streets to heal someone else. Veronica explains that it was as if time had stopped and she were no longer on the planet and that there were no others around … only Jesus and she, having a personal conversation.

The Young Merchant loses his composure, starts crying, lifts her head by gently raising her chin with his hand, and says, looking into her eyes, "Thank you, Veronica, for sharing that sacred experience with me. I love you as well and am so incredibly grateful that you are not harmed."

Veronica reaches down, pulls up her dress to reveal her now bloodied knees as she says, "Yes, but I have received some injuries, but they were worth it. From the moment I was placed here I have been on my knees. I have been praying you would come rescue me." Veronica looks up into the Young Merchant's eyes and declares as she lets her dress drop back to the floor, "I have an important question."

"Yes."

"What is your name?" She looks in his eyes with expectation.

The Young Merchant had not considered he had never told her his name. *How could that be?* he wonders as he looks back into her eyes again and before he can respond, he is overwhelmed at how clear and beautiful they are—a deep green, as if a gentle breeze was moving fields of lush grass. Without taking his eyes off of hers he responds, "My name is Joshua. Joshua of Jericho." Veronica sits straight up, not releasing his eyes from hers and taking his hands into hers, says, "Joshua … the Lord is my salvation."

Veronica holds that declaration in the air for several moments and says, "Please, I have been waiting for you. I need some clear, pure water. I need strength from you."

Joshua has already brought his water bag to his knee and is ready to satisfy Veronica's request. She thanks him and drinks deeply.

Neither of them knows how long they are in the small room under the temple together, but they exchange a world of experiences and an infinite number of ideas, plans, and possibilities.

They stop talking and simultaneously decide they'd better leave and leave quickly. They walk to the door holding hands. Joshua leans his head out, looks toward the exit path, and says in a hushed but urgent tone, "OK, let us move, now." Veronica tells Ognir, "Good boy. On alert."

In a moment they are passing temple worshipers going the other direction the day after Passover. Veronica reflects, while touching Ognir's head with her fingers, *It seems very cruel to discover, plan, and use a holding chamber for someone who will become a slave inside a temple storage room.*

MOMENTS LATER, TWO FIGURES APPROACH where Veronica had been held. "Something's wrong!" a strained voice exclaims. "The watch guard is gone! I told them I would be arriving after first prayer!" The smaller of the two picks up his pace while all the taller figure needs to do is lengthen his stride.

They make two turns, arrive at the outer passageway, and quickly move to the door, which they find ajar. The small man looks in so quickly he almost falls over. "They are gone! She is gone! How did this happen? We were so prepared. The guards were hand-picked. We practiced so many times ... so many times."

The taller figure keeps his composure and says calmly, "OK—no merchandise, no money. Return the deposit now if you please; I have other important errands to deal with before everyone leaves Jerusalem." He puts out his hand and barks "Now!"

VERONICA'S NEW TEMPLE APPLICATION

OGNIR IS READY TO GO and looks at Veronica as if to say, "I am ready, I am always ready. Why does it take you so long to get out the door early in the morning?"

"Ognir, you look genuinely nice today. I like the coat you are wearing. I will be a minute," Veronica says. She reviews her mental checklist, *Hair up in a bun—check. Blue dress—check. Shawl with tassels that Joshua likes—check. Sack with lunch for two—check. Ognir's snack—check. Have I forgotten anything? … No, let us go to the Temple and meet Joshua later. I cannot forget to take the longer route to say hello to Elias and Gabriel. I hope Jacob is keeping busy wherever he is. It was such a miracle to have him visit. It was only a year ago, but it seems like yesterday. What do resurrected people do all day? I suppose they are kept occupied so they do not get into mischief.*

Ognir is at Veronica's side as they walk. He is particularly attentive of Veronica's need for assurance in her quest to prepare and make application to work in the temple once again. Of course, he has no clue about his mistress's intentions, but he can feel her energy, the same way he had sensed when she was sad or lonely or in pain in years past, when he would be found next to her touching her leg or with his head on her lap.

Ognir even knows when Veronica has nightmares, sleeping on the floor at her side. She experiences bad dreams, which include scenes from her abduction, and she once dreamed of Joshua getting swallowed into the sand. Today, Ognir senses Veronica is visiting a sacred place because of the type of energy she has. They arrive at the top of the hill with the two benches.

"Elias! How are you this fine morning? You look good!" Veronica says, seeing Ognir had already placed himself directly in front of Elias.

"I will answer your two questions in a moment. I need to reacquaint myself with your guard here. Who knows what he would do to me if I did not pet him and let him know I am not a foe?" Elias replies.

"Oh, OK. I did not ask two questions. Is Jacob here playing jokes on you?"

"So, there is the third question. You need to slow down and let me answer the first two!"

"Yes sir. I wait upon you as I wait upon the Lord. I am patient," Veronica says peacefully as she sits down and watches Elias interact with Ognir while thinking, *It looks as though they have known each other for one hundred years. Where is Jacob? Oh, that was the second question.*

Without looking up, Elias says, "I am doing well, as usual. I like many parts of getting and being old. You can get up when you please, eat what you want, and even drink more wine than you should. I do not. But knowing I could brings a satisfaction you cannot gain when you are young. When you are young and drink too much, certain crude appetites take control, and you can do foolish, and sometimes dangerous things. When you are old, you may think of stupid things, but mostly you fall asleep somewhere, like the keeper of the records of old who was found missing his clothes, his sword, and his head! Nope, none of that for me." Elias has gotten sidetracked as usual, looks up from Ognir at Veronica and says, "Did I answer question one?"

Veronica is smiling, "Yes, Elias, you did a good job. Thank you."

She is about to remind Elias what question number two was when Elias says, "Gabriel is late today because he got a spurt of energy along with an unrealistic amount of optimism. That is the answer to question number two."

"What is he doing? If I may ask," Veronica asks in hopes of slowing Elias down a bit.

"Yes, you may ask, but I will not answer until I inform you about your third question; question number three, the eternal question. Ready?"

"Yes."

"Jacob is not bothering me very often. He visited, and we had a nice chat, the four of us, only a couple of weeks ago."

"That is lovely!" Veronica replies in a soft tone. "Who were the four? Jacob, yourself, Gabriel, and Lidia?"

"Why, of course. Should I count that as one question, or five? Who else do you think would put up with him? He had some funny things to say. Some surprising things as well. He could not stay long. He has way too much work to do where he is. It seems that the 'rest' they promise when you are there is not so accurate. I believe that is why my sweet wife has not visited; she is too busy doing things for others, and she knows I will not be long," Elias reports.

"My goodness," says Veronica, "I appreciate that you feel you can share these things with me." Veronica offers a smile as she looks into Elias's eyes. She then sees Lidia arriving, "Lidia! So good to see you!"

"Thank you, Veronica. Every time I see you, there is more light in your eyes," Lidia remarks.

"She has more meat on her bones, Lidia; she is getting her 'battle muscle' back. That's what it is," Elias adds.

Lidia grins at Veronica as she sits next to her. Ognir comes over to say hello.

"Hello, Ognir. So nice to see you today," Lidia says as she pets the top of his head, bends over to look into his eyes, and asks, "Are you taking good care of Veronica?"

"So, where are you off to?" Lidia asks, sitting back up and looking at Veronica.

"I am going to the temple for a visit today. I decided to come this way to say hello. You look well. I hope you feel that way," Veronica replies with a loving smile.

"Oh! That is wonderful. I hope you run across Gabriel. I saw him at morning prayer! He was there very early, and they allowed him to help prepare. He was practically running," Lidia says as Veronica glances at Elias, who nods his head yes, communicating to Veronica, "That's what I told you, right?"

Lidia also glances at Elias as she concludes with, "I do not know whether to laugh or cry … Gabriel has such a pure heart."

"Well yes, a pure heart but foolish pride. He is going to kill himself overdoing it. If he dies inside the temple I told him, they will take his body and offer it as a burnt sacrifice, right next to the goats! That's what I told him; I did," Elias declares.

Lidia retorts, "I will have nothing to do with this talk Elias. Gabriel has tried to do more since Jacob passed. You know that he was told to do as much temple work as he could by Jacob. He is trying his very best."

"Yes, you are correct, Lidia; however, the fellow Jesus told His followers that burnt offerings were to be stopped. After His followers get baptized, they are doing baptisms for their ancestors … nobody knows what they are supposed to do any more … such a strange world … everything is changing," Elias observes.

He knows about that? Veronica asks herself.

Lidia adds, "Yes, and the Pharisees and Sadducee leadership have engaged people to track down and arrest His followers."

"Such a sad state of affairs. His followers have been seen doing healing out in public. I also heard that He came back and taught His senior followers for some forty days … but alas, no warfare, no battles … telling people to love one another. The Pharisees do not want the competition. Makes you wonder, Lidia," Elias comments.

"Well, it is a very personal thing. You are all witness of my healing. Go and ask God himself to tell you what to believe. The invitation is always there … always," Veronica says with her peaceful smile. She then stands up and says goodbye to Lidia, then Elias.

"I am so happy to see you both and will pass your regards to Gabriel when I see him at the temple," she offers.

"Do not tell anything to Gabriel from me! I will not come to his funeral, either!" Elias yells after Veronica.

As Lidia is about to jump at that comment, Elias looks at her as if to say, "I got you!" with a big grin.

Lidia shakes her head.

Elias chuckles.

WHILE OGNIR AND VERONICA ARE walking, she thinks, *Hmmm, how many paces from here to the temple?... I cannot remember.... I hope Aaron is at the guard stand today; he likes it when I leave Ognir next to him. Ognir sits at attention and looks everyone in the eye. Last time Ognir almost launched himself after Mordechai. The guard thought it was hilarious.... I wonder what has become of Mordechai ... such a sorry story.*

She begins to consider what Lidia and Elias had said as she ponders, *I am so worried about the followers of Jesus, especially those who can congregate. I have been able to participate several times and love the feelings it gives me. The people to whom I gave dresses are so appreciative. I wish I could do more.*

Veronica's thoughts turn to her destination as she rounds the corner and sees the wide and tall stairsteps rising before her. She looks up and says to Ognir, "Yes, there is Aaron!"

Veronica bounds somewhat unladylike up the stairs with Ognir, who knows exactly where he is going. Aaron is on the right at the top, so they have to go up and traverse to the right. They receive several stares from others arriving or leaving the temple as they make the climb.

"Hello, Veronica! Great to see you!" Aaron exclaims. He then looks down and says in a military-like tone, "Ognir, my temporary companion, please, I have saved your spot. Come and sit. I remember when you gave Mordechai a good scare ... staring him down and baring your teeth. It was great entertainment. You probably will not see him around today. He has taken up a new hobby: turning in followers of the Rabbi from Nazareth. Mordechai's personal trail is always on a downward slope."

Ognir looks at Veronica who says, "Done." Ognir is in his place at attention in an instant. Veronica thinks, *Mordechai? I thought he had been placed in prison. He is turning in people who follow Jesus?* She turns to Aaron and smiles.

"Well, hello, Aaron! You two look as official as official can be. I hope you are doing well."

"Thank you. All is well. As you are aware, there is always something going on around here. Sometimes funny things, sometimes sad things, and these days, some things are miraculous," Aaron replies.

Veronica's eyes widen, "Really, what happened? What was the miracle if I may be so bold as to ask if that is ok?"

"Well, a while back, after I thought things had settled down, I observed two men start to walk up the stairs while a lame beggar yelled out to them for money—nothing out of the ordinary. I saw one of those men converse with the lame man, which is always the beginning of trouble as you know. So, the next thing I know, I see one of the men reach down and grasp the lame man's outstretched hand. It was amazing," Aaron reports.

Veronica responds, "Yes? So, they shook hands?"

"No. Yes," Aaron says as he looked at Veronica with wonder in his eyes and leans slightly forward, lowers his voice, and says, "Veronica, the lame man stood up, hugged the man whose hand he was still holding, started crying, and walked away. He stood and walked down the stairs. It all happened in only a moment."

"Oh my," Veronica said in a soft voice. "What happened next?"

"The two men quietly walked up the steps and entered the temple, and the lame man was gone. There were a few people around, coming and going, but there was no fuss—they were not from here, and they had not seen the lame man before, so they probably did not know what happened ... but I saw it all, and I know," Aaron elaborates. He stands back up straight and nods a confirming nod.

"Aaron, thank you kindly for sharing that with me. Please keep an eye on Ognir for me," Veronica says as she reaches in her sack, grabs a couple of snacks for Ognir, and hands them to Aaron, saying, "Here are some treats for Ognir if you so desire. I plan to give you yours at the end of your shift, so you will not get in trouble."

Aaron grins and says with emphasis, "Again."

Veronica grins and replies, "Yes. Again. I am still sorry about that, Aaron."

"No, it was actually hilarious, Veronica. Enjoy your visit," Aaron replies and then adds, "We all hope you will come back to work at the temple soon."

"Ahh, that is what I hope as well, Aaron. See you in a while," Veronica responds, then she turns to her right to enter her "home."

MIRACLES HAVE NOT CEASED. PEOPLE *with faith are all over. That was such a touching event, right at the gates of the temple,* Veronica thinks as she walks into the Court of Gentiles toward the Court of Women inside the walls of the temple.

Looking in awe at the sights of the temple, Veronica reviews what she understands about this sacred place, *There are the cloisters, all in a row, neat and tidy. There are several groups of people gathered in them. I wonder what they are talking about. Lidia took Mary and Joseph to a similar group gathered around the young boy Jesus one day long ago. She has seen so many important things. They are all simple and of seemingly little import, but when you see them together, they tell the most important story ever.*

"SO, WHERE ARE YOU? I have been standing here looking at you for five minutes and you have that 'faraway' look on your face," Joshua says to Veronica, who is startled when he speaks.

"Oh! Joshua! Hello! I was reflecting on the wondrous things which have transpired in this magnificent temple. It feels as though God has set to do His work among His people once more. I am so glad to see you. Thank you for coming," Veronica says in a peaceful tone.

She wants to hug Joshua but instead looks into his eyes thinking, *He is so gallant and handsome. I love him for saving me. That day seems so far away....*

Joshua, standing in front of Veronica, cocks his head sideways and says, "Hello? You are drifting away again." He smiles when she acknowledges him and then asks, "Are we not going to walk together and then eat something delicious you have prepared for me, er, us?"

"Yes, my dear friend Joshua, whom they call, 'the Young Merchant,' I will show you the temple's fine jewels and elegant clothing. She is adorned with beautiful, holy accessories, even as she is still being completed. Her people love her. She is my closest friend."

"Your closest friend?" Joshua asks with a quizzical smile on his face.

"Yes," Veronica responds with confidence. She then adds, "You will need to stand in line." She provides a thought-provoking smile with her face as well as her eyes.

As they walk, Veronica cannot help thinking about what had brought them together, *I know so little about this man. He has spoken briefly of his mother, grandmother, grandfather, cousins. Has he no siblings? No uncles? No father? I suppose he has similar questions about me. I hope he does not ask.*

A poet could not script what wonderful conversation and views are shared between Veronica and Joshua that afternoon. They feel they are alone with wonder all around.

"Yes, I will be well prepared, and yes, I will make application to the committee next they meet. When do they meet these days, Dinah?" Veronica confirms and asks.

"They meet twice a year to organize the temple volunteer teams. The applications must be approved by the subcommittees one hundred days prior. What position or group do you wish to join?" Dinah replies, knowing full well what Veronica wants to do as she thinks, *Veronica will certainly want to teach. She will ask for a group of twelve-year-olds. I worry, though, that she may not be welcomed.*

"Of course, I will gladly do anything they wish me to do," Veronica replies with excitement in her eyes. She considers for a moment and says, "If they ask me to tell them where I feel in my heart I would be of most worth and value, I will tell them 'With the first and second-year girls, dear sirs, the twelve and thirteen-year-olds.' Those are the children most trainers are afraid of. Such untethered energy contained in small spaces.

Of course, the boys are nearly as frightening, but at the same age, they are mostly clueless and starting to mumble when they talk and stumble when they walk," Veronica replies in her customary lots-of-details manner.

It is a delight to see such beaming light coming from Veronica's face. She is actually looking years younger. The past few months of peace and calm have done her good. I will need to poke around to know the general disposition of the subcommittee members toward Veronica's desires, which are as pure as could possibly be. I wonder how she will be accepted by them since her healing was noised about in so many neighborhoods, Dinah ponders as she completes folding the Egyptian fabric Joshua retrieved for her when he went south.

Dinah then offers some assistance. "Yes, I agree. I believe you would love to work with them, and they will love you dearly. You need to keep two things in mind; One—you will not be allowed to discuss, while you are in the temple, your healing with Jesus and, Two—because of that experience, regardless of the miracle that it was, it may keep you from being accepted by the committees," Dinah says, then she looks over at Veronica.

Veronica's eyes are clear and filled with light as she ponders what Dinah shared. She looks directly at Dinah and replies, "Yes, I understand. I wait upon the Lord and ask that His will be done."

VERONICA ARRIVES AT DINAH'S WORKSHOP with an armful of completed fabrics. "Have you spoken with them?" she asks before even saying hello. She sets the finished goods on the designated shelf. Prior instances when she had asked the same question were not quite as enthusiastic as this time. She turns and waits as calmly as possible for Dinah's response.

"Yes, Veronica, I have spoken with each member of the subcommittee as well as two members of the full temple committee." Dinah pauses for an instant and says, "Why do you ask?" with a broad smile.

Veronica is frozen with anticipation, her hands now in fists, arms straight down, her eyes as big as a puppy's eyes anticipating a cookie. The energy inside her builds up as she is trying to capture a response to the honest-but-mischievous question and get it out in a somewhat dignified way.

Sophie had stepped in and stands watching the drama, which instantaneously fills the room. She reviews the situation and recognizes, *At least they are both smiling, so perhaps no crisis today.*

Veronica gains enough control to speak after taking a deep, controlling breath. She softly responds, "I am asking, Dinah, because I appreciate all the efforts you have been taking on my behalf. I also wish to apologize for bursting in on your day without notice. Please accept my sincere expression of love."

Veronica stops speaking, but she is not done. Dinah does not respond as she is laying fabric on the workshop design table. Veronica stands for a moment and, in a tensely restrained voice, "So," she gulps, "What did they say?" She asks the question quietly as she releases her fists, drops her shoulders, and gently brings her hands up to her chest. She tries to keep her palms open and place them together, and she is successful for only a moment before her fingers intertwine and become a double fist. Her eyes remain wide open and pleading.

All eyes are on Dinah, who seems to be in no hurry. She moves the fabric slightly so that each piece is in the correct position. Without looking up, she asks in a soft, motherly-education-moment tone, "Veronica, when you design a garment, what is the first step?"

"Speak to the recipient, or the customer. You need to know what it will be used for and in what season and what fabric and design ideas ... to start," Veronica responds, caught a bit off guard.

"Yes, you have done that step many, many times," Dinah confirms. She adds another piece of fabric and asks, "And when you have this important information, do you begin cutting so you will get this important garment completed as quickly as possible because you have three other clients waiting in line?"

"If you only wanted this particular client once and they were going to a land far, far away, like Greece or Ethiopia, and they ask for it immediately, perhaps yes, but word would spread quickly, and the three clients you have in line would go elsewhere," Veronica responds with grand gestures. Her hands are no longer clasped with tension.

Dinah listens and says, "And?"

Veronica takes a step forward and explains, "It is advisable to procure the fabric, show it to the client and get their ideas while you offer your suggestions. You then come to a mutual agreement before you begin."

"I understand," Dinah says, still working. "So, what is my answer to your original question then?" She adds her own question, feeling Veronica and Sophie have already sorted out where she is going.

How ... did ... she ... do that? Veronica wonders. She looks at Sophie and smiles, then replies, "You have interviewed your customers and are reaching an agreement favorable to, in this case, your desires to achieve excellence and a very happy customer ... relationship."

Dinah looks up at Veronica and pronounces, "No."

Veronica is surprised and her mind races, *No? What happened? They said no?*

Dinah continues and tries to get to her punch line before Veronica breaks down, "I am influencing our clients. At this point, all the subcommittee members agree that you should become a member of their staff with two of the full temple committee members offering to suggest an acceptance of the subcommittee's recommendation. Lidia is working on, er, with the remaining old, er, distinguished members. We fully expect a successful outcome dear Veronica."

Veronica bursts into tears. She runs to Dinah and embraces her. She is shaking and speechless and sobbing heavily. Dinah embraces Veronica and sheds tears as well. She looks over at Sophie, who is also crying. The spirit of joy unspeakable cannot adequately be described in any language.

Veronica is cleansed in preparation for temple service four months later after the approvals are administered and recorded. The next eighteen months are as a passing dream for Veronica as well as her young Temple students.

The World Changes

"Dinah, I tell you; I saw it with my own eyes!" Daniel says, his voice filled with fear.

"Daniel, calm down. Bolting in here and declaring, 'Veronica's in danger!' does not help me understand what is going on. Sit down, take a few deep breaths, and explain exactly why you feel that way, and thank you, Daniel, for taking time to come all the way over here to 'warn' me. Give it to me one … piece … at a time," Dinah says in a reassuring voice.

Daniel sits down and starts breathing slowly and deeply to calm down. Dinah hands him a cup of water and thinks, *This has to be serious. I have seen Daniel upset with "elites" before, but never so disturbed. His face is pale as if he has seen death itself.* She pats his knee and asks, "Feeling better? There is no hurry. Take your time and tell me what you can."

Daniel looks better than when he arrived. He takes another sip of water, places the cup on the table, and looks at Dinah as if he would begin to explain. Instead, he starts crying, which would have turned into sobbing had Dinah not handed him the cup again. She consoles him, "Take your time; we can get through this together, Daniel. I trust you. You know that, right?"

Daniel is looking at the cup. He looks up at Dinah and says sheepishly, "Yes. Thank you." He takes another sip, lets out a sigh of relief, sets the cup back down, and starts slowly.

"I was in the office of the temple committee delivering the new draperies—you know, the design you did for them. Well, I also needed to discuss the materials they need for the next temple construction step. Well, I was sitting in the small reception area—I was not eavesdropping at all; I was sitting there, out of sight, and they were inside the committee meeting room." Daniel stops and looks up.

"How many of the committee members were there? Do you know?" Dinah asks Daniel, coaxing him to continue.

"There were four or five of the senior members. I do not know all their names, but Ezra was there, and I was there to speak with him."

"Ezra! I know Ezra. I have worked with him for years. So, what happened next, Daniel?" Dinah says in as calm and reassuring a voice as she can.

"I know exactly what they said and will remember it forever.... Someone asked 'So, are you keeping an eye on our little angel? How is she doing?' Another person replied 'How do you think she is doing? She is perfect. She assumed her assignment as she has always assumed her assignments. What else would you expect? You should have more respect for her. She could teach your grumpy, old temple staff a thing or two. She knows how to serve with love and compassion, and she does not forget where she is, or who she is.'" Daniel reports, gaining some composure.

"Were they talking about Veronica?"

"Yes, of course. Who else would they be talking about?"

"Yes, go on." Dinah says reassuringly.

"The person they were interrogating was excused, leaving Ezra and two others, I believe. Ezra never said anything to them. The other two gave away the trap they had placed Veronica in ... the trap!" Daniel exclaims and begins to get shaky again as he looks up to Dinah.

"Daniel, how do you know it is a trap?" Dinah asks in a soft voice.

"They discussed how they approved the subcommittee's recommendation to bring Veronica back as a temple worker so they could keep an eye on her and see if she would preach Jesus to the children. If she did, they would arrest her. Well you know she would not do that contrary to the rules, but they do not know that, so they are keeping her at the temple so they know where she is, where she will be for when they collect enough evidence or get people they pay to give false witness.

They want to arrest her. They pay people to do that now. Where have we come to, Dinah?"

Dinah asks using the same calming voice, "Daniel, do they know you are a close acquaintance of Veronica?"

"No. After they were done, the two committee members went out the back door while Ezra came out and saw me. Luckily, I acted as if I had only just walked in, so he has no idea what I heard. I am so fearful for Veronica. She is so innocent and pure."

"Daniel, listen to me. Look at me Daniel." Dinah says in a calm but direct way.

Daniel looks up as he is wiping tears away from his now-red eyes as she asks, "You have dealt with the committee for a very long time, haven't you Daniel?"

"Yes. Way too long. It is exhausting," Daniel replies.

"Yes, the reason it is so exhausting is because they take forever to make any decisions, correct?"

"You can say that again. Yes," says Daniel.

"I know people, your boss for example, and others who are fully aware of what is going on. I promise you that we will prepare an escape for Veronica. The moment any decision is made about her welfare, we will know about it. How does that sound? Are you with me on this, Daniel?" Dinah offers as she invokes her sales skills.

"I think so. I am so upset they could do something like this to anyone, but to trap Veronica, who thinks she is working in heaven and who loves her little temple workers. It is evil … not at all what they should be doing," Daniel says, looking again at Dinah and continues, "Thank you for listening to me. Sometimes I feel forgotten, always doing everything everyone else hates doing, so I do it, day after day, year after year … all alone."

Dinah consoles her longtime friend. "Daniel, you know you are not alone. We know all the good you do, and most of all God himself knows you and appreciates your work. You have possibly saved Veronica's life today. We will say nothing of this to her but will prepare for the worst and pray for the best to come of all this. OK?"

"Yes, I know who they are and where they frequent. You need to place them on your list. They will be easy to snare, and to make it worth your while, I will pay you, not the other way around this time," Mordechai nervously tells Saul from Tarsus while his eyes dart around.

"I have associates who know you, and they have all told me not to trust anything you say or do and especially to distrust anything you want to pay me to do," Saul replies to Mordechai's offer, adding, "I will consider your generous offer, and we will be in touch. Have a good day, sir." He turns and leaves, hoping the stench of the conversation does not sully his reputation.

Two additional opportunities to capture, and cleanse. What has been growing in the darkness? I suppose they will be worth looking into as soon as we gather enough support to have a mobile "cleaning team" who are always ready to evict, arrest, or stone. I believe we will be ready to trap Stephen in the next couple of weeks … maybe sooner, Saul reasons as he makes his way to the predetermined meeting location.

"You cannot tell them; it is not your place, Reuben. It must be their mother. Not you," Lidia emphasizes, looking into Reuben's eyes with authority he cannot refuse.

"They are going to want to get married. That cannot happen. It would be a grievous sin," Reuben replies.

"So, prior to any marriage, they will go to his home, and she will meet his mother and grandmother. Let it be." Lidia is still looking into Reuben's eyes, which will not stay focused on her. He looks down.

Lidia continues, "You are no longer responsible for her destiny. She needs to progress by making her own decisions … as she has been doing so remarkably for many years, Reuben."

"Lidia, I know and understand that. I am so proud of her. I was terrified when I heard that she went, on her own—well, with Sophie—to meet the Rabbi from Nazareth, or Capernaum at the time. He was nothing like my brother.... He had the power to rid us of the Romans and rule if He was who he said He was. If He had done what He should have done, we would be better off. His following was growing. He healed Veronica, and she knows some of His followers."

"Reuben, you will not lose her. She has a business here and loves to work in the temple. She will be back. All will be well." Lidia then responds to Reuben's reflections, "You should know that the Rabbi ministered to the individual. He only did what He was told by His Father to do, and the entire world is better because of His sacrifice. He did not force anyone, He only invited."

Reuben hears what Lidia is saying, but his mind is reflecting on the potential disaster which awaits Veronica if she stays at the temple. He looks out the window of his office and thinks, *How is this possible? I received a little baby by surprise, found a nurse-mother caretaker for her and have made sure she is safe. She has a natural tendency to choose the right path growing up, and then, she endured the debilitating illness with courage and strength. I love her and cannot bear to see her go. Now we are pressed by glorious possibility on one side and disaster and imprisonment on the other.*

"Reuben," Lidia says in a calmer voice that reaches through his thought-fog, "I need to go. Keep your eyes open and send a runner should they try to make any moves." She touches his arm. He looks at her and motions, "Yes. Thank you."

As Lidia makes her way out along the open breezeway that overlooks the temple, she contemplates how complex life has become in Jerusalem, *If Veronica can learn of her beginnings in a gentle, natural way, it will make her stronger. If that knowledge is thrust upon her without mercy, she may never recover.*

She notices that the gathering is beginning for evening prayer and thinks of the many hundreds of times she has been there, at this exact moment, preparing for God's children to participate in sacred ordinances, *I loved being there. I hope Veronica finds peace. I do not believe she will be there for many more months.*

"Before you arrive at the temple for your assignments, children, how do you prepare?"

Several twelve-year-old girls' hands shoot up. Veronica nods at the first girl and says, "Yes, Judith?"

Judith stands and replies, "My mother and I talk about what I learned last week. She asks me how I feel when I am here, and I tell her."

"And how do you feel today?"

"Well, if I concentrate on what you are saying and try my best, I feel warm inside."

"Thank you, Judith," Veronica says with a smile.

"Samantha, would you like to share?"

"Yes, Miss Veronica. I try to think about the temple alone, when it is quiet, and go over what we do and think of why it is important to God that we do it properly."

"Samantha, thank you, and thanks to all of you who do similar things as Samantha and Judith to prepare to come and work in the temple. We all appreciate everything you do. Your work is important to all those who visit, and ..." Veronica changes the tone of her upbeat voice to a more serious tone, "it is very important to God, who knows and loves you. He even knows your names."

Veronica smiles and stands as she looks at all the girls dressed in white dresses and announces, "Today we will start with laundry and folding and delivery! Then, if we complete all our tasks with excellence, we may get to see where the birds are. Does that sound like a plan?"

The girls eagerly shake their heads yes. Veronica is thinking, *I love these girls with all my heart, mind and soul. They are wonderful and want to learn everything at once. My life has been so very blessed. Hmmm ... I wonder what Joshua is up to.*

She engages in her lesson again, "Each plan is made up of a sequence of steps which allows you to move forward toward your goal. If a plan only includes your goal, and no steps, you may actually end up going, exactly ..." Veronica jumps up and turns facing the opposite way as she exclaims, "backwards!" All the girls giggle.

Looking at Omari the Camel Herder, Joshua explains, "You see, I don't exactly want to leave yet; there are things I need to sort out first."

"Oh, and would those things have anything to do with someone named, 'Ve-ron-i-ca'?" Omari quips with a wry smile.

Joshua blushes, looks straight at Omari, and affirms, "Well … yes, of course. I cannot stop thinking about her. There is something about her eyes."

"So," asserts Omari, "you are the same fellow who, for many kilometers, told me I was not in my right mind for being prepared, and now it is you who has fallen to the 'eyes of the enemy.' Ha!"

"After all this time, you have a lonely goat … that's all."

"Ah, yes my Young Merchant," Omari retorts, "my camel is not as lonely as you say, because it is you who rides her when your Veronica wants to go somewhere with us! She loves you … my camel does." He looks up at the sky and adds, "It is so beautiful to see my bride on my camel, hahahaha!" He lowers his voice and with a somber look, shakes his head, saying, "You are the one who is unprepared my friend."

"Well, 'Camel Driver,' we will see where this goes. Before anything permanent happens, Veronica will need to meet my family. Then we will see, now, won't we?"

Omari looks down again to add some drama and says, "Oh, you have no idea what it will be like to marry someone who is smarter than you are, has more connections than you do, and" he looks up at Joshua quickly, "is prettier than you, no matter what my loyal bride camel says."

"Omari, you are correct on most points…." Joshua says before Omari interjects with, "And imagine what will happen when, after you have been riding my bride camel all the way up north, your Veronica meets your mother and your grandmother and they fall in love with her and no longer pay any attention to you. You will be resigned to spending all your time with your grandfather before, and especially after, the lovely marriage you are secretly contemplating. But do not worry ... my bride camel, Miskah, will be looking for you and will always know where to find you!"

Joshua smiles and responds, "You do have a point there. Your camel does like me more than he likes you. You should treat him kindly. He likes to munch on Veronica's licorice cakes. You should try that and see if it will mend your relationship." Joshua stands up, slaps Omari on the shoulder, and walks outside, chuckling on the way.

"Sophie, do you think Joshua would make a good husband, a good father?" Veronica asks in a soft, reflective voice as she is laying out some fabric on her worktable.

Sophie sets her crochet on her lap and responds with a dreamy, light voice, "I suppose, if I were approximately your age and had potentially strong feelings about said gentleman, that I would seriously consider such import-ant questions before making a dreadful mistake." Veronica is grinning at Sophie's sophisticated, overstudied response that tells her nothing at all.

"Please, go on, my dear confidante, Sophie; your reflection is enchant-ing," Veronica teases as her smile continues to light up her face.

Sophie giggles and says, "Yes! He is a bit old for me, but someone who was old like him would find him to be a perfect husband and a very good father, but his children, especially the many girls, will wish to spend most of their time with their charming mother," she observes, smiling while looking up at Veronica and batting her eyelashes.

"Now that was a full and complete answer to my simple 'yes-or-no' question. You, Sophie, have been very observant as you visit your elite clients and are beginning to sound increasingly more like them...."

Veronica changes to a feigned-old-man voice and lowers her chin to look at Sophie with a comical frown, "Be careful, my senior assistant or there will be those who wish to 'take you down.'" She then bats her eyelashes as Sophie had done.

They both start laughing together and as they continue working, chat about the grand possibilities of the future.

Dreams are being fulfilled.

NEW BEGINNINGS

"WE ARE RETURNING TO JERUSALEM to where you-know-who lives, in freedom, since Ognir saved her months ago, and you are not paying attention to your loyal camel except when you-know-who is around my friend, the Young Merchant, who is hopelessly in love and has not thought a single practical thought for days."

"That is not true at all! I have not had a clear mind for weeks, not days. I have no idea what has come over me. I am useless ... and am afraid I will be 'pitifully useless' when we get to Jerusalem tomorrow. All my plans have been disrupted. Why? Perfume and the smile of a woman ... such a sad state of affairs."

"Ha! You forgot to mention a few primary facts which make you not only 'pitiful' but also a noticeably clear sort of 'underling.' Number one—you gave her the perfume she wears, but I am positive she shared it with her camel ... what is his name? Yes, Smooshy Face."

"It is Squishy Lips, not Smooshy Face."

"Yes, of course. You will need to be careful when you want a kiss in the dark to not follow the scent of the romantic perfume they both use because of you, or you will get a great, big, slobbery kiss, and the camel's magnificent camel eyelashes are many times longer than hers," Omari declares in a practical, "sound advice" sort of way.

"You are having way too much fun with my despair."

"Number two—This woman who has distracted you temporarily has many more valuable skills than you do.

    A. She is a senior camel master trainer officer … with a Roman medal … a medal of honor.

    B. She can make anything out of nothing with ease, and she will be smiling all the while.

    C. She knows people of enormous influence.
      and

    D. Her character is upright, and she is humble … when she needs to be."

Omari continues, "You are treading on territory you know little about, and now you have also lost your mind! Hahahaha! I cannot stand by and watch this Greek tragedy happen before my eyes. I will need to gather all the young ladies once again and entertain them once again, each … and … every … one. I will dust off my amazing turban and will show you how it is done."

"Yes, remember, you will have only two old gentlemen observing your theater unless they have talked someone else into hanging out with them. Do not forget to bring your sweet cakes … brother," Joshua says with a smile of reconcilation.

"This was delicious, Veronica, thank you. I love being with you … when you have the time," Joshua says calmly as he and Veronica finish eating together.

"You are very welcome, Joshua. That is your real name, isn't it?" Veronica responds. She gathers the platter and as she turns to take it away, adds, "I mean, you did not change it during your trip, did you? I am glad you are passing through and did not quickly drop your orders off then continue on to Alexandria and Cairo." She turns with a smile back toward Joshua adding, "And I am also happy to be with you as well."

Joshua's face blushes, and he passes back a huge smile. Veronica turns away again while arranging what she had gathered while Joshua's mind is busy, *My name? She wonders about my name. Should I ask her? Should I ask her now? She is pleased I am here? …*

Her hair is amazing when it is down ... it reminds me of my mother's hair. I should not think like that.

Veronica's mind is doing the same thing, *When is he going to ask me? It has been months and months. Maybe he is going back on the trade route and needs some time. Maybe he thinks I will become ill again and that I am going to be a burden. Why am I so busy doing so many things that I have spent hardly any time with him? I have been ignoring him. Why do I push people away? Why do I abandon them? He is too good for me. He knows every merchant in every town ... everywhere. Why would he want to be with me?*

So, there they are. Joshua looking at Veronica's back, distracted by Veronica's hair, which she let down out of the bun she normally has it in. Veronica is frozen in self-doubt. Time stands still for each of them, until Joshua breaks the silence by slowly asking, "Veronica, I would like it if you would ..."

Veronica asks herself, *Is this it? Will he ask me?* Veronica turns to face Joshua with, "Yes?"

Joshua clears his throat and continues, "I would like to ask if you would be willing to come with me, to meet my mother and family, up north, near Mount Hermon ... when you are free." He looks into her wondrous eyes with a boyish smile, full of anticipation.

Her mind races, *He finally asked. I am so proud of him. Of course, I will go. I need to sort out some business affairs, and tell ....* Her response has not made it to her mouth yet so Joshua adds, "Of course, if you are too busy, I will understand, and ..."

"Of course! I would love to have you escort me to meet your esteemed family. Thank you sincerely for asking a lowly seamstress. She would be delighted," Veronica says in Sophie-style as she curtsies. Her green eyes are shining with delight.

They both are thrilled beyond measure and feel like they should embrace each other but are fine with having the joy of being in each other's company.

Sophie looks up from her work on a set of draperies and asks, "I do not want to be in your way, but I would really like to be with you as you work in the temple a few days, Veronica. Every time you describe what it is like, I feel as if I am missing something sacred in my life. Do you think it would be acceptable? I mean am I allowed to visit and watch your amazing group of girls? What do you think?"

"How long have you wanted to ask me that question, Sophie?" Veronica replies without looking up.

"Oh, about since you first mentioned how you love working there about …" she looks up to the ceiling, "yeah, about twenty …" she looks directly at Veronica and completes her response with confidence, "thousand years ago. Not long. Not long at all I must say."

"Well, if it has been that long, I suppose I could put in a request with the Committee, but since you are the daughter of the esteemed Dinah, and, of course, the granddaughter of the legendary Lidia, I believe they will certainly approve more quickly than they would for any 'common' person."

"Yes? They will say yes? So how long will that take? A week? When will they meet again?"

"They will meet again in the fall."

"What?"

"But I can make special arrangements and get you in with me through the south gate … uhmmm … tomorrow. How does that plan sound?"

Sophie squeals with delight. She also has a plan of her own that she has been working on with Lidia's help. "Yes! Thank you! I will be there before morning prayer."

"Good, I will come meet you at the guard station. Aaron will be waiting for you. I will come with my girls, who will be thrilled to meet you," Veronica confirms.

"Thank you, thank you, thank you. A thousand times thank you!" Sophie says as she thinks, *I have already met each of your girls, and we have something wonderful planned for you my sweet Veronica, whom I adore as if you were my older sister.*

"You are older and more sophisticated than I was led to believe, miss. Are you the very same Sophie that Veronica was talking about with me this morning?" Aaron, the guard at the temple gate, asks.

Sophie blushes and curtsies as she responds, "Why yes, sir, my name is Sophie. I am here to meet Veronica. I am very excited to be here and am very glad to meet you, sir."

"You look familiar. Do you have family who have worked in the temple in the past?"

"Well, yes, sir. My mother is Dinah, and my grandmother is Lidia. They have both worked many years inside these magnificent walls," Sophie responds as politely as she can while also commenting about the structure of the rebuilt temple.

"Young woman, you have a mother and a grandmother who are both as solid and as steadfast as these 'magnificent walls.' God has His eyes on you." He looks at Sophie, who is watching through the gate for Veronica, who at that very moment is striding toward her.

"Sophie! Please come in. The girls are waiting for you," Veronica says as she greets Sophie. She looks up at Aaron and says, "Thank you for your kind assistance, Aaron."

"You are welcome, Veronica. Please have a good day," Aaron the guard responds without leaving his station.

Veronica and Sophie walk quickly and are soon at their destination. The girls are thrilled to see Sophie, and they spend the rest of the day tending to their temple responsibilities. Sophie is trying to soak it all in and keeps an eye out for Lidia, who should be arriving toward the end of the shift.

Sophie's mind is busy, *I will need to remember everything we did today so I can tell mother how orderly it all is. Veronica is a master teacher, and her girls are so attentive and precise with each task. They all look like miniature Veronicas. I cannot wait to tease her about that. Grandmother should be here any moment.*

Veronica is thinking as her girls complete their last tasks for the shift, *I am so happy Sophie is here, especially today. The girls are on their best behavior and seem to have more energy than usual.*

Veronica notices the level of energy rise as the girls all see someone arrive. One of them calls out, "Miss Lidia!"

Indeed, it is Lidia, who sets a package on the table before being surrounded by twelve girls, each vibrating with energy and excitement. Veronica wonders what unusual treat Lidia brought this time. Sophie's face lights up watching the commotion with pure joy and anticipation.

"Girls! I am so happy to see you all!" Lidia exclaims as she reaches out to greet each one of them.

"Do you have it?" One of the girls asks as she looks at the package on the table and reaches over to touch it.

"Yes," Lidia says. She then looks at Veronica and says in a grandmotherly way, "Veronica sweetheart, please sit down. The girls have prepared something they wish to present to you."

What? I am so surprised. I better sit quickly before I faint, Veronica thinks as she looks for the nearest chair and begins to sit as she glances over to Sophie, whose huge smile gives away that she is part of the surprise.

"Go ahead girls," Lidia says as she nods her head.

The oldest girl reaches for the package Lidia had set on the table, carefully picks it up, and motions to the other girls to join her as she brings it over to and stands directly in front of their beloved teacher. The girls stand together with beaming faces.

"Miss Veronica," the student begins, trying to be as formal as possible while not forgetting what she planned to say, "We, your humble temple workers, wish to thank you for all you have given us." She looks at her fellow students and then back to Veronica.

"We have prepared a gift for you that we all helped create. It is not perfect like what you make, but we hope it will remind you of how we love you and appreciate all you have taught us." She pushes through the words and carefully sets the package on Veronica's lap, because Veronica's hands are busy wiping tears away from her eyes. All the girls are crying at this point, including Sophie and Lidia.

Veronica tries to gain some composure as she looks at each of the girls with a full heart. She carefully begins to open the package as she thinks, *My joy is full. I have never felt such pure love in my entire life. I wonder what precious item they have created ... with their own hands, oh. I love their hands; they have continually sacrificed their time righteously working here in God's temple.* She opens the gift and pulls a cloth item out of the package, looks at it with wonder, and cannot believe it.

"Oh, my goodness, girls!" Veronica exclaims as she lifts it up.

"It is magnificent. It is beautiful!" she happily declares as she looks at each of the girls, who are brimming with joy as well. Veronica thinks, *Where did they find the purple embroidery thread? This reminds me of the tunic I created that ended up on Jesus.* She looks at Lidia, then at Sophie, thinking, *Well done my dear friends, Well done. I love you both. You are my strength, my hope and my dearest friends.*

Veronica pulls the fabric to her heart and gushes, "Thank you, thank you, thank you! I love it! I will always treasure it."

She spreads it out for everyone to see and as the master teacher, says, "Please, come. Show me what wonderful things each of you have made. Please come close. Let us look at this perfect piece of work together."

Sophie looks at Lidia, who looks back with a smile. It is hard to tell who is happier. Lidia, however, knows what is ahead.

"I AM SO HAPPY TO see you once again. Do you have my order? Did it make it without damage? Without sand? Please, come in and take a seat. My wife made these for you," Ezra says as he reaches over, picks up a small packet, and hands it to Joshua.

Joshua sets the fabric order on the table and looks around as he slides his sales pouch to his back, takes a seat, and offers, "Thank you! You have made some nice changes around here, Ezra. How did that come about?"

"I will certainly tell you because it is all your fault, but first let's settle business."

"Of course!" Joshua says, "Let me get them one … by … one for you. I am sure you and your clients will be pleased." Joshua opens each package and lays them on the table so they all can be seen at the same time. Ezra is visibly pleased with the delivery.

"Oh yes, we have done well, you and I. Thank you for bringing these to me." He stops, looks up at Joshua, and asks seriously, "You did not bring these patterns of beauty to anyone but me.… Is that correct, Joshua?"

"Ezra, you are correct as usual. These patterns are not found at any of my merchants' shops between here and the great city of Byzantium. You are a privileged man."

"You speak the words of good business, Joshua. I trust you and appreciate you, even if you are only a young boy," Ezra declares.

Joshua is thrilled to hear such kind words, but his interest is still piqued by the improvements which have been made, so he asks, "Ezra, tell me what inspired you to part with the substantial costs needed to turn your shop into a showplace of grandeur?" He looks around again and settles on Ezra's eyes, which are glistening with joy.

"Ha! You ask me what inspired all this?" Ezra says waving his arm across the display and cutting room. He places his hands on the table, looks at Joshua, and declares, "That woman you enchanted, she came here with her young friend. I cannot remember her name.…"

Joshua interrupts with, "Veronica? You saw Veronica and Sophie? They came into your shop?"

"Oh yes, my young friend, and they were so cordial, with such wonderful smiles, I was happy to agree with all their suggestions. You are incredibly lucky I am not fifty years younger or else you would have no chance with her at all." He grins like a young lad as he nods a confirming accord with the improvements; he had let Veronica and Sophie complete their suggested improvements and adds, "Yes, they told me that 'times were changing and my clients need to feel they are walking into a sophisticated business which,'" he looks up to retrieve a thought, "hmmmm … 'caters to their needs.' Yes, that is it. They are supposed to come back before winter to change to a different 'seasonal' color scheme."

Joshua's look of surprise is all he can muster when Ezra confirms the success of "catering to his clients' needs" by saying, "Yes, business has been better ever since. I have been selling to the younger generation too … they have more money than we did in our youth, if you want to know."

Joshua is trying to sort it all out as his mind searches for clues, *How did she know? What would give her the idea of reaching out to my clients? How…?*

His thoughts are cut off when someone at the front of the shop yells, "The movers will be here in the morning to take all this trash out the east gate and dump it in the garbage heap! The Committee on Joyful Living has determined this establishment to be a hazard to the well-being of too many of Jerusalem's residents. It needs to go, and it needs to be shut down sooner rather than later!"

The intruder walks toward them as he is delivering his raucous speech, grabs a chair as he completes, reaches over the table to shake hands with Joshua and glances at Ezra with a big grin and asks, "How did you like it? Pretty convincing do not you two fine gentlemen think?"

They all stare at each other until Joshua exclaims, "I love visiting with you both! You are so entertaining! So worth having as friends. Great to see you!"

Ezra and Josiah look at each other as if confused. Together they both look over at Joshua and react toward him as if he had insulted them. They glance at each other again, seem to decide, look back at Joshua, and declare simultaneously, "We are not your friends. We are your 'clients.'" They hold their gaze. Joshua has no clue what to say so he looks back calmly with a smile. The stare down continues until Joshua says quietly, "I am truly sorry, gentlemen…" at which point Ezra and Josiah burst out laughing and pat each other on the back exclaiming, "We got him! That was a good one!"

Joshua laughs with them ... again as he realizes, *They certainly have not lost any of their wit since last I saw them; that is a good thing. We all need humor in these difficult days. I need to get to everyone else soon so I can complete the trip down to Alexandria and get back to take Veronica to meet my family.... I hope they like her.... I know they will love her.* He completes his visit with Ezra and hurries to make his delivery to Josiah and gives his wife a gift as well.

THERE ARE MANY PEOPLE OUT and about this evening although the sounds seem subdued. Joshua is thinking, *The colors are disappearing as they do every night at this time ... seems like the world's light is put out as well. So sad my friend from long ago was taken away....*

"Joshua, stop daydreaming and pay attention to your surroundings," Eran says in a quiet but stern voice as he appears right next to Joshua, who is stunned and replies, "I hate it when you appear with advice and counsel."

"I know you appreciate it when I save your life, time after time. When you are an officer in the Roman army, you will learn to 'appear,'" Eran replies, then, without hesitation, says, "We are going directly to wherever Veronica is. Take me to her right now."

Joshua is shocked. *How can he be so abrupt, and how does he believe I know where Veronica is at this very moment?* He replies, "I don't know where she is...." He is cut off as Eran picks up the pace and says, "I know exactly where she is, hurry!"

Joshua runs to catch up to his determined guide.

"WHAT BRINGS YOU TWO GENTLEMEN here, together, when it is not dark? Should I be delighted or frightened?" Veronica asks as she glances at Dinah and Lidia and then over to Sophie who is walking in ... with Daniel ... and Reuben.

Both Veronica and Joshua's jaws drop. Veronica now has all she needs to know which emotion she should feel. She reaches out her hand and takes Joshua's, then quietly moves to sit on the bench with him and whispers, "Frightened."

Reuben steps forward as is his custom, scans those present, and focuses on Veronica and Joshua as he announces, "We have come to know that there are evil forces at work in Jerusalem and beyond."

Veronica thinks, *I am with my clients or in the temple working with my children and have heard nothing evil, besides what recently happened to Stephen. Where is this going and why is Reuben here? I remember he came to my ceremony at the training grounds. Why is he looking at us?* She glances at Joshua and squeezes his hand tighter.

Joshua is as puzzled and worried as he thinks, *What is going on? My plans, our plans…. It feels as if they are going to be rendered useless. Stop introducing a speech and get to the point. Better yet, let Eran get to the point. He can say what needs to be said in one short sentence.* He glances back at Veronica and then at Eran. Joshua's thoughts conclude with, *Eran is focused on Reuben as if he knows what he is going to reveal … and by the look on his face, it won't be good.*

"Veronica and Joshua …" says Reuben, who now has their full attention, "You are being set up for arrest and possible stoning. You will need to escape in two days."

Veronica's world collapses. She switches instinctively into battle mode as she stands and takes the floor, "What? How could this be? Who are you to march in here and make such outlandish declarations!" She is staring directly into Reuben's eyes, which feel this danger more deeply than she could ever realize.

Oh, my sweetheart, I wish I could tell you who I am and why this is as painful to me as it is to you. I can only pray that God will watch over you, along with the entire Ninth Regiment, Reuben thinks as he looks back at Veronica then at Daniel, inviting him to gently provide what he has observed.

"Veronica, we all love and appreciate you more than words can tell. Thank you for listening to us. We know you will make the right decision," Daniel begins in an unusually calm and peaceful tone of voice.

Veronica looks back at Joshua, who motions for her to sit back down next to him. She does so and he leans over and quietly says, "Let's listen to everyone's story as if we were in a battle council tent." Veronica looks straight into his eyes and whispers, "I love it when you talk like that." She sits and nods her head to Daniel to say, "Please go on; you have my full attention."

Daniel begins again. "Thank you. You work a regular shift at the temple. You are a wonderful mentor to all your students, who love you dearly and look forward to coming to join you on a regularly scheduled basis. I have seen you from my office walking across the temple grounds with your little ducklings following after you. Thank you for your service."

"You are welcome. I love being there. It brings me peace. Please go on," Veronica responds to Daniel's kind remarks.

"There are others, Veronica, who you do not know, who also know your schedule. They have been plotting with the same group who stoned Stephen to have you arrested … I believe the day after Sabbath. I heard them plotting with my own ears. I am sorry to tell you this, but we cannot allow this to happen," he explains while shaking his head. He looks at Eran.

Veronica is sitting straight up. She nods her head to show she understands what he has said. Her military training is coming into full force. As she looks at Eran to gather more intelligence she says, "Please."

Eran invites Veronica and Joshua to stand with him at what has become the Escape Strategy Planning Table. They come forward, and he motions for all to join as well. It is an impressive gathering, and lives depend on what they will plan and execute in the next forty-eight hours.

Eran begins, "I can corroborate what Daniel and Reuben have said. My team confirms that Mordechai not only met with Saul to sell your souls, but he plans also to confirm your escape plans with them as soon as he knows them. We will tell him your plans, or the plans we wish him to know. We have the resources to execute, so please do not feel you will be in any immediate danger. It will go in a series of steps as follows...." Veronica is anticipating what will follow and has already come up with a couple of ideas herself. Eran continues and engages all present as they discuss saving Veronica and Joshua's lives....

Eran concludes with, "The 'perp'? We will then collect him no matter where he is. There are no worries about that. You can be sure."

THE ESCAPE

"VERONICA, WE HAVE GATHERED EVERYTHING you will need so you can spend some time with us before you go," Dinah says the following day after Veronica, Sophie, and Lidia arrive from the temple late in the afternoon. "We do not want you to have to think about anything. Consider us your ... quartermasters. We made a checklist if you would like to review it," she adds with a smile.

Veronica is sitting, holding the gift she received from the girls, caressing it softly. She looks up at Dinah. "Thank you, Dinah. You are too kind. I appreciate everything and wish I did not have to leave under such circumstances. You deserve better ... so much better."

Dinah comes over to sit next to Veronica, takes Veronica's left hand, brings it to her lips, and kisses it, saying, "We have the same wish, Veronica. We all love and appreciate you. You have taught us many valuable lessons we will forever cherish."

She brings Veronica's hand down and holds it on her lap, looking at it and running her index finger slowly down each of Veronica's fingers one at a time, "Your hands have always been in the service of others, even when you were desperately ill ... every day ... even when you were exhausted, or upset or feeling alone, you were there, looking for some way to help someone, even in little ways, lifting them up with a smile, saying a kind word, creating something which would make them happy. You were there."

Dinah lifts her head and looks deeply into Veronica's eyes, which are welled up with tears, and shares, "I love you as my own daughter and pray the days of your safe return will speedily arrive, but until then, we want you to remember us as fellow temple workers working hand in hand with you." She looks at Lidia and nods, "it's time."

Lidia perks up, motions to Veronica to stand, and takes her over to the design table. Lidia reaches over and holds up a stunningly beautiful yet simple and elegant long dress with long sleeves and says, "We have a little something for you. Here, put it on so I can pin the hems." Veronica is speechless once more as she gazes at the dress with long vertical lines of various fabrics.

"It is so lovely! Look at this fine taffeta. It looks like the …"

Dinah interjects, "Yes, it is from the temple. We needed to replace it when it was shorn during the earthquake, but we did not have to destroy it. It represents the sacred covenants made in God's holy edifice."

Veronica looks up at Dinah in amazement. Tears still flowing, Dinah adds, "It also represents going into God's presence after fulfilling covenants."

Lidia adds, "Yes, we all designed this together. Sophie oversaw the sleeve design. Hold your arms out and see how it falls with elegance."

Sophie is already at Veronica's side and shows her the nearly invisible seams at the end of the sleeves, along with the tiny rows of beads. "See these beads? They stand for your classes of twelve girls, all in a row. See, are they not so cute?"

Veronica looks at Sophie and agrees, "Yes, they are all so cute, all standing in a row. This will help me remember."

Lidia agrees and says, "This entire dress is to remind you of your service in the temple." She touches each of the styles of fabrics as she explains, "Lines of this fabric represent the temple walls. Lines of this fabric represent the work being done in the temple and this fabric represents the many people who come to worship in the temple."

Veronica is admiring how it is designed and touches the small, horizontal pleats equidistant apart across the upper bodice.

Dinah says, "Go ahead. I know you want to count them. They represent the southern staircases going up to the temple gate."

Lidia stands and steps back admiring what she sees and says, "You can move gently around now; the pins will not come out."

Veronica looks down at the flowing skirt, holds it out with one hand, and twirls to make it flow outward as little girls do when in their best dresses. Everyone's heart is full once again as the tensions of the past several days are vanquished momentarily, until there is a knock at the door and everyone freezes, not knowing what to do.

The door opens quickly, and Daniel comes rushing in saying, "I am so happy you are still here; I was so worried you would have left already and would have died if you were not here." He stops talking, looks around and asks, "Why are you all staring at me? I have my clothes on, but I could not wear my formal attire because you never know who is watching. Speaking of which, do you know that you have secret guards?"

"What?" Veronica asks.

"Why yes, they are all over the place. They are in the dark of course, but they are there. I will say they are Eran's team, keeping an eye out to keep you safe."

Dinah confirms Daniel's observation, "Yes, they have been assigned to us, so we should relax as best as we can and get some rest." She looks at Daniel as she completes that sentence to convey, "We are not going to stay up all night chatting."

Daniel remarks, "Yes, of course." He then looks at Veronica and exclaims "Oh Veronica, you look so lovely! Who did your dress? Was it that famous Jerusalem Design Team 'Dinah, Lidia, and Sophie?' Or was it 'Sophie's Dresses and Draperies'? Please tell me."

Veronica and Sophie giggle while Dinah replies, "Daniel, you are not making a sales presentation, you can calm down. Please … sit." She picks up a chair and sets it down again as only a not-so-pleased business associate can do.

"Of course, yes. I understand." Daniel sits quickly and instantly points his knees toward Veronica and announces, "Veronica. I know you have received a glorious gift from these girls, and I know you are aware of the enormous amount of time and skill it took." He looks for an approving smile from Dinah, Lidia, and Sophie then continues.

"Well, I tried to imagine what you would be thrilled to have accompany you on your trip and came up with something that you and I have had the greatest conversations about ... construction work." As Dinah and Lidia's brows are furrowing, Veronica and Sophie's eyes widen in expectation.

Daniel reaches into his small travel bag and pulls something out as he says with subdued enthusiasm, "I worked with a few of my senior craftsmen from Nazareth, the ones who craft intricate stone monuments as well as tiny amulets. They designed and created this for you. A necklace with slivers of the northern wall stone on each side of a piece of fine silver steel representing the temple with the earth beneath." He beams with joy as he holds it out to give to Veronica.

"Oh Daniel! You do not know what this means to me! It is amazing!" She gently takes the precious gift with glowing admiration, holds it up, turns to Sophie, exclaiming, "Look! Isn't it beautiful? Daniel, thank you with all my heart!"

Sophie smiles and exclaims, "Yes, I have never seen anything like it, except some of the jewelry they make in Egypt, but that has gold. This is so unbelievably beautiful!" Sophie then looks at Daniel and says, "Daniel, this is so amazing. You are so kind."

A deeper voice is then heard in the room, which gives everyone a start.

"We need to get ready for tomorrow. You ladies need to get some sleep. You will have a long day tomorrow," Eran says authoritatively.

Veronica looks around to see who else had come in so silently and smiles when she sees Joshua. He smiles back and says, "Everything is ready for our escape." He stops talking and looks at Veronica in her new dress remarking, "Veronica, you look like the Queen of Heaven." He is then speechless.

STEP ONE

"THE TIME HAS NOW ARRIVED. My moment of greatness will astound my followers. I will exercise my persuasive powers and they will say 'Yes, lead us to those who must be removed, and we will cleanse them from our midst,'" Mordechai whispers to himself.

He continues his speech alone, in both third and first person, "His shifty eyes are darting as he makes his way through the crowd, listening, observing, watching for opportunities. Always vigilant. Always superior. I know more dirt about each one of these people than they know about themselves. I can snare anyone, any time, for anyone, at any moment ... especially when it is dark. Dark, you ask? Yes, I say. Darkness is my friend, whether it is the lack of light in the square or the more useful darkness inside people's minds and hearts. Shadows are my specialty. I can disappear in a shadow in the morning, the evening, and also midday, in a corner, looking out. Always looking, forever watching, listening...." He stops to take his bearings and takes count of who is there. "Where are the cleansers? The time is at hand. We must meet. I have a plan."

Mordechai feels the presence of power and realizes, *Someone is watching me. They have had their eyes on me far too long. I cannot retreat. I need to locate my next partnership and settle a deal*, he says to himself as he takes inventory of the crowd. *I feel as though the angel of death has chosen me. Perhaps I must perfect the plan more before I present it one last time.... Who is watching me? I am in the open but feel surrounded by darkness.*

His eyes dart once more through the crowd, *I must have solitude. I must find it now.* He looks around once more then quickly shoots his piercing eyes to the rear.... *No eyes can I find, but I still feel someone is here. I have to move before they strike.* He darts out of the shadow and makes his way as fast as possible toward his personal hideout, all the while whispering, "Solitude. Silence. Perfect ... the ... plan...."

The feeling of being watched turns into fright. By the time he reaches his destination, it is fear. He looks to the right and left before he stops, precisely walks through his security check, and reaches for the door observing, *The stick leaning against door is in place with the small sliver of a rock lodged between the top of the stick and the door. Good.*

The now intense dread gives Mordechai reason to push the heavy door open and practically jump inside. Once out of view and in his own space, he leans against the door to close it and does not want to move until the feeling of dread leaves thinking, *I am safe. I cannot be watched by anyone when I am here, in my own command center. Nothing can touch me.*

Still, the feeling of being watched does not dissipate as it normally does when he enters his personal space to contemplate dark deeds. He slowly slides down to the floor with the door against his back and sits perfectly still as panic grows in his heart and mind.

The deep and menacing voice that welcomes him home almost kills Mordechai. "You are not safe. You can be watched. This is my command center, and I could kill you in an instant so you would not be aware you were dead until well after I depart. They may find your body in ten or fifteen years. 'Who is this?' they will ask, but there will be no answer because there is not a soul who cared for Mordechai. His evil was complete. Exactly what he aspired for. I am here to help you reach your wicked goals. You must listen attentively, or you will die now! … Are you ready to listen?"

As wide as he tries to open his horrified eyes, Mordechai cannot see the source of the voice who has taken possession of his very soul. He tries to make sense of what is happening, *My heart is going to explode. Who is this? I thought the angel of death would be floating in the air with a sword unsheathed and at the ready. I am going to faint, or die, I am sure.* Breathing becomes difficult but he manages to push a response out, "Yes. Give me my errand."

"I doubt you are worthy of the instructions I have been commanded to pass to you…. You are to receive secret knowledge which comes from the Roman commander Felix, for your ears only. Do you place your honor on the altar of duty?"

"Yes, sir."

"The Roman army has decided to work with the Jewish directorate and not hinder actions they and their agents take to apprehend and punish the Rabbi and now His followers. You know that John the Baptist, the Rabbi himself, and Stephen, among others in recent days have been dealt with."

"Yes, sir."

"I am Eran, the senior Roman officer who has been watching you. As you have accepted your duty and have received secret knowledge, you and I are now compatriots in the same cause."

"Yes, sir."

"The two individuals you wish to sell to the group searching for followers have made plans to leave Jerusalem. You would expect they would leave following the Young Merchant's trade route to Cairo and Alexandria as is common at this time of year. I am here to tell you that they will leave from the north, not the south."

"Yes, sir."

"You shall tell those you are dealing with that they will be successful following them to the north. Do you accept this charge and swear with an oath you will be obedient?"

"Yes, sir."

"Close your eyes now and when you wake up in the morning, seek out those you wish to do your bidding."

"Yes...."

Eran waits fifteen seconds, stands up, walks out the door, and nods to his team who then replace the sliver of rock and stick in their proper place and disappear into the darkness.

STEP TWO

"OH, MY HEAD IS GOING to explode!" Mordechai exclaims as he awakens with both hands holding his skull surrounding his temples. He is lying on the cold stone floor next to the door. He is afraid to open his eyes for fear that any visible light would blind him and finish him off. *Where am I?* he asks as he realizes he is moaning in pain. *You must take control! Try to sit up ... now,* the small functioning portion of his brain commands him. His muscles refuse to react in any way as his stomach is again sending pre-vomit fluids to his mouth. He blacks out once more.

TWO MEN IN THE SQUARE converse while standing, looking around the square, "So, where is Mordechai? He promised he would give details about two followers he wants to turn in. Wasn't he supposed to be here earlier?"

"Yes, you have that right. I do not know where he is. Someone saw him in the southern square yesterday. They said he was looking more nervous than he always does, but he darted away as they were going to approach him to get an update."

"Well, we can't wait on him all day, regardless of how sneaky he believes he is."

"I have new news," Mordechai says from directly behind, causing them both to jolt with surprise. They turn to face the source of the raspy-sounding voice, and both have the same thought: *This man looks and sounds like death himself, and he smells worse than death*. They both take a step backwards as they watch his bulging eyes dart around.

"The news is that they are going to leave from the northern gate, and it will be tomorrow, not next week. You have already been paid. You will complete this assignment, correct?"

They look at each other and then back at what is left of Mordechai and in unison say, "Yes. Confirm with us when they have departed. If there are any changes, you know where to find us."

Mordechai nods, says, "Yes," turns around, and is gone in an instant.

Step Three

OGNIR SENSES THERE ARE IMPORTANT actions taking place and has been on high alert since the unusual gathering last night. He watches Veronica prepare to leave, and from what he sees, he knows they will be going over the hill and then on to the Roman Training ground.

"Let us be on our way, Ognir. We have important tasks to accomplish," Veronica says as she places her riding shawl over her head, opens the door, and steps out. As is her custom, Veronica does a survey of her surroundings as she begins her trip, *The left and right are empty. The top of the buildings are empty as well. If anyone is watching me, nothing should look abnormal.*

Veronica and Ognir head for the hill the exact same way they normally traverse the city so as not to cause any suspicion. She notices, *The air is crisp and dry. I love it crisp and dry when riding Squishy Lips. Sounds travel clear and fast when the air is like this. His breath can be seen and heard. The leather has a certain squeak to it with his every step. The outsides of my legs are cold, while the insides feel the warmth. When it is hot and muggy, none of those contrasts are as clear.*

How did I get up here so quickly? The benches are empty. I hope they slept well last night, Veronica observes as she arrives at the top of the hill. She looks west at the instant the rising sun behind her strikes the hills on the horizon and turns them a blazing orange. She reaches for the bench and sits down to take it in. "Oh Ognir, look! Isn't that the most beautiful sunrise you have ever seen? The blaze of light seems to be overtaking the entire horizon. I want time to stop right now. I never want to leave this moment. It seems so peaceful. I remember His eyes looking at me and calling me His 'daughter.' This is that peace. I never want to forget it. I want to take it with me...."

Veronica reaches up to wipe tears from her eyes, sits up straight, and says, "Ognir, we are now going to rehearse the entire riding commands sequence on our way down to the Training Grounds. I want you to pay attention as we walk so you can remind me if I forget." She stands up and asks, "Are you ready?" Ognir is already standing, looking down the path they have taken perhaps one thousand times together. He observes, smells, and listens all the way there.

Veronica decides to give Ognir free rein as they approach the Roman Training Grounds. His nose captures the smells of the livestock long before they arrive, and she sees his excitement rise the closer they get. "Ognir, done." He is gone so quickly; he is already next to the trainers' assistants before Veronica reaches the gate.

With Ognir's arrival, the crew knows Veronica will be right behind him, so they make sure they are ready to greet her in a formal way ... perhaps with more strict protocol than when they greet Roman officers. Veronica still commands great admiration from the soldiers of the Ninth Regiment.

As Veronica is watching the bustle of readiness on the right side of the grounds, she knows that the senior trainer is sneaking up on her right side. She is already striding as an officer would, back straight, head held upright and straight forward. Her ears pick up the minute sound of his stride approaching hers. She prepares her move so that he will be caught off guard ... three ... two ... one ...

In one fluid action, Veronica places her right leg in the path of his advancing left leg, catches it and pushes it behind his about-to-retreat right leg. The reverse-fulcrum move is flawless so that the body's center of gravity keeps moving forward without the support of the legs and ... plop! The senior trainer is facedown in the grass.

Veronica stops and extends her hand down to him, so that when he rolls over, she grasps his hand and lifts him up faster than his legs can adjust to. As she launches him into the air, his laughter gives a signal to the shocked crew that they too, are free to laugh.

"You never cease to amaze me Madam Veronica, Senior Master Camel Trainer Officer and holder of the Civilian Medal of Honor."

She looks at him thinking, *He said madam? Not Miss. Since when have I gained the prestige of being a Madam? Probably Dinah's doing. It also means I am getting old. Not sure I like that part.*

"You are very welcome," Veronica says to him as they start walking together then adds, "You are lucky I chose not to show them how I could have taken you out with a knife, a boot, and a quick twist of the head, but that one would take two hands, and I always like to keep one free, for various reasons."

"We will have your camel and the support camels ready tonight in the location as you requested. They will be fed and loaded with two weeks' supplies when you arrive in the morning."

"Two weeks? We are only going ..."

"In case. You know."

"Yes, I know. Please thank your troops for us. I wish we could have given you more time."

"We are always ..."

"Yes, I know. Thank you anyway. We will be back as soon as we can."

"I understand. Thank you."

"For what?"

"For everything you have done over the many years you have supported our mounted training operations ... and for not making me look like a fool in front of my team."

"Of course. You are welcome. I love being here and wish you all well."

Veronica greets the senior trainer's crew, looks Squishy Lips in the eyes, scratches behind his ears, and says, "Good morning, Master, shall we show these fine men what amazing things you can do? ... Huph Huph." She looks at the senior trainer again and says, "We will not be long. We need to show those watching from the top of the third building to the north that something odd is about to happen."

"Yes ma'am. Eran's team is already behind them."

"Doesn't surprise me," Veronica replies as she begins standard exercises with her favorite camel. Ognir has finished saying hello and is watching Veronica (and those on the roof) attentively. He moves to Veronica's side and is a bit closer than normal. Veronica thinks, *Something is up. Be aware.*

As they are looking at the buildings, the entire training team comes to form a circle around Veronica and the senior trainer.

What are they up to now? Veronica asks herself as she sees the circle open and ... *What?* Joshua walks in with Jari, the Roman armorer. *Why does Joshua have that smirk on his face?* Veronica dismounts and sees that Squishy Lips returns to standing at attention, which makes Veronica realize, *So, my steed is in on this event, is he? I will need to have a word about loyalty with him ... soon.*

Joshua stops while Jari takes three more deliberate steps to place himself directly in front of Veronica. *He is at attention, so at least he has something formal to say,* Veronica observes as she looks him in the eyes and considers, *His eyes are so kind looking. I wish I would have been able to learn his craft. I know Joshua has spent a lot of time with him when he has been here.*

Jari begins speaking in a very formal tone, "Veronica, I not only represent the Ninth Regiment today; I represent all Roman regiments as well as the League of Master Armorers who serve everywhere in the Roman Empire. We are committed to our craft and are committed to serve those of our league who may require assistance at any time and in any place."

Veronica glances at Joshua, who nods once, communicating, "Yes, this is real."

"On behalf of all league members, I present you with this token of our appreciation." He raises his hands and from nowhere there appears a shiny knife with long slender blade and ornate handle, sitting on a beautiful sheath.

As Veronica looks at the intricately crafted tool, her breath is taken away. She looks back up at Jari in amazement. He continues, "Accepting this will unite you with the league, which will give you the responsibility to assist, in time of need, other members of the league. They too, will be constrained to assist you, should the need ever arise, as long as you live."

Veronica is now standing straight and replies, "Yes, I accept this as well as the responsibilities which come with it."

"At the end of your days, you must pass this to someone you trust, who will take the same oath and who will carry out the same tenets. Do you understand and agree to this oath?"

"Yes sir, thank you sir," Veronica says as she remains motionless.

Jari changes his tone to a more familiar voice and continues, "You are a beautiful woman. The only woman who has ever attained the rank of Adjutant Armorer. Understanding that it may not always be possible for you to wear the full knife day and night, I made part of it which can be removed and worn as a pendant necklace. It is found here, at the center where the handle and the blade cross." Jari explains, after which Joshua steps forward.

Joshua holds a necklace chain in his hand, walks up next to Jari who moves something on the knife, removes an amulet, and places it on the chain. Joshua steps behind Veronica and places the necklace on her while thinking, *Oh please do not do this wrong. She will never forgive you.* He completes his task and as he is stepping back to his place, Veronica whispers, "Perfect."

Joshua looks into her eyes and thinks he has died and gone to heaven.

Jari places the knife in its sheath, hands it to Veronica, and says, "Welcome to the League of Armorers. Thank you for accepting." She takes the knife and responds, "I am honored. Thank you, kind sir."

An instant later the entire training team is cheering.

Veronica smiles, looks at Joshua, and winks.

Joshua is frozen and speechless. He is sure he will die in an instant.

STEP FOUR

AS THE DARK RUNNER DISMOUNTS and ties his horse, he thinks, *This person called Mordechai has a process for everything. He is obsessed with structure. He believes he is sneaky, but there are any number of Romans who have had him as their primary assignment who can tell you where he will be on any given day and at any specific hour. His daily routines are written in at least fifty "handy observation notebooks." I will move through this passageway, lean inside this small corner alcove, and he will be trying to take my place in a moment or two.... I can feel he is near ... there is his smell....*

Mordechai whips around the corner and bumps squarely into the Dark Runner with an "Umph!"

"What are you doing here? In my spot I have been using for more than three years? You don't deserve to be here. Go back to the night where you belong," declares Mordechai.

They have known each other for decades and had both started as street cleaners then graduated to become runners for the influential and sometimes famous residents and dignitaries. For Mordechai, who has a taste for the darker side of tasks, this led him to become more familiar with and then more at ease with evil doings. The Dark Runner, on the other hand, whose name is Jeremiah, tended to carry messages outside the city, and his specialty evolved into carrying secrets. People trust him, and he is exceptionally good at stealth. He has twice been trusted to carry an infant out of danger in the middle of the night.

These two practitioners of darkness stare at each other for a moment when Jeremiah says, "The Roman spy has deceived you. He visited you last night, correct? His name is Eran."

"Eran. Yes, we had a friendly conversation and parted in agreement on a certain situation."

"I am here to tell you that he lied to your face."

"You do not know what you are talking about. The Romans have had what we would call 'a change of opinion.' Your news is too late. You are too late. He told me all about it. And you know nothing!" Mordechai glares at Jeremiah and starts breathing through his gritted teeth.

Jeremiah watches the transformation and feels he can now reveal the message, "I know what you are up to. Eran told you 'they' are leaving to-morrow evening through the north gate. I am here to tell you that they are leaving through the south gate tomorrow before sunrise. Eran lied to you."

"How do you know this? Who do you represent today? Who is paying you to take me off the path of success? Who is it, Jeremiah?" Saliva is now escaping his mouth with his frantic demand. Jeremiah knows he has him in exactly the right place.

"It is very simple, my friend. We are, you and I, trained observers. We have been cast out of society; we do not enjoy power and prestige. People do not come to us for advice, they come to us for information. We have information they are willing to pay handsomely for. You and I are both particularly good at what we do, so we are the ones who actually have power, and we are paid to wield that power. Don't you agree?"

"Yes, power is what we have, and information, and secrets are our best assets. They have none of that, except we provide it to them, at a price."

"You are absolutely correct! You are wise, and you are the best there is in this essential business. You have allowed kings to stay in power, and you have also dethroned them because you are an expert observer. That is why I knew you would want to hear what I personally observed. The secret I must share with you will make you more powerful than anyone, even more powerful than the Roman army. Do you want this information? Because we share so many interests in common, I will give it to you absolutely free."

"Yes, share this little secret with me my brother and we shall see who has power in this mighty city," Mordechai agrees.

He has calmed down, we are now a team, he trusts me, he is ready, Jeremiah reasons as he looks at Mordechai. He divulges the crucial information…. "Do you know where Omari and Joshua keep their personal camels near the north gate?"

"Yes. I have been there many times. I have also seen Omari in his ridiculous turban entertaining very lovely and vulnerable young girls. He should be arrested for doing that."

Good, he knows the turban, Jeremiah ascertains. He completes the transfer of information, "Well, I was passing by the stable and saw their camels being loaded with merchandise and supplies. What does that mean to you?"

"Of course, they are getting ready to leave through the north gate."

"Yes, but they never pack their camels this far in advance of a common departure. I believe they are moving their camels and merchandise, with their supplies, as they always do, to the south gate. They are leaving through the south gate; this is the staging move, and they are doing it now, so you will not see them! Come, let us get to the best place where we can observe them! Quick, let us go now!" Jeremiah steps away, motions for Mordechai to follow, and encourages him by adding "We will catch them in their childish little lie!"

Mordechai follows, gaining enthusiasm with each step.

Step Five

"I TOLD YOU THAT YOU need to bring your lovely turban. It must go with the Egyptian camel team in the morning. They will take care of it, and your brothers will kill them if they do not show up with it when they do the transfer at the Shokeda forest," Joshua asserts as he looks over Bindi's back at Omari, who is cinching his saddle on Revolk.

"If you say so, but I will not be able to 'arrive in splendor' when we get to your family's compound. I suppose it will turn out fine because your mother and grandmother love me more than they love you, and they've never admired you, no matter what you say," Omari responds, thinking, *I have my new black and silver turban, which I was planning to wear for the grand entry anyway. The women will love it.*

Joshua glances at him again with a certain look on his face that brings Omari back to reality. Omari feels compelled to add, "But of course, we are bringing you-know-who, so neither of us will get any attention, that's for sure."

"They will probably not even look at us for fifteen or twenty years. That is what I think, my desperate camel driver," Joshua shoots back.

"You are the desperate one, not me, and I am your Camel Herder, not driver," retorts Omari.

Joshua grins as he infers, "Yeah, I am not the one who trails a lonely 'bride's camel' all around the world. If you are not desperate, it is because you have forgotten what your goal is. Your brothers will have a wonderful time setting up Miskah the lonely camel with potential bride candidates. I wonder how they will 'interview' them."

They complete loading, mount their camels, and quietly begin moving southward toward their normal southern trade route staging area. There is no moon and no shadow.

Step Six

Jeremiah the Dark Runner slows down and feels the need to engage Mordechai. He looks at him and asks, "You are the expert in the city; where do you suggest we station ourselves to get the best view of them?"

"I know the best place. I used it to observe their last staging for their southern route. Follow me. Be quiet," Mordechai responds.

Jeremiah is satisfied thus far and thinks, *This is going as well as can be expected. He is now taking charge. I hope the boys are on the move. We cannot miss them.*

"We'll go left and up those stairs to the abandoned room with openings to the passageway they will take," Mordechai instructs. Moments later he adds, "We're in the best vantage point; you should see them coming from that direction," pointing with his right hand across Jeremiah's face, almost hitting him in the nose.

Jeremiah wants to start a conversation with Mordechai, but Mordechai is so intently focused that Jeremiah decides, "So, how's your family?" is not appropriate. They both sit in silence.

The sound of loaded camels on a stone road is very particular, and once you hear it, you will never forget it. Jeremiah faintly hears them coming and thinks Mordechai has not heard yet; however, Mordechai starts whispering, "Yes, we hear them coming. Yes, one, two, three camels, four, five, six. There are six camels coming. Do you hear them? Three are heavily loaded, two have riders, and there is a camel with no load at all. They are coming. Be quiet." He grabs Jeremiah's arm, who nods in agreement.

I cannot believe it. He has senses like a jackal. I am so glad they are coming through. This fellow still gives me the creeps, even after so many years. He is almost not human any longer. So sad, Jeremiah ponders. The small caravan comes into view in the moonless night.

Whispering slowly, Mordechai says, "There they are. Look, do you see the rider with the Egyptian turban? Why he is wearing that when there are no girls to impress, I do not know. He is an idiot. There's Joshua. Did you know he has an exclusive contract with Daniel and Dinah? It is disgusting. I have tried to break that up but keep getting stopped by the fat guy, Reuben, who is no fun at all. Do you see them? We caught them, and they have no idea we are on to their little secret. You will never come to this spot again, do you understand?"

"Yes, thank you for bringing me here so I would know what really is going on. Thank you," Jeremiah offers.

"I can teach you things. You can have more power than you ever realized. I will find you and will teach you some intriguing secrets, first about this city, then about the secret lives of those who live here. I will teach you more than you can imagine. Now, we need to leave. Never stay in one place longer than five minutes, twenty minutes if you are doing a lame beggar. Do you understand?"

"Yes, thank you," Jeremiah replies softly.

"I need to leave now and find someone fast. Do not go back out the same way you came in, ever. Never do it. Now go and stay silent. I can show you things...." Mordechai continues talking as he makes his way to warn "The Cleansing Team." He thinks, *I have found the truth. I need to be vigilant when dealing with such dishonest people. I am glad for this discovery and must get the word to the right people. The morning will arrive quickly. The trap will be set and ready.*

STEP SEVEN

"WELL, MY FRIENDS. WE ARE happy to see that you did not get lost coming all the way down here to hand your camels over to us," the Egyptian camel team leader says as Omari arrives on Revolk, followed by lonely Miskah, followed by Joshua, riding Bindi. Members of the Egyptian camel team receive the loaded camels.

The Egyptian camel team leader continues, "You know, we were getting hungry and were discussing this very moment which of our camels we were going to need to eat, but now you arrive, with enough camels for several weeks. We are so happy to see you arrive but not as happy and relieved as our camels. Look at them; they are grinning ear to ear!"

"You are not eating anyone's camels tonight, or any other night," Eran says as he steps forward out of the darkness. "You will leave before sunrise as we planned," Eran confirms to the camel leader, then he turns to Joshua and reports, "You were seen by Mordechai, who passed the information to those who will track 'you' down."

He turns back to the leader and asks, "You have your birds?"

"The vultures? Yes. They are hungry too," he answers with a grin.

Looking back at Omari, Eran says, "We will need your turban, and Joshua, we need Veronica's bright red shawl." Both items are produced, which sets off a competition among the Egyptian camel team's smaller members.

"I want to wear the turban!"

"No, I want to drape the shawl over my beautiful hair and ride like the Queen of Egypt!"

"Me, I already volunteered to wear the turban, and you heard me!"

Eran looks over at them and shakes his head. He walks up to the Egyptian camel team's leader and quietly commands, "This is up to you to resolve, and we will be watching as you leave, on time, in the morning. Please thank your hilarious team for their professionalism and astute capabilities to execute their mission."

The camel team leader takes one step back, stands at attention, and salutes Eran, saying, "Thank you sir. We will be ready." He glances at his men and adds, "It's the way they act under pressure." Eran nods with a smile and says, "I know."

Eran motions Joshua and Omari to follow him outside, where horses are ready to take them northward where Veronica's camels will be arriving soon.

STEP EIGHT

MORDECHAI CONSPIRES AS HE MAKES his way back to his command center. *All is set. All is well. My people are ready to follow the fugitives out the southern gate. This is a fine trap. The Roman officer who believes he knows me is not a friend at all, and we do not share the same goals. No, never. He shall pay for lying to me. Pay dearly.* He looks around and double checks his stick and stone safety device before he opens the door, very slowly. The door swings wide open, so Mordechai sticks his head inside, sniffs around, and once satisfied his den is empty, gives a furtive glance around and then disappears into the darkness.

"HE HAS RETIRED TO HIS residence, sir."

"Good. We have all his runners 'occupied,' so there will be no one out looking for movements around Jerusalem—except us, of course. The camel team is already in place and the night should be quiet. Confirm our guard to watch Mordechai is in place so we can track him in the morning. If he sleepwalks, apprehend him before he slithers even one paw out of his hole. Thank you. Dismissed," the commanding officer states.

Mordechai wakes with a start. He had been dreaming of being followed by angels of death, with drawn swords raised in the air and flaming
helmets on their invisible heads. He carefully considers, *Must be what I ate
before coming home last night. I am being watched by exactly nobody.
Eran believes I am going to watch to the north, but I taught Jeremiah,
the Dark Runner, how to discover their real plans. I now have them all in
place. We will watch them leave out the south gate: one naive merchant,
one turban on top of a useless Egyptian head, with one arrogant woman
who thinks she owns Jerusalem. I do not care if the extra camel comes along
or not. If we end up with it, I will give it to Jeremiah when he comes to me
for the training I offered. He may be useful. I have ideas for him.*

Mordechai walks to his door and cracks it open to allow only a sliver
of pre-dawn light to come in. His eyes dart in every direction. Assured he
is not being observed, he slips out and is gone to ensure that all is in place.

"This is the perfect place to spend a delightful day observing the refugees leave through the south gate in all their innocence ... with an ample
sprinkle of terror mixed with dread. They should be leaving any moment,"
Mordechai mutters to himself as he climbs a lone tower from which he can
see the south gate very clearly. He sets down the food and drink he carries
with him, which he plans to eat as if on a picnic.

Mordechai leans back against the stone wall and takes a bite of bread as he
watches in silence. He has never been happier to orchestrate a snare; this one
he feels is perfectly planned. His attention is caught by movement, *Hmmm,
something happening. Oh, there is one camel, there is another, with the turban
and, yes, there she is, all dressed up in her red shawl. The Queen of Jerusalem.*

Mordechai counts the cargo camels with delight, *There is the empty
camel that I will give to Jeremiah if he is a good student, OK, there are
two cargo camels, two more ... yes, we have part one of the perfect plan
moving into the trap. Such a perfect plan I have to admit. I am glad I am
doing this for free; well, I paid them, but it is worth it. The Cleansing Team
may prove to be of use in the future.* He takes another bite of bread as he

watches the camels and petrified riders move away in a single line to the south, dust being disturbed as they progress.

He lies down to wait until the afternoon when his Cleansing Team will begin their chase. "A nice nap will do me good. The past several days have been unusually exhausting," Mordechai says aloud as he positions himself on the stone floor. Sleep overtakes him quickly.

"WHAT'S THAT NOISE?" MORDECHAI WAKES to someone yelling abruptly. The stone walls which encircle him amplify noises coming from the southern gate. He hears a whip crack and jerks as if it is right next to him. He rises to look out of the tower to see what he guesses will be his Cleansing Team passing through the gate. Observing the commotion, Mordechai thinks, *City boys trying to ride camels without a camel team expert leading them. They are cheap and arrogant. They should have taken horses; they are not in a hurry. Horses cost more. Good grief.*

The team with dark deeds in mind manages to get moving all in the same direction over the next several minutes, and begin what appears to be a small, organized caravan of southbound travelers.

"Good, I am glad they have that sorted out. Now all we need is time to follow the refugees into the perfect trap. I am so happy everything is going according to the perfect plan. Time for another nap; I am so tired after pulling this magnificence together," Mordechai congratulates himself and once again, and is content, and asleep.

STEP NINE

"HELLO ELIAS AND GABRIEL! WE hope you are doing well this evening! Do you feel we will be able to see Mount Hermon Road tonight?" Sophie asks as she approaches the patriarchs sitting, as usual, on the west-facing bench.

Sophie sits on the empty bench facing east. Ognir sits in front of her next to her right knee. Ognir then turns his head toward Sophie as if to say, "Please give me permission to say hello," to which Sophie says, "Oh, sorry. Done." Her new fulltime companion joins Elias and Gabriel in one swift leap.

Elias does not look at Ognir but gives him a pat on the head while he focuses on Sophie. He waits a moment and then says, "Sophie. You have come alone today. And your Roman-trained companion has also climbed the hill alone." Elias is tapping his left heel ever so slightly on the ground under him. Gabriel is stroking his beard as Jacob used to do.

Sophie places a smile on her face, looks at her two trusted friends, and says, "Yes, I am so sorry to worry you both. There has been no disaster. A parting perhaps, but no disaster." Sophie tries to say it in a reassuring way, then adds "Not yet" as she looks down at Ognir.

Gabriel's heart is breaking. He is aware of the tangle of tension Veronica has been thrust into, through no fault of her own. He offers his heartfelt wisdom. "Sophie dear, we know, and we understand. There are many evil happenings these days, and they will continue. Veronica loves you dearly. You have been a source of strength and courage to her for several years. That relationship will never end, and she will be back, and you will be reunited as close friends once more."

Sophie, now crying, looks up with her tear-filled eyes and says, "Thank you. I appreciate your kind words and love coming up to visit with you. Thank you ... for everything." Both Sophie and Elias wipe their tears away, and a moment later, the silence is broken by Lidia's salutation.

"Ognir! Come to see me boy! You are looking so handsome today! Sophie is taking such loving care of you!" Ognir is thrilled to leave the men and bounds down to see Lidia, who knows where to scratch.

Lidia looks at Ognir as she greets him with a scratch behind the ears, and as she leans over, she says loud enough for the group to hear, "So, Ognir, did you bring your new mistress Sophie, or did you escape and come all alone?"

Sophie springs up and dashes to give Lidia a grand hug. Elias says in an extra loud voice to Gabriel, "She did not give us a hug like that when she arrived! Lidia, why is it that you always get the hugs, and we are left wondering?"

"Elias, neither of you receive hugs from young women because your beards are too bristly and you have not trimmed your eyebrows in thirty-seven years," Lidia declares as only a woman of her age can get away with.

"Humph. Well Gabriel, should we cut or pluck the eyebrows? We will need to find someone who can see. What do you think?" Elias asks in a comical tone.

Gabriel reminds Elias of their past episode with several young women. "Elias, remember when the Young Merchant came to visit with Veronica, and he reminded us of when we were given treats and kisses by all those young women down by the camel stables? Did you forget that again?"

Elias's foot stops hitting the ground as he looks up to retrieve the memory and says, "Yes, but that was Joshua, with the Camel Driver Omari family prince from Egypt. That fellow sure knows how to gather the girls, that is for sure."

"Yes, mostly correct Elias. We need no trimming. We need to know when Omari is in town," Gabriel says, looking confidently at Elias next to him.

"OK Gabriel ... forget the beards, remember the girls," Elias returns, then looks over at Sophie and Lidia and adds, "Yes, Joshua handed the girls the best sweet cakes. They danced over to us, handed them to us, and as we were accepting them with pleasure, we were kissed! Kissed! And they all giggled!" He looks back at Gabriel, seeking confirmation, "Isn't that correct my friend?"

"Yes. Stop thinking about it, or you will start talking about it in your sleep and frighten someone." Gabriel pats Elias on the knee while looking him in the eye, then turns his attention to the two lovely women and says, "I am sorry we went astray ... again. We are back with you. Go on. You were saying?"

Both men's attention focus on Lidia and Sophie, who, they discover, are paying them no attention at all but are having an animated discussion of their own. They both sigh, look at each other, and return their regard to where they had been looking before anyone else joined them ... the western hills and rough horizon, the Mount Hermon Road being out of their view.

Sophie and Lidia are chatting on the bench, almost facing each other, their knees touching. Lidia is telling Sophie, "I remember when you were a baby, I would hold you up here, so your head rested on my shoulder, and I'd bounce you lightly to coax a tiny baby burp from your cute little cheeks."

"Did it work?"

"Most of the time, but if you felt like it, you would burp a very large burp, with some milk to go with it."

"Really, I spat up?"

"Uhm, yes. That is why I always had a cloth laid over my shoulder. It was best to be prepared."

"I am so sorry!"

"Those are the exact words I told your mother one day when I had arrived and was not prepared."

"What happened?"

"Well, I came in after you had been feeding, and your mother needed to run out of the room to receive a client, so she handed you to me, saying, 'Sophie needs to burp.'"

"Yes?"

"I was thrilled to get you to myself, so I lifted you up to my right shoulder and started to pat you when I realized I had nothing to catch a little milk in case it happened."

"Oh.... so?"

"Yes, well I reached out to the nearest piece of fabric I could easily and quickly snatch. It was perfectly timed...."

"How was that a problem?"

"Your mother was not happy."

"Why?"

"The fabric I grabbed ... was already cut for a project, and it had gold embroidery in it, so I said, 'I am so sorry.'"

"Did you need to throw it away?

"No, of course not, I have cleaning oils that work well. I blotted it, soaked it with water and lemon oil, rinsed it, and set it to dry ... it was simply fine."

"Oh, I am so very sorry I caused you all that trouble!" Sophie says.

Lidia responds with counsel, "Sophie, you know very well that all babies do that. You have adopted one of Veronica's habits. You need to stop thinking that everything bad that happens anywhere in your circle of friends or even in the world is your fault."

"I did that? Well, it was a kind reference to causing harm…. Oh, I guess I am apt to do that very often."

"It is fine. Be aware when you do it, and do not take yourself too seriously. Be aware, and do not give it too much weight or value. It is good that you are observant, but let God assign fault … let Him take the lead and provide relief, comfort, and healing when you cannot do those things."

"Yes, ma'am. Thank you."

Gabriel looks over and warns, "The sun is going to go down sooner than later Sophie, and you will not have a view of Mount Hermon Road from here. You will need to get up to the northern vantage point, almost at the new wall they are building, but do not go into the construction area, especially alone."

"Yes, Sophie, I knew you would want to see them off, let us go. We have plenty of time, especially if we leave these two strong gentlemen here to guard the benches. Be on the lookout, boys!"

Ognir knows a hike is happening and dutifully places himself to Sophie's right side with Lidia on his right. They both stand, offer their goodbyes, and set off with a good pace. Roman soldiers are watching them from the rooftops.

Step Ten

ALL IS PACKED, ALL IS well … a sense of relief comes over the north-departing caravan team.

"Joshua," Veronica says, nodding and looking up at the adjacent buildings, "We are being watched by Roman soldiers."

Veronica ponders, *I wish Ognir was by my side, as anything could happen. They are detaining Israeli citizens more often, and rumors have it that they are being turned over to the Leadership for lashing, imprisonment, and possible stoning.* She flows into battle-senses mode.

"We are ready. There is no need to fear, Veronica," Joshua says quietly as he places his hand gently on her forearm.

Veronica feels his strength and is grateful Joshua is near, as well as Omari. She turns in his direction and says, "Thank you Joshua. I know. Please help me up."

"Of course, I will help you. Thank you for asking."

Eran walks in and announces, "Everything is in place; the southern caravan team is being followed as planned, and Mordechai is asleep in the southern tower. Time to go."

"SHE HASN'T WORN THE RED shawl since the rabbi healed her!" Mordechai yells aloud as he jumps to his feet, almost knocking himself out as his head hits the stone wall while losing his balance jumping to his feet so quickly.

"They lied again! They are all liars! They left from the north! Where are my runners?"

He regains his footing and scampers down the stairway to the open ground. He stops, takes a long breath, and begins racing as fast as he can to the northwest wall construction site. The frantic race almost kills him.

THE NIGHT IS QUIET AS the sun sets to the west, casting an orange glow. There are nine long shadows cast as they leave calmly and orderly through the city gate, one at a time. Sophie and Lidia watch them go off into the sunset.

Sophie ponders, *I am saddened to watch this; however, I am excited to be asked take Veronica's place, and I look forward to learning the higher-level skills of craftsmanship and business my mother does. I am mostly glad they have escaped unharmed.*

"They have a Roman guard watching over them, Sophie," Lidia offers assuredly while she puts her arm around Sophie's shoulders. Ognir stands at attention, ears alert and muzzle sniffing the surrounding air. They both continue to watch as their loved ones start a new adventure.

"I know, Lidia. They also have God and His angels watching out for them," Sophie says as she points in the camel caravan's direction and announces, "Look! Do you see the eagle crossing in front of them? How magnificent that God would send them a sign! Do you see Lidia?"

"Yes, I am glad you pointed that out; my eyes have trouble seeing details that far away. You are clearly 'a watchman in the tower,' Sophie."

Sophie leans into Lidia again and says, looking down, "We will count the days until they return, won't we Ognir?"

Ognir licks his lips in response.

ON A NEWLY COMPLETED PORTION of the north wall, standing in the shadow made by the setting sun hitting the second tower, the exhausted and sweat-drenched Mordechai is also watching the small caravan of travelers taking the road west. He is not sure if he is pleased or saddened to see their departure. He watches as they make a silent trail of dust and muses to himself, "Vengeance and revenge are my favorite synonyms. I feel lonely without them."

Mordechai slowly turns in retreat to his hiding place for the night and is stunned to see twelve Roman soldiers standing silently and motionless in line only five yards behind him. Eran steps forward slowly as darkness arrives.

THE TRAVELERS NOW OUT OF sight, Ognir nuzzles Sophie's hand and then pushes it backward telling her it is time to go. Lidia sees and nods to Sophie, "He's right, let's go."

The three companions walk slowly home and pass by the area Sophie and Ognir have played in many times, Ognir sniffs around a corner, picks up a stick, brings it and drops it at Sophie's feet. They start playing, and Sophie is heard laughing and giggling as they relieve the tension which they have both been feeling for so many days. Lidia watches patiently in the faint light of a new moon.

Epilogue

ON THE NIGHT OF THE escape, after joining the resting place of the caravan they come to a stop. While the adults are setting up their night shelters, the sounds of children scampering around and giggling is like music, which lifts everyone's spirits. Being even a short distance away from the city and its related tensions is strengthening to all present.

Joshua, Omari, and Veronica take travel blankets and spread them to cover the sands under the shelter, and while they do so, there is silence until each member of the party is sitting as if contemplating what they have been through. Veronica looks at her companions and, referring to their recent discussion, poses the unanswered question about Joshua and Omari's experiences many years before while in Nazareth.

"Why did you two look at each other as if a deep history has been shared?" It is not an unexpected query.

Omari is looking down, and neither of them move a muscle. He looks up at Joshua with a question in his eyes. Joshua looks over at him and with the slightest nod, gives permission ... it is time.

Omari gazes up at the top of the tent to gather his thoughts, looks at Veronica, and explains, "Growing up ... visiting Nazareth ... having friends in Nazareth ... we loved swimming." He looks over at Joshua who is watching him with interest as if to request Joshua take the lead.

In a soft and kind but direct voice Joshua speaks carefully, "One particular friend ... always had a straightforward approach to everything ... he would naturally choose the right ... he seemed to be somehow connected to the history of our people, of all people."

Omari interjects, "He could cite his amazing oral genealogy directly to King David, and he knew everything about the patriarchs … everything."

Veronica reflects aloud, "You have a great respect and, I would say, honorable love for this friend."

Joshua affirms with a nod and says, "Yes."

He continues, "One day in early spring, on our way back north from Jerusalem a couple of weeks after Passover, the three of us were exploring, walking outside Nazareth near the active quarries where we would go swimming in the flooded old sections.

"The morning was crisp and unusually clear. It seems we could see forever across the valley," Joshua says as he looks at Omari who nods several times slowly as if to say, "Go on, my brother."

Joshua takes a long, slow breath to decide how best to communicate what they had experienced. His voice changes to a reverent tone, as if what he is about to say is sacred and of eternal worth.

"As we were wandering, the morning silence was shattered by the sharp sound of a sheep's bleat. Not the normal sound you hear in the fields where young sheep were romping in the grass calling for their mothers, but rather, a frightened and terrified young sheep bleating desperately for help.

"Although the sound was echoing off the many quarry walls, and Omari and I could not locate the sheep in distress, our friend calmly walked over to exactly where the sheep had fallen into the water, frantically trying to get out.

"Because of the high, straight walls on that side of the pool, the lamb could not catch hold and was destined to perish. We, on the other side of the rainwater-filled pit, could not reach the lamb from any direction. The lamb's cries brought us to feel a fear of its helplessness, and our urgent anxiety grew by the moment.

"While our internal commotion was heightening and we were paralyzed with fear that the young lamb would die, our friend remained calm and peaceful.

"Our companion kept his focus on the lamb as he confidently stepped over the edge and walked directly toward it … leaned over, grasped the flailing lamb, pulled it out of the water and held it close to his chest. He then turned to our direction.

"As he walked across the water back to our side of the pool, the lamb became perfectly calm and nuzzled against him. It seemed as though time had stopped as we gazed at what was happening right before our eyes.

"He reached the edge next to where we were standing, stepped off the water up to the stone, looked at us, and said, 'Tell no one.'

"Without breaking stride, he looked down at the then-peaceful lamb, caressed its coat a bit, looked up toward the pathway out as he continued walking, and softly told us, 'Come, let us take this precious lamb to where it belongs so it will be safe and warm.'"

Joshua glanced at Omari, then looked into Veronica's deep green, tearful eyes and said …

"So, we followed Him."

END OF BOOK ONE

CREDITS: CAST

HUMAN CAST MEMBERS

- **Veronica:** the anonymous woman in Mark 5:34 (*bearer of victory*)

- **Joshua:** "the Young Merchant" (*the Lord is my salvation*)

- **Mariah:** Joshua's mother (*the Lord is my teacher*)

- **Nehemiah:** Joshua's grandfather (*builder of the walls of Jerusalem*)

- **Ruth:** Joshua's Grandmother (*compassionate friend*)

- **Omari Shadek Zinhah:** Egyptian; "the Camel Herder" (*of high birth*)

- **Onur:** Camel stockade supervisor (*man of integrity*)

- **Ece:** Supervisor's wife (*the queen*)

- **Altan:** Supervisor's thirteen-year-old son (*crimson sunrise*)

- **Duman:** Supervisor's seventeen-year-old son (*helpful*)

- **Aylin:** Supervisor's daughter (*moon halo*)

- **Adina:** Veronica's young friend serving in Jerusalem temple (*gentle one*)

- **Kaleb:** Veronica's young friend serving in Jerusalem temple (*bold*)

- **Hannah:** Veronica's young friend serving in Jerusalem temple (*favor, grace*)

- **Dinah:** Lidia's daughter (*judged and vindicated*)

- **Flavius:** Senior trainer, Ninth Dromedarii Battalion (*yellow hair*)

- **Senior Roman training ground officer**

- **Lidia:** from Lida, the mother of Dinah (*one who loves people*)

- **Boaz:** Caravan master (*swiftness*)

- **Theseus:** Senior caravan guard (*heroic Greek mythology king*)

- **Sophie:** the daughter of Dinah (*from Greek word for wisdom*)
- **Elias:** One of the three old men on the bench (*from Elijah, Lord is my God*)
- **Judith:** Elias's wife (*woman from Judea*)
- **Jacob:** One of the three old men on the bench (*supplanter*)
- **Gabriel:** One of the three old men on the bench (*God is my strength*)
- **Tobin:** Peter's apprentice (*God is good*)
- **Muriel:** Peter's mother-in-law (*shining sea*)
- **Jari:** The Roman armorer (*helmeted soldier*)
- **Eran:** The Roman Army recruiter/spy (*alert, on guard*)
- **Mordechai:** The Jewish spy (*small man*)
- **Daniel:** The Jewish leader's senior assistant (*God is my judge*)
- **Reuben:** The Jewish leader (*behold, a son*)
- **The old man in the rain**
- **Jeremiah:** The Dark Runner (*Yhwh will rise*)
- **Susanne:** The Dark Runner's mother (*graceful lily*)
- **Ezra:** Merchant #1 (*help*)
- **Josiah:** Merchant #2 (*Yahweh supports*)
- **Maccabee:** Merchant #3 (*hammer*)
- **Abraham:** The Rabbi of Veronica (*father of nations*)
- **Gad:** Reuben's brother (*fortune*)
- **The Roman field commander**
- **Jeremiah:** The fraudulent tax collector (*the Lord Exalts*)
- **The Roman corporal**
- **Naunet:** Omari's Mother (*goddess of the ocean*)
- **Omari's father:** Micah Sharif Zinhah
- **Omari's grandfather**
- **Omari's grandmother**

- **Omari's brothers**

- **Hiram:** Veronica's childhood friend (*exalted, noble*)

- **Lila:** Veronica's childhood friend (*God is my oath*)

- **Peter:** The fisherman called by Jesus (*the stone*)

- **Andrew:** A fisherman, Peter's brother, called by Jesus (*strong and manly*)

- **Aaron:** Jerusalem temple guard (*teacher, mountain of strength*)

- **Michael:** Merchant #4 (*Who is like God?*)

- **Ruth:** Michael's wife (*compassionate friend*)

- **Egyptian Camel Team leader:** who leads his small team of available business mercenaries

- **The old gentleman and young boy in the snow**

- **Saul:** Persecutor of Jesus' disciples (*asked for/borrowed*)

- **Jesus** (*The Holy One of Israel*)

ANIMAL CAST MEMBERS

- **Bindi:** the Young Merchant's (*Joshua's*) camel

- **Revolk:** the Camel Herder's (*Omari's*) camel

- **Miskah:** The future bride's camel

- **Squishy Lips:** Veronica's Roman Ninth Camel Dromedarii training camel

- **Ognir:** (*from Ogna*) Veronica's Roman-trained scout dog (*fearsome*)

- **Gallus-Gever:** Sophie's neighborhood rooster belongs to a Roman, so she calls him Gallus-Gever which is 'rooster' in Latin and Aramaic.

Post-Credit Stinger Scene – Screenplay Script

SCENE FORMAT — CAMERA — SOUND — DIALOGUE — LIGHTS

EXT. — Tent — Night

CLOSE behind EIGHT RAIDERS, follow them into a tent expecting a tense encounter. Raiders are men in their late twenties—early thirties. Period dress.

INT. — Tent — Night

PAN to show inside of tent with the EGYPTIAN CAMEL TEAM in the exact same location as the Egyptian Camel Team 1.

CLOSE PAN — EGYPTIAN CAMEL TEAM LEADER (ECTL) in his mid-fifties.

> ECTL
>
> Welcome! We have been expecting you!
> Please! Make yourselves at home and be our honored guests!

ECTL CLAPS

His men move into position behind him for his 'Kill Me First' speech.

PAN BACK — Over the shoulders of the raiders to ECTL, who speaks in a welcoming tone. Lights increase to show details of the Egyptian Camel Team wardrobe with camels in the background.

ECTL

We have slain those you seek, the man and the woman, and have eaten both their camels—one with a pepper sauce and the other with tangy fruit sauce. We took all day because we knew you came to kill them because of what they believe, and, since they are buried deep in sand and since you want to kill someone because they believe differently than you, you must now, to keep your honor, kill each one of us, so we now will die happy, with our bellies filled. Thank you kindly. We are ready … Whom would you like to kill first, or should I ask for volunteers?

The Egyptian Camel Team stands in line with hands folded together submissively with solemn looks on their faces. The moment the word 'volunteer' is said, they all began to jump up and down, asking to be first.

EGYPTIAN CAMEL TEAM MEMBER 1

Me! I want to be first!

EGYPTIAN TEAM MEMBER 2

No, me, please pick me!

EGYPTIAN TEAM MEMBER 3

I am always picked last. I want to die first this time!

EGYPTIAN TEAM MEMBER 4

I deserve to die first; You were killed first last time!

The raiders are frozen in position. The Egyptian Camel
Team Leader walks up to the raiders' leader.

ECTL

You are the ranking member of this vigilant group
here, so you must fulfill your responsibility and
kill us all for taking your bounty before you
could. We admit it and deserve to die at your
hand now … or … we will take down our old tent
and go home to our wives and children. I believe
my wife is fixing tender goat with red wine and
couscous … would you like to join us?

PAN to view from behind ECTL to show ROMAN LEADER entering
first, then ROMAN GUARD of eight soldiers in their
mid-twenties briskly enter the tent behind him.

ROMAN LEADER speaks directly to the raiders' leader.

ROMAN LEADER

What are you doing in my precinct with weapons
and obvious intent to kill?

ROMAN LEADER

Oh, um, we have not killed anyone sir.

ROMAN LEADER

You SAY that in all innocence, yet I SEE the
vultures circling the sands you have passed
through … and you DENY any mal-intent? WHAT are
you doing inside this tent? You were not invited.
You have your weapons drawn. First you attack from
the rear and take out two of these poor camel
tenders. THEN you bury them to hide your misdeeds.

ECTL

Sir, if I may suggest a solution … These gentlemen
descended from Jerusalem in search of shadowy
characters who were escaping with their lives
and desired to kill them forthwith. We took care
of the dastardly deed for them and apologize for
the birds. They have swords, knives, and spears,
which they have sharpened with great care to
efficiently shed blood of horrible fugitives.
The fugitives are already gone, so, to retain
their honor of gallantry, they need to kill all
of us. We have interrupted their well-laid plans
and deserve to die, one at a time. I was asking
for volunteers when you happened to join us.
This gentleman, standing right here, is trying
to make up his mind whom to start with.

ROMAN LEADER

I have told you before … never leave innocent
carcasses in my area of responsibility.
Guilty carcasses, yes, but not innocent ones.
There is way too much paperwork. I am going to have
to fine you for this infraction. I have no choice.

Roman Leader TURNS AROUND to face the dumbfounded Raiders.

ROMAN LEADER

You gentlemen are in way over your heads. What gives
you the right to chase after anyone you please with
the only goal of dispatching them? Did they steal
from you? No! Did they molest your daughters? No!
Did they eat corn from a field on your Sabbath?
No! As far as I have ever heard or seen, all they
do is preach love and service to those who need
help. Now, put your sharp toys away and leave
this tent, and my guards will escort you back to

the city where the commander will decide what to do with you. If he lets you go, I will admonish you to get real jobs and stop harassing the good citizens of Jerusalem. I never want to see any of you out here again. Do you understand?

The raiders all SHAKE THEIR HEADS YES, RETIRE THEIR WEAPONS, and LEAVE QUICKLY. Four Roman soldiers FOLLOW THEM OUT of the tent.

ECTL's team places CUSHIONS on the ground then FOOD TRAYS out for dinner.

ROMAN LEADER waits until the raiders have left under guard escort and turns to ECTL.

ROMAN LEADER

I only have one question for you sir. Be careful how you answer because your life depends on it. What is for dinner?

ECTL

You are always welcome! Please sit and dine with us. My men will take dinner to your troops outside. Come. Relax. How is my friend the commander? Everything going well? Passover is soon upon us, so if you need any additional assistance, please let me know. I am always at your service. Do not worry one bit about my birds; we will take them in right after dinner and feed them handsomely. They adore spicy sugar cakes. So, tell me how is …

SOUND fades.

CAMERA pans back and the scene closes.

Appendix

W E NOW ARE IN A time that is a hundred generations from the king who wrote the Psalms, achieved great heights of power, and whose rule is still talked about in universities, churches, and synagogues around the planet. At the height of his illustrious career, he fell. He fell because he lost focus on the truths enshrined in the virtuous and uplifting verses he had penned when he was a humble servant-king. This story began over three thousand years before King David, in the sands of Canaan.

Abraham was the son of Terah who lived in the upper region of what was called Canaan, a sparsely populated region of the Arabian Peninsula. Although it is surprising to many in our day, life in that land at that time was more similar to our times than we are apt to consider.

Within a week's travel time by the prevalent camel transportation method, you could arrive in marvelous places. Anywhere around the Mediterranean region you stopped you would see, smell, and hear a vibrant society composed of various cultures, languages, and religious persuasions. As today, the primary force behind most of this activity was money.

To the north was the metropolis of Troy, where an estimated 250,000 permanent residents lived. Troy also housed between 60,000 and 80,000 temporary visitors who were there on business or were transient travelers or tourists.

Southward into Egypt, you would find treasures of knowledge, to which Abraham, Joseph, and other Israelites contributed greatly over hundreds of years. People would look to Alexandria and Cairo in Egypt for highly developed historic, legal, and political writing systems which were quick to compose and took up comparatively little space on building columns, frescos, tombs, and papyrus records.

Westward was the Mediterranean, which gave access to the entire known world. Ports were thriving; ocean-going vessels were built, launched, and commissioned to carry loads of merchandise hundreds of kilometers. When goods needed to be brought inland, rivers were navigated by barge, and land navigation was accomplished using camels, the most underappreciated and most reliable form of transportation ever used by man.

The history of the Jewish culture began with Abraham, who was contemporary to King Melchizedek, to whom Abraham paid tithes. Abraham developed a personal relationship with Elohim in his quest to receive the priesthood blessings and authority of the ancient patriarchs Shem, Noah, Methuselah, Seth, and Adam. He desired knowledge of all truth and was willing to wrestle for it.

In his development and preparation, Abraham learned that to receive great blessings from God, he must be willing to receive, understand, and keep promises made to God. He learned to live according to covenants, which are a formal contract whereby God sets the standards and those involved accept the conditions and live a new standard.

The name Abraham means *father of many nations*, and this was the result of his covenant and the beginning of a people who became a covenant people. When Abraham's offspring kept their adopted covenant, they prospered; when they faltered and rejected the covenant, they were afflicted.

The covenant made with Abraham was and still is in force.

These links may be useful for information relating to first century AD:
The Galilean Fishing Economy and the Jesus Tradition
Author: K.C. Hanson
www.kchanson.com/ARTICLES/fishing.html

Biblical Archeology Society
www.biblicalarchaeology.org

About the Author

D ENNIS MCKASKEY AND HIS WIFE Catherine have been married 48 years. Dennis has a BS in Marketing and a BA in French. The McKaskey's raised 7 incredible children and have 20 amazing grandchildren who have inspired (assigned) Dennis to write poetry. A selection of his poems can be found at: www.grandpasunplannedpoems.blogspot.com. They're worth checking out.

Dennis and Catherine have lived across the US where Dennis has held leadership positions in Engineering, Manufacturing, Marketing and Process Excellence. He has been a servant leader with Manufacturing Executives and Professionals in 26 different countries.

Dennis' debut novel, *The Hem*, offers profound insight into the life of the mysterious woman from Mark 5. This compelling narrative takes the reader through her journey, her struggles, and her faith.

THE HEM

www.thehem.faith